THE SILENT I

A Jo Wheeler Mystery

Guy Sheppard

S✺CCIONES

ISBN: 9781090197634

Cover design & typesetting by Socciones Editoria Digitale
www.socciones.co.uk

Other mystery novels set in Gloucestershire by Guy Sheppard

Countess Lucy And The Curse Of Coberley Hall
Sabrina & The Secret Of The Severn Sea

Bristol. Sunday, November 24, 1940

That dull drone in my ears is deafening. It's half monotonous machine and half grumbling monster as it thrums over St Peter's Church and shakes me rigid – it feels far too massive, cumbersome and heavy to stay in the sky. Whole colonies of maddened bees are swarming my way? My other thought is a growl of thunder. But this noise is everywhere in the walls, in the floor and in my bones. I twist and turn on my polished wooden pew because the very air itself is beginning to tremble all around me. Whatever this is, it's not usual.

My wristwatch says 6.30 p.m. Reverend Lovegay's booming voice breaks off from reading Evening Service. He gazes in awe at the fiery flicker that suddenly illuminates the nearby stained glass window like daylight – it could be a light from hell.

Next minute he's urging us politely but firmly to find refuge in the vaults of nearby St Peter's Hospital. Still everyone is surprisingly slow to stir. Others insist on arranging their hymn books on their shelves quite neatly. The person beside me can't find their gloves. We've all grown a bit blasé about false air raid alarms, so why should this one be any different?

But not me. Not this time. I'm first to wrench open the heavy church door and stride down the road.

That doesn't mean I'm not as stunned as the rest of the congregation. I can't think straight, either. All those heavy ack-ack guns starting up at Bath and Weston fill me with confusion and panic.

I break into a run even as something else screams, whistles and hits a house close by me. It flares like an obscene firework in an upstairs window. Frantic screams break out as shadowy hands claw at blazing blackout curtains. I summon the courage and dive past. Whatever just hit home went straight through the roof. A red clay tile smashes to smithereens at my heels, slashes the back of my boot. I utter a cry: it's half profane oath and half childish yelp.

But that's not the worst of it. Something singes my hair and scorches my cheeks. A blizzard of burning embers blows my way like hot fireflies.

Reverend Lovegay was right – no one can afford to get caught in the open. I have to be more careful.

These first German planes must be dropping some sort of flares in their thousands. Half the city is going up in flames. One canister misses its target and explodes in the road not two hundred yards before me – it spills its load of thirty-six metal cylinders like toys on the tarmac. The individual sticks might be small but each incendiary burns like crazy. On the angry air comes a pungent smell – of burning aluminium and iron oxide.

Well, I don't know what to say.

I'm suddenly haunted by the conviction that I've taken a wrong turning.

I can't see much for smoke and flame. Can it be? That street up ahead is mine.

Castle Street is aglow already.

A half-naked woman staggers from a blazing doorway, clutches her face and screams, 'My eyes! My eyes!'

But I have no time for her. Each firebomb is fuelling a ferocious firestorm.

Can't you see what's happening?

This whole idea's crazy.

Better get myself to the nearest shelter, I'd say.

Yes, but my baby and husband are right in the middle of all this.

I should be at home with them this very moment – the three of us should be safe and sound in the stone cellar of our sweet-shop.

That blind woman is a terrible warning.

'Emmy! Jack! I'm coming.'

ONE

Gloucester, Autumn 1943

As Sam Boreman struck another match in the cathedral's gloomy nave, he wondered whether his innocent action would attract the one-eared woman's attention. To do any good, each flame had not only to burn but to dazzle. Ordinarily it would be too normal, too commonplace? Not worth a second glance. But for a ten-year-old boy who knew bad things, this was no mere prayer candle he was lighting.

Each bright little beacon was a signal-fire, somewhere between a guide and a warning, should she glance his way? They both knew she wouldn't. There had to be something slightly solemn, even broken-hearted, about her walk up and down the north aisle. But for the miniature bull terrier at her side, she might have chosen to be alone. No matter how oppressive the weight of surrounding grey stone, she seemed happiest pacing cold shadows cast by towering pillars.

Those words on her crimson and gold badge said FIRE WATCHER, he noted, while those on her white-on-blue armband said FIRE GUARD. The black cat Craven "A" packet of ten in her blackberry coloured fingernails gave her a somewhat rebellious air, as if here was someone who didn't care too much for authority. She puckered her bright red lips and waggled a cork-tipped cigarette at her stainless steel Zippo lighter that she worked with one hand. She broke her own rules in this place of prayer.

Sam reached across the ranks of votive offerings to place his hot candle in its waxy hole. His nervous breaths caused its flame to waver dangerously on its crooked black wick. Had he not already tried to do the right thing and confess all? Yet here he was. Even his school teacher had warned him not to be so stupid. 'But, ma'am, I've seen things. In the Forest. I don't know what to call it. I never even knew it existed.' She'd literally looked at him as if he were possessed by the devil.

No, the woman with one ear had to be his best hope, if only he had the courage. Dressed in long brown coat and scarf, she conjured up images of the ghostly monks of the Benedictine Abbey of St. Peter going about their daily services. She flared like a moth in shafts of white light that pooled below the Great East Window's empty, stone tracery.

His head already buzzed. He could feel a panic attack coming on. If it wasn't the fire watcher's eyes that followed him everywhere, it was others. They latched on. That was because impressive monuments bore witness to violent and bloody deeds that most definitely did still haunt dark corners now. Whether it was the effigy of a king or a crusader, or the statue of monk Serlo, founder of the very slabs on which he stood, they all kept vigil on behalf of eternal time.

Or he fancied he heard the jeers of mischievous Civil War soldiers, the ear-shattering reports of their muskets and the clip-clop of tired horses upon the nave's grey pavement.

For, whatever tragedy this cathedral was witnessing right now had been carved much earlier in stone – he craned his neck and saw a curly-haired apprentice with open arms and twisted knee forever plunge with a frozen scream to the floor of the south transept far below.

But it was no good. The very reason he had come here was the same reason he should leave as soon as possible. The minster's guardian angel carried her gas mask over her shoulder and settled her unwieldy steel helmet on her head as she emerged in front of the choir. He listened to her shiny black boots tap the stones. *Patrolling.*

She hissed a few words to her mangy dog and disappeared in the direction of the south aisle. By way of response, the ugly, partly bald bull terrier sat down panting within sight of the burning candles. It remained fixed to a grimy stone slab, as if in its own act of religious devotion. An animal like that, once roused, could be hard to dissuade. He couldn't say if it was his keeper or protector.

Relax. There was no reason to worry.

Oh, but there was.

Seconds later a shadow appeared at his shoulder. It was the mutilated woman, smelling of jasmine, rose and lilac. She'd used the dog to distract and outflank him.

'You hungry, at all?'

'….'

'I take it that's a yes.'

The unfamiliar wrapper in her outstretched hand caught his attention.

'What is it?'

'It's a Hershey Bar.'

'What's a Hershey Bar?'

'It's chocolate, silly. Go on, take it. It won't bite you.'

'All I ever get is liquorice or fruit gums.'

'That's because you don't know any American GIs.'

'Don't you want it?'

'It tastes too sour and tangy for me.'

'Thanks.'

'If anyone asks where you got it, tell them that Jo Wheeler gave it to you. And don't throw the wrapper on the floor.'

It was all over in a few seconds, before she departed as swiftly as she'd arrived. Who else would have done that? *Nobody*. It was a blatant bribe from someone who wanted him gone – she was like every other treacherous adult he'd ever met? She threw him the bar of milk chocolate the same way she tossed her dog a bone?

But that didn't mean he shouldn't have come clean with her about something.

*

'You seen the brat, or what?'

Jo stopped dead and looked round. Anyone with an ounce of sense could see that she was in no mood to chat right now, but not the verger John Curtis, who was refusing to get out of her way in the cathedral's chilly cloister. Red-faced and agitated, he buttonholed her beside one of the perfectly preserved stone receptacles once used for towels in the monks' lavatorium.

'Seen who?'

'The boy, damn it. He's lighting more prayer candles.'

'That's what people do.'

'But why does he have to light so many?'

'How the devil should I know?'

There came that twitch in John's lip that she'd come to expect and dread. Ever since he had lived through the London Blitz, he had given up his job publishing bibles and prayer books in the capital and moved to this new, distinctly less well paid position in Gloucester Cathedral. It was seeing other people's children blown to bits in front of his eyes that had destroyed his belief in pacifism. As a result, at the age of thirty-five he'd belatedly tried to enlist as a soldier, but his poor eyesight had let him down. That's how badly he needed to rethink things now. Other people might say he was, like her, still in shock. If the war ended in victory – if it ever ended, that is – *then* there might be a slim chance of them both forgiving the bombers. She hadn't the foggiest idea when that would be.

She admired his stubbornness, though. God might have deserted this world at the present time, but John Curtis still thought it his duty to help protect His place of worship. Not that it was without considerable risk, not when a ten-hour bombing raid had practically levelled Coventry Cathedral of St Michael in November 1940. Since then there had been the so-called 'Baedeker' raids. The enemy was using the well-known international guidebook to target cathedral cities all over England. Exeter had been badly hit on 24 April 1942 and Canterbury had burned on May 31. It could conceivably happen here in Gloucester any day soon. As caretaker to these hallowed walls John was making himself a target. He'd be here when the bombs fell, which worried her sick.

'Do me a favour, Jo. Get rid of him. It'll be blackout in half an hour.'

'Me?'

'I don't like it. Why isn't he in school? Who is he? Does he have his Identity Card with him, I wonder?'

'The parents look after the cards of all children under sixteen. You know that.'

'So where are they? Do they even live in Gloucester?'

'Perhaps they're d…' A wave of guilt broke over Jo for even having this conversation. Her heart raced. Perhaps someone the boy knew had just died in an air raid. Perhaps someone was suffering. Maybe the boy himself was terminally ill. Speculation knew no bounds.

John stroked one end of his black moustache.

'It's unnatural, I tell you. What boy his age volunteers to come to church every day for a whole week?'

'Tell that to the choristers.'

Jo looked down the corridor of magnificent fan vaulting and thought of all the monks who had once chosen to find inner peace here. She still hoped to find answers, too. Being thirty years old, she was, by most people's reckoning, well and truly 'on the shelf'.

It was hard to see how to disagree. Had she not once spent too long in the company of handsome Hooray Henrys who had complimented her on her exceptional beauty? Huh! They wouldn't be doing that now, would they! She'd rebuffed innumerable offers to woo her at parties and pheasant shoots held on her father's estate high on the Cotswolds, only to fall madly in love with someone completely different and get married.

Look how that turned out.

Since then she'd resisted becoming anyone's passing conquest. Not well enough, apparently. So here she was, pregnant again. Was the father of this child likely to marry her? Not as far as she knew. Her *absobloodylootely* fantastic stud had a war to fight which had nothing to do with her 'condition'. Not that she had told him yet. As if anyone deserved love when so many were dying! If needs be, she could always do what London's mothers were doing and give the baby away at the local fish shop?

Or so rumour had it.

That's because people had no time for children any more, they were already on their knees simply trying to survive. They were tired, *to their souls*. She could see why. Since Russian soldiers had driven the Germans out of Stalingrad and the Allies had chalked up an impressive success at Alamein in Africa, she was not the only one to hope that the war was about to enter a decisive phase. The worst of the bombing might have stopped for a while, but 1943 had proved harder than ever as shortages of just about everything had become *so* much worse. Why, you couldn't even find a pint glass in some pubs, which was why she sometimes took her own jam jar with her in which to sup her beer.

While she had few motherly instincts left – she was dreading having another child – some dark incubus did seem to pursue this odd little boy in the cathedral today. You'd think the verger could be more sympathetic.

'Can't *you* have a word with him, John? Man to man, and all that?'

'It's your turn to do fire watch tonight and I want to go home.'

'Won't it look a bit strange?'

'Strange?'

'Me stalking him, I mean.'

'How come?'

'Oh, never mind.'

'Soon we won't have a candle left in the place.'

'I doubt that very much.'

So saying, Jo whistled Bella.

'That's another thing, Dean Drew only allows Guide Dogs in the minster. He really means it this time. So do I. Bella's as bad as the boy.'

'Oh, come on, you know you love her really.'

'Don't play the innocent with me. You know how I hate it.'

It was true, the thin little boy did resemble some sort of stray animal, thought Jo. Was it because he had nothing better to do?

No. He came here for a reason.

Thought God might listen, did he?

That had to be part of it.

And fear?

The dark-eyed lad didn't exactly look afraid. Nor was he badly dressed in his grey flannel short trousers, school cap and duffel coat. Something important had to be going through his head as he placed one candle next to another. No wish, name or spoken invocation accompanied whatever the devotee thought he was doing, though, only some never-ending humming.

John was right: perhaps no one had ever explained to the wretched child that one candle equalled one prayer? Didn't he *know* there was a shortage?

But he became very agitated if anyone approached too closely. That humming soon became a buzzing. Like bombers overhead.

Obstinacy was written all over his face, thought Jo, as she did an abrupt turn back to the north aisle and choir. Obstinacy was good. But that didn't mean she wasn't plain out of patience.

*

Sam's lips trembled as he dodged vast pillars, as if darting from one enormous stone tree to another, on his way to the South Porch. His lungs beat like bellows. He knew how crazy it must look, but his mind was made up.

Today was proving to be like all previous days. Whenever he visited this place its roof reared almost sixty-eight feet above him and its transepts yawned like a great whale to devour him whole. No ant or beetle could feel so small. So feeble. Every time it rendered him timid and dumb.

That's why he was leaving right now, while he still could. But what was this? The one-eared woman and her black and white dog were also heading for the font by the door? She kept looking his way. Fire watcher Jo Wheeler. She whose job it was to keep the cathedral and everyone in it safe from enemy incendiaries. Was she cross with him about something? She seemed like a person who might lash out without warning. Her hollow, chestnut-coloured eyes struck him as unpredictable, her voice even more so.

'Hey, boy! Come back here! I just want to know who you are.'

Sam bolted. If anything, he was cross with himself. Tomorrow his school would close for the foreseeable future because of the war. From now on he'd be stuck at home, could confess nothing to anyone.

Daylight dazzled after the cathedral's muted shades. A chill ran down his spine as the wintry air blew fresh in his face. Not that he cared. He pushed on past busy shoppers along one of Gloucester's oldest, half-timbered streets. Many a medieval pilgrim had come this way to unburden themselves of their intolerable guilt, just like him. They'd prostrated themselves before the minster's holy tomb of King Edward II to beg for his help.

He came to a halt on the narrow path between the quaint, overhanging houses and felt his confusion grow. Monks had once filed through here, carrying their dead to be buried. But it was all right, pursuer and dog must have gone another route.

Next instant he felt his right shoulder twist and crumple under him like paper. He did not so much as freeze as feel the rest of the world cease to move all about him. Blackberry-coloured fingernails literally ringed his upper arms to lift him clean off his feet.

He was a bag of bones in two claw-like hands.

He was immobilised by this human anchor. He blinked hard in the mixture of sun and rain. Did he have a choice? Strong arms curled round him, not so much crushing as cradling, in case he fell. One vigorous shake saw his box of matches tip from his pocket.

'You don't want to be carrying those around with you any more,' said Jo. 'That's a terrible idea.'

'Let me go, damn you.'

'Not until I know your name.'

*

'Don't tell me they're still talking?'

John Curtis popped his head round a pillar and peered down the nave; he positively tried not to be seen as he pressed his cheek to bruised, red stonework – evidence of a great fire when the cathedral was consumed by flames hundreds years ago. He was appealing to Canon Bill Jones, the cathedral librarian, whom he had just overtaken on his way to the deanery.

From where they were standing under the organ, they could observe woman and child deep in conversation on the tiled floor of the choir. Jo had removed her helmet and briefly placed it on the boy's head. In so doing she revealed her curling, shoulder-length black bob. Being so tender, she looked every bit like family. Like mother and son.

Bill raised a bushy grey eyebrow. The rest of his head was bald.

'What do you expect? The boy won't stop effing and blinding. It could still go either way.'

'She might at least have left him where she found him, *outside the cathedral close.*'

Bill eyed him somewhat harshly as he hugged a heavy, leather-bound book entitled "Memoir of Abbot Froucester" – its original manuscript was one of the cathedral's great treasures.

'You told her to deal with it, so that's what she's doing.'

John huffed and puffed and grew redder in the face.

'Strange, isn't it? Mrs Wheeler is usually so stand-offish and touchy.'

'Isn't she just. I blame the war. Try asking her to make the tea – she loses her rag something rotten. Hits the roof. Tells *me* to do it. Can you believe it?'

'Never would have thought it possible, I must admit.'

He meant the helmet, not the tea. It was the sort of game he had played with his landlady's sons in London when he had first shown them how to wear gas masks. They'd been about ten, too. Before the bomb struck.

'What do you suppose they're doing now?' asked Bill, fidgeting.

'Hard to say. I can't see that far. How about you?'

'Looks like she's getting pen and paper out of her bag.'

'Really? What for?'

'I have no idea.'

'What in heaven's name are you doing with that smelly old book you're carrying?'

'Dean Drew wants it. Hasn't he told you? He's writing his new history of the cathedral.'

'God help us all.'

TWO

Sam stared admiringly at the red and gold fountain pen in his hand. Called a Waterman Commando, it was clearly American, like that half-eaten chocolate bar that filled his pocket. It certainly bore no resemblance to the crude pen and inkwell he used at school. It was almost too sleek and smooth for his hand to hold.

He drew his knees together to support his borrowed notebook, then pressed the pen's gleaming gold nib to its page. It glided like a dream across the paper and there was absolutely no scratching and blotting. He had no choice but to draw something, now that he had been compelled to sit in the choir's canopied stalls – he felt inspired to do it by the picture carved into the chair-cum-perch of the hinged, dark wooden seat right next to him. It showed two wild pigs eating acorns under an oak tree. He could not take his eyes off the boars' bristly backs and very sharp tusks that protruded from their greedy mouths.

The one-eared woman would have him not only show her why he was there but how he was feeling.

The instant he started, he waited to see in her gaunt, troubled face what he fully expected.

He expected condescension. What else? But what did it matter? There was little reason to believe she would ever understand. Why should she? He secretly ached to rewind the moment. If he could go back five minutes, he would, because he feared what might happen next.

But it was too late: he had already freed something from its cage. He was giving it sufficient flesh and bone to make it half real. His picture reawakened the dangerous thing that had to be kept under lock and key. He was already shaking like a leaf and needed to pee – he was feeling sick to the pit of his stomach.

Very soon he felt sure he'd drawn a good likeness, in black ink. Then he went to tear it to pieces. But Jo leaned sideways from her stall and pinned the drawing to his knee with the ball of her hand. She turned it full circle with a quick twist of her sharp fingernails and dragged it back her way. He watched her strained, pale features for a reaction.

'Go ahead, Miss, have a good laugh. Everyone thinks I'm a bit dippy because I'm so different.'

Except she was being deadly serious. Wrinkles on her brow turned to deep furrows. Was that a tear he saw in her eye? He literally had no idea.

'I won't laugh at you, Sam.'

Clearly she had never thought to see anything quite like it. From him.

'I've got to go now, Miss.'

'Go where?'

'Back to the Forest.'

'Shouldn't you and I talk about this?'

'Not if I can help it. Bye.'

'So what's changed?'

But Sam was off like a frightened rabbit. He ran out of the choir past an astonished John Curtis and Bill Jones and sprinted straight down the centre of the nave – he ran the same way he ran out of school midway through a lesson. At the South Porch he glanced behind him. Was he making the biggest mistake of his life, by surrendering to abject panic?

Might be for all he knew.

He couldn't wholly explain it to himself. No one could. They had no idea.

He didn't have time to think like that right now.

Jo went to chase after him. She tore the drawing from her notebook and waved the page urgently in the air. She dodged from one soaring Norman archway to the next in disbelieving horror, but the boy vanished in the mixture of light and shadow, dissolved as if into the stone's deepest mysteries. She should never have taken her eye off him. Damn it.

'Sam! Come back! It's all right. No one will hurt you.'

Her shouts reverberated to the grubby, radiating arches of the vaulted roof high above her. To the heavens. The echo of her voice lasted a full ten seconds in the cathedral's unique acoustics, but Sam knew it couldn't be helped – he was already heading for the nearby Gloucester (GWR) railway

17

station until it was time for his mother to pick him up in her car. Where else? For was that not where he'd told her he would be as usual, watching those green express engines with the fancy brass names such as 'Ivanhoe', 'Knight of the Thistle' or 'Lady of the Lake'?

Or he could take the long footbridge that led to the other, LMS railway station where he could see bright red engines as they steamed south to Bristol or north to Birmingham. Except nearly all the overworked, tired-looking locomotives were painted in drab wartime black – their cab windows were plated over so that no German bomber could see the glow of their fires at night and the coaches they hauled were absolutely filthy.

He had lit the candles to pray for great strength in order to do what he needed to do – he'd asked God to be the next Flash Gordon or Buck Rogers, but the truth was that he was neither.

Now someone else knew it, too.

The ferocious reality.

He might never have done it, had it not been for that weird, medieval misericord of two pigs in the stall right next to him.

The resemblance had been uncanny.

What were the chances of that?

Fire watcher Jo Wheeler had told him that whenever her baby daughter had been upset she had drawn her a picture to make her smile. Why didn't he draw her one, to show her how he felt now? That's why she had sat him down beside her in a 'mercy seat' in the choir. She'd looked so sad when she said it that he'd decided to take up the offer. He hadn't wanted to draw anything. But he had. He'd shocked himself and her. On his piece of paper was his best attempt to draw something as accurately as possible. As a result, he felt laid bare, ugly, exposed.

He hated her for persuading him do it.

But she hadn't laughed.

That meant a great deal.

Best of all, she had let him go.

THREE

It was a lovely, bright winter's morning, but she hardly thought so. No matter how much Jo tilted her felt hat forward at a jaunty angle against the wind, its flimsy veil could not stop her eyes filling with tears as she, Bella and John Curtis skidded across wet cobbles in College Street. She really should get herself those new mittens she kept promising herself. That icy blast had to come from the east, so chilly did it leave her inside her one good coat. If only she'd thought to wear her bottle green cardigan made from recycled wool.

'Bella! What did I just tell you? Don't run off like that, do you hear me?'

Bella shook her egg-shaped skull and stopped dead outside a menswear shop. It was closed for repairs and its door was locked. She knew the routine. Frost-covered pieces of cardboard and a grubby blanket lay along the shop's narrow step, while from the untidy bundle issued a snort and a snore. She pawed at the bundle quite roughly – smelt dubious smells. Some things were to be expected, she supposed, when a man spent the night on a frozen pavement in Gloucester's city centre.

That's not to say they had a minute to lose. Not right now. She had a free sausage to collect from the grill room in the Cadena Café in Eastgate Street.

Jo kicked the sleeper, too.

'Rise and shine, Noah.'

A mop of black hair was visible on the pillow of damp newspaper.

'What the hell?'

'No fish paste today, I'm afraid. You'll have to make do with a cheese muffin.'

Noah sat upright and scratched his armpit.

'What time is it?'

'Eleven-thirty.'

'Considerate as always, Mrs Wheeler.'

'Can't stop. I'm late as it is.'

'Who's your friend?'

'Sorry. What was I thinking? Noah, this is John Curtis. He helps to spot enemy planes with me from the cathedral tower.'

'Delighted, I'm sure.'

'The pleasure is all mine,' said John, tapping the rim of his grey felt hat before he carefully skirted the pile of belongings at his feet. He was in favour of helping the unfortunate, but this was the first he'd heard about Jo's so-called friend.

What was he doing here?

Was he ill?

Everyone had their breaking point.

Noah had somehow reached his?

Yes. Could be.

'Any Fire Guard of Jo's is a mate of mine,' said Noah, biting his muffin. Strictly speaking, it should have been eaten hot but he wasn't fussy.

'I do keep watch with her on the roof of the cathedral,' said John hastily, 'but I'm no Fire Guard. I'm filling in for someone. Really, I'm the new verger.'

'That a fact?'

Bella wrinkled her nose and licked her sharp teeth. While it was never a dog's place to comment on its owner's sexual proclivities, it did seem to her that John had protested a little too loudly when he declared that he and Jo were not exactly comrades-in-arms. As if he only accompanied her to the top of the cathedral out of the goodness of his heart, on account of somebody else's unfortunate absence!

'How are things with you today?' asked Jo. 'Any more trouble?'

Noah pulled a face. Rubbed his bearded chin.

'You were right, some geezer on the city council wants people like me off the streets by Christmas. Anyone found sleeping rough faces being rounded up by the local police and CMP. You'd think I was a deserter, or something.'

Jo pressed her finger to her pillar box red lips and looked concerned.

'Never forget you have rights, too. I'll help you any way I can.'

'Don't worry about me, I have prospects.'

'Prospects?'

'I can't believe it, either.'

This was not exactly a boast, but that was the gist of it. He might have just won a lot of money on the horses or something.

'All the more reason to look after your health?' said Jo.

'As I say, don't mind me, Mrs Wheeler, I've got me a whole new future.'

'Just like that?'

'Isn't it a miracle?'

'Care to explain?'

'I'd rather not. It's all hush hush.'

'For what reason?'

'How shall I put it? It's been a while since my luck changed.'

Bella laid a paw firmly on Noah's knee. A rough sleeper like him brought back fraught memories of her own time on the streets. Granted, she had been lucky to survive the bomb that killed her first owners, but sitting on a pavement in Bristol in all weathers had left an ache in her bones. You had to live it to feel it. Bare skin was a mass of tiny shivers where her coat refused to grow back in bald patches scorched by fire. It was so embarrassing – she looked like she had the mange.

She whined impatiently.

They'd be right back.

That sausage would be getting cold.

'You still not going to the men's hostel, then?' said Jo.

Noah's dilated pupils shone a rich jade colour that could be truly disconcerting.

'You know I don't feel safe in those places.'

'They're predicting the coldest Christmas for thirty years.'

'At least on the street we can look out for each other. In the hostels you never know who's going to rob or attack you. You get some right nutters in there.'

'That cough of yours isn't going away.'

'That's what you said yesterday.'

'I mean it.'

'Don't worry, I've had worse.'

'Well, all right then. But if you find you need help in a hurry, you know where to find me.'

Jo jerked her thumb at the great grey tower that loomed over the rooftops; she pointed to the cathedral's four spiky pinnacles as if it were home.

Noah cleared the rattle in his throat.

'Nice of you to stop by.'

'As I said, winter's come early this year. They're predicting heavy snow in the next few days.'

'I'll think about it.'

Bella barked. Well, it was not her decision.

*

'Who on earth is the smelly vagrant, Jo?' asked John, as soon as they turned the corner.

'Noah's Spitfire came down in a dog fight during the London Blitz. At the time there was a problem with the planes' fuel pipes that iced up and cracked at high altitudes. His fighter stalled and he was forced to bale out. Broke both legs. Lost his nerve. Doctors said he would never walk again. He has proved them wrong, but he can't sit in a plane's cockpit anymore and misses flying. For a while now he's had a bad drink problem, ever since his wife left him on account of his constant nightmares and dark moods. Really he just needs a bit of help and understanding, but some people find beggars like him too intimidating. They don't consider him to be really destitute and ill. They say he goes home to a nice house to sleep every evening. Actually, he never even asks them for anything, he just sits there.'

'Since when do you give a damn?'

'Because sometimes there's no going back when you reach a real low.'

'You sound as if you would know.'

Didn't she, though.

But knowing wasn't good enough.

Not at present.

She had to maintain her belief in action because she'd lost virtually everything, too.

John shook his head and quickened his pace; he clutched his double-breasted tweed overcoat at his throat against the creeping cold.

'Your good deed won't do him any good. I'm surprised at your naivety.'

Jo called Bella to heel. A rattily horse-drawn cart, as well as a convoy of US army lorries in the streets made her nervous. But not as nervous as John's brusque matter-of-factness made her. Nobody knew anything until they had 'gone under' both mentally and physically. It wasn't pretty. Sometimes there was not nearly enough booze in this world to bring you oblivion.

'Who the hell am I to judge, anyway? My own family has cast me off except for the small allowance that my father secretly cables me once a month now that I'm pregnant again. As for my mother, I might as well be dead to her already. Her last tirade went something like this, *"You look like a tart in those silk stockings and we all know what you've been doing to get them – I'm surprised you're not chewing that awful gum like the rest of the girls, now you're a 'Yankee bag' just like them – I hope a bomb falls on you – why can't you show more backbone, you've brought disgrace to us all. Your father can't even show his face at the golf club."* Need I go on?'

'Best not.'

'Noah might look like a lost cause, but the least I can do is to bring him a sandwich every morning. Keep an eye on him.'

'It's still got to be a huge mistake.'

'Noah or my baby?'

'Stop being so bloody uppity. I don't think I can bear it today.'

'Say what you have to, but sometimes a little act of kindness counts for more than the airy-fairy twaddle that we hear from our so-called betters.'

'Isn't that the truth.'

Bella barked.

'Don't worry about her,' said Jo. 'She just wants her sausage.'

*

Jo ordered a freshly roasted coffee in the Cadena Café and shot Bella a smile as she lay down obediently at her feet.

'What's up?' asked John, opting for hot chocolate and a sticky bun. 'Don't tell me you're going to be nice today, after all?'

'First thing this morning I stood in front of my mirror and told myself: Jo Wheeler, you are slim, you are fabulous, you are brilliant.'

'No change there, then.'

'I was brought up to be a nice, obedient girl. I went to a good finishing school for polite young ladies, but for too long I never thought for myself. No one has a right to expect everything to be tickety-boo any more.'

'Can't answer that.'

'Being happy is all about choices, not constantly worrying if I'll put a foot wrong.'

'My view exactly.'

'For too long I've silenced the sound of my own voice.'

'That before your mother called you a whore, or after?'

'Too much 'poshness' is depressing. It's time to cut the navel-gazing. Suppress my negative feelings.'

'You think?'

'I've joined "The Women's League of Health and Beauty".'

'I'll say.'

She could never tell if John was taking her seriously or not, but she pressed on.

'From this day forward I'm going to make sure I keep fit and healthy for the sake of the baby. What about you?'

John's pencil-thin moustache was a sudden mess of frothy, hot chocolate.

'I can't take all these government 'Keep Fit and Eat Healthy' posters seriously.'

'Happy as we are, are we?'

'It's not all good news. I've put on three pounds already. I must be one of the few people getting fatter despite rationing.'

Bella lay on the ground and chewed the end off her sausage. She knew what it was like to be on a restrictive diet. Hers had come with beatings and confinement and still she'd been expected to give birth to puppies in her former home. Nor had she been safe when she crawled out of the wreckage after that bomb hit them all. You didn't meet many dogs in big cities nowadays. In London, for instance, it was official policy to gas pets to save food.

All that was behind her, but she still found it hard to take readily to strangers.

John was one such person.

Yet he seemed kind enough.

Not that you could always tell.

'So what are we really doing here?' said John. 'What is it you want to tell me that you can't in the cathedral?'

Jo lit a hasty cigarette.

'As you know, the Dean's sister is being buried tomorrow in Westbury-on Severn.'

'Oh dear yes, everyone's talking about poor Sarah.'

'You have to admit she died rather brutally.'

'But nobody I've met so far can say *why* it happened. Can you?'

'From what I've heard she was driving home at night through the Forest of Dean when she swerved off the road and struck a tree. Stray animals roam wild. She could have met a sheep or a deer.'

John took a moment to bite his bun in half.

'A bit of a puzzle, definitely.'

'Fire watching on the cathedral roof won't be the same without her.'

'You two struck me as very good friends.'

Jo wanted to say that Sarah had been her *only* friend until John had come along. But she was afraid it might give him the wrong impression. She didn't want to come across as a moaning Minnie.

'Sarah might have, for all I know, never really liked me, but we talked a lot while looking out for the Luftwaffe. Did you know she was fearless at rock climbing? She was ready to clamber anywhere on top of the cathedral to dowse incendiaries.'

'Everyone speaks very highly of her.'

'As I said. A lovely person.'

'Take my advice.'

'What's that?'

'Don't go.'

'That's just it. I really do want to do the right thing by my fellow plane spotter. Also Dean Drew isn't coping too well with his loss.'

'You mean you know you should attend but can't see a way to wriggle out of it.'

'I've seen enough funerals to last me a lifetime. I detest them. What would you do?'

'I just told you.'

She eyed him truculently over her carrot cookie.

'No, really.'

'Should I go with you, Jo?'

'No, I'll be fine.'

John traded looks with Bella who shut one eye. She laid her head on her paws and sighed. Jo was frowning at her – so now someone wanted her opinion? By all means. She closed her other eye. Squeamishness should come before loyalty at all times.

John reached for his hot chocolate again.

'Tell me one thing.'

'What?'

'How old was she?'

'Sarah would have been twenty-six this Sunday.'

'Better take some flowers. Do it for all of us.'

'Flowers? Are you mad? All those have been dug up to grow vegetables. Have you seen the price of violets, lately?'

'Leave it to me. The archdeacon won't miss six of his best blooms from his rose garden.'

FOUR

'You first, my love. Your palace awaits you.'

Freya Boreman forced a smile at her husband's brisk words – they were less invitation than command. James was holding open the door of their new house in the Forest of Dean. Dressed in his striped worsted business suit he managed to look rather self-absorbed and bookish with his slightly hunched shoulders. A certain handsomeness featured in his large, square head, rugged jaw and blazing red-rimmed eyes. He was not a young man, but he knew how to live well. That's because he had the money to do it.

Her show of enthusiasm was not exactly voluntary, but self-control won. Self-control always won. That's why she was wearing the platinum and diamond wristwatch that he had just bought her, as well as the new eau de toilette with its hint of perfumed verbena. She wore her blonde locks gathered and waved with curls on top and rolled into a fashionable chignon at the back of her neck for the special occasion.

It was at times like this that she knew to consider the risks before uttering a word – she held back and went in on herself like a snail.

'Well James, it looks big and bright, I must admit.'

'I thought we'd call it Beech Tree Grange.'

'How lovely.'

Freya secretly shivered. So much clean, perfect white plaster struck her as cold and unfeeling. It would need an enormous dining-room suite and a lot of easy chairs and sideboards to fill all the stark, empty angles. Such things weren't that easy to come by as the world went to hell in a handcart.

Nevertheless, she tiptoed from one vast space to another, marvelling.

'Can it really be true?'

'What's not to like, my darling?'

'At Drake's House we have pleasant neighbours and a great view of the boats on the River Severn.'

'You got that right.'

'And?'

'Our so-called neighbours are always watching us come and go. They're too interested in what we do. In what *I* do.'

'What about me, James? I'll be all alone in this woodland glade. I won't have anyone to speak to all day.'

'You'll have our maid Betty. And Sam has no school to go to for the moment.'

'You know what I mean.'

'It's only a matter of fitting the oil-fired Aga.'

'We should decide what paper to hang on the walls.'

His face clouded.

'Would that be better?'

'I don't know. Are you telling me not to?'

'Isn't it fantastic!' said James, removing his Homburg to stroke his slicked and neatly parted scalp. The use of so much shiny, lilac-scented Brylcreem to tame his shock of bristly white hair was threatening to ruin another, otherwise perfectly good hat. 'It's a whole new step up for both of us. Our future belongs here in our very own sylvan mansion.'

No matter where Freya turned her head, to whichever window, the nearby Forest stared back at her in silence. Ancient oaks and beeches cast long shadows over the new home whose walls were all metal and glass, even futuristic.

But James was too busy running his hand admiringly along red and black painted wall cupboards and creamy white worktops in the kitchen to notice. He trod the fashionable black and white checkerboard flooring and came to a stop at a freestanding, large metal box in a corner. With a loud hurrah, he levered open its door.

'Come here Freya.'

'Is that a …?'

Words failed her.

'Isn't it the cat's whiskers, darling?'

'But where on earth did you get it?'

'Never you mind.'

She studied the shelves inside their latest acquisition and was genuinely astonished. While she might have the newest Goblin vacuum cleaner at home, she didn't know anyone with a refrigerator. She stored all her meat in a wire mesh safe in the pantry while vegetables were left to wilt on a rack.

'How beautiful.'

'It's a Frigidaire from America.'

'But wasn't it hideously expensive?'

'Don't worry your pretty little head about that.'

Freya flinched. The kitchen was a marvel of new design but she hated it when he talked down to her. Not that he seemed to notice.

'You might at least have consulted me on the colour scheme.'

'Take care with these drawers and doors, won't you. I don't want you staining them. Whatever you do, don't use bleach on them or you'll ruin the finish. Just try a cloth and warm water. That's goes for Betty, too. Make sure you tell her.'

Since she'd had no say in it, the length of the brightly coloured room came as a genuine shock. Back at Drake's House everything was, by comparison, quite tiny.

'But James, don't you think it's a bit *too* big and swanky?'

'Who wouldn't want a kitchen this size?'

'To do what exactly?'

'Trust me, it means we can have bigger and better parties. Be as noisy as we choose. Invite the right kind of people.'

Suddenly her worst fears were confirmed. In this bright new tomorrow at the heart of the silent Forest, her job was to play 'hostest with the mostest' to his business associates and their saccharine wives. It meant more expensive cars, champagne and haute couture clothes.

She was going to have a hell of a time.

FIVE

'Look lively, the Chapter Steward is after us,' said Jo, buttonholing John Curtis on her way to hear singers rehearsing for Choral Evensong at 3 p.m. 'The British Red Cross and the Order of St John want to raise funds for the sick and wounded in the cathedral cloisters. He wants to know if we'll help out?'

'I will if you will.'

'Okay, but I might have to run off for a pee every now and then. Something to do with the baby, you know.'

'No, I don't know. More importantly, no one else round here does, either. The dean will have a fit if he finds out you're pregnant by some random soldier and not by your dead husband.'

'That would indeed be a miracle.'

'You know what I mean. Unmarried mother and all that…'

'Yeah yeah, tell me about it. The whole world is going up in flames and all anyone can worry about is my GI baby.'

'My lips are sealed.'

'It won't all be hush-hush for long, that's for sure. My breasts are getting larger and so are my….'

'Spare me the details.'

'Who else round here climbs 225 feet up the cathedral tower every night? Who else freezes their ass off on the roof to watch for German Heinkels?'

'Don't I always?'

'Without your flasks of lovely hot tea I'd die, it's true.'

She felt a bit sorry for John. As verger there was no denying the demands of the chief operating officer. He was also in the Home Guard. What he really dreaded, though, was not marching about with a wooden rifle but dressing up as Father Christmas for the specially sung Eucharist on 25th

December. He had not yet been in his current job a full twelve months, but it had to be a racing certainty that on account of his avuncular size he would be the one saying 'ho ho ho' to the children again this year. At least he wouldn't have to dish out any presents, not when everyone was being encouraged to donate funds to help finance the armed forces instead. Besides, there was no wrapping paper to be had for love or money in the shops. And what was a present without the surprise?

They'd arrived at the font by the cathedral's main entrance. Blackout was not far off, despite two extra hours of daylight every afternoon ever since the clocks had not been put back since 1940 and 1941 to save fuel. John rattled the big bunch of keys that swung from his belt. Ancient keys. To doors and history. They had to be doubly careful to keep everything safe, ever since they'd caught some chancer trying to help himself to one of two silver-gilt candlesticks from the altar last month. It was a myth to suppose that everyone was patriotic or actively supporting the war effort. Some people had an eye for the main chance.

'So, Jo, what did you do about the boy? You still haven't said.'

'Sorry?'

'You never told me what happened. Was he casing the joint, or what? He was, wasn't he?'

She had no idea. There was no point lying to him. She could feign great concern or none at all. Nobody would know. Probably meant nothing. But she wasn't behaving as if it meant nothing. Because their budding pyromaniac, although gone physically, hadn't vanished. He'd somehow stayed behind in the shadows, incorporeally. By talking to him she'd established a link and now there was no going back. The genie, sprite or goblin was out of the bottle. It was called worry.

Nothing placated it. Not the Preces of Evening Prayer, nor its prose psalms ending with the Gloria Patri. On the contrary, the monotone chanting of the Apostles' Creed stirred something ghost-like in the air which even the combined joy of twenty choristers, twelve adults and an organ could not quite dispel: Credo in Deum Patrem omnipotentem, Creatorem caeli et terrae…

'It turns out his name is Sam Boreman.'

'And?'

'You're not going to believe it.'

'Try me.'

'We can talk about it later.'

'Bullshit.'

'Don't worry, he'll be back.'

John stepped up the pace. For a big man, he could move surprisingly quickly.

'You were meant to scare the hell out of him, remember.'

'Because he left something behind.'

'Such as?'

'The Ian Allan "ABC of GWR LOCOMOTIVES".'

'Are you serious?'

'The boy is obsessed with trains.'

'Really? That's your answer?'

'It's not so bad.'

'It's not so good.'

'Clearly you've not met many boys. Trainspotting is the new rage.'

'Time to check the close,' said John, with exasperation and signalled her outside.

And Jo obeyed. They walked out of the South Porch into the bitterly cold air to the car park, beneath whose paving many a human skeleton still resided. It wasn't only monks who lay interred in shallow graves at the foot of the minster's walls, but the medieval citizens of Gloucester in their very own lay cemetery.

Or so it was said.

John might be right about the boy after all, thought Jo. They could be missing something. Could he be a thief? She didn't think so. But should she have interfered? She'd done what she had to do. Now what? She should really throw Sam's book away and forget all about it. That especially went for the very odd picture he had drawn her. Undecided, she watched John slip a rude note under the wiper blade of a badly parked, green Riley 9 Lynx Tourer that was doing its best to block access to the cathedral.

Damned shoppers.

It was all the distraction she could do with right now.

Bella, meanwhile, slunk off to nearby College Green where she began digging grass furiously for more coffins.

Sunday November 24, 1940

The fires haven't left much for the looters, that's for sure. Here, Woolworths is wrecked and smouldering. I'm treading all sorts of boiled sweets, fruits and bars of chocolate whose pretty silver and gold Christmas wrappers lie scattered among the shop's broken glass on the pavement.

My hair is burnt and one ear hurts like hell. I'm stumbling along past wrecked buildings and overturned cars, willing the next bomb to fall on me as I try to see where I'm going through soot and tears.

All I know is that those enemy planes have been passing over Bristol for hours now.

Do you want to die tonight?

Yes, I actually do.

The firefighters don't stand a chance — there aren't nearly enough of them to cope with so much destruction. Burst water mains everywhere tell their own story. It's 9 p.m. and the city is one blazing inferno. That goes for St Peter's Church as well. It won't be long before its bells fall down.

In front of me the flame-lit river is a mass of dancing light on a cruel mirror. I plunge my head and hands into water but it might as well be liquid fire. My fingers, I realise with curiosity, are covered in blood.

As are my best Sunday clothes.

My whole body shakes, throbs, burns.

Emmy and Jack are gone. That much I can be sure of.

But what can I do about it now?

I'll sit here all night under this bridge while the battle rages on and on.

That might work.

I have to try, at least.

The combined noise of guns, planes and detonating explosive is utterly deafening. That's when something hits the river not too far from where I'm kneeling. I have no idea what's happening. The water erupts in a spectacular fountain as I tumble head over heels backwards. Coming straight at me is a wall of roiling liquid. I have to hang on to the bridge's pier to stop myself being taken — I have to cling for dear life to an iron boat ring on the wall in the tsunami.

Soaked, choked and profoundly shaken, I somehow resurface for air.

That bomb was meant for me, but it missed.

That has to count for something.

SIX

The outside of the elaborately named Church of St Mary, St Peter and St Paul in Westbury- on-Severn had seen better days, all right. Sizeable sections of render peeled like scabs to expose rough stone patches beneath ochre-coloured walls that struck Jo as positively rusty. The heavy oak door creaked horribly on its black hinges despite her best efforts.

She was here to pay her respects like any other mourner but behaved more like a thief. That's because she felt like one. This wasn't going to be easy. She had to slink in the back without being noticed. A coward was what she was. Perhaps one day she would be able to mourn other people in a way they deserved. First, though, she would have to quell the rage in her heart.

Exuberant singing reached her ears from the nave's somewhat gloomy interior. By the sound of it, relatives and friends of Sarah Smith had all come together to give her a good send-off in her home town.

She unfortunately had not. Thanks to her troublesome Brough Superior Combination motorcycle she was horribly late – she'd been obliged to use her Automobile Association key to unlock a phone box at the side of the road to summon help. The problem was dirty petrol blocking the carburettor, since clean fuel was increasingly hard to come by. Next time, she'd know how to fix it herself, though – she'd make damned sure she had the right tools.

She peeled off her leather cap and goggles with relief. Walking into a church dressed in her heavy oilskin coat and leggings was hardly appropriate, she feared, feeling somewhat mortified. She felt like a seal.

Actually she was just being diplomatic.

'Did you just go wee on that wall, Bella?'

Bella lowered her tail.

Might have for all she knew.

'Remember, not a sound.'

She bared a canine.

'It's a funeral. You got a problem with that?'

Not me, whined Bella.

Jo led the way across the uneven stone floor to rest six pink roses on the nearest pew. Up to one hundred mourners faced the chancel whose pretty arcades, each with seven bays, lined the aisle. Either it was her hangover or those very old, pointed limestone arches on the north side leaned decidedly outwards?

Not only had she failed to see the arrival of the coffin, she had just missed all the eulogies. As the message of hope was read out prior to the time for reflection and remembering, she pictured Sarah's bittersweet smile as they had sat on the cathedral roof scanning the night sky through their binoculars. It was too soon to call them memories because her friend was hardly yet gone, but some impressions flooded her mind. Her fellow fire watcher had very red, curly hair and freckles. She was always busy yet somehow inwardly calm – whenever she directed her large, aquamarine eyes at her, she did so with a laser look that brooked no nonsense.

If she'd been allowed to speak in church today, she would have said how much Sarah had loved people.

She'd say how lovingly she had nursed her terminally sick sister who had sickle-cell anaemia.

She'd say how much she'd worried about a German invasion.

She'd recall how she was equally happy going shopping with her in Gloucester on Saturdays or climbing Welsh mountains.

Most importantly she treasured her raunchy laugh that was gone forever. She'd taken it for granted because she'd thought it immortal. She didn't know what to believe now. That tall, thin, somewhat awkward woman who never hesitated to voice her opinions right or wrong lay cold in her coffin. She only hoped that someone had thought to dress her in those colourful, not to say dreadful, tops and trousers that she was always wearing.

Was it possible to see into someone's soul without truly knowing them? Sarah had struck her as unusually shy and nervous the last week she was alive, but she had put it down to the fact that, like her, she had just found out that she was several months pregnant.

Now Sarah had been silenced. Perhaps she should have shown more interest, thought Jo? Been more curious? Asked her a question or two?

Looked for that clue? Next moment she felt very sad that her friend had not chosen to confide in her more. Her eyes misted. There was a strange hole where her stomach should have been; her heart fluttered and her breathing quickened. An uncontrollable tremor took hold in her bottom lip. Both eyelids did the same. The power of speech deserted her. All she knew was, the sooner this was over the better.

Her thoughts went back to the Bible reading that echoed along the nave: 'For everything there is a season, and a time for every matter under heaven: a time to be born, and a time to die; a time to plant, and a time to pluck up what is planted; a time to kill...'

In a matter of moments, it seemed, she was staring at the grey-faced pallbearers who bore the coffin down the aisle. The graveyard being a 'closed' one, everybody began to proceed along the lengthy stone path that led away from the church. She could do no better than join the last mourners to exit the building?

She was all set to walk down the lane to the new burial ground that lay behind the village school when Bella barked.

'Be quiet, damn you.'

But Bella uttered a more urgent growl that commanded her attention. A little boy was peering round the corner of the unusual church tower that stood all by itself in one half of the graveyard. He was eyeing the funeral procession very keenly from his careful vantage point.

'The devil!' said Jo, rather too loudly and gazed again at the tall stone structure-cum-watchtower overlooking the curve in the river. 'Sam? Is that you?'

Not who she was expecting to see today.

In her confusion she missed her chance to place her flowers on the coffin before it left for the lane.

At first she thought their spy must have entered the ancient tower itself, but the door proved firmly locked for repairs. Instead, she trod several cedar shingles that had shed their copper nails and tumbled from the fragile 160-foot high timber spire.

Suddenly Sam broke cover. Jo saw him race down the path that wound its way past ancient, ivy-clad table tombs in the graveyard.

'Damn the brat,' she thought and followed.

She saw him double back to the mourners, then leave another way.

Should she not simply return to her motorcycle?

What was she to this silly child anyway?

That's assuming she was the one being spied upon?

Perhaps she was wrong.

How should she know?

It was the cathedral all over again.

Suddenly she lost patience.

'Bella. Come here. We're going home.'

But Bella had already exited through a wrought-iron gate in the middle of a hedge at the back of more tombs. Jo dived after her. To her surprise, she at once found herself standing before the entrance to a very large house that looked all shut up for the winter.

A green Riley 9 Lynx Tourer was parked in the driveway.

Not for the first time she sensed that Sam might be leading her on. The spy wriggled past wrought iron gates, then set off across the extensive grounds of an unusual Dutch-style garden. She did the same. A two-storey red-brick tower afforded her an elevated view of a very long channel of water, but nowhere among all the very neat rows of yew and holly topiary that were cut into pyramids and balls could she see her quarry.

It didn't add up.

Should she worry? Could be no one. But now she felt obliged to descend the pavilion's steep steps, then walk the length of the ornamental canal as a duck waddled her way. Greedy fish surfaced from deep water and tried to catch her attention.

Which was when she saw Sam dart towards a small, brick summerhouse that overlooked a second T-shaped canal and its mass of glittering ripples.

'Wait!' cried Jo. 'What the devil do you mean by creeping around the churchyard like that?'

Beyond the summerhouse lay a small walled garden of bedraggled and otherwise dying cottage plants. From there she entered an old-fashioned orchard. She had just ducked the low hanging branches of several pear and cherry trees when she heard the sound of urgent voices. A willowy blonde leaned off a small bridge above a fast-flowing stream lost in shadow. Sam stood beside her, talking rapidly in whispers.

Jo's astonishment was not lost on Bella who flattened her ears, bared her teeth and all but snarled. The scent of the woman's eau de toilette with its hint of perfumed verbena drifted into her nostrils.

'Forgive me. I don't mean to trespass, only I met Sam just now and….'

The water gazer gave a start. Her square look, knee-length winter coat with its mix of green, black and maroon herring-bone tweed was immaculate. On her head she wore a multi-coloured propaganda scarf with 'Save to Make Bombers' sewn into it in patches. Round her neck hung a green Coronet Midget camera. All the same, Jo was astounded by the bloodless, very white colour of her face – there was something so blanched and unnatural about it that she might have lived her whole life in perpetual gloom. Yet, to dismiss her as ill or worse, anorexic, was not to diagnose but to misunderstand her, so poised was she in her calf skin court shoes with their rounded toes and solid heels. She cuddled her pet dog very closely.

'Don't worry, I'm not the owner. This house belongs to the Colchester family, but they are hardly ever here because they own another, grander home elsewhere in the Forest. They have been reviving the water gardens, however, and said I simply must photograph them. Aren't they lovely, even in winter? Photography's rather my thing, you see.'

'I'm sorry to intrude.'

'Sam tells me you're the chief Fire Guard at Gloucester Cathedral. You're Mrs Jo Wheeler?'

'That depends.'

'On what?'

'On who you are.'

'I'm Freya. I'm Sam's mother.'

'You are? Then I'm pleased to meet you.'

'He says you were very kind to him.'

'Not really. He was lighting every damned candle in the cathedral and I was sent to investigate.'

41

'That your miniature bullterrier?'

'It is.'

'What's her name?'

'Bella. She rode here with me today in my motorcycle sidecar. We've been firm friends for a while now, ever since I found her wandering about with her coat half burned off during the Blitz on Bristol.'

'Where are her owners?'

'Dead, I would imagine.'

'Something you didn't see coming?'

'Never considered myself a dog lover.'

'But I can see you do now,' said Freya. 'You can tell a lot about a person from the pets they keep.'

'And yours?'

'Her name is Ruby. I've been told she's descended from dogs once kept by the Aztecs.'

Bella curled her lip. A dog might embarrass or otherwise let down its owner, but that was only because it had not been properly introduced. But this newcomer was well-versed in canine etiquette. She pulled off a glove and offered her bony fist for her to sniff, all the while clutching her bug-eyed, six-inch-high bundle in her other arm. It was a Chihuahua, all right. Yap. Yap. Yap. Hmm, how fitting.

'Sorry,' said Jo. 'Bella can be wary of strangers.'

'Tell me, Mrs Wheeler....'

'Please call me Jo.'

'.... did you give my son an American chocolate bar?'

'Well, all right then, I know a few GIs who have access to such things.'

'Much obliged.'

'For what?'

'Sam's not like most other boys. He doesn't seem to need friends. Don't get me wrong, he likes company but he doesn't seek it out. He's happiest on his own which can make things difficult at times. Other children won't take the trouble to understand him. They either ignore or tease him. Did he mention it, at all?'

'Never said a word.'

'It's like this. His fellow pupils at school try to push him around because they consider he gives off an air of defensive hostility, I suppose. I can't say what it is. They take him on just to see what his reaction will be. They bait him like a stray dog. You've no idea. Some of the girls are the worst because they throw stones. They see him alone in the playground and have a go.'

'OK, I didn't know.'

'But most children do that, don't they? They have a pack mentality. There's nothing they like more than to prove how tough they are by picking on some easy target who's all on his own.'

'Which reminds me,' said Jo, 'I have his book of train numbers. I retrieved it in the cathedral just after he and I had our little chat. It was on the floor of the choir.'

'Thank God, he's been going crazy about that book. There's never been anything like it before, you see – the publisher only just started compiling lists last year.'

'I'll make sure he gets it.'

'Will you?'

'Soon as I can.'

'His father thinks it shows he isn't quite right in the head.'

'And you? What do you think?'

Suddenly Freya turned her face and her scarf slipped back on her hair to reveal a patch of white scalp above one ear. Either she had scratched her head bald at this point or a large tuft of hair had been torn out recently by its roots. The wound still looked red and sore in the middle. Whatever her accident, it had left her bruised.

'I don't know, Mrs Wheeler – I mean Jo – he's just Sam to me. Yes, he finds being around people awkward and is pre-occupied with very narrow interests, but he's still my Sam. Always will be. Some people might want to call him unusually serious and focused, but that implies that he's somehow deficient when all he is, really, is a bit different. Different can be good. And he's not often so frustrated that he gets violent. We can all learn a lot from

Sam. He's very resilient. Which reminds me. Where is he? Sam! Oh dear, he's prone to wander off at a whim.'

'I last saw him over there with Bella under those black Poplar trees.'

'I do hope he hasn't walked down to the river.'

'Let's go find him.'

'Please, that's not necessary.'

Freya hid her head in her scarf again. Dark circles round her sunken eyes had been artfully masked in part by make-up. Something about her pale green irises suggested another deeper shadow behind the gloss. Whatever she was giving, doing or sacrificing to talk to her like this came at a price, thought Jo, like someone long out of practice when it came to idle chit-chat.

'At least let me walk with you for a while.'

'Goodbye Jo.'

'You're right, I really should leave you to your photography. Sarah's wake will be starting any minute.'

'You knew her well?'

'For the last two years we looked out for enemy planes flying over Gloucester Cathedral.'

'She and I went to the same school together.'

'Then you're coming to the wake, too!'

'No, I'm not.'

'No?'

'*No.*'

More Freya would not explain. Yet here she was. That she was avoiding someone was suddenly obvious; it had to account for the blushing under the rouge on her cheeks. She didn't believe all that nonsense about photographing the gardens. Evidently, she had come here to give vent to her feelings in private.

Which she'd so carelessly interrupted, thought Jo.

It wasn't her fault.

Yes, it really was.

She envied her tears, though.

To cry was not to fear emotion.

Since the mention of Sarah, Freya was much troubled. It was as if they had just traded, thanks to Sam, some sort of secret. They paused to go their separate ways at a gnarled evergreen oak that looked so cracked and old, it could have been the world's oldest.

'Hurry up and send me my son's book, Mrs Wheeler, if you can. I will, of course, refund the postage.'

'Thank you. Please take my card. I'm in the middle of looking for new digs, but you can reach me via Gloucester Cathedral at any time.'

'I'm about to move home, too. My current address is Drake's House in Gatcombe. It's just a few miles from here, by the river. Folklore has it that Sir Francis Drake once stayed there when it was still an inn, which is one reason I've always liked it.'

'Had I known I'd meet you like this I would have brought Sam's book with me.'

But Freya was no longer listening. A fresh cloud crossed her face as she successfully recalled her son to her side. They hurried away past the canals and pyramidal yews where they somehow managed to look very lonely.

'Drat!' said Jo aloud, unable to forgive herself.

She last caught sight of mother and son at the parterres by the pavilion, where Sam would have stopped to feed the lame duck had Freya not hurried him on.

That strange picture that he had drawn her in the cathedral shook in her hand. Too late, she pulled it from her pocket.

Either it was her imagination, or it had changed its beastly mien. She hesitated to say what it represented exactly, except to say that it reminded her of those fearsome creatures that were to be seen carved in medieval oak misericords of the choir stalls. Its ugly eyes had, in the last few days, grown more malign? As had its teeth.

SEVEN

It could be a rotten business rustproofing guns for the army, Raoul discovered, as he donned his clumsy rubber gloves and leather apron. Next minute, with a deft swing of his shovel, he began to scoop white dust from a sack and decant it carefully into the tank's hot liquid beside him.

A sour taste filled his mouth, while his tongue was all bumps and cracks like rough sandpaper.

There was an awful churning in the pit of his stomach and his head throbbed.

He was confused, heady, even giddy. He wondered whether it was just the searing heat from the workshop's gas burners or the haze of chemicals in the air that made him feel so peculiar. Or the steam. The sickly steam. It wasn't always that easy to breathe.

His constant retching and choking recalled the seasickness he'd suffered when his boat sank during the hurried evacuation of Allied troops from Dunkirk, two and a half years ago. His chest tightened as he relived the day he failed to pluck his brother and fellow soldier, Pierre, from the treacherous tide. France might have fallen to the Germans, but the Devil was not done with him yet – he was still punishing him. And he deserved it.

In this hell.

The viscosity of the liquid in the tank was his biggest cause for concern because it was liable to erupt like lava. He could not afford to let the solution dry out, yet to add water from a bucket was to play a cruel game of chance. The crimson salts soon hissed and spat at him like a nest of vipers.

One hot spray of liquid could cook his eye's cornea in an instant. One drop of boiling caustic soda could burrow to the bone.

But today all he could think about was the manner in which Mr Devaney, the factory foreman, treated him – he could not but resent the fact that he was no better than a slave.

His spade stirred the thick layer of crimson sludge in the bottom of the tank – his blade detonated intermittent plumes of steam like geysers to release heat from the burners below. The tank's rusty metal sides shivered and quaked most alarmingly as their metal plates expanded.

'Why?' he cried out each time he prodded molten fire. 'Why should I, who should never have been plucked from the English Channel when I was going under for the last time, expect to have any dreams left now?'

Thousands of French soldiers like him had made it safely to England, but he would gladly have given up his life to save Pierre. Had he not promised their mother to keep him safe?

Now he simply didn't want to fight any more.

It hadn't always been like this, but people were inferring that 'his sort' had surrendered to the enemy far too quickly. They had the nerve to say that French armies hadn't had the stomach to fight Hitler's advancing tanks when he personally had helped destroy Panzer after Panzer at Hannut in Belgium, even though they had been heavily outnumbered.

He shovelled faster. The more reason he had to condemn himself, the more motive he had to toil hard.

To work was to forget. Of that much he could be sure.

Not that he had much choice. Clearly, unmistakeably, he saw loom over him the broad, ugly shadow of the pipe-smoking foreman – dark, threatening, demonic, forever attendant! The rifle bolts he was working on had to be coloured black to stop them reflecting the sun on desert battlefields in North Africa. One flash of bare, silvery metal could betray a man's position from miles away, get him ambushed. It was said they were destined for a special raiding squadron called the 2nd S.A.S. whose training camp and headquarters were only thirty miles north of here, in Hereford.

Raoul bowed his head. He shunned Devaney's contemptuous gaze and smell of tobacco. Remained silent. For now.

Monday, November 25 1940

I hobble past more bombed out buildings. It can't be far in this lunar landscape, but I'm struggling to recognize anything anywhere. I try to focus on one step at a time before I lose my nerve completely. I didn't sleep last night. Even now, to close my blood-soaked eyelids is to feel a black fog stifle me, blanking out the smoky sky. The smell, taste and feel of the burning ruins constrict, suffocate and fill my chest with pain until I can barely go on. All strength drains from me.

Someone, somewhere, has bandaged my head, but I can't say who or when.

Thanks to censorship by the Ministry of Information it is terribly hard to know what's really happening. It would be a relief to be able to say that while we have been utterly devastated, other places remain unscathed. But newspaper headlines simply say "Germans concentrate on west towns", which is an insult since everyone knows that it was Bristol that got hit yesterday. Such deliberate vagueness might deny the enemy details of damage done, but it doesn't help morale. Everyone here is feeling totally abandoned.

Doesn't look good.

Eleven days ago, when whole areas of Coventry were flattened, The Ministry of Information did not hold back then, it gave the raids maximum airtime on the radio and front page coverage in the national newspapers. So why not be truthful about everywhere else? It's a fine line to tread between stirring up patriotic resistance and fuelling despair. Today I heard people talking in shops and at tram stops. 'Of course we can't win. We're only a small country' or 'We won't win this war unless we have underground shelters – it will drive us all skatty.' A chorus of dissent is building. I feel the same.

I'm so frightened to come back to Castle Street. The broken walls are not just bricks and mortar but visible proof of a lost world which I so recently inhabited. That prevailing smell has to be escaping gas? It's not just my own physical pain. This is where happiness and hope lie buried, along with my loved ones.

No one can predict the future, but at this moment all I know instinctively, horribly, is that I feel like a different person.

I'm in a tail-spin.

It's all a dark, bloody dream. A woman dressed in a dusty coat and torn headscarf heats soup in an open-air cauldron at the side of the road. Another, older woman sits on a mountain of rubble and takes time to light a much-needed cigarette. Elsewhere a little girl is busy rescuing a black and white doll's house from the wreckage of her home. She breaks into a big smile at my approach. She's delighted with the toy house which, miraculously, appears to be totally undamaged. I gaze back at her, aghast. But I get it. These aren't people whose spirit is hopelessly broken, they're just carrying on.

EIGHT

It was just gone midday when the sun in the otherwise wintry sky cast a welcome glow over Westbury-on-Severn, the half timbered Red Lion Inn and its beer garden. Having missed most of Sarah's funeral she was determined not to return home without downing at least one drink. Or two. That's not to say she wished to chat to any of the mourners at the bar. Another ten minutes and she, Jo Wheeler, would be gone.

She was about to let Bella lick the last of the stout from her glass, when a middle-aged man lurched from one table to the next while desperately trying to stay upright across the lawn. It didn't work. Next minute he crashed into a parasol beside her.

The drunk was definitely fixing her in his blurry focus.

He had all the right in the world to breathe straight in her face.

Hers alone, in his opinion.

There was something he had to say to her and no one else?

'You Jo Wheeler? You that fire watcher my wife liked so much?'

Her heart sank, but what was she supposed to do? His voice was slurred, not to mention over-excited. He clawed wildly at empty air like someone drowning. Damn it. There was no escape. Not that she could think of.

This had to be Sarah's husband, Bruno.

'I am a fire watcher, yes, but strictly speaking only within the environs of Gloucester Cathedral.'

'That's not what I heard.'

'How do you mean?'

'I heard you tried to rescue a child from a burning house in Bristol. Newspapers called you a hero.'

'That depends.'

'On what?'

'You're the one doing all the talking.'

Bruno tore loose his tie and his single-breasted CC41 Utility jacket, with its skimpy lapels, already hung off one shoulder. His bloodshot brown eyes, wide and unfocused, had in them a mixture of disbelief and panic. His mop of gingery hair, much ruffled, was all over the place, his cheeks were inflamed with a livid blush as he hammered the wooden planks in the garden table with his fist. The beer in his glass went flying.

'Sarah should never have died. Do I make myself clear?'

'You tell me this now, because?'

Bella, who had not yet finished licking stout off her nose, rushed forward to face Bruno with a snarl. She did not like the widower's ugly look, his loud voice, his deliberately provocative stance.

She heard Jo bark her name.

Too late now.

She had hold of Bruno's heel.

'Leave, Bella!'

It was every dog's duty to defend its owner.

'I said leave.'

'....'

'You know what happened last time. *No sausages.*'

Bella let go. 'Woof,' she said, acknowledging the gravity of the situation with a still graver frown.

Jo hooked Bruno's arm in hers. He was terribly shaky, confused and worried. Paranoia was no less obvious as she sat him down on a chair.

'Sorry, I haven't a clue what you're going on about.'

'Sarah always drove her car so slowly and sensibly.'

'You mustn't talk like this. Not here, not today. Not at her funeral.'

Whatever had prompted this unseemly outburst had Bruno all fired up about something. Somebody had put some crazy notion into his head, she could say that at least. Clearly he needed to tell his version of events to anyone who would listen.

'Her car didn't just simply skid off the road and hit an oak tree.'

'That's not what the police say. They think your wife swerved to avoid a wild animal.'

'Bullshit.'

'She would have had absolutely no warning.'

'Blast you, Mrs Wheeler.' Unclenching his fists, Bruno clawed wildly at his hair before he dissolved into tears. 'I'm not wrong.'

'Are you serious?'

'Somebody knows the truth…'

'Please lower your voice.'

'…and I know who.'

Jo sat him back down at the wooden table. He appeared in less need of counsel than a cuddle.

At that moment a well-dressed couple entered the beer garden to say their goodbyes.

'See you soon, Bruno,' said the young brunette briskly. 'We'll give you a call.'

Bruno clasped both hands to his face and bowed his head; he appeared completely overcome by the terrible conviction of some deep evil – a conviction which his friends found hard to fathom.

'Whatever is it, old chap? What's wrong?'

'You don't know anything.'

'No need to worry,' said Jo, quickly taking the mourners to one side. 'Our friend here has had a bit too much to drink. He's feeling a bit dismal. Alcohol has that effect on some people, as we all know. It's understandable, given what's happened.'

'We should call a doctor. He looks ill.'

'As I say, the beer is making him a bit maudlin, that's all. I'll sort it.'

'Are you sure? Only we have to catch our train back to London.'

'No need to apologise. Have a safe journey.'

'Sarah was an excellent driver,' Bruno called after them very loudly.

With little hope of it doing much good, Jo rejoined her grief-stricken companion.

'Do you have any more surprises? Think before you speak, Mr Smith.'

As if on cue, the widower pulled half a dozen black and white prints from his pocket and slapped them on the table's weather-beaten planks for her to see. His breathing quickened and his eyes narrowed.

'You're never going to believe it.'

'Try me.'

'It's worse than I thought.'

'Say what you have to calmly and quietly.'

'Last week I was sorting Sarah's things when I found her PRONTOR II camera in a drawer in our bedroom. These were with it.'

Whoever had taken the series of images had done so in the dark, hence the underexposure. Even so, they were pretty good quality, as photographs went, though she never had much time for all the fancy things cameras could do.

They were looking at a Vulcan 5ton drop-side lorry parked in a forest of mature oaks and beeches.

'Any idea whose truck it might be?' asked Jo, trying to make out the company name painted on the cab door.

'No, but keep looking, Mrs Wheeler.' Bruno was still visibly upset but completely focused.

Half loaded on to the lorry was a stack of neatly cut timber. That the driver was a little grey-haired man was plain enough, Jo observed. He sported long, old-fashioned sideburns and a thin moustache; he was probably in his fifties, lightly built, with a crooked right leg. He could have been a veteran of the First World War trenches. Climbing into the lorry's cab, he didn't seem an obvious criminal. His long-haired companion, on the other hand, was all brawn. His padded shoulders bulged inside his black donkey jacket as he threw lengths of timber about with ease. His steel-capped black boots looked enormous. This gorilla helped stack the wood in a distinctly slow, heavy and awkward way which indicated a certain stupidity or clumsiness.

'So tell me Mr Smith, why would your wife stop to photograph two men loading a lorry with planks in the dark?'

'Right now the Royal Engineers are bulldozing trees like crazy from the Forest of Dean for the war effort. Nearly all of it goes for pit props since we need to mine the coal to power our ships, etcetera. What we have here are war profiteers. Somebody has done a deal with someone to sell a load of timber on the black market. Funeral directors, especially, can't get enough sandpaper let alone sufficient wood to make coffins. In some cases, they're having to use cardboard. They're not the only ones who might pay well to keep their businesses going. Sarah would have hated that. The war effort is one thing, but she loathed anyone who treated her beloved Forest with disrespect.'

'Sarah was someone of high principles, that's for sure.'

'More than that, she was fearless, even headstrong. Ours wasn't a perfect marriage, I grant you, but it's not as if we were totally estranged – she was carrying my child, for God's sake – so why didn't she tell me about it?'

'How would I know?'

'What was she doing out there, anyway?'

'Perhaps you're asking yourself the wrong question?'

'I need to understand what's going on, that's all.'

'Can't disagree with you there.'

'Will you listen to me, or not, Mrs Wheeler?'

'So she's driving through the Forest of Dean one night when, as bad luck would have it, she comes across these men and their lorry. She stops the car…'

'A red ACA Pearl Austin Seven Cabriolet.'

'…and begins to photograph them framed in the light of her vehicle's dimmed headlights.'

'Until they chase her.'

'But she escapes unhurt?'

'As I said, she never said a thing to me about it.'

Bruno scratched hard at his neck which caused Jo to fidget, too. He was expecting her to go along with every word he said as if it were the gospel truth, which struck her as ridiculous.

'This concerns me how?'

'You want to know if this can possibly have anything to do with Sarah's death, Mrs Wheeler?'

'I should say so.'

'Not long after she came across that lorry – I can say this for sure now – someone left a pig's head on her car's bonnet.'

'Like a trophy?'

'Written in blood on the windscreen were the words: *Say Nothing.*'

'Any idea why that might be?'

'I know it was a callous thing to do.'

'Just get to the point.'

'Isn't it obvious, Mrs Wheeler? That boar was a warning.'

'Sorry, you've lost me.'

'It can't be a coincidence. Sarah witnessed a crime being committed. Those men saw her photograph them and wanted to silence her. She never said so at the time, but they were sending her a message. A few weeks later she ends up roadkill, too.'

Jo took a closer look at the prints. The truck's number plate was either broken or covered in mud because she could not make out any letters, only the numbers 442.

'You've been to the police, naturally?'

'Oh yes, but these things get lost in paperwork. I even doubt they took me seriously. This war takes up all their time.'

'Did Sarah have any enemies?'

'Everyone loved her because she was so bubbly and kind.'

'That I can vouch for.'

'See here,' said Bruno, with the same indignation in his voice that he had in his eyes. 'Who else but these men had a motive to hurt Sarah? I reckon they set out to follow her home. I believe they went so far as to run her off the road when she next drove that way at night.'

'Or she went back to gather more evidence.'

'Exactly.'

'But we don't know that, do we?'

'Nobody saw a thing.'

'Good luck with that.'

'Then tell me what to do, Mrs Wheeler.'

'Just to be clear, I don't think it's any of my business, but did anything else unusual happen in the days before Sarah's death? Did she mention anything at all?'

'Come to think of it, we were shopping in central Gloucester when she suddenly ran off into the cathedral.'

'Did you confront her about it?'

'I did, but she went very quiet. She behaved as if she was being followed.'

'So she didn't admit anything?'

'No.'

More mourners entered the garden to bid Bruno goodbye. Sensing her opportunity, Jo stood up to go. She gave Bella a cursory whistle which she obeyed with a cursory bark. Sometimes a dog could be taken too much for granted. This whole business of Sarah's car crash was most bizarre and unwelcome. Bruno was forgetting that she was terribly upset, too.

There was something almost manic in the widower's emphatic conviction that his wife had been deliberately targeted, which was not helped by the hard twist in his mouth and the cold look in his eyes. All the passion that had been unleashed by drinking too much beer was tinged with an unusual bitterness – he appeared unnaturally vengeful.

Perhaps when he had sobered up he would have forgotten all about it.

Wouldn't that be lovely.

On the other hand, that boar's head and message left on Sarah's car had to mean something?

But she did not move fast enough.

Bruno came after her, seized her arm.

'Sarah admired you a lot, Mrs Wheeler. You think you might look into it for me? As I say, I literally have no one else to turn to.'

Which was why her answer was no.

Which was why her answer was yes.

'Suppose I do ask a few questions about her, what then?'

'You'll have to do more than that, Mrs Wheeler. As soon as you start investigating you'll see how serious this really is.'

'You think?'

'Don't we owe it to her to discover the truth because I'm convinced that her death goes way beyond any accidental hit-and-run.'

Jo felt a shiver go down her spine.

'What exactly are you trying to say?'

'I'm not mad, Mrs Wheeler! Please help me. You'll see something's wrong as soon as you delve into it, I know you will. If I'm mistaken, then so be it – I'll say sorry in advance for bothering you. But I'm not wrong. Someone has to speak out, because I'm quite sure Sarah has been murdered.'

NINE

Nora Kelly had never heard such a piercing scream, not since her dead baby had been torn from her arms. Back then, that scream had been her own.

She let go the stainless steel basket that she was about to tip into a deburring barrel and its load of gold-coloured finger rings and necklace chains spilled everywhere – she trod half-moon earrings with decorative fretwork patterns like flowers as she peered at the factory floor. What with the deafening stamping press banging out fresh pieces of metal nearby and the general fug in the air, she was confused as to what awful accident might have occurred.

Someone else took up the cry. It was the Frenchman Raoul wondering, like her, what the hell was going on.

Bridget and Mary were next to shriek. They stopped gluing imitation sapphires on to rings and brooches, threw down their gummy paintbrushes in ashtrays full of water and mounted their stools. There they stood clutching their knees as they peered all round. A few yards further along the workshop, the ex-soldier with the nervous tick and explosive temper who went by the name of Nigel (not his real name) looked up from his Startrite five speed drilling plinth. He was just bringing its diamond-tipped bit to bear on a brass plate in a shower of gold dust, when something ran over his feet. He let go the long metal handle and the drill recoiled with a bang.

'What the Devil?'

Raoul's compatriot, Thibaut, also stopped what he was doing. He eased his foot off the pedal of his electric soldering and demagnetising machine when, in the general confusion, he banged his brow on the hot, bare bulb that hung over his bench.

'What is it?'

Nora saw something pause and look up through the slots in the wooden decking at her toes – she caught the glint of a shiny black eye. Whatever it was squealed. Rather, its constant scream was cut short by rib-crushing contractions. Its body pulsed with pain as it arched its back to stave off each terrifying spasm.

Soon it was off again, driven by the next convulsive movement. The wretched animal was trying to outrun its death throes, she realised, it was seeking refuge beneath the wet wooden boards on which everyone walked in the workshop. Instinct drove it on towards the door, to air, space and freedom as pain devoured its vital organs.

Factory foreman Kevin Devaney marched past with his pipe in his hand and shot her a nasty look.

'Get back to work, you whore.'

'But that rat is dying. It could bite someone.'

'I couldn't care less about that.'

'Did you poison it?'

'What do you expect? The boss is due here at any minute.'

'What if someone gets bitten?'

'My point exactly.'

So saying, Devaney opened the shutters to the workshop just as a two-seater SS Jaguar 100 sports car cruised to a halt in the yard. One tyre went over the blinded, bewildered rodent. It popped it like a balloon. Bloodied the wire spoke wheel. Nora saw the foreman run round the car to open its driver's door, only to stand back respectfully. Even a bully like him knew his place in the pecking order.

'Miss Boreman?'

'What does it look like?'

'Er...'

The driver extended a long leg over the car's curvaceous, red running board; she emerged from its low-cut door wearing her fox fur coat and a bulbous red beret trimmed with a pompom.

'What's wrong, Mr Devaney? Cat got your tongue?'

'We don't see you very often.'

'My brother couldn't make it today, so here I am.'

Thibaut made a face at Nora who stifled a giggle. She desperately urged him to resume work at the electric furnace where he melted a block of metal into silver lava, ready to pour it into rubber moulds. She was reminding him how necessary it was to err on the side of caution, something she had learnt polishing dormitory floors with beeswax for hours on end under the watchful eyes of flint-faced nuns. She, especially, had reason to feel nervous about unexpected visitors, ever since she had run away from "St Mary's Mother and Baby Home" in her native Ireland.

Devaney reminded her of the redoubtable Mother Odile who had never once stinted on the use of the rod.

Best to look busy, she decided. Other workers did the same. They set about wiring, drilling and electro-plating more jewellery in a great hurry.

Devaney kicked aside the fallen basket on the greasy duckboards that led past the benches. He was all fingers and thumbs suddenly.

'Do please watch how you go, Miss Boreman, or you'll ruin your shoes.'

'Thank you so much.'

The unexpected visitor trod cautiously in her lace-up, brown brogues which she always wore to the factory, on account of their robust heels of stacked leather. Effluent from acid and rinse tanks flowed along an open gutter. Each bang from the metal press shook the ground like a small earthquake.

'Shall we go straight to the office?' urged Devaney, anxiously.

But Miss Boreman had come to a halt beside Thibaut. She watched him open the mould to reveal a profusion of delicate, spidery grooves which cast fancy brass fretwork in the shape of lace-like shells. Idly, she picked up a paintbrush used for cleaning the finished article. She rolled its stem between finger and thumb like a miniature witch's broomstick. Then she placed it very carefully back on the bench before her.

'Fact is, Mr Devaney, my brother and I are not happy. Ever since The Jewellery Quarter in Birmingham was mostly turned over to making munitions, it has been up to us to fill the gap in the market. Women still want to buy pretty things. It's good for morale.'

'But more and more orders are coming in for army buttons. We have government contracts to fulfil for soldiers' uniforms…'

'This war won't last for ever. I'm thinking of the future. Now's our chance to establish a whole new business. Demand for our jewellery continues to grow, yet our production is slow.'

'If you could just step this way for a moment, Miss Boreman…'

'So tell me what's wrong?'

'The weather's bad. People are falling ill.'

'Say that again.'

'One of the older women can't stop coughing. Fingers split and don't heal in the cold…'

'That wasn't what I asked. I'm here to see the books.'

Devaney looked flustered. He really didn't want a dressing down in front of the workers.

'I'll get right on it, Miss Boreman.'

'Yeah, I suppose you will.'

TEN

Freya knew when not to speak out of turn. James didn't like any noise at the breakfast table – he wouldn't even let her tune in to the radio. Heaven forbid that her knife should squeal on her plate as she sliced the rind off her bacon. Generally, reticence was her magic cloak. She could hope to 'vanish' by not revealing character, feeling or even intuition.

She listened to her husband gobble his food while he pored long and hard over dates in his diary. Now and then he uttered a piggish grunt as he geared himself up to deal with whatever problems the day might bring. She admired his entrepreneurial steeliness. His willpower. Even his heartlessness. He fiddled with his 9-carat gold tie pin or rang the bell for Betty to bring him some more toast or pour him fresh coffee from the new percolator. He swore as his tongue slurped the dregs from his mug.

Her own tongue was a fleshy, muscular slug in her mouth which threatened to choke her as she tried to remain calm.

The solution to his nervous tension today, she wanted to tell him, wasn't more threats, extortion or violence. They were his stock-in-trade, but they only created more problems at home.

'I don't know when I'll be back tonight,' said James without looking up.

Freya's hand froze on her fork. Its prongs stopped at her lips. Was he really going to leave her to pack all *his* things by herself? Moving home was a complicated business and they still had lots to sort out. As it was, there were half-filled boxes and portmanteaus of belongings still awaiting her attention, here, all over Drake's House. She looked down at the table and coughed. It was a quiet, prudent choking sound which she could pass off as a piece of stringy meat.

'But you said…'

'I know what I said.'

James continued to make a pig of himself. If it was one thing that he appreciated, it was their maid's cooking, thought Freya. She listened to him tasting, masticating, swallowing. His greedy tongue was a mockery of hers; it had in its arsenal all sorts of ferocious weapons – sharp, caustic, dangerous, short. It could snap at her like a crocodile. Then again, it could be ironical, humorous, facetious, tender.

The problem this morning was Sam. School classes might have been suspended for the foreseeable future, but still he wanted to sport his old cap which was far too small, frayed and falling to pieces. James had snatched it off his head and thrown it away.

'Ignore him. He'll soon forget all about it. If school resumes after Christmas, which I doubt, he can wear his new one.'

Freya fidgeted. Had she not already stressed that Sam couldn't do without it? Last night he had struggled to go to sleep for the very thought of it. That old cap was his crutch. A reassurance. A mark of continuity and stability. It was worse than his book of trains.

'Please, James, be kind for once.'

'No, he can't have it. He has to stop being so silly and learn to let go. You see, it'll be a milestone.'

But it wasn't all right, it was a contest. She knew it. James knew it. In consigning the cap to the dustbin in the backyard he had issued a challenge: it was his word against hers and he was winning.

'By the way, Freya, we move into the new house on Saturday.'

'Saturday? But we agreed Monday.'

'I decided to bring the date forward.'

'Without telling me?'

'Now I have.'

She carefully sliced more bacon on her plate. She cut it into little pieces. Anatomized it. She did it the same way a pathologist sought to examine something dead part by part – she analysed and criticized it in minute detail.

'I won't wait up for you, then,' she said, referring back to his original comment.

James nodded and left the table, whereupon Freya expressed an inaudible sigh of relief.

Not until she watched him leave for work did she own up to that festering scream that she kept locked in her throat.

Her spine sprang back into shape after sitting so tensely at the kitchen table for so long.

She picked up the ignition key to her Riley 9 Lynx Tourer and stepped outside. She rolled her head and felt her aching neck. There might be no school to which to drive Sam any more, but that didn't diminish the burning temptation to take off somewhere new, wild and unfettered.

Instead, she ran as far as the dustbin, lifted its lid and dipped her hand into the still warm ashes from last night's fires. Suddenly she felt as if she could breathe again. She returned to the house just as quickly.

'Don't let your father see it, Sam.'

'Don't let my father see it.'

'It's our secret.'

'It's our secret.'

She was striking the first blow to foster what might never be more than a small reprieve, by doing something very risky. No one, not even Betty, had seen her do it or so she hoped. In retrieving the dirty old school cap from the rubbish, she had scored a minor victory which somehow shaped her resistance.

But there it must stay for now, under wraps, so to speak.

Like that strange business of the candles in the cathedral.

Monday November 25, 1940

Roofless, half-collapsed houses all look the same. One ruin merges with another as vast quantities of loose bricks and timbers spill into the road. A few firefighters clamber like ants up and down the scree. I'm walking in a wilderness of smoking rubble. Here a multi-storey building, doorless and windowless, has been disembowelled while a few paces further on, over all the trailing hosepipes, someone else's home has been turned inside out – I'm gazing in disbelief at blue wallpaper on bedroom walls that now stand open to the drizzle.

Here's what I've done. I've come as far as I can into what was the commercial heart of Bristol.

So where are the restaurants, dress shops, tobacconists and tailors, to name but a few? A few hours ago you could buy almost anything here.

But there's nothing left of any of it.

Not a damned thing.

With the daylight comes an awful silence. Those noisy burglar alarms and barking dogs cannot contradict the grotesque absence of noise. Then I realise. My head still rings with the scream of sirens, the heavy drone of enemy planes, the thumps of ack-ack guns and the earth-shaking blasts of exploding bombs. The sky might be empty but that doesn't stop me listening for the whistle of incendiaries. That silence is fear.

There's still some blood in the gutters, but it's the smell I can't stand. Flesh, both human and animal, smokes under debris that has yet to be cleared.

I'm here to find Jack and Emmy.

Only I have the right to lay claim to their blackened bones.

ELEVEN

There was no going back now, thought Jo. She just couldn't. The Boreman Properties' advertisement in the local fishmonger's window promised somewhere that had all the hallmarks of a historic town house of high quality.

When someone like her found themselves all alone, they owed it to themselves to make the best of their predicament without burdening other people. That went for war widows especially. Which was why she was so determined not to make such a hash of it this time. To put it bluntly, this was her one chance to make a new home for herself and her baby, now that her previous landlady had so thoughtfully evicted her with one week's notice – not everyone would tolerate an unmarried mother under their roof. It was entirely her own fault – she should never have opened her big mouth, been truthful!

She was feeling distinctly upbeat when a smartly dressed woman drove up to the door of 18A Edwy Parade in her red sports car.

'Mrs Jo Wheeler? How lovely! We spoke on the phone. How-do-you-do. My name is Tia Boreman.'

'How-do-you-do. Thank you for agreeing to show me round the property so soon.'

'Of course it needs a bit of work,' said Tia and ignored Jo's outstretched hand to look in her bag for a key. She peered past the brim of her blue trilby trimmed with petersham ribbon, while she struggled to unlock the door to the little, red-brick terraced home. As owner and landlord, she was keen to get in off the street as soon as possible, evidently.

'I'm not afraid to get my hands dirty,' said Jo, with a laugh.

Bella sniffed a rusty ironing board lying abandoned in the tiny front garden. A dog should be able to trust her owner's judgement without question, she supposed.

'There, we're in,' said Tia and flashed a gold tooth at them both.

Some hard wood blocks from a child's box of Picabrix blocked the hall.

'Previous tenant leave in a hurry, did they?' said Jo.

'War widow, like you. Fell behind with the rent. I had to sling her and her five kids out on their ear.'

'I can tell.'

Bella barked. Someone needed to take a good look at the peeling wallpaper. No, really, they should. What dog could be expected to live in such squalor? Yet here they were, about to slum it. She couldn't rule it out.

Tia, smelling of jasmine, clutched her ruched, shell-shaped handbag close to her red, knee-length fur coat. She sidled like a crab down the narrow hallway, should any of the filthy black marks on the wall somehow leap out at her. She might turn up her nose at the glassy-eyed fox fur round her landlord's neck, thought Jo, but she recognised a bargain when she saw it. A fur with its legs and head still attached was classified as a pelt and not subject to rationing.

'What you have here, Mrs Wheeler, is a rare opportunity to rent a charming property which is only a ten-minute walk from Gloucester city centre.'

'About the décor…'

'I haven't finished. It occupies a peaceful backstreet location much in demand by bombed-out people such as yourself.'

'Is that drains I can smell?'

Tia kicked aside a tin bath with the 4-inch heel of her black suede and snakeskin shoe.

'All houses of character have their peculiarities, Mrs Wheeler. This way, if you please. In here we have the impressive parlour.'

Are you serious, thought Bella? It was not big enough to swing a cat.

Three's a crowd, definitely.

'I know you'll like it,' said Tia, retouching her lipstick in a mirror over the fireplace.

Jo sniffed again more loudly.

'I was hoping for something a little larger.'

'So cosy, isn't it?'

Say what she had to, but the house had no electricity, no 'Wizard in the Wall'. She should have known as much when she passed the grubby little gas lamp in the hall.

It was not so good.

It was not so bad.

A buff wicker chair, upholstered in flowery cretonne, was the parlour's only furniture. Its reversible cushion lay loose on the filthy, threadbare carpet.

'I'm just not sure that I can live somewhere quite so – how can I say – *tired*.'

'You don't know anything yet, Mrs Wheeler. You'll soon transform it into a modestly chic abode.'

'Modest is right.'

'Perfect for a downsizer like you.'

'Shouldn't someone – you know – give a place like this a bit of a spring clean before letting it to anyone new?'

Tia's eyes widened. She rose, teetered and subsided momentarily on her peep-toes. Her look bore down sternly on both her and Bella.

'Time is money, Mrs Wheeler. Boreman Properties manage a great many dwellings. We can't possibly afford to run after all our clients and do their housework for them. Besides, there's a war on.'

They headed for what Jo hoped might be the kitchen.

'I see something has gnawed holes in the skirting boards.'

Tia buried her nose in her fox fur.

'What's a few mice?'

'Could be something else.'

Bella was of that opinion, too, as she eyed suspicious gaps in the wainscoting. Her nose led her on a trail of black, lozenge-shaped droppings. Either the mice round here were enormous or…

'Moving on,' said Tia, with a click of her heels. 'A house like this always has such a lovely lived-in atmosphere, don't you think?'

Jo kept away from peeling plaster and bare brick.

'I can smell that smell again.'

'Nothing a little bit of tender loving care can't fix, Mrs Wheeler.'

'That's what you said last time.'

'I wasn't lying.'

'Admit it, it's a bit of a ruin.'

'You said it yourself, how many other landlords in Gloucester will let you keep a dog in their property?'

'That much I admit.'

So now it was her fault, thought Bella and slunk off.

'Welcome to your very own urban retreat,' said Tia proudly. 'Here we have the dining room/kitchen/breakfast room/living space.'

Jo stared at the tiny back room off which led an even tinier scullery.

'….'

'Handy, isn't it. Bespoke solutions make the most of the smallest places.'

She stopped at a gas-heated copper and gave its tank a tap. It held water all right. Nearby lay a washboard and mangle. At least she'd have somewhere to boil and dry dirty towels and nappies. There was even a fold-up wooden clothes horse on which to air her bras, girdles and slips. Well, everyone had to start somewhere.

She opened a cabinet complete with flour box and scoop.

'Does the cooker work, at all?'

Tia stared at her very hard before her voice came back as a growl.

'How should I know?'

'Just curious. The hotplate looks a little black to say the least.'

Tia wrinkled her nose and opened the cooker's fall-down door very cautiously. Then she quickly let go of it again with a bang.

'You might want to replace it.'

'I will.'

'Moving on. Note the spacious garden.'

'Is that a water closet I can see in a corner?' said Jo as they entered a small brick yard bounded by crumbling walls that were overgrown with ivy.

'Consider it your very own private privy. No sharing with neighbours…'

'It has a cistern, at least.'

'…in your very own garden.'

'We're standing on cobblestones.'

'It's the perfect place for stargazing on a clear night. Take a tip from me, Mrs Wheeler: always buy medicated toilet paper. It's hard and shiny and doesn't go damp in the frost.'

'This is where that foul smell is coming from, isn't it?'

Tia turned on her heels.

'An ideal space for your dog. Think of that. And in that corner is your very own Anderson shelter.'

Bella looked mournful. If it were left to her, she'd get straight to the point – she couldn't help but wonder where a dog was to dig if this was her garden. As for the prefabricated air raid shelter buried in the ground, she was pretty sure it had rats.

'I could have tubs of flowers, I suppose,' said Jo. 'I could win the best-planted shelter award for the neighbourhood.'

In actual fact, everyone she knew had already abandoned their garden shelters for the filthy, damp holes in the ground they really were. Nowadays people favoured sheltering from bombs indoors – they were taking refuge like animals in reinforced cages that doubled up as dining tables by day in case the roof fell in. More fool them. It was a sure way of burning to death if your home caught fire.

'Please, this way, Mrs Wheeler and I'll show you the rest of the house.'

'Bella, come.'

'Do mind the stairs. As you can see, there's no carpet.'

They trod steep, narrow treads whose wood had worn black and slippery over the years.

'Please observe the compact linen cupboard on your way past, Mrs Wheeler. So handy.'

'How about a bathroom?'

'You saw the tub. A wash by the fire in the parlour is so much cosier.'

'Headroom's a bit on the low side,' said Jo, ducking a sagging ceiling. She was already trying to work out how many pans and kettles it was going to take to fill that tin bath she'd seen earlier. Where she'd grown up, she'd once had maids to do all that for her. In recent years, newly installed gas heaters had heated water in more than one bathroom.

'Here we have a lovely bedroom with calming city views,' said Tia, opening blackout curtains to let in some light through a grubby window.

Jo blinked at the sight of a vast stadium. It was, Tia pointed out happily, Kingsholm's Gloucester Rugby Ground.

'Just think, Mrs Wheeler. You'll be able to soak up the atmosphere of the game from the comfort of your own home. There have already been fundraising matches for the armed forces held in the Odsal Stadium in Bradford. Who knows, it might happen here, too.'

'And if I don't like rugby?'

'Don't worry, with the war on there hasn't been much activity lately.'

It was true, teams such as The Worcester Warriors were taking a break for the duration of the war, but Hereford Rugby Club were continuing to play as many games as possible. Who knew if she would have to listen to the sound of men's animal screams any time soon? Already "We are the Gloster boys, G-L-O-U-C-E-S-T-E-R – GLOUCESTER" rang in her ears as fans roared their traditional song.

She was all in favour of men playing their silly games.

That's not what she feared.

She feared hearing screams inside her own home.

Would thicker blackout curtains at the windows shut out the noise, because she didn't sleep too well at night?

No, probably not.

'Is there anything else I need to know?'

Tia refolded her fox fur scarf at her throat, then led the way back downstairs.

'You have here an immensely popular place to live.'

'That's what worries me.'

She was still thinking of possible cries from the stadium. She might be half deaf in one ear, but one scream could soon recall others never to be forgotten.

'Think of it as a unique opportunity to restore this lovely little house to its former glory.'

'It doesn't look good.'

'Do you want it or not?'

'I do wonder.'

'How do you mean?'

'If you could just reduce the rent a little to reflect the condition?'

With half a smile Tia locked the front door behind them after a wrench and a bang. Her 4-inch wedge heels clomped about on the short garden path back to the pavement.

'Must dash, Mrs Wheeler. I'm late for my next appointment. Who doesn't want to rent Boreman Properties' characterful lettings?'

'Sorry to ask?'

Tia walked over to her shiny red SS Jaguar 100. Before she opened the car's low-slung door she turned her head and her hard blue eyes stared straight at her.

'Maybe you weren't listening.'

'Okay, I'll take it,' said Jo, 'but only because it's not more than ten minutes' walk to the cathedral at night for my fire watch duties.'

'Good for you, Mrs Wheeler. You won't regret it. I take it your husband died fighting?'

'Like to think so.'

'You'll be reclusive but not remote,' said Tia and promptly shut herself in the open-topped roadster. 'You'll be homely but not…'

'I get it. I really do.'

Jo stroked her as yet not very swollen belly. She had no more words to account for the chill that had just run down her spine. It was a sensation of panic – once alone in the house she would have to confront who she was, start over on her limited budget. No more lies. She would finally face up to the fact that there was no doctor to stand between her and the everyday business of coping alone, ever since she had been discharged from the burns hospital, not to mention her short stay in the mental asylum after she'd threatened to shoot… Well, never mind. Each time the air raid sirens went off, her head felt on fire as though she were back in Bristol amidst the bomb blasts, shrapnel and falling rafters. Already she felt a familiar shadow stalk, mock and get ready to test her – she felt as if she were dealing with the Devil himself again, but the car's two-and-a-half litre engine suddenly roared into action to distract her.

'Rent is in advance,' shouted Tia above the deafening blast of all six cylinders. 'No buts. Do I make myself clear?'

'That won't be a problem.'

'Glad to hear it. I'm sure you and your bow-legged, scrawny, flea-bitten dog will be very happy together.'

Bella watched Tia race away a trifle coldly, then she entered her new abode hard on the heels of her mistress. She did so in a mood of dumb disappointment. Even your average bow-legged, scrawny, flea-bitten pet had her standards.

TWELVE

Overripe fruit – that's what it most reminded him of, thought Thibaut, wrinkling his nose still harder. That strange perfume pursued him everywhere he went in the muggy factory. He could only think that it had something to do with the open gutter that drained the workshop floor. There, cyanide met acid and turned the water blue. The fumes were worse than the dirt and noise; they ate at his nostrils and left them red and sore.

Of one thing he was quite certain: the rotten air he breathed was daily more obnoxious and disgusting.

He sat on his stool at his bench and picked up a pair of red snips. This was monotonous work. As he cut a length of 22-gauge soft copper wire, the stamping press went thump, thump, thump without a break at the far end of the workshop. Each heavy, percussive thud banged like a drum in his head. The vibrations ran through the concrete floor and into his feet to give him pins and needles.

He had not yet spoken much to the boy who worked the press, but he knew his name. It was Adrian, a deserter from the British Army. Since he scarcely considered himself a soldier any more, he bore the youth no great grudge. There had to be thousands of Adrians who had run away from the fighting because they couldn't bear the carnage any longer.

Thump. Thump. Thump. The press was a huge hammer: it came crashing down to spit out shapes from a long strip of metal that was continuously fed through its jaws. It was what he imagined war did to people. Each sliver of brass passed through a forming tool which bent it into shape to make the next brooch, badge or button. Actually, it was no use trying to talk to Adrian, since he was already deaf, such was the effect of the stamping press on his unprotected ears.

At that moment Nora shot him a smile. This was the second time today that she had risked looking at him this way. But Thibaut recognised in her blood-shot, tired eyes something of which he daily recognized in himself – the increasingly ghastly glaze of never-ending worry. Of course, any meaningful conversation was difficult in the din. Besides, it was forbidden.

That didn't stop her trying.

'Where did you say you're from again?'

'I was born in a small place called Blesle in south-central France. It's a pretty little place up one end of a picturesque valley with a circular Romanesque church. I was training to be a policeman with the local gendarmerie until I had to join the army. When the Germans invaded I managed to escape capture at Dunkirk. I consider myself lucky, luckier than Raoul, for instance – he saw his brother drown before his very eyes.'

'You did what you could.'

Thibaut shook his head wearily. Ever since Marshal Philippe Petain had moved the French capital from Paris to Vichy, he'd felt totally ashamed. If she really wanted to know, a "Free Zone" had been established in the southern part of the country free of German troops in some sort of accommodation with Hitler. Now that Allied troops had made big gains in North Africa, though, the Germans had occupied the whole of France anyway and French policemen were being ordered to round up Jews. Women had lost hard won rights. The Catholic Church was not being much help. This was scarcely the France he had known and loved, so much so that he wondered if it was even worth fighting for? But he didn't tell her all that, he didn't want to scare her.

'How did you end up working here?' asked Nora.

'I was begging outside Gloucester Cathedral when someone came over and said he could find me a job.'

'Me, too.'

'What made him choose you?'

'He just did.'

'Haven't you noticed? Almost everyone here is an ex-soldier or a homeless person seriously down on their luck.'

'Yeah,' said Nora, 'we all have one thing in common.'

'You think?'

'No one will miss us when we're gone.'

'I was so happy not to die on that French beach but now….'

Nora had a story, too.

'I left Ireland after falling on hard times and ended up living on the streets. Work here and all would be well, I was told. It was either that or become a prostitute with my shameful past. I had an ID Card and Ration Card, but Devaney took them from me and won't give them back. One worker threatened to report this place to the police, but we haven't seen him since. I've had enough. I don't know what to do. Will you help me?'

'Watch out, here comes the foreman now.'

They both busily resumed sorting jewellery for wiring onto copper jigs for electro-plating. It paid to be diligent, Thibaut realised. Kevin Devaney was a heavily built bully with an ugly face rendered still uglier by his broken nose. He was also a drinker who liked to down a few pints every lunchtime and, as a result, he had an uncertain temper. Today his shirt hung loose from his trousers and his flies were undone. His wild, staring eyes seemed to swim in his face.

'All of you – get on with your work. What do you think this is, a holiday camp?'

A soldering iron weighed threateningly in Nora's deft fingers. With a cloud of stinging smoke, she melted flux on metal to solder a red heart to a ring.

'I said fucking get on with it. You know how the boss likes his orders to go out on time. You know what happens when they don't.'

Everyone redoubled their efforts to work faster as the foreman walked along the wet, slippery duckboard that covered the gangway. His heavy boots creaked on the wooden planks, his steel-capped toes got ready to kick someone.

Next minute Thibaut left his bench and crossed the workshop with his jig of fifty brass earrings in order to degrease them prior to plating. They jingled on their long copper wires like little Christmas bells. Instead of making soldiers' buttons as per army contract, a lot of valuable metal was being redirected into these gewgaws for private gain? But what could he do about it? What could he say?

Mary, also busily wiring jewellery onto jigs, had warned him not to breathe the foggy clouds that issued from the heated tank before him. Pale-faced Bridget said the same – the white mist into which he was about to dip his hands was something dangerous called trichloroethane.

'Take my advice,' she hissed in his ear. 'Don't lean in too close.'

'Is it poisonous?'

'The fumes give you a lift which can be addictive.'

It explained why, every morning, Devaney stood over that particular tank and took a deep breath. He liked the analgesic rush that went to his head.

'What about the foreman?' asked Thibaut.

Bridget smirked.

'Who cares if he dies?'

But avoiding the fumes wasn't so easy. The ghostly white vapour tingled in his nose, scorched his throat and set fire to his lungs. At ten o'clock break, he ventured outside into the walled area at the back of the factory to smoke a cigarette with everyone else. Adrian, Raoul and Nigel all huddled together at one end of the enclosed space that was stacked high with leaky drums of used toxic waste. It occurred to him that while the factory gates were kept locked, he could climb these metal drums and hop over the wall? Beyond it lay a vast river and forest. More than that, he couldn't say.

Meanwhile Nora, Mary and the red-haired Bridget talked together on the other side of the yard. They were looking at him and giggling.

'Merde,' said Raoul, 'I hate this shitty war.' He, too, liked to rail against the Vichy government back home but only because he was a Bolshevik. As such, he could be political and dangerous.

'Tell me about it,' replied Thibaut, grimly.

'If our generals hadn't relied so heavily on the Maginot Line we wouldn't be here now and my brother might still be alive.'

'I can't believe you just said that.'

'They owe us.'

'I don't even want to think about it.'

'We should have been better prepared.'

'Nobody expected Hitler to Blitzkrieg us via Belgium.'

'Only the Russians can save Europe now, you mark my words. Only they have a big enough army.'

'Doesn't exactly help you and me here.'

'Okay, but watch what you do with that degreasing tank. It's very dangerous.'

'You know this how?'

'It can catch fire. It's definitely illegal. You shouldn't apply heat directly to trichloroethane. They say it's not inflammable but that's not altogether true. Devaney is buying reconstituted liquid on the cheap. It isn't right, I tell you, there'll be a disaster. And by the way, in case you haven't noticed, that Irish mademoiselle is sweet on you.'

'Don't be ridiculous.'

*

Back in the factory Thibaut did his best to learn the names of the chemicals that set his trachea on fire – sulphuric, nitric and hydrochloric acids. To walk back to his bench was to move through their bluish fog. He was scared and confused, not only by the filthy conditions in which he worked, but by the rash on the lower part of his arm; the skin prickled bright red. It was like a thousand stinging nettles. This was no ordinary rash due to heat – more often than not the workshop was extremely cold – but a more worrying inflammation. He suspected dermatitis.

So quickly did he have to work, dipping jewellery in and out of different tanks full of evil-looking liquids, that it was all too easy to splash his hands and face without even noticing. His nails were perpetually black because there was only one small washbasin in one tiny toilet that served all the workers.

Now his fingers craved to scratch the back of his wrists. Today a million itch mites were burrowing into his skin. His flesh was already scabby; he really had to work hard to ignore the constant distraction of his body. Scabies couldn't have been much worse.

Nora scratched herself, too. Because one of her jobs was to heat the vats of chromic acid every morning and polarize the lead anodes, she breathed in a lot of fumes whenever she stirred the hot, steamy liquid. The fine droplets of chromate salts collected in her nostrils where they had begun to burn her septum. Co-worker Mary, who had toiled in the factory for much longer, had already suffered a hole from one nostril to the other.

Thibaut grew increasingly aware of Nora's presence at the bench beside him. It was disturbing but somehow challenging. When he at last summoned the courage to smile at her he knew only one thing – he did for a second or two escape the hellish predicament in which they both found themselves. But it wasn't that simple. Any momentary reprieve was immediately shattered by the arrival of a flatbed lorry loaded with brass, copper and steel billets at the front entrance of the factory.

Devaney was all derogatory shouts suddenly.

'What's up, Frenchman? You daydreaming again? Go help unload the truck at once. Or you'll be working nights again.'

'Yes, Mr Devaney.'

To disobey was to lose pay.

'That a problem?'

'No, Mr Devaney.'

'Because if you ever lay a finger on Nora you'll be in trouble. She's mine.'

'Don't kid yourself.'

'What did you just say?'

'You're the boss, Mr Devaney.'

'Because you do like her, don't you?'

'Want me to go, or not?'

'Should I worry?'

'Please let me pass, Mr Devaney.'

But the foreman eyeballed him with a sense of simmering grievance that could only be said to be downright vicious.

'Don't step out of line, Frenchman. You remember that, or you could meet with an accident. All it takes is one word to the boss and you're finished here.'

Thibaut walked, head bowed, to the waiting lorry. There he climbed aboard a forklift truck and began to unload billets of metal on their wooden pallets. He'd never had any training in driving the clumsy vehicle apart from a few lessons from Devaney. No one had. They were expected to get on and do it. No wonder terrible accidents had occurred.

It was then that Nora's words came back into his head. They burned in his mind like all those acids in his throat. She was right: they had to look out for each other. For the foreseeable future they could be certain that no one would rescue them.

Which meant seizing the initiative. They had to come up with a plan before this place killed them both. It mustn't be too long. For now, though, he could only rack his brains as to how, not when, escape might happen. Nora should let him talk it over at once with Raoul.

Monday 2 December 1940

This is the first time I have ever held an incendiary bomb in my hands. It's definitely a dud but I still finger it with care.

It can't weigh more than a bag of sugar.

Frankly, it has to be insignificant next to a massive Satan bomb that can flatten a whole row of houses in seconds.

This finned metal tube is no more than a very large firework.

I couldn't be more wrong.

It was an incendiary bomb just like this that began the fire that burned Jack and Emmy to death. The Imperial Eagle on the side is a nice touch. It gives the stamp of officialdom to the business of killing innocent people.

As if the dead care.

My fingers pass from hole to hole in the bomb's side. These let out the gas when the detonator begins to burn.

So I've seen.

Now I'm a Fire Guard, I know that these incendiaries have a weakness – they can be extinguished.

6.30 p.m. It's been nine days since the first raid on Castle Street. The bombers are back, which is why I'm standing on the roof of St Mary Redcliffe Church with Canon Sidney Swan and his trusty team of fire watchers – we're all busting a gut to stop the roof catching fire and melting the lead. I have the tools and training. All I need now is the will to fight back.

That's not to say I don't feel awfully exposed up here as fire rains down all around us. Together, we're frantically priming our stirrup pumps. These bombs burn like mad for about a minute, but after that we can get in close enough to douse the flames with water and sand from our buckets.

Tonight we're going to fight like fury against 'Firebomb Fritz' to save a little bit of Bristol.

THIRTEEN

It never rained but it poured, thought Jo. First there was that queer business of Sam at Sarah Smith's funeral, then the delusional Bruno with his accusations of murder and now here she was about to give herself a dreadful chill, to be sure. At least there was, by the sound of it, a happy and convivial atmosphere coming from Victoria House at 136 Barton Street, even if the pub's windows were all painted black for the blackout.

Why should she not believe it?

All was obviously right with the world.

What's more, it was her night off from fire duty.

Yes, but she did worry.

Time to leave Bella round the corner in Victoria Street.

'You watch over the motorcycle. Understood?'

Bella curled a lip and immediately joined her on the pavement.

'Just asking,' said Jo, and threw her cap, goggles and gloves into the sidecar. Her gas mask she kept slung over her left shoulder.

Every roof and chimney glittered and glistened with frost. What's more, the total absence of streetlights magnified the glorious, star-lit sky in a way not seen before the war. But she wasn't here to wonder at the beauty of night-time Gloucester, she was hoping to solve a bit of a mystery.

She gripped her No. 8 pocket torch. If she hesitated to shine it for long at the inky pavement, it was because replacement batteries were so damned hard to come by! Besides, given the obligatory piece of tissue pasted over its glass to dim its beam, it was next to useless, not least because she was forbidden by law to point it anywhere but directly at her feet, even when flashing it twice to hail a bus. That's why so many pedestrians had taken to wearing reflective buttons, so that fewer people like her bumped into them.

Many a male head turned the instant she entered the pub. She did not so much feel cold as chilled – one was less explicable than the other. Hers was an unfamiliar face in otherwise familial surroundings.

It wasn't just the sight of her shrivelled ear which she did nothing to hide.

Not that anyone looked at her disfigurement for more than a second or two.

One embarrassed, horrified glance at her 'badge of shame' proved sufficient, usually.

Everyone soon resumed their drinking.

Never said a word.

She called for a stout at the bar. Some days she liked to drink until she could no longer stand; *sometimes* she lay on the ground in a drunken stupor while Bella sat like an incubus on her chest, keeping guard.

Tonight could turn into one of those nights, if she decided to 'let go'.

Wouldn't be the first.

Wouldn't be the last.

Admit it, not much else dulled the pain that screamed silently inside her. The outbreak of war had brought some advantages, though. At least now she could visit a pub all by herself without being called a whore.

'Hey there, you seen Noah lately?'

The long-chinned barman wiped a glass with a rag.

'Who wants to know?'

'I'm Mrs Jo Wheeler. Victoria House is his regular.'

'Then know this, Mrs Wheeler, we don't much care for the likes of you in here.'

'Don't get me wrong, I don't mean him any harm. I'm a Fire Guard at the cathedral. I'm not here to cause any trouble.'

'Those oilskins you're wearing say different.'

She had spoken too soon, it seemed. Not every publican thought lone women deserved a drink in wartime, not everyone thought she should ride a motorcycle, especially.

'Listen, chum, I'm a friend of Noah's. I'm worried about him, that's all. I can't find him anywhere on the streets any more.'

The barman went on polishing the same glass with slow deliberate hands until it shone.

'You asking me to rat on him?'

'As I said, this is where he likes to come for a drink.'

'Noah didn't turn up to play skittles last Sunday.'

'Should I be worried?'

'Never known him miss his eight o'clock game before.'

'Can you think why?'

'I've already said too much.'

The barman shifted sideways to serve another customer. In that moment he might as well have been a mile away.

With no clear strategy in mind Jo drank her stout and took a walk from one crowded room to another. An over-sized toucan with its comical red and yellow bill beamed at her from a Guinness advertisement, while the picture of a silver Grand Prix racing car hurtled across a wall. She started asking around but no one would say when they had last seen Noah. Not that they knew of. Not that they cared.

That left the drunk, brawny man who sucked on his black Bakelite pipe and blew smoke in her face. He had a swarthy skin and a crooked nose, while his unmistakeably mean look was accentuated by an old burn above one eye whose lid drooped heavily. He tried to pat Bella's head and cooed baby noises at her as she dodged his exceptionally large feet on the floor's spongy sawdust.

'Here poochy, poochy. Who's a lovely doggy, then?'

The presence of a canine reduced some people to simpletons, it seemed.

You had to hear it to believe it.

Did these people not know how to engage a miniature bull terrier in meaningful conversation?

Had they no self-respect?

Not that she could tell.

Jo came to a stop before a dartboard. It might mean nothing. She could not honestly say, but her eyes stared hard at the wall. All she could tell was that they did not lie.

A large blackboard hung behind the target on which someone had chalked lists of players and their scores. One particular name read 180 in blurred white dust.

Back at the bar she signalled the barman for another bottle of stout.

'You lied to me just now about Noah.'

The barman's look was both churlish and rude. His whole inconsiderateness had to be a little cynical.

'I'm just not sure there's any more to say.'

'Noah played darts recently. His name and score are still chalked up on the blackboard over there.'

'So he's gone now.'

'Where to?'

'Why would I tell you?'

'You don't seem very bothered about a vulnerable ex-RAF pilot whose lungs suffer in weather this cold.'

'And naturally you are?'

Jo left her bottle half drunk on the bar. It tasted too sour. Or she was about to lose her temper.

'The slightest chest infection can soon end in pneumonia. If you see Noah in the next few days, tell him that Jo Wheeler misses their little chats every morning.'

No sooner had she turned to go than the barman called after her.

'Hang on a minute.'

'Yes?'

'Last I heard, our friend got himself a job. That's all I can tell you.'

'Doing what?'

'Seriously, you don't want to know.'

*

The blacked out street struck her as doubly bleak and icy as Jo pulled on cap, goggles and gloves. Things were not much better on the motorcycle as she did her best to kick-start it into action with a hard thrust of her instep on the reluctant pedal. She had to wait for the 1096 cc, side-valve V-twin engines to burst into life with a great roar.

Suddenly someone came striding round the corner. She might not have seen him at all in the night, had it not been for the cherry red glow of his pipe. At first she assumed that he stopped to take heed of the poster on the wall whose boss-eyed, black cat stared straight at him with the slogan: UNTIL YOUR EYES GET USED TO THE DARKNESS. TAKE IT EASY. But no, he paused only to tap his pipe on the brickwork, emptied its hot ash and began to refill its bowl. Sure enough, he was soon unscrewing the disk-shaped, Bakelite lid on some Fine Shag in his 'baccyflap'.

To her horror she saw him strike a match. Blackout had begun hours ago and no one was meant to show even a cigarette's meagre glow.

Suddenly he looked up and made a beeline for her motorcycle and sidecar. One hand was tucked inside his black donkey jacket as he fixed his eyes on its canine passenger and rider. He could have been carrying a knife or gun.

He appeared intent on noting everything about them.

'What the hell are you doing?' said Jo out loud.

She recognised the heavily built man who had called Bella 'poochy' in the pub. His steel-capped boots glinted in the dimmed light from the sidecar's own, masked spotlight. The hard, lumpy mass of scar tissue weighed upon his eyelid which gave him a perpetually lopsided look, especially as his untidy hair fell across one temple.

Without speaking, he walked all round the Brough Superior Combination with great interest. Okay, that was rude but forgivable, thought Jo. After all, you didn't see the 'Rolls-Royce of Motorcycles' very often. Not even the famous T.E. Lawrence could buy one of these any more, had he still been alive, not since their factory on Haydn Road in Nottingham had been turned over to making crankshafts for Rolls Royce Merlin engines for the war. Their observer said nothing, however, only stopped beside the sidecar.

Bella bared her teeth. Went wild. The man's breath reeked of beer and stale tobacco as it misted the air. His clothes smelt the same. His one good, unobscured eye was unblinking.

Jo wasted no time. She had little reason to trust the intense, manic look on this person's face – she could have been about to go head to head with a murderer. No woman felt safe after blackout. But she was not a coward.

'Say what you want, or else. I'm serious.'

At that, he took a step back. He no longer lodged one hand inside his jacket in a strangely threatening manner, but neither did he cease to study the motorcycle in detail.

'Damn you,' cried Jo and opened the throttle.

She'd got this. She should just go. This drunkard couldn't possibly have anything to do with her.

It had to be a case of mistaken identity, or what?

You'd think he'd say.

Still Bella snarled, frothed and barked her hardest from the sidecar. As Jo rode past Barton Street's bombed-out houses her odd encounter seemed unclear and unremarkable, as having happened in seconds and for no very good reason. Blackout meant she was limited to twenty miles per hour and she was obliged to navigate by the white lines painted down the middle of the road and along the kerbside – it was confusing, frightening and occasionally downright dangerous.

Next moment she blew hot and cold. Her heart roared like that Grand Prix racing car she had seen pictured on the pub wall – she felt her guts twist like an octopus inside her.

The thought was not madness but seemed to float straight down from the cold, frosty roofs of the city itself.

'Of course, Bella! He's the brute in those photographs that Bruno showed us at Sarah Smith's funeral. He's one of the timber thieves that she encountered shortly before she met her death in that car crash in the Forest of Dean.'

As soon as she could, she stopped at a public telephone box to make a call.

'Hi John. It's Jo. I need you to do something for me. *Tout de suite.*'

She'd never intended to take Bruno's rants seriously.

It was a really bad idea.

Now, out of the blue, there was something concrete to go on.

FOURTEEN

Never had she felt so lightheaded and dizzy, thought Nora. The workshop's bluish, acidic atmosphere was giving her a bad throat. Above all else, she mustn't rub her sore eyes. Everywhere in the factory was so filthy it was easy to transfer dirt from one place to another – she could soon give herself conjunctivitis. Instead, she concentrated on scratching the hellishly red spots on the backs of her hands.

Her job today was to sort rejects from hundreds of freshly made miniature Buddhas, boys on crocodiles, lions' heads, shells, highwaymen's pistols and miniature fighter planes. Nearby on her bench lay a pile of pixies with impish grins, large ears and pointed hats, but her favourite was a naked woman reclining in the curve of the moon. None of these brass stampings looked anything much yet, but soon they would all be transformed into eye-catching jewellery coated in silver and gold. First, though, she had to deburr the rough edges from each trinket in a revolving wooden barrel. The hexahedral tumbler was not unlike a greedy little ship. If she did not keep sufficient water in it, its planks would dry out, shrink and leak.

She had just opened a sack to begin ladling cream-coloured burnishing powder into a bucket, when she saw the diminutive, dark-haired Adrian open a storeroom door marked with a skull and crossbones. Soon he was wrestling with a large blue drum of chemicals. This she had to see. It really was quite comical. Talk about King Sisyphus trying to roll a boulder up a hill! He needed to hit the drum with his hammer and screwdriver to unclip its lid, but it was obvious that a puny young man like him was not fit to move something weighing well over one hundred pounds.

Of course she should go over there and help him, but she had her quota of work to finish. Bang, bang, bang went Adrian with his hammer. He tried again to drag the drum a few inches away from the wall to give himself more room. Honestly, he was wasting his time.

At that moment her friend Mary gave her a shout. She, too, worked a deburring barrel just like hers, but she was having trouble emptying it. She literally hadn't a clue.

'Turn it to the top,' said Nora, with her long hair tied up in a red scarf to keep it safe from whirring cogs. 'Use your iron bar to loosen the clamps. Then you can pull out the plug. Now tip.'

'Thanks Nora, I don't know what I'd do without you.'

'Don't forget to put your hand inside the drum to pick out any remaining pieces that have stuck to the sides.'

'Bloody gloves leak.'

'Tell me about it.'

Nora focused her itchy eyes on Adrian again. All efforts to lever off the retaining ring from the top of the impossibly heavy steel drum had finally paid off. Good for him. She turned back to the barrel she had just set in motion. There, she set about silencing its squeaky bearings with a flick of a stick that she dipped in a jar full of grease. She listened to the drum's constant swishing and swashing. At each lurch of water, she let herself be transported away from the factory to a once happy childhood.

She was listening to the rush of seawater up an Irish beach as she trod warm sands with her boyfriend. They were kissing with the break of each wave. To complete the illusion, she closed her eyes and imagined what might have been if only she hadn't 'sinned'… In a small town like hers there was little understanding, let alone forgiveness. You 'got yourself' pregnant, as if no one else was involved.

When she opened her eyes again, Adrian was standing triumphantly beside his open drum. But he was awfully still – rigid, frozen and without sound. Disbelief filled his face. Panic was no less obvious. His body was in shock. Next, he tore at his throat in an effort to breathe.

'Adrian? You okay?'

With no clear understanding she ran to help him, only to see him make dire rasping sounds as he clutched his chest like someone drowning.

She could in no way explain the colour of his face right now. The only other human being she had ever seen turn so blue had been a dying baby. Her own.

It half paralysed, then galvanized her into action.

'Mr Devaney!'

The ape-like silhouette of a man loomed out of the gloom.

'Get back to your bench at once.'

'But something terrible is happening to Adrian.'

The foreman, as clumsy as ever, fixed his hand upon Nora's shoulder and glared at her with that special look he reserved for all troublemakers. His breath reeked of beer. But even he appeared frightened now.

'Hurry. Run to my office. Fetch the First Aid Box.'

'But he's choking to death.'

'So will you if you don't do as I say.'

His reaction was that of a panic-stricken but quick-thinking medic. That's not all he did, noted Nora, as she looked back across the workshop. He already had hold of Adrian by his heels. To her horror, he was dragging the stricken youth through the workshop ready to deposit him outside on the icy ground. The yard was a great pyramid of metal drums and globular glass carboys set in straw and metal frames, a toxic minefield and dumping ground for everything that had outlived its immediate usefulness, but its air had to be fresher than inside.

She hurried back and saw veins swell horribly on Adrian's head and neck. His breathing became noisier. Each gasp proved a struggle to get past the cramp in his chest.

'Is he dying? Should we call an ambulance?'

Devaney shook off her imploring hand.

'No ambulance, Nora. Do I make myself clear?'

'You haven't answered my question.'

'Pass me that bottle labelled amyl nitrite and some cotton wool.'

She literally had no idea what was really happening. But Devaney did. As soon as she gave him the bottle from the medicine box, he transferred some of its liquid to the cotton wool. Then he held the gauze flat in his hand as he waved it under Adrian's nose for him to inhale the vapour.

'He's going to die, isn't he?'

Devaney growled.

'Like to think not.'

So saying, he thrust the bottle and cotton wool into her hand.

'Whatever you do, don't touch his mouth, or else the liquid will give him a nasty rash round his nose and lips.'

Still Adrian went bluer and bluer.

Nora was watching him asphyxiate for lack of 'air'.

Meanwhile Devaney hurriedly cut the stricken man's shirt from his chest and pulled off his trousers. He did it in such a way as not to drag his clothes anywhere near his face.

'Adrian? Can you hear me? Can you tell us what happened?'

But Adrian only rolled his eyes.

'I feel sick to my stomach.'

Nora held on to his shoulders as a fresh seizure arched his spine with severe cramp.

'We should definitely call a doctor.'

'Please, no doctor,' said Adrian.

'But you look very ill.'

'No one must know who I really am. They'll send me back to the army.'

'The army is better than an early grave.'

'From what I've seen, there's little difference.'

'We should get you a coat. You'll catch cold out here.'

'Have mine,' said Devaney. 'The important thing is that he gets as much air into his lungs as possible.'

'It's as if he's drowning.'

'That's what cyanide poisoning does to a person.'

'Cyanide?'

'Yeah, I'm afraid so.'

'Do we have any more amyl nitrite?'

'It's very expensive. As are doctors.'

'Is that what you want, Mr Devaney...?'

'Can't be helped.'

'…to see him die?'

'Too much of that stuff can be dangerous.'

She ignored her own safety and felt for a pulse in the young man's wrist. It was racing like a train. She feared for his heart. He complained of nausea, thirst and blurred vision. She shook him hard before he fainted. She had to try to keep him awake – if he was conscious there had to be hope.

'Stay with me, Adrian. What did you do in the storeroom?'

'The zinc plating solution needs strengthening. Mr Devaney told me… mix cyanide and caustic soda in a bucket of water.'

'You ever do this before?'

'Yeah, but it was a new drum. Instead of hard eggs of cyanide which I could pick out by hand, it was full of fine, white powder.'

'So what happened then?'

'As soon as I dug into the drum the salts took off like snowflakes. They were so fine. They floated right up past my face. Like a blizzard. I must have inhaled something.'

'You bet.'

Devaney went off to secure the door to the storeroom.

Nora ran after him.

'Wait. What if the worst possible thing happens?'

'We'll know in two to six hours. Meanwhile, dip a cigarette in the last of the amyl nitrite and get him to suck it. Make sure you throw it away afterwards because it will be highly flammable if anyone tries to light it.'

'You can't be serious.'

'At least he's not dead yet.'

'Why take that risk?'

'You heard what he said, he doesn't want anyone to find out that he's an army deserter. Neither do I.'

Nora stopped short of the door to the workshop. For a moment she watched the foreman march away and was outraged. A young man's life hung in the balance. But what could she say? Ashamed of her cowardice, she had no excuses. Instead she sensed in her own attitude a cruel pragmatism not unlike Devaney's. To call an ambulance was to invite unwanted questions for which she had to have some very good answers – if this factory shut down she would be back on the streets.

In the next few hours she grew gloomier, not to say sullen. She knew in her heart that she should report her employer to a factory inspector.

About this, however, she literally said nothing. Was this not what Adrian, as much as Devaney, wanted? Nor was the foreman all monster – in the heat of the moment, had he not given him his coat knowing that it would have to be burned afterwards?

Thus were they all bound in absolute obedience to their real master which was silence.

It was "St Mary's Mother and Baby Home" once more.

FIFTEEN

'Please, granddad, tell me more about the phantom boar.'

Sam's request saw a smile cross the old man's bearded lips, rendered more crooked by his jagged cheek bone. Jim Wilde had once been a freeminer digging coal beneath the Forest of Dean, when the adit's roof had fallen in and nearly killed him.

'You know your mother doesn't approve of my silly stories.'

'But you promised.'

They were seated before a glowing fire in the parlour of Tunnel Cottage. Much as he loved to visit his grandfather, his home always filled him with a sense of eeriness and foreboding. The tiny, two-storey sandstone house with its oddly shaped roof – like a grey school cap with its peak pulled down – guarded a level crossing on the railway branch line that pierced nearby Bradley Hill. The occasional coal train rattled the ill-fitting windows as it steamed through the tunnel within sight of their front door. You could hear other echoes in the dead of night when a fox screamed or a stag bellowed near the sinister opening. To enter that subterranean passage was to visit another world; it was a way into the silent Forest and all its secrets. That's what it felt like to him, anyway.

'It's all right, granddad, mum won't be back for ages. She's gone to put flowers on her friend's grave. She says she can't rest until she has talked to her one last time.'

'Whose grave would that be, Sam?'

'Sarah Smith. She crashed her car into a tree.'

'Oh yes, I read about it in the newspaper a couple of weeks ago. A gruesome business. But I had no idea Freya was still in touch with her old school friend. She never said. Did your mother not attend the funeral, then?'

'Dad wouldn't allow it, but we went anyway. Sort of. Mum sent me to spy on the service while she hid in some gardens nearby – I had to tell her how many people sat in the church and how many flowers decorated the coffin.'

He didn't mention being chased by the one-eared woman through the graveyard – no one needed to know what he thought of the untrustworthy fire watcher who had not yet returned his book of trains.

Jim Wilde raked coals furiously with a poker. Into his one good, grey eye there came a flash like flint on fire. He growled through gaps in his twisted, blackened teeth as he resented his age and lack of strength. A man did not crawl through the bowels of the earth for decades without acquiring a few broken bones that mended badly. Yet it was not arthritis alone that caused him to shiver.

'I said there'd be trouble if Freya ever married James Boreman.'

Sam knew enough to say nothing. Instead, his eye wandered to a nearby oil lamp that glowed on the mantelpiece. This late in the day there were no trains due, but the hand lamp's black wick burned every night in case of trouble. Sometimes they heard the sound of faraway gunfire carry across the treetops from the direction of Lydney. Talk was that the GIs were learning how to shoot their new M1 semi-automatic rifles at a woodland target range in readiness for a fresh assault on the enemy next year.

Suddenly Jim Wilde smiled at him again.

'You want a cup of tea, or what?'

'First tell me that tale of the magical boar.'

Jim Wilde wrinkled his nostrils and sniffed loudly.

'Do you know the best way to protect yourself from a wild boar?'

'Yes, granddad, I do. You've told me ten times already. You collect human hair from a barbershop. Then you sprinkle it all over the entrance to your house and garden.'

'That way the smell repels them.'

'Like vampires and garlic.'

'I suppose.'

'You do believe in the legend of the phantom boar, don't you, granddad?'

'Would I even tell it to you if I didn't?'

'*Please*, granddad.'

'Are you sitting comfortably? Okay, then listen to me. Many, many years ago the queen of King Cilydd Wledig is frightened by some pigs. She goes into premature labour and dies giving birth to her son in the pigsty, but not before she names him Culhwch. As a result, the prince is raised in secret by a swineherd...'

'Where did you read that?'

'It's all written down in a very old book called the 'Red Book of Hergest'. But how can I start my story if you interrupt me?'

'Did you just stop?'

'Here's the deal. With Culhwch's mother dead, King Cilydd Wledig is free to marry another king's widow. However, the new queen wants to marry her own daughter to Culhwch but he refuses. The new queen becomes so terribly angry that she puts a curse on him. Now Culhwch has to marry the beautiful Olwen and no one else.'

'So what's the catch?'

'Olwen is the daughter of the cunning and treacherous giant named Ysbaddaden Bencawr who lives in a high, almost impregnable castle.'

'But that's what princes do, isn't it, granddad? They rescue beautiful princesses from spooky castles?'

'Culhwch doesn't want to go there. Believe me. That's a terrible idea.'

'Why not?'

Jim Wilde sat so still, with such an inclination to stop and listen to the Forest all around them, that Sam feared he would refuse to go on with their adventure.

'Because the giant is under a curse himself, that's why. He'll die if his daughter ever marries.'

'So what happens next?'

'Culhwch is already hopelessly in love with Olwen but her father is very cunning – Ysbaddaden sets Culhwch a set of difficult tasks before he'll consent to give his daughter's hand in marriage. In particular, Culhwch must cut the giant's hair and beard so that he can look his best when he walks his daughter down the aisle.'

'Sounds easy enough.'

'It's not, though, is it? The giant's hair is so thick and tangled that no ordinary blade or comb will cut or straighten it.'

'What's all this got to do with the phantom boar?'

'I'm coming to that in a moment.'

Sam listened to the trees scrape and scratch the roof of the house – some wild creature was rooting about in the garden quite close to the window? Then again, it was most probably a rush of the wind through the nearby tunnel; it could have been some bird or deer calling or something else.

'And Culhwch? What does he do?'

'He learns of a magic pair of shears, comb and razor that will do the trick, but there's a problem: the magical items reside among the poisonous bristles on the head of the ferocious Twrch Trwyth.'

'What's that?'

'That's the name of the phantom boar. 'Twrch' in Welsh means 'wild boar'. So Twrch Trwyth means 'the boar Trwyth'. But this is no ordinary boar, it's an Irish king whom God has changed into an animal on account of a quarrel.'

'Sounds scary.'

But even as Jim Wilde opened his mouth to reply he gave a shiver. An involuntary contraction of arms and legs took hold of him briefly – it might have been his arthritis, after all.

'Twrch Trwyth does not fight alone. He's accompanied by seven young hogs all of whom are really men under a spell. Culhwch seeks the help of his cousin, the famous King Arthur of Cornwall who immediately selects six of his finest knights. To defeat 'the boar Trwyth' they take with them a magic sword, a boarhound and a boar's tusk. Meanwhile Twrch Trwyth is laying waste to a large part of Ireland. A great fight follows but the supernatural boar proves far too strong for our heroes on the battlefield; it crosses the Irish Sea and lands safely in Wales. All the way across the coast to the Amman Valley the two sides are locked in ever fiercer fighting. More men and pigs are slaughtered until, by the time they reach the River Severn, Twrch Trwyth stands alone.'

'Then they kill it?' said Sam eagerly.

'Culhwch and Arthur overpower him. Take the razor and shears.'

'So *yes*, then.'

'Not so fast. The great beast wriggles free. By a miracle it escapes again to Cornwall, where it is caught once more. There, the comb is retrieved at last. After that Twrch Trwyth is driven into the sea and is never seen again.'

Sam took a deep breath.

'So it *is* still alive. I knew it.'

'Why do you say that?'

Sam hesitated. There was a sudden thundering in his head. His ears sang. His nostrils whistled. He sensed all the power and panic of an immortal beast on the run. Then, despite the catch in his voice, he made his confession.

'I think I may have seen it.'

'What's that? Where?'

'Here, in the Forest.'

'Describe it to me.'

'It's massive.'

'You kidding me, or what?'

'No,' said Sam indignantly. 'I really have seen it, I tell you. Its bristles glow white in the dark. When it moves it weaves its way through the trees like smoke.'

'How many times have you seen it?'

'Twice so far.'

'Hardly conclusive then? It was the Forest mist playing tricks on you.'

'I've done a drawing of it.'

'Show me.'

'I can't, I gave it to someone else.'

'Whatever is the matter with you today, Sam? You fret so.'

But Sam had never told anyone before, not in so many *words*.

'I'm afraid Twrch Trwyth wants to kill us all.'

'That's not very likely.'

'It is though, isn't it? No one saw the boar drown, only vanish from sight a thousand years ago.'

Jim Wilde frowned. This was not the first time he had registered such intense enthusiasm in his grandson's eyes. He went back to goading the hellish flames in the fire with the tip of his poker. Once the boy got a passion for something there was no shaking him. It was just like his weird fascination for trains, it came out of the blue. Now he regretted putting the whole idea of a phantom animal into his head. He hadn't meant to excite this childish curiosity – this fixation.

'That's not what happened, Sam. I swear the magical boar was never seen to leave the sea again. How else do you think Culhwch married Olwen? They lived happily ever after. You have to forget all about it.'

'Don't see how I can.'

'This time of year, you must expect to see farmers' pigs roaming freely in the Forest. They eat the acorns and beechmast.'

'I should tell my dad. He'll pursue it and kill it.'

'Your father keeps very bad company. Nor was he born in the Dean. Those of us who really love the Forest respect its old ways. That's because it contains places where humans should rarely go. Many a hidden glade is 'blessed' and offers peace to those that would live together in harmony and freedom. Druids once worshipped there and like them we should abide by Nature's boundaries that guard its secrets.'

Jim Wilde spoke with a ferocity that filled Sam with awe.

'Maybe we should get that cup of tea, granddad?'

'That would be nice.'

'Perhaps go for a walk later.'

'Is your mother so very unhappy, Sam? You can tell me. It's all right.'

'Ever since I lit too many prayer candles in Gloucester Cathedral.'

'Seriously? Prayer candles?'

'Oh never mind.'

'I did try to be a good father to her, you know, but Freya turned very wild. She met James Boreman and now I can't get any sense out of her.'

'If I see the great white hog again I'm going to speak to it.'

'There is no such thing, Sam, believe me. It's only a figment of your vivid imagination.'

Jim Wilde's stern words came with a look that urged great caution: this was to be their own special fancy and it shouldn't go any further.

'If you say so, granddad.'

SIXTEEN

Next time anyone told him, John Curtis, to go on a wild-goose chase they could jolly well do it themselves. He was trying to find his way along a busy basin crowded with ships, lighters and oil barges. That wheezy little steam engine that was shunting trucks past towering brick mills and warehouses had nearly run him over twice already– it had come puffing along North Quay without so much as a whistle. He had not visited here since he had come to marvel at a Royal Navy submarine that had sailed up the Sharpness Canal to promote the War Savings Campaign. Strictly speaking he had no jurisdiction this far from the cathedral close, anyway.

That hadn't stopped him marching down to Gloucester docks in his gown and purple cassock. He was particularly proud of the badge that he wore on each sleeve of his gown. Not only did it confer authority but its mitre and cross earned him a ten per cent discount on purchases in certain cafés and gift shops near the minster. For someone whose duties ranged from chalice bearer and doorkeeper to sacristan and gravedigger, he could put on quite a show if he had to in all his regalia.

He stopped by a coal-carrying narrowboat called 'Free Spirit' and tapped on its roof with the silver cap of his Malacca cane. It might not be the posh staff he carried in church processions, a reminder of a time when vergers like him had once walked ahead of their fellow churchmen to clear the streets of animals and vagabonds – but it would have to do today.

'I say, anyone at home?'

Every single person he had interviewed had said the same thing: Sarah Smith was as nice as pie. She had no enemies. No mysteries. She was an angel. So they'd *said*. Fine. Here, then, was where he could finally sign off from what had proved to be a stupendous waste of his time, so far.

Did a hand just hook a curtain in a porthole?

Something like that.

There came the increasingly shrill whistle of a kettle coming to the boil.

No mistake, someone was on board.

'Hello – I'm Gloucester Cathedral verger John Curtis.'

If he still sounded a bit brisk, that was too bad. A door suddenly flew open at the back of the boat and a young, ash-blonde woman dressed in a close-fitting, mustard yellow jumper looked out from her cabin.

'What do you want?'

'My name is John…'

'I heard you the first time.'

'You Susie Grossman?'

'If you say so.'

Her hazel-coloured eyes grew wider; her face was round and freckled while from her ears swung two oversized silver hoops that were very bad taste to his eyes but had a certain panache, he supposed.

He tried his best smile.

'You knew Sarah Smith, I believe?'

'Where did you hear that?'

'From the Very Reverend Dean Drew. He's her brother.'

'He was. Now she's dead. What more do you need to know?'

'You tell me.'

'Don't see how I can.'

'Am I that scary?' said John and worked the toe of his box calf boot over the edge of the boat's wooden counter.

Next minute he was standing in the hatchway.

'Where the hell do you think you're going?' asked Susie.

But John had already pushed past the colourful castle landscapes painted on the cabin's door, where the first thing to strike him was heat from a stove. If he stretched out both arms at once he could touch the sloping sides of the boat; he bumped gleaming brass lamps and horseshoes and ducked fancy lace frills that hung literally about his ears.

He'd seen bigger Wendy houses.

'How about you make us a nice cup of tea?' he said and sat down gingerly on an upholstered dog box which passed for a bench. 'It's perishing out there.'

'….!'

'Please. I'm here as Sarah's friend, too. I have a few questions, that's all. Won't take long.'

Susie picked up the steaming kettle from the stove and filled a rose-painted teapot with boiling water. Her eyes shone with more obvious sorrow than she meant to admit.

'It was a bloody car crash, for Christ's sake. There's so much military traffic on the roads at night at the moment. No driver can see past their nose on account of the blackout and dimmed headlights.'

'I can't disagree with you there. Bloody Yanks.'

'So there's no case to answer.'

'The thing is, there's not a lot to go on – no one saw it happen.'

'Then why bother me?'

'Someone was trying to scare Sarah into silence about something.'

'And you know this how?'

But he kept mum about the severed boar's head, as well as the threat that had been written in pig's blood on the windscreen of Sarah's car – he still couldn't quite believe it himself.

'I'm looking into it on behalf of her husband Bruno Smith who suspects foul play. You want to find out the truth, don't you?'

'And you turn up making ridiculous suggestions?'

'That remains to be seen.'

'Huh?'

'Can you help me, or not?'

Susie unhooked two white china cups decorated with red poppies and gold from a cupboard. She seemed all at sixes and sevens suddenly. Never mind that she was also doing her best not to cry.

'Oh bloody hell.'

She'd just spilt hot water everywhere, John realised. He let her bustle about in her blue satin slippers as she mopped the floor in a hurry. Besides which, the cramped conditions in the cabin were bringing on a shortness of breath in him. That bullseye porthole set into the cabin-top above his head might let in a glint of sky, but it was hardly a proper window as such. Two people had to be very intimate to share such a home, he decided, tapping his bark-tanned heels together as he pulled at the collar of his shirt.

'How would you describe your relationship with Sarah?'

'Why should I tell you?'

'Why not?'

'And if I refuse?'

'Then I'll go away and let Sarah rot in her grave.'

'We met at a book club until her husband made a fuss.'

'Why would he do that?'

'Bruno found out that Sarah and I were more than mates.'

John fanned himself with one hand. Blinked hard.

'Were you?'

'She wasn't going to leave him… Just so you know.'

'How long were you and Sarah seeing each other, if you don't mind me asking?'

Susie took a deep breath.

'Two years and one month. She stayed here on the boat whenever she could. They were the best two years of my life. Sarah loved being on the water. By ferrying coal to Birmingham we were two people doing our bit for the war effort. We would lower the door on that cupboard right behind you and make up a small double-bed. We'd snuggle up together on its mattress next to the engine bulkhead. Nor was she afraid to get her hands dirty – last year she helped me lift the 'Free Spirit' out of the water and paint its steel hull with bitumen-based paint to discourage any rust. She was my beautiful girl but also a grafter.'

John tried not to watch walls slide towards him as he fought for air.

'Did you notice anything unusual about Sarah before her accident? Did she say or do anything different?'

'Not to my knowledge.'

'Did she have any enemies?'

'All I know is that one day she told me that she couldn't see me any more.'

'This was when exactly?'

'Just over two months ago. I couldn't believe it. We'd been so happy. Suddenly it was as if I didn't exist. I said to Sarah, "What is it you're not telling me?" but she seemed so excited and secretive. She wouldn't help me shovel coal or fill the water tank. I began to realise how thrilled she was about something. I could see it in her eyes. I felt certain she had found someone else, but she wouldn't admit it. I thought at the time she just wanted to be cruel, or she was undecided.'

'So you didn't see or hear much of her after that?'

'We had a big quarrel. Sarah stormed off. Then, shortly afterwards we bumped into each other again in the Cadena Café.'

'And?'

'I could see at once that she'd changed. That look of awe in her eyes had faded. At first I was glad. She'd left me in the lurch without explanation, but now she knew better? It was not as if we'd been apart very long and I hoped we could get back together.'

John finally set aside his tea which was much too bitter.

'So you *did* notice something odd about her?'

'Yeah, well, you could say.'

'What did you talk about exactly?'

Susie fiddled with one of her hoop earrings.

In an instant it came loose at the lobe.

She expressed surprise.

That's not what she'd intended.

'I told her I'd missed her terribly.'

'What did Sarah reply to that?'

'She told me that she didn't know what to do, but she was going to fix it one way or another. She'd teach them a lesson, she said.'

'Them? Was she scared of her new partner, do you think? Had they quarrelled?'

'I'm not sure.'

'Perhaps her husband turned nasty after all?'

Susie shook her head very quickly. It was the same astounded look she had just given her errant earring.

'That's madness. Bruno was a fool but he was never violent.'

'How can you be so sure?'

'I never saw any bruises.'

John raised his eyebrows.

'I need you to be totally honest with me.'

Susie smiled thinly, then replied with some gusto.

'Bruno secretly hated me but he worshipped Sarah. He always thought he'd win her back one day. It's not as if they ever stopped sleeping together. Not quite. Sarah desperately wanted a child. Either that or he was prepared to have a threesome, I guess. I took her hand in mine and begged her to tell me what was wrong.'

'And did she, this time?'

'If I do, you might suffer, too, is all she said.'

'So what happened?'

'She simply stirred the spoon in her teacup endlessly on the table between us and stared blankly out of the café's window.'

'Really? She said nothing?'

'Next minute she took my hand and held it long and hard. That scared me. She was shaking, as if she were working herself up to say a final goodbye: "I may have to go away and lie low for a while," she said.'

'And you? What did you say?'

'That's when I swore to God to keep any secret. But she said, "It's no use. It's not me, it's someone else." Then she ran off.'

John felt hotter and hotter as he gripped the cabin's dog box for support. His lungs felt blocked and his ears wanted to burst. He put his hand on his neck and rolled his head because he found the lack of headroom so constricting.

It didn't mean he was about to suffocate.

What if it did?

'So Sarah didn't mention any particular name that you might want to tell me about? Man or woman? Who was this mysterious *someone* who loomed so large in her life in the final few days before her crash?'

'I don't know, but she was scared shitless on their behalf. She dreaded what might happen to them if she stayed around, yet she's the one who ended up headless in her own car.'

'It's still not a lot to go on, but thank you all the same. Here's my card. If you think of anything else, please give me a ring at my cathedral lodgings.'

'Do you really believe that someone killed her?'

'I believe she veered off that road for a very good reason.'

John stepped ashore from the narrowboat in a hurry. Then with a careful and deep inhalation, his lungs came back to life. He quickened his stride along the quayside as his wobbly legs regained their strength. Soon, only his spine ached from having sat too long bent double in a cabin fit for dolls.

*

'Bruno never told me that his wife had a lover,' said Jo, sipping stout in THE MONKS' RETREAT bar beneath the Fleece Hotel in Westgate Street. She liked to think she was upholding a fine tradition: she was drinking in the same vaulted undercroft where pilgrims to Gloucester had once drunk their ale after visiting the tomb of King Edward II. Romantic legend would have it that it had once been part of a secret tunnel that led to the cloisters in the nearby abbey, but that was bunkum. 'He never let on that his marriage had landed him in such hot water.'

John swallowed a mouthful of rum and lime as clouds of cigarette and pipe smoke befogged medieval stone arches. He took a deep breath to savour the atmosphere. Honestly, how was he meant to cut down on smoking?

'Bruno was prepared to settle for a threesome, by all accounts.'

'Open marriage, eh? I wonder how that works.'

'I wish I knew, but Dean Drew says that his sister and her husband fought a lot.'

'We can't rule out that Sarah was scared of Bruno, no matter what Susie Grossman says. We can't rule out that she crashed her car deliberately.'

'Suicide? Surely not.'

'Why else was she driving so fast?'

John struggled to make himself heard in the crowd of WAAFs and Auxiliary Territorial Service women who were drinking the non-rationed beer in the company of bus drivers, housewives and shop assistants.

'How about she misjudged the corner because she *thought* she was being chased by someone?'

Jo let the idea hang in the air.

'Susie told you Sarah wanted to protect someone. No idea who?'

'What about Freya Boreman? She's still on our list of possible workmates and friends. We know she went to school with Sarah. I've tried ringing her, but only her maid or husband ever answer my calls.'

'Don't worry, I'm working on it.'

'You are?'

'Ever since Sam introduced us.'

John thought about leaving his hard wooden chair to buy them both more drinks, but he could scarcely see past all the people as their legs crowded the row of green painted beer barrels that supported the bar.

'Never seen so many women having such a good time in a pub before.'

Jo lit a cigarette between her freshly painted fingernails.

'Why shouldn't we be entitled to the same drinks as men? We're doing just as much in this war as you.'

'Doesn't mean I was complaining.'

'Doesn't mean you weren't, John.'

He smiled. What she said was perfectly true, but after three year's absence many husbands and lovers had not yet seen home and many women were becoming increasingly lonely, depressed or downright restless as the strain took its toll.

'So Jo, how's "The Woman's League of Health and Beauty" coming along? Are you feeling like a new person yet?'

'It turns out they're particularly strong on bust exercises.'

'Ouch. So how do you do those, exactly?'

'We whirl our arms about like frantic windmills which is supposed to strengthen our pectoral muscles. Of course, being pregnant, my breasts just keep growing larger anyway.'

'Some way to go then?'

'You can scoff, but it should improve my hourglass figure.'

'Not if it kills you first.'

'You're the one to talk.'

'I don't understand it. Everyone else seems to be losing weight since rationing, whereas I'm still twenty stone.'

'You see, John, you'll be doing the Superman press-up yet.'

'Superman?'

'Sorry, I forgot not everyone gets to read American comics. You alternate your knee out to your elbow as you lower your chest towards the floor.'

'How is your boyfriend, by the way?'

'He's practising shooting guns in the Forest of Dean.'

'Your romance is still on, then?'

'Mostly off, if my parents have their way. Enjoying a one-night stand with a black man from Mississippi is a big no-no in their eyes. Not quite right for a posh Cotswolds girl by a long chalk.'

Sensing thin ice, John switched back to the subject in hand.

'Why are we doing Bruno Smith's dirty work for him anyway?'

Jo frowned.

'Because who else will?'

'That's meant to make me feel better, how?'

'Think of it this way. Before Bruno we had nothing.'

Friday December 6, 1940

I'm on my knees with my back to the wall. The tunnel repeats and magnifies the chorus of voices in endless echoes. There's absolutely no sleep to be had in here tonight — once one infant starts crying, another does the same. I can't hear myself think for all the screams that mock and taunt me; they wrench at my brain as if they would tear it apart.

Will nobody in this rocky hole let me forget that a few weeks ago I was also a wife and mother?

Everyone warned me that this place would be hell.

I should never have come.

It's a very bad idea.

Fact is, there's nowhere else safe in Bristol to go. Those pathetic, little brick shelters that continue to pop up like mushrooms on pavements all over the city are cracking whenever a bomb explodes too close — rumour has it that penny-pinching builders have skimped on proper mortar to cement the walls. In a direct hit, everyone gets blown to smithereens. Besides, there aren't nearly enough of them to protect so many needy people.

So Portway Tunnel it is for me. A railway once ran through here at the side of the Avon Gorge. It's not an official bomb shelter, at all — no sign even advertises its existence. I found it through word of mouth alone. Hundreds of people are braving this stone bore to feel secure, they huddle together in the gloom like primitive cave dwellers. That's what blanket bombing does to us all: it bombs us back to the Stone Age.

I can barely see anything, but I feel icy water run down the walls. Everyone's wheezing and coughing in this winter cold. There's literally no space to lie down and no respite from the awful smells of dirty nappies, urine, sweat, damp bedding and even people's filthy clothes. Sandbags exude their own peculiar stench at the tunnel's entrance. It smells like dead dogs to me.

The two small water closets are proving woefully inadequate. I can't say for sure, but there has to be at least one thousand adults and children in here while the war rages on in the world above us.

I'll try to sleep again in the morning. For now, though, I'll drink another bottle of beer. Better some fuzzy stupor than the sight of my baby in my husband's arms.

The trouble with dreams is that they're so silent.

I see the flames but can't hear them crackle.

It's like drowning in that river of blood that flows down the street in the rain. I'll never get there in time....

Before that falling rafter strikes me down.

...to my burning daughter.

By day this place – and my nightmares – can be better kept at bay. It's not a lot to be going on with. One young man coughs violently beside me and spits red phlegm into his handkerchief. That's the scariest thing. Who knows how many of us are already dying from tuberculosis?

SEVENTEEN

That sudden noise of something shattering was too close for comfort. Blacked out windows made it hard to tell if it was night or morning. Jo sat up in bed, still grinding her teeth. Her head ached. There was no smell of smoke. No fire. It wasn't a bomb exploding. So was it only she, not her house, who was shaking?

The half open door to her bedroom still exerted a terrible hold on her dreams – grievous shadows massed there like fretful friends, forever stoking painful memories that she could never satisfy. Or, rather, they became in the cold winter air the awful suggestion of something worse.

'Jack? Emmy? Is that you?'

There was no unsecured way into the house.

Not that she knew of.

Not even for ghosts.

She threw off the bedcovers and listened hard. *Nothing.* Only an empty beer bottle slid off her pillow and bounced about at her feet on the floor's bare boards.

'Bella?'

An owner might indulge a dog with a great deal of attention and comfort, but in return she expected her to be at her side in her hour of need. It was like an unspoken pact, especially when she had the mother of all hangovers. There was something gloriously selfless about what a dog would do. So she was decidedly aggrieved to see no sign of her on the blankets or in her basket.

'Hey, Bella? Hey, girl? Where are you?'

She didn't pretend that she could go back to sleep now. Upending a brass Arctic Lamp complete with sprung loaded candle from her bedside table, she raised it aloft like Thor's hammer. Was this really such a good idea? She was shivering as it was.

Most likely Bella had simply knocked over her water bowl.

That's not what she'd heard.

'Who's there, damn you?'

She used her bare toes to open the door. She did it like a blind person would. Next, she worked her free hand crablike to the gaslight on the landing wall and turned up its flame inside its grubby shade. Made sense. She shouldn't have. Not then. At the tips of her toes lay an enormous brown rat. It moved not a muscle yet seemed no less conscious for all that. Its astonished gaze mocked her pitilessly. Her heart fluttered. Her brain swam.

There was not a trace of blood on its fur, no slur of red from its long front teeth as she stepped over it and ran, hell for leather, downstairs.

Once she was in the scullery she had to force herself to be rational. Something had to be sufficiently big and square to throw over the slumberer, tail and all? If the rat revived and shot beneath her bed she might never get it out again, or equally unhelpfully, it would die under the floorboards and stink to high heaven.

She settled on her new metal sink basket from the Army and Navy Store. There was something else. She finally thought to rip a piece of thick cardboard from the box of groceries that she had bought only yesterday.

The possibly stunned rodent had not closed its beady black eyes upon her return.

Not that she chose to linger.

She threw the bowl over the body and slid the cardboard beneath it in a sandwich that she could transport more easily to the rubbish.

She had just lifted the ashbin's lid in the backyard when Bella raced up the steps from the cellar.

'Is this your doing?' cried Jo. 'It is, isn't it? Next time, don't *bring* it to me, don't *leave* it on the landing.'

Bella barked happily and wagged her wiry black tail. She let her tongue hang out while she pricked up her ears at her urgent interrogation. However, the sight of genuine fright in her otherwise belligerent owner did impress her. It proved that some jobs were better done by a dog than a human.

But Jo had no time to stand and brood. It was necessary to scour the perforated sink basket with bleach and boiling water – she had to wash away every trace of dirt and disease; she had to do it before she threw up all over the scullery floor.

That's when her eye settled on the nearby window. Its old metal handle had been left open. She didn't examine it for long. She didn't need to. Clearly somebody had entered the house by way of the makeshift kitchen – that sound of something breaking a few minutes ago had been the sound of them taking a screwdriver to putty and glass as they chiselled out a pane. Whoever it was had squeezed past the mangle and helped themselves to some of her precious, homemade honey biscuits from her cake tin. It could have been worse – they could have gone off with her date and nut loaf, or her sultana pudding.

Bella was too busy sniffing for more vermin in the cellar to notice.

Jo lit a gaslight in the parlour and waited while its incandescent light grew brighter inside its mesh mantle.

Had she really been burgled?

It was hard to say.

She had no idea.

Everything seemed to be where she had left it, except for her notebook. In it, she had jotted down everything she and John had discovered so far about Sarah Smith and her unexplained car crash.

That was missing.

EIGHTEEN

Something wasn't right. She had a bad feeling about it, which she couldn't entirely pass off as vertigo. A climb this high inside the cathedral could not be rushed. It was a mad thing to do. Yet here she was, thought Jo, edging her way along its narrow, elevated galleries at practically roof level, while all those people on the pavement of the vast, echoing nave far below her looked tiny.

Ever since she had eaten eggless pancakes for breakfast she had suffered from gut-wrenching nausea. She couldn't altogether blame it on the hundreds of twisting, stone steps, however, since it had been the same when she was carrying Emmy. Perhaps they should call it morn, noon and height sickness.

All the same, to gaze into the void before the biggest East Window in England was to fly like a bird. To peer at the gaps in the planks where beautiful stained glass should have been, was to feel as if she could walk on clouds this far above so many sculpted arches, jambs, mullions, perpendicular tracery panels and scalloped capitals.

She could have been in the gods of a vast medieval theatre. Stretching before her from boss to boss in the minster's ceiling were fifteen carved angels, each one with a different musical instrument accompanying the great Gloria in Excelsis in the blue vault of heaven.

Only the fact that the window was missing, like a hideous wound, was a sad reminder that the whole country was at war.

The next tiny room proved equally frustrating – she and Bella found no one and nothing except a Last Judgement 'doom' once used as an altar-piece in one of the chapels of the nave. The dramatic, post-Reformation picture was due to go to London in the New Year for repair, or so she'd heard. Painted on wood in tempera on oak planking, Our Saviour sat on a rainbow. On his left was a lily, a symbol of mercy, that was directed towards the saved, while on his right a sword pointed at the cursed.

Not stopping to study the poor lost souls being cast into hell – it could have been a depiction of her stomach right now – she ducked and squeezed all the way round to the north ambulatory, only to find her path blocked by the mysterious mechanical paraphernalia of the 32-foot organ stop.

No joy there then, but she could hardly be expected to wait about forever.

She stifled a curse or two and retraced her steps back to the small choir-gallery known as the Abbot's chapel. There, she looked down into the Lady Chapel below. She didn't know what else to do.

Suddenly, Freya Boreman stepped from the shadows. She was dressed in her long, beige-coloured coat and toffee brown, felt hat whose peak she carefully tilted over one eye. She carried her dog next to a zippered, circular handbag with 'Prystal' plastic, twist-ring handles which had to be American. Ruby's eyes grew bigger and bigger.

'So glad you could make it, Fire Guard Wheeler. I didn't have great hopes.'

Jo came to her senses at once and wiped sweat off her brow.

'Why... would... you think I might not come?'

'I thought you wouldn't bother.'

'It's been a while since the funeral. *I* was about to ring *you*.'

Bella growled.

Jo frowned at her and mouthed a few silent words.

Will you give it a rest?

Bella continued to stare hostilely at the Chihuahua. No pet worth its name could call itself a proper dog when it rode about like a baby on its owner's arm.

Freya did her best to smile at her, but to what extent it amounted to a concession, it was hard to say. It was within the hushed confines of the cathedral that her haughty reserve suited the occasion very well.

'You know, Mrs Wheeler, you really ought to look after yourself a lot better. I was afraid you were going to have a heart attack just now.'

'I'll have you know that I'm trying every fitness programme I can find.'

'You're following fads. It's not the same. Never mind me, though. Did you bring it with you?'

'....?'

'You did promise.'

'Of course, how rude of me! You're here for Sam's ABC of trains.'

'You did say you'd send it to me by now.'

'I haven't had time. Let me nip home at once and fetch it.'

'No matter, it can wait.'

'That is the reason you asked to meet me up here, isn't it?'

'Why wouldn't it be?'

'It would have been easier to go for a drink in 'THE MONKS' RETREAT bar', you must admit. We still could.'

'We could, yes.'

'So why don't we?'

Freya glared at her. What else was she waiting for? Why did she not say? There could only be one way to describe her. That word was uncompromising.

'I just want to take this chance to say thank you again for looking after Sam. I might never get another.'

Jo blushed some more.

'I'm here to help if I can.'

'That's good to know.'

'I mean it. I do hope we can be friends?'

'You'll regret it.'

'Really?'

'It's not easy having a boy like Sam. To most people, he's awkward, pedantic and pre-occupied with the steam engines that run by our house, but you are one of the few people I've met who sees him for who he really is.'

The words hung heavily on the air, thought Jo. They only emerged at all because Freya impelled, dragged and forced them from her throat – like some bloody, tubercular bacillus. She reached for a cigarette and held out the packet to her. Freya's eyebrows met in another frown. She was not a smoker. Not here, anyway. Next minute, that half of her face shaded by the tilt of her hat lit up in the flare from her lighter. Enigmatic she may have been, but this was no game. Hers was a particular kind of reserve, a most careful silence. Her left eye was black and bloody in the new illumination.

Jo sensed the horrid crimson slash creep between them. It cast its spell to attract, fascinate and threaten until she could no longer be immune to its sinister presence.

'You flatter me, Mrs Boreman. The thing is, I can't say I entirely know the lad…'

'On the contrary, you know exactly what I mean. I see it in your eyes. You're prepared to be his friend whereas… whereas…'

'I'm all in favour of that.'

'Whereas my husband James isn't.'

'I'm sure he loves Sam as much as you do.'

Freya stared fixedly into the void below. There was not the slightest hint of self-pity, but there was panic, an emotion hard won since she lived her life in such perpetual alarm? It might have been desperation or a call to arms.

'I can't rightly talk about it now.'

'You didn't climb hundreds of steps for nothing.'

'You could say that.'

'So I'm listening.'

Seconds later Freya recovered, but talked very low. Perhaps she was aware of how far her voice might magnify and carry, so near were they to the Whispering Gallery and its vocal trickeries.

'James takes Sam poaching deer in the Forest of Dean. It's both illegal and dangerous, yet he won't listen to my worries.'

'So what don't I understand?'

'James's hunting expeditions are all based on the idea that he can 'cure' our son, Mrs Wheeler.'

'Please call me Jo.'

'The way he talks, you'd think that he was about to remedy some dreadful evil, not that I expect you to understand.'

But she did understand. There had been a time, not so long ago, when she herself might have spoken in terms of a spiritual charge – a cure of souls – just after she'd suffered her nervous breakdown but before she'd found out that she was blessed with child for a second time. It hadn't proved very helpful.

'I doubt if your husband considers Sam to be possessed by the Devil.'

'Don't be so sure. He's been reading about an Austrian psychiatrist called Leo Kanner. There is a condition he calls autism. He describes it as "lack of affective contact, fascination with objects, desire for sameness and non-communicative language before thirty months of age". He calls it "extreme autistic aloneness" and says the problem is a cold mother. While I accept that many things about Sam's early life fits Kanner's description, I can't accept that I've ever been cold towards him. Why must men always blame women? Nor do I think 'blame' is the right word for any of this. Sam is just Sam. But James doesn't agree. He wants to subject our son's brain to electroconvulsive shock therapy. He's willing to take a chance on something on the basis of very limited evidence, so much so, that I live in fear of his pitiless benevolence. James will seek any remedy that cures Sam's 'disease', 'condition' or 'problem', no matter what I say. It is my own powerlessness I fear most, that I cannot stop someone else labelling our child as ill. James will have Sam suffer medical experiments in a foreign land to test someone else's hypothesis.'

'Is electroconvulsive therapy even accepted medical practice in Britain?'

'It has gained a lot of credence ever since someone called Kalinowski toured England in 1939 to extol its virtues.'

'But is Sam ill? He doesn't look so to me.'

'Some people think that electric shocks can cure anti-social behaviour.'

'But where would James send him?'

'To America, Jo. He'd send him across the Atlantic while there's a war on! I might never see my son alive again.'

'Really? That puts you in a difficult situation. I'm so sorry to hear it. But what about you? You look as if you've been in the wars yourself? Have you been in an accident recently? Is that why you insisted we meet up here, away from curious eyes?'

Freya was all purported horror and disbelief as she touched her bruised face.

'Oh that. I walked into a door while looking round our new house in the Forest.'

'…?'

'No, really.'

'Forgive me, I don't mean to pry. But there's something I'd like to talk to you about, if I may, while I have the chance. You told me, when we last met, that you were an old school friend of Sarah Smith? I was wondering what else you could tell me about her.'

'Does it matter?'

'Fact is, I'm not at all sure why she died the way she did.'

'Is this what you do, Jo? Meddle in things you can do nothing about?'

Jo threw up both hands in mock surrender. It didn't mean she didn't still feel that odd sensation of whirling and general imbalance at the precipitous drop beside them, in the pit of her stomach.

'You really won't have that beer with me, then? For Sarah's sake? She was my friend, too. Or bring Sam to the cathedral and I'll show him the crypt. He might like that.'

Freya's words came in fits and bursts now; in her throat she was audibly choking and rasping.

'Fact is, Sarah is the real reason I came here today. To warn you. You and the verger must stop asking questions about her. What's done is done. None of us can bring her back. We should let her rest in peace. I'm begging you.'

'You know something I don't, Mrs Boreman?'

'I'm sorry, but you've got it all wrong.'

With that single denial their meeting was at an end. Jo was taken aback. She wanted to take her hand, but Freya resisted.

'Mrs Boreman. *Freya*. Wait. Don't go yet. Please explain yourself.'

Jo set off along the dark, narrow galleries in pursuit of her new and baffling acquaintance, only the stone steps down to the floor of the south transept proved far too steep and slippery to catch her in time. Nor was there anything to grip on the smooth, downward spiralling walls. She slipped and cursed her own ineptitude.

Never for one second had she meant to scare Freya off. But she had. Except *Freya* had meant to frighten *her*.

Saturday, April 12, 1941

At last Bristol is allowed to be in the news! I'm ridiculously, even violently, excited. Yesterday witnessed the sixth, large scale raid on the city since November 1940 and today Winston Churchill is on the streets to boost morale. It's not only me, there's a whole new public mood – a burning anger. 'They will have to pay for this' still rings in my ears.

I'm not sure any official visit will help much, though.

There's been too much strain on morale.

That booing I just heard was for real.

Why should we believe anything the great man says now?

Maybe it's because Bristol is such a small city that the devastation feels so complete – its commercial heart is all but gone. The old buildings, those reliable witnesses to the past, have been wiped from the Earth. It's not only people who lie in pieces but centuries of history.

One refrain occurs over and over: 'Things will never be the same again.'

Yet Bristolians have been quick to organise. The Civil Defence Services are now fully co-ordinated. When a report comes in of a bomb exploding in a particular street, an officer decides which services are needed. I'm not alone any more, I'm linked to Engineers (Light Rescue, Heavy Rescue, P/C squad) or Medical (F.A. Parties, Ambulances, Trailer Unit). That's what counts from now on. We're all in this together. If anything sees us through the war successfully, it will be our newfound resilience.

It's our best chance.

I'm doing it for Jack and Emmy.

NINETEEN

'*Now* you call me, Mrs Wheeler? It's been ages.'

Jo had ridden her Brough Superior Combination to the Forest to see where precisely Sarah had crashed her Austin Seven in such mysterious circumstances. Now she was on her way back home. Simple as that. Well, not exactly. She should never have stopped at a public telephone box to ring Bruno.

'Nothing definite to report yet, I'm afraid, Mr Smith…'

'What the hell have you been doing?'

'…except I am following a possible lead right now.'

'You do *know* what has to be done, don't you?'

'And if it's not that simple?'

'Damn it, Mrs Wheeler, I'm depending on you.'

'Mr Smith, will you please be patient…'

'You want payment up front, I suppose? Fine. I'll even make a donation to the cathedral…'

'No, I don't want your money. I said I would ask a few questions for my poor friend Sarah's sake, which I'm continuing to do…'

'Don't you think there's a bit more to it than that? Or are you just being stupid?'

You don't know what I think, thought Jo and hung up. Okay, Bruno's wife had most definitely got under someone's skin and they needed to find out why, but she never meant to raise his expectations. That's not to say she was about to give up, either.

She kick-started her motorcycle to follow the road beside the River Severn. Whatever God-awful mess Sarah had been involved in, she wouldn't shy away from it. She was just getting started.

*

Nothing about the concrete walls and plywood doors of the utilitarian factories that lined Lydney harbour looked obviously suspicious at first sight. Jo pulled off her goggles and long leather gloves. She pushed up the fur-lined peak on her helmet, took a good look around, then crossed the quayside cobblestones in her oilskin coat and leggings.

One long row of arched sheds appeared particularly bleak and bland and went by the nondescript name of Factories Direction Ltd. But it wasn't hard to see that something special was going on, given the vast stacks of timber that kept arriving by boat along the estuary – since when did anyone import wood to a forest?

She'd first noticed the barges on her regular visits to the American camp and quartermaster depot at nearby Lime Walk.

In reality, these were 'shadow factories' built off the regular routes of the Luftwaffe bombers, one of which, she'd been told in strictest confidence, made plywood for the fuselages of the De Havilland Mosquito aircraft and gliders. Such idle talk could earn a person a lengthy time in jail and she took care not to repeat it.

'Stay in the sidecar, Bella. I mean it this time.'

She made a bee-line across the car park for a factory whose green and white sign read Wellbrite Metal Finishing. In her hand was a bag. This was her cover. It was called killing two birds with one stone.

What could possibly go wrong?

Suddenly a large and cumbersome forklift rumbled at speed round the corner of the factory.

It came at her like a bull with straight horns.

A blast on the truck's hooter pierced the air, but it was too late. One of the twin pallet forks flew past her ear like a lance.

Another step and she would have been gored in half.

She wanted to chase after the driver at once and give him what for. Instead she stood where she was, in total shock. She had her hand clamped to the factory's door and her whole arm shook like crazy.

Nowhere could she see any signs to warn visitors that loading and unloading went on in this part of the yard.

She took a deep breath and held herself lucky not to be skewered.

She should have thought of it before.

All things considered.

*

A brunette, her hair freshly set and still in pin curls under a turban, lounged at her desk in reception. She scarcely left off varnishing her nails as Jo entered the office. Blue eyes shone with cool impoliteness.

'What?'

Jo deposited her snakeskin and leather bag on the grubby counter.

'I've been told that you do plating jobs for the general public?'

'Says who?'

'You advertise, don't you?'

'What about it?'

'I want to restore something off my motorcycle.'

The receptionist rose reluctantly to her feet, prodded one corner of the bag with a blazing red fingernail, but did not look inside.

'Wait here. I'll fetch the foreman Kevin Devaney. He'll decide. He's the expert.'

'Worked here for a while, has he?'

'From since before the war.'

The brunette struck Jo as too tall, too well-dressed and altogether too exotic to inhabit such humble surroundings. The same could be said about the tropical fish in the nearby aquarium. She pressed her nose to its glass and a glossy black head floated level with her own.

'You remind me of Bella,' she said and tapped the tank's side. 'Same bullish head.'

She really shouldn't have. Not then. Next second, water boiled in a frenzy – a perfect storm of bubbles exploded before her eyes. She jumped back as the fish tried to shred her face through the glass. So sharp were those bright, white incisors that they could have been filed.

'Don't go putting your finger in the tank. He'll tear it to pieces.'

Jo spun round and felt the hairs rise on the back of her neck; there was a sudden thumping in her heart. Her fists automatically tightened. She gave a gasp. The rich aroma of shredded, course tobacco blew past her nostrils. The man with the gravelly laugh breathed beer at her while his eyes accompanied his timely advice with a wary glare. One upper eyelid hung heavy with an old burn. To her astonishment she was looking at the pipe-smoker who had admired her motorcycle outside the Victoria House pub in Barton Street not so long ago.

The very same.

But if he was aware of who she was, he said nothing.

She didn't think she should, either.

Sometimes, silence was all that needed saying.

'What kind of fish is it?' asked Jo, rubbing her cheek with a shudder.

It had, after all, just gone for her throat.

'That, my friend, is a black piranha.'

'Lives by itself, does it?'

'He already – how shall I put it – sampled his brother and sister.'

The big man's smile faded as his hand travelled to the tan-coloured bag on the counter. Jo beat him to it. Whatever had roused the factory foreman to mount his drunken foray the other night, he seemed to have no beef with her now.

Or he'd forgotten all about her in his drunken haze.

'This it?' he said, seeing Jo slide a piece of metal from one of the bag's inner compartments.

'It's a badge for my motorcycle.'

'Classic, definitely.'

'1936 Brough Superior. They only made 187 that year. It belongs to my brother Hugo. He fitted it with a BS Petrol Tube Sidecar whose supporting frame contains extra fuel. He loved to ride it until he was blinded by a grenade while fighting in France.'

'Now I feel sorry for you.'

'He can't bear for it to leave the family or have it sitting around doing nothing, so I use it on condition I look after it and take him for rides. I was hoping you might be able to re-chrome the BS badge which sits on top of the sidecar frame and acts as the fuel cap. It has taken me forever to find it because the factory has stopped making any new ones. The old one snapped off after I had a spill. I want to fix it for him for his Christmas present because I know it will make him very happy. No one else is interested. They only do war work.'

The big man puffed more Fine Shag in his pipe while he examined the rusty badge in great detail.

'Stones fly up from the road and chip the chrome quite badly. That lets the rust in.'

'Can you help me or not?'

'Personally the Norton WD16H is the bike for me.'

'I take it that's a yes?'

'Nothing we can't handle.'

'I'd like to see how the restoration is done,' said Jo innocently.

'As I say, the Norton is the more rugged machine.'

'It would interest me a lot, it really would.'

She was still reeling from this most awkward reunion. Four times she had visited Victoria House public house to track him down, but no one would tell her a blooming thing except to say that he restored motorcycles somewhere in the Forest of Dean.

Then this happens.

It was too good to miss.

Hence the subterfuge.

She could finally put a name to the face.

So why didn't she come straight out with it now while she had the chance: *Did you kill Sarah?* The words formed soundlessly on her lips which didn't make them any less absurd. It was pride, she supposed. She didn't want to make a complete fool of herself, so she said nothing. What did she really have against him, anyway? Not much, and she was still wrestling with how far to push her line of inquiry.

She went on playing the perfect stranger.

Hedged her bets.

As did the foreman. He definitely wasn't stringing her along without a reason.

He knew all the time.

The piranha floated back into sight and filled her with caution.

Well, two could play that game before one of them got eaten.

'Forgive me. I suppose the boss is about? Is he?'

'No, actually he isn't.'

'No one knows more about restoring quality bikes than you, Mr Devaney, I'm sure. I bet I could get you a first-class write up in next month's Motor Cycling Magazine.'

'You could?'

'I have connections.'

'The real question is, who are you?'

'My name is Mrs Jo Wheeler and I'm chief Fire Guard at Gloucester Cathedral.'

'You sound very posh.'

'How can I forget?'

'That's funny.'

'But I can tell you're busy…'

'Relax, I'll give you a quick tour of our factory, Mrs Wheeler. My pleasure. We've nothing to hide. Nothing at all.'

'That would be nice.'

Because she had more to discover.

Beyond a rusty metal door, a foul taste in the air straightway caught in Jo's throat. So much so, she wanted to spit, cough and choke. This chemically based atmosphere was all acid and steam, the floor was wet and slippery; something about the warm, bluish fug prickled her face and blew up her nostrils.

It was hard to say what it was exactly.

Meanwhile condensing steam dripped on her head from the workshop's rusty roof. Worse still, all windows had been painted black to hide any glow from enemy planes and the artificial light was scarcely adequate.

The result was horribly gloomy, not to say depressing.

'First we'll degrease your badge, then we'll strip off all the old plating in here,' said Devaney, pointing to the dirty green liquid that seethed with electrical current inside the nearest tank. 'This stuff is so strong you could dissolve a body in it.'

'You don't say.'

The foreman, as crafty as ever, wove a dangerous path along slippery wooden duckboards beneath whose slats flowed an open and evil-looking drain.

'Trust me, it's almost pure sulphuric acid.'

But his exaggerated boast was lost on her because she had become aware of shadows shrouded in the factory's misty veil. These were living human beings, but not as she knew them. Their faces were drawn and grey, their eyes deeply sunken, their skin deathly pale without so much as a hint of a smile. Busy hands, impossibly deft, tied jewellery to wires on copper jigs with a speed that was positively unnatural. Workers' eyes, peculiarly blank, stared straight ahead, almost totally blind to her presence.

They might have been absorbed in their work or completely indifferent.

She couldn't tell which.

Two more women stood at a noisy, double-ended polishing machine whose spindles spun at great speed. A deafening extractor fan attempted to suck up all the dust, fragments of cloth mop and polish that flew off pieces of hot brass that each worker burnished at her fingertips.

'Don't go so close,' warned Devaney. 'Someone only has to lose their grip on a button they're buffing and it can fly like a bullet absolutely anywhere. You'll never see it coming.'

That made sense. Or he was still trying to work out what she really wanted.

'This dust not trouble you, at all?' asked Jo, her tongue feeling as if it were about to blister.

'Not that I know of.'

'But you must worry?'

'How do you mean?'

'It's a tough environment. Not every worker would want to get their hands quite so dirty. Not even for the war effort.'

His lips twisted with an ugly grin. It was more dry, mocking humour as he puffed heavily on his pipe to block all other smells.

'I couldn't care less about any of them as long as they do what I want.'

'Good to know.'

All other conversation was lost in the din of another machine starting up. Next moment the air blew thick with additional dust and sparks.

As Jo coughed and went to cover her mouth with her hand, so Devaney was feeling quite chatty.

'In my previous place of employment in Birmingham, we had a polisher who broke his arm while buffing a toast rack for our boss. The first person on the scene saw all the blood and fainted. That's because the toast rack had collapsed like a pack of cards and wrapped the worker's arm twice round the spindle. After that I had him sweeping floors one-handed for a while, but he had to retire shortly afterwards. Lung cancer got him.'

'The dust?'

'Who knows?'

'Shouldn't these women at least wear masks?'

'There's always a first time for everything.'

Jo retreated further from the storm of fire and dirt. Walls were strung with black growth-like debris thrown up by the row of machines. The floor was the same. To brush against any surface was to touch something like a living, greasy moss or lichen; it was millions of very fine fibres that had come loose from staple and finishing mops and flown through the air to attach themselves to every surface. There was also much greyish-black soot everywhere.

'It's emery grit,' explained Devaney. 'We glue it to the polishing mops where it dries very hard. Then we use it to abrade away the pits in the metal. Your badge is a case in point. Only when it is mirror bright can we put on new layers of copper, nickel and chrome.'

'How long will it take?'

'Give me a few days.'

'Thanks. I'll see myself out.'

'Not that way, Mrs Wheeler. I'll escort you off the premises, just to be safe.'

One of the workers glanced up from his bench and caught Jo's eye as she passed by. He was very calm but utterly lost. His gaze met hers with a stare that did not spare her. She couldn't say it was the look of the faceless damned since everything else appeared so humdrum.

Or she didn't choose to see it.

That's not to say it didn't bother her.

Even as she walked out the workshop, she saw Devaney rush to dial somebody's number on the phone on the desk in reception.

*

At least she had thought to bring her bag of stripy humbugs with her. Jo sat astride her motorcycle in the factory car park and waited for Bella's return. Peppermint tasted warm in the cold. Sweets were her one weakness.

Her mistake had been to expect that good-for-nothing dog of hers to stay put on the quayside. Now she was missing.

She was really berating herself for not being bolder – she should at least have cross-examined Kevin Devaney about where he was on the night Sarah died. But she was no police officer. He could simply refuse to answer her, or run a mile. Better to keep quietly digging for information than show one's hand too soon. For all his brainless brawn he didn't look the sort to kill lightly – he'd have to have orders from on high?

No, there had to be more to this than met the eye.

'Bella! Come!'

Where most dogs had an uncanny ability to sense their owners' slightest change of mood, whether sad or happy, she had noticed something was missing in Bella as soon as she got to know her better. In a word, she could be semi-detached. And that detachment could happen at the bat of an eyelid. There would forever be deep inside her the desperate urge to break free. They had that in common, at least. That's why she usually let her go off whenever she wanted.

That didn't mean that right now she wasn't being a bloody nuisance.

'Oi! Where are you?'

Suddenly there came an excited woof.

'Uh oh.'

She knew that sound.

Bella had found something.

The nearer Jo drew to a large metal skip on the quayside, the more her eyes fixed on a mop of black hair that fell across someone's face.

Bella indeed looked ecstatic. She might have been a miniature bullterrier bred for ratting not fighting, but she could still be roused to attack. That's why her captive was not going anywhere until she said so. She wasn't being aggressive, as such, she was just showing him her less gentle, affectionate side next to the bin of dented, empty oil cans.

'What's up with your dog?' came a feeble voice. 'What do I do next?'

Jo knew that devious, hangdog look.

It wasn't so much buck-toothed as toothless.

Yes. Could be.

'Noah?'

The cornered man's hands were clasped at the back of his head, his knees were drawn up to his chin as he hid behind his elbows.

'It *is* you, isn't it, Noah.'

'That depends.'

'Whatever are you doing all the way out here in the Forest?'

'Nothing I can't handle.'

It was her missing friend all right, but he was horribly flustered. Worry and guilt were all over his features; shame was no less obvious. His old raincoat had gone in favour of a smart zip-up, one-piece siren suit. Just about everyone including Winston Churchill wore such suits nowadays, for those long hours spent in dirty holes underground during enemy air raids. He wore equally new box leather shoes. Whoever had fitted him out with his striking wardrobe had given him a grey scarf, grey balaclava and matching knitted mittens.

'You been avoiding me these last few days, or what?' asked Jo.

Bella gave a bark, then licked Noah's chin.

'Trust me, Jo, I can't say a thing to you.'

'Okay, so now I'm concerned.'

'Please go away.'

'Better question, why?'

'If I'm seen talking to you they'll beat me.'

'Who the devil is 'they'?'

Noah rose to his feet and clasped his hands together as he started to bow and scrape. He behaved as though he were face to face with a regular bobby, but he made a very bad liar.

'Please, I haven't done any harm. Honest.'

'So why are you so scared of me?'

'You've been asking all sorts of questions in Victoria House pub, haven't you?'

'No more than I should.'

'Please don't interfere in things that don't concern you. Let me go. It's not safe here for either of us. You don't know what you're getting yourself into.'

'Suppose I do leave,' said Jo with less conviction in her heart than her voice. 'It's clear to me that you're in some serious shit and someone has to talk you out of it?'

He nodded vigorously, but she wasn't finished with him yet.

'I don't like the look of you. What's going on, Noah?'

'Not now. Not here. I'll meet you somewhere safe – soon – in the cathedral. I promise.'

With that, Noah ran into the plating factory. Bella wanted to chase after him, nip his heels. But first she conferred. She looked up and rolled her head. Pricked her ears. It was one thing for a dog to be able to act decisively in the absence of its owner, but quite another to have her standing right next to her and daring her to move a muscle. Should she really lose the initiative due to someone else's imprudence? They both knew Noah was up to no good.

That said, she eyed Jo critically.

'*What!* Okay, so I was a bit harsh, but there's no way round it. If Noah's so smart, he'll show up when and where he says he will, or else.'

Bella curled her bald tail between her legs, as if to say: 'You *think?*'

Jo frowned. Clearly news travelled fast in Gloucester. This was the second person in forty-eight hours to urge her to call off her investigations *and keep quiet.*

TWENTY

Sam simply couldn't sleep for brooding about it. The best he could do right now was to go to his window, lift the blackout curtain and scan the horizon one last time. Why shouldn't he, from the safety of his own bedroom?

In the morning he and his parents would leave Drake's House forever, bound for a new home deep, deep in the Forest. He was going to miss living by the river and railway so much.

He had never moved home before, but not even that could quite explain the wild thumping of his heart right now. An odd ringing noise reached his ears, as of metal on metal.

Was he sure it was only a shout and not a call? What's more, there was that ghastly ripple of the blood-filled moon on the River Severn's restless water.

His window was glinting and flashing. He could just about see to the water's edge if he stood on the tips of his toes. Was he even truly awake, or was that a clash of weapons that he heard?

Soon there came the sound of someone's piteous wails. Giddiness turned to vertigo. The sight of it all was both eerie and spectral. But who'd believe him? The room rocked from side to side and his head started to reel. His arms ached; his lungs heaved fit to burst; he felt pain, exhaustion, fear and excitement. This was no dream. Embattled men were combing the Forest in murderous pursuit of something? How long had this been going on? He had to have the answer. Their rallying cry died on the wind as he pressed his nose flat against the cold glass. The moonlight shone red in his face, the blowing of horses' nostrils blasted hot in his ears. They were all knights of the Round Table.

Suddenly King Arthur held his long sword aloft and sounded his war trumpet.

'The white boar has killed too many of our men already. I will not chase him any more, but will challenge him here, face to face.'

Slithers of ground mist coiled from dark forest to muddy beach, Sam noticed. Trees rattled and boomed like thunder. Then he saw step from the fog the large, misshapen silhouette of some animal or other. It both shocked and shook him to his core. The razor-back crest of hair along its spine suggested some sort of pig. With its broad snout and muscular shoulders, the angry hog hunched its short, powerful neck in a confusion of malice, outrage and pain.

But formidable tusks told him that this was no ordinary swine. Fiery red eyes glittered like garnets. It swivelled its ears forwards and raised its great head in the air to smell and take stock of its ambushers. Or rather its entire stance changed to a charge as it lowered its brow, all white bristles, like a battering ram.

And yet, with its obvious brutality there came intelligence, courage and stamina.

He could have been mistaken for thinking that this was one creature created from a mishmash of others.

The outcry from the knights was unanimous.

'Mabon,' cried Arthur, 'ride forward. Goreu, you do the same. Menw, you follow me. Together we'll drive it into the river.'

So saying, Arthur whistled to his two boarhounds Aned and Aethlem. He ordered the slobbering, black Great Danes to circle behind the beast at the river's edge and bite at its heels.

Sam saw it stamp its cloven foot, paw the ground. Then it snorted. During this time, the knights shouted louder and louder to bolster their spirits, for they had been fighting their enemy all the way from Ireland and were weary to their souls.

'Go to the devil, you filthy pig!' shouted Menw, son of Teirgwaedd.

'We've got you this time, you coward,' added Mabon, son of Modron, even as he struggled to rein in his mount Dun Mane, the horse of Gweddw.

They were not alone.

Goreu, son of Custennin, screamed:

'You eat little children.'

Sam heard the boar let out a growl. Immune to insults, it tracked the two boarhounds with its flared nostrils. The brutish stubbornness and brave, blazing eyes lent this Hogzilla the nobility of a worthy foe.

It ground its lower tusks against its upper ones, whetting each razor-sharp tip while its mouth filled with foam. The longer it stood its ground, the more it gained courage.

Then it charged again.

The knights did the same.

The crash was awful and gory. The air was rent with screams of men and hounds. Drake's House shook to its very foundations. Osla Kyllellvawr attacked with Manawyddan, son of Llyr. With them went Kacmwri, Arthur's servant.

'Grab it by the ears,' cried Gwyngelli, the instant they closed in from all sides.

Mabon spurred his horse to the boar's head and there he leaned down and plucked the magic razor from its bristles. Kyledyr Wyllt charged on his own mount until they all fell into the river – still he managed to hook the shears. In the confusion Gwyngelli upended the hog by its feet and plunged with it beneath the currents.

Sam held his breath, saw the great boar disappear. But its feet somehow found the riverbed and Kacmwri trod too close. The beast speared him with its tusks – it tossed him several yards into the river in the blink of an eye. All efforts turned to Arthur's servant to stop him drowning. Too late, Kacmwri was dragged away by the surging tide before he could be reached.

Horrified, Sam watched the knight slip under, weighed down by his armour.

'Help!' cried Osla Big-knife. He also had been gripped by the wall of water. It raced at him with tremendous speed. No horse could have galloped faster than this tidal bore. In running after the hog, he had lost his weapon. Now the steep-fronted wave filled his sword's sheath, unbalanced him and dragged him down for a third time.

'Where is it?' cried Arthur. 'Where is the devil?'

But this great creature, like all wild boars, was an excellent swimmer. Neither knight nor hound could go after it across the wide river. Once safely ashore, it ran at a steady thirty miles per hour in the direction of Cornwall, Sam observed with wonder.

But he'd already seen too much.

'Sam? Whatever's wrong?' cried Freya, as she burst into his bedroom in her blue, crepe-de-chine nightdress. She switched on a bedside lamp and crouched beside him, smelling of lemon cleansing cream. 'Why did you just scream?'

Still craning his neck at the window, Sam stared with stupefaction through its glass grown dim again.

'It's the wicked king, turned pig, called 'the boar Trwyth'. King Arthur's boarhounds Aned and Aethlem have gone after it in the river but won't catch it.'

'You've seen King Arthur hunting a boar?'

'Yes, a big white one. He and his knights have to retrieve the magic comb from its bristles. Without it, Prince Culhwch can't comb the giant's hair and marry his beautiful daughter Olwen…'

'Wow. Slow down. What is all this about knights and giants?'

'Don't you see? King Arthur never killed Twrch Trwyth when they drove it into the sea off Cornwall. They never knew where it went after that. No one did.'

Freya stood stock still for a moment, baffled by the conviction of Sam's revelation. Only gradually did her eyes fix on a book that lay open on his bedside table.

'Did granddad give you this?'

'Yes.'

She picked up 'The Mabinogion' and turned a few pages of her favourite Welsh stories.

'I might have known it. My father has been telling you more crazy tales, hasn't he? You do know that he is obsessed with wild boars? He collects reports about them from all over the world. A boar has only to chase a diplomat up a tree or invade the French Riviera and he cuts the article out of the newspaper for his scrapbook. Last time we spoke he insisted on telling me all about how they're laying siege to Rome and raiding the dustbins for food. He really can't be trusted to talk sense at all.'

'Twrch Trwyth is alive, mum. It's stalking the Forest. I've seen it.'

'I blame granddad. His silly stories are giving you nightmares. Please go back to sleep immediately.'

'Why won't you believe me?'

'Because there are no wild boars living in England. They were hunted to extinction hundreds of years ago. Go to sleep now.'

Next minute James arrived in the room clutching a cricket bat with both hands. 'What the hell is going on? Why are you both still up at this time of night? I thought you were burglars.'

Freya hurried Sam into bed as he made urgent, pleading signs to say nothing.

'It's just a childish dream, no more,' said Freya, sternly.

James retied the strings on his silk brocade dressing gown.

'Be that as it may, the removal van will be here first thing tomorrow. Sam needs to be up and about by seven for his breakfast. You do, too.'

Freya pulled blankets up to Sam's chin and planted a kiss on his forehead.

'Daddy's right. We all have a busy day ahead of us.'

Sam half closed his eyes in the darkness, but before Freya could move away he grabbed her arm and hissed a few words in her ear.

'I see the white boar most nights now. What do you suppose it wants from us?'

Freya's eyes blazed with rightful outrage.

'We all have our monsters.'

Sam tried shutting his eyes harder and buried his head in his pillow. Downstairs he heard James shout furiously at Freya about something, until she successfully urged him to lower his voice.

After that, anything his father said descended into grunts and snorts.

It was because of times like this that he wished he'd said more to that woman with the withered ear when he'd had the chance, in Gloucester Cathedral.

TWENTY-ONE

No one could like a stray cat quite so filthy and repellent, Thibaut had to admit. He watched its lithe, black body descend the pyramid of drums that stood rusting in the fenced yard and dodge into the factory for warmth and shelter. The tomcat always entered the same way, he observed. Its nose was crisscrossed with very old scratches and one ear was split in two. Its large, strong head had protruding from it a bump more worrying than its missing tail – it had to be a big abscess about to burst.

But for some reason the moggy had allowed him and no one else in the workshop to feed it scraps.

'Don't let that thing in here,' warned Devaney, 'or I'll wring its bloody neck.'

'Good luck with that.'

'Cats and chemicals are bad news.'

'Since when do you care about either?'

'I've told you before, Frenchman, don't try to get clever with me.'

There was something about the stray that fascinated him. Perhaps it was the wild defiance in its blazing eyes. Or it was simply the animal's ability to survive that was so inspirational?

Certainly the cat had nine lives. There was, in an annex to the main machine shop, a room where hot tanks simmered all day over powerful gas burners. It was the warmest part of the factory, unbearable in summer but not so bad in winter. So hot, steamy and rank was this place that no one much cared to visit it too often. The women workers said it smelt like cow dung. Only the ever reliable Raoul toiled there all day for little reward, blacking guns.

All burners were turned off each night, which meant that, by morning, a white crusty coating formed on top of the vats' cold, viscous liquid. This could look deceptively solid. No one ever thought to cover the tanks when not in use, of course. So it was that he saw the cat venture on to the surface of the nearest solution; it walked on its claws across the snow-white layer, like an ice-skater, on its way to its warm lair on some stairs nearby.

He held his breath. One crack and the cat would plunge into the sludgy caustic soda below and be dissolved alive.

There was something diabolical in its devilry. It lived for reckless mischief and daring.

Not for the first time the stray made it safely across. He uttered a small prayer of thanks. For did not everyone in this awful place perform similar feats every day? They gambled with their health – they were like that cat but without its nine lives.

He'd somehow plucked up the courage to mention his escape plan to Raoul.

Better still, he should have appealed for help to that one-eared woman with the sad eyes, whom Mr Devaney had shown round the factory earlier. There had been a moment when he thought he might have seized the opportunity, but he hadn't dared.

No one had.

TWENTY-TWO

Her hand was shaking like a leaf as she mounted the shallow steps that led to the cathedral's north ambulatory. She needed this quiet corner to reread the telegram that had just arrived from her father: *"Primrose seriously ill. STOP. Doctor says TB. STOP. Come home at once. STOP."*

Why on earth would she do that, thought Jo? She and her mother had hardly spoken since she'd threatened to blow her head off with her father's shotgun a year ago. They'd spent all day screaming at each other. Since then Primrose had told her to pack her bags and not come back.

Ever.

Perhaps, having been reminded of her own mortality, the rich, well-connected and God-loving matriarch had suffered a change of heart? Fat chance of that. More probably this was simply her latest ploy to lure her home so that she could harangue her some more about getting 'rid of that brat' she was carrying. Bit late now. And all because she was supposed to play the part of the respectable widow.

Well, her husband Jack wasn't ever coming home, was he? She had last seen him disappear in the smoking ruins of their shop in Castle Street during the bombing of Bristol. With one arm broken, he had rushed back into the fire to try to rescue their baby daughter but had succumbed, like her, to the inferno. Hundreds of people died that night. Their blood mixed with the molten lead from nearby St. Peter's Church that flowed past her feet like red lava.

Jack had died the real hero, not her. Now she was expected to live like a nun for the rest of the war to do him justice. At best she was meant to know her place, stay at home and look after her wounded brother day and night as if she were Florence Nightingale.

As if that had anything to do with it.

Put simply, she and Primrose had always clashed. She should have blown her head off her while she'd had the chance. But there was disobedience and disrespect – they weren't quite the same. Really, her mother had always been jealous of her. She couldn't stand the fact that, unlike her, she had somehow 'got away'.

Well, she wasn't the only one, was she! Since this war had begun, many a young woman had discovered there was more to life than they'd ever thought.

Suddenly she stopped dead. Someone was leaning heavily against the slender stone pillars that formed the back of the presbytery. The devotee's eyes appeared to be devouring the sanctified effigy of King Edward II.

Then again, a genuine pilgrim wouldn't look so unhappy, would they?

'With me, Bella. No barking.'

Bella knew this role. She was to be her non-judgemental provider of security.

But she was not meant to interfere.

The would-be worshipper gave a groan and stared at the effigy's open eyes, curly hair, beard and crown. He pushed his face forwards as though he would kiss the graffiti scratched in the murdered king's polished marble chest or simply stroke the two winged angels at his head – he seemed beside himself with worry.

Jo cleared her throat, rather loudly.

That didn't mean she was sympathetic.

'So Noah, you've decided to show your ugly face, after all?'

Light from the choir lit the penitent's siren suit. A mass of black, unwashed hair fell forward on his brow to hide half his ashen face. He was panting.

'Sorry, Jo. You startled me.'

'You surprised me, too. You look terrible.'

'As do you. Is it bad news?'

She hurriedly slipped the telegram back into her pocket.

'I'll let you know.'

At that moment Bella bared her teeth. She did it, she thought, pleasantly enough. Not for the first time Noah looked ready to take to his heels.

'It's okay, she won't bite you,' said Jo. 'Why are you lurking here? Why not go somewhere else for a nice cup of tea?'

'Screw you.'

'Have I not helped you out in the past? Are we not old friends?'

'I should hope so.'

'So you do trust me?'

'Otherwise I wouldn't be taking such a risk.'

'Put the knife down and follow me.'

The better they all behaved, the better this would go.

Bella flattened her ears and narrowed her eyes while she watched Noah very carefully. It was all well and good to expect a dog to be forever brave, loyal and self-sacrificing in the face of human folly, but not even a reassuring pat on the head entirely restored her faith in her owner's dubious judgement of character today.

Framed in white light from three large, plain glass windows, Jo sat down on one stone bench and directed Noah to another, in the south ambulatory chapel.

'Okay, let's hear it. What do you have to say for yourself? How did you come to be outside that factory in the Forest of Dean when Bella cornered you?'

'Oh, man.'

Bella stood guard in the chapel's entrance.

This could take a while.

Noah cast nervous glances. Scratched his chin.

'Please, I can't do this without a cigarette.'

Jo cast her eyes to heaven.

'Okay, but if Dean Drew catches us we're both for the high jump.'

Noah hastily pulled a Wills' Wild Woodbine from the dog-eared packet in his pocket and lit it between his filthy fingernails.

'I never should have agreed to tell you anything.'

'But you're here now.'

'Sadly yes.'

'You know something I don't?'

Noah sucked smoke deep into his lungs and let it steady his nerves for a moment.

'If you want me to go on breathing, which I do frankly, then you'll never mention my name to anyone ever again.'

'Fair enough.'

'As you know, until recently I was sleeping rough in shop doorways. One night shortly before you and I last met, this toff in a smart business suit offers to buy me a coffee and a bun. It was freezing cold so I was very grateful.'

'This 'toff' have a name?'

'I found out later that he was James Boreman.'

'*The* James Boreman? Gloucester's best known businessman?'

'The very same.'

Jo curled her lip. She hadn't expected to hear that name again quite so soon. That's because she couldn't connect it with someone so deserving as Noah.

No one could?

Yeah, maybe she could. Had not Mr James Boreman helped pay for the dismantling of the Great East Window for the duration of the war? Thanks to him, all its fourteenth century saints and martyrs, kings and abbots had been safely stowed in wooden crates – likewise, the Apostles who stood on the same tier with the Saviour and the Virgin Mary had been hidden from the bombs that had rained down several times on the city already. He was one to espouse a good cause.

'So what did he want with you, Noah?'

'He pointed at my grubby clothes and said, "It doesn't have to be like this, you know."'

'And you. What did you do?'

'I got up to go.'

'Him?'

'He said, "What's the hurry?"'

'You?'

145

'Trust me, I was beginning to think he was one of those awful blokes who wanted something for nothing. Once you live on the streets you get all sorts of weirdoes trying to proposition you. They think that because you've been bombed out, or are otherwise down on your luck, that they have the right to add to your misery. It's even worse for the women – they get attacked.'

'So what happened, exactly?'

Fresh anxiety creased Noah's face as he almost bit the end off his cigarette.

'He came across as quite the philanthropist and suggested we might be able to help each other out, because I could reach all sorts of people he couldn't. You know, wounded ex-airmen like me or destitute soldiers who lived on the street. The way he told it, he was making lots and lots of money and felt it was time to give some of it back to the community.'

Jo looked round the chapel. Shadows crept up the walls like dark water growing deeper and deeper. If the cathedral wasn't sinking, why did she feel that it was about to take her with it?

'James Boreman wants your help to help others?'

'You can say that again. He's paying me to persuade rough sleepers to go and work in his various businesses. Most say no. Some are too off their heads to bother. Others want the money for booze or food. Either way, we're all vulnerable.'

'Does he pay well?'

Noah raised his eyebrows.

So did she.

'Does he pay at all?'

'We receive ten bob per week.'

'Did I hear you right? *Ten shillings*?'

'If anyone protests they get beaten with a shovel or broom. Boreman's second-in-command, Kevin Devaney, has free reign to treat everyone like dogs. I was given new clothes, but others are lucky if they get second-hand boots and overalls. He confiscates their Identity and Ration Cards and plies them with beer and free cigarettes to keep them sweet.'

'Kevin Devaney works for James Boreman?'

'Who do you think owns that engineering and metal finishing factory in the

Forest? It sure as hell isn't Devaney.'

'I'm sorry to hear it. I saw inside. Conditions there looked downright hazardous.'

'I can almost guarantee it.'

'So, Noah, are they doing much legitimate war work, or what?'

'Yes and no. Boreman siphons off metal supplied to him by the government to make buttons for army uniforms and uses it to make trashy trinkets. It's a nice little sideline. Sounds harmless enough, as black marketeering goes, but talk on the street is that in Birmingham and Bristol he has links with gangs who loot bombed-out houses. When they get caught and sent down for eight years' hard labour he denies all knowledge. What judge is going to believe a petty criminal against a respectable businessman who is apparently working hard for the war effort? He's not alone. You read about people who earn £7 or £8 pounds per week in well-paid jobs who leave them to go looting. Can you believe it?'

'Better question, why?'

'Because he can get away with it in all the chaos. Word is, gangs raid the ruins and take anything from stair carpets to mangles and whole suites of furniture, not to mention any jewellery or other undamaged valuables to sell on before they can be traced back to the real owner. Trusted workers like Devaney get the perks, or so I'm told. Don't ask me to prove it.'

'You mean Boreman's robbing the dead to pay the living?'

'You said it, not me.'

'How can this be possible?' asked Jo, growing ever more resentful.

Noah had smoked half his cigarette already.

'That's not all. He gets people to pose as home owners who have lost their houses during an air raid. That way they can claim an allowance from the government of £500 with another £50 for furniture and £20 for clothes. One man claimed he had been bombed out nineteen times in five months before he was caught by the National Assistance Office. He and his gangs split the money between them.'

'Tell me more about the people you get paid to hire.'

'They're no better than slaves.'

'So why not complain?'

'I already told you. Most rough sleepers are sick or have shattered nerves. They've either run away or been dismissed from the armed forces, only to lose their way completely. None of them wants to make a fuss, not officially, they just want food and a roof over their heads until the war ends.'

'For ten bob a week?'

'They don't always view themselves as victims, as such.'

'How do they live? *Where* do they live?' asked Jo.

'I don't know. Somewhere in the Forest. I know for a fact that if anyone poses serious trouble they get to disappear without explanation.'

Jo raised her eyebrows.

'Disappear?'

'You don't see them back on the street. You don't hear of them again at work. They simply vanish into thin air amid a lot of secrecy and silence.'

'You listen to me, Noah. I'm sorry I got you into this but have faith, I *will* get you out again. Meanwhile, keep your eyes and ears open for me. Take care, okay?'

'Why do you think I've been praying to royalty?'

'One last thing. In your opinion, is Boreman dealing in blackmarket timber from the Forest of Dean?'

'You bet.'

*

'You've obviously been shopping,' said John, pulling up a chair at a corner table in the Cadena Café.

Jo took care not to break her newly painted butterscotch nails as she examined a large grey, galvanized cage and solved how to work its wire door.

'Now we're in business!'

'Whatever is it?'

'It's the answer to all my prayers.'

Bella lay down on the floor and placed her nose on her paws. She shut her eyes and flattened her ears. Not only did she have to tolerate idle chitchat this lunchtime, she was also about to be put out of a job, apparently.

John rattled the cage's bars.

'What makes you so sure?'

Jo looked triumphant.

'This is a humane rat trap.'

Bella gave a sniff. Resented the implication. No dog could guarantee to give its owner their daily tally of dead rodents when she felt so humiliated. Besides, were those not orange drop cookies she could smell on a nearby trolley?

John stroked his pencil-thin moustache, savoured his ground coffee.

'I don't know what to say.'

Jo explained.

'The rat enters the funnel at this end of the cage. When it steps on a metal pad, the trap door drops shut behind it like a seesaw.'

'A rat that big will never take the bait unless it's very stupid.'

'Talking of rats, you and I need to crosscheck a few things about James Boreman. His business interests appear to be very unusual to say the least. We need to verify what Noah says. You can start with the black market.'

'What does ANY of this have to do with the death of our friend Sarah Smith?'

'As we've seen, she used her PRONTOR II camera to photograph two men stealing timber in the Forest of Dean and now we know who they are.'

John leaned sideways to slip Bella a piece of his toasted sandwich under the table. She refused. She only ate food if Jo gave her leave to. It was her choice, not his.

'We know *who* they work for, at least.'

Jo looked thoughtful.

'If Boreman isn't Mr Nice Guy, what is he?'

John finished his coffee.

'Okay, I'll look into it. But only because it's you.'

Jo consulted her platinum and diamond wristwatch, a twenty-first birthday present from her grandmother before she had stopped being 'a good girl'. Let's face it, she would soon have to pawn it to buy baby clothes.

'Tread carefully, John. I get the impression that someone likes to stay ahead of the game.'

'Meaning what exactly?'

'Whoever burgled my house the other night took only my notebook. In it was everything we know about Sarah Smith so far.'

'Don't tell me you think James Boreman lifted it?'

'Call it intuition.'

'Why should you believe that? Houses are getting broken into all the time. No one's safe after blackout these days.'

'This is different.'

'You say this because?'

Jo reached for a fresh slice of brown bread. She preferred white, but who was she to grumble when there was no choice on shop shelves? At least brown bread had not yet been rationed.

'Most of the putty and broken glass were outside, not inside, the scullery. That suggests someone broke the window to cover their tracks after they let themselves in with a key.'

'Boreman's sister, Tia?'

'Precisely.'

'Relax. It's most likely a coincidence.'

Jo tried to eat normally but choked at the attempt.

'Except it happened right after my visit to the Victoria House pub in Barton Street. It can't be coincidental that Kevin Devaney overheard me asking questions about Noah. He came after me in the blacked out street where he pretended to admire my Brough motorcycle combination, until Bella growled at him from the sidecar. Later, when I tracked him down to that factory in Lydney, he pretended not to know me, but I saw him put in an urgent call to somebody the second I left the building. That somebody is keen to know what we're up to?'

John wrinkled his lips in disgust.

'Naturally James Boreman won't want anyone to delve too deeply into his business affairs if it does turn out that he's a serious racketeer. The thing is, how far will he go to keep people quiet?'

'Or how far did Sarah go to threaten him? Whatever it was went very wrong.'

'….'

'What?'

'It means Bruno might not be so crazy, after all.'

'Can't say. But things just got a lot more complicated.'

She was thinking about the last time that she had met Freya. Something about the troubled woman's words suddenly rang horribly true. So she had really been warning her in no uncertain terms not to cross her husband James? It seemed almost inconceivable. Most of all, why did someone like that marry such a man in the first place?

On that unhappy note, she was glad that she had accidentally-on-purpose misplaced Sam's ABC of trains. That book was her one chance to meet Freya again before things became any weirder?

TWENTY-THREE

'For Pete's sake,' said James, flexing his 18 carat gold Rolex watch round his wrist in a hurry. 'Where's that all new jewellery I bought you?'

Freya teetered on her shiny black Louis heels. This again. Why didn't he tell her that ten minutes ago? They were about to open the front door of Beech Tree Grange to the first of their guests for the evening.

'I'm sorry, I thought this dress looked so much better without it.'

'Do you really think I'm going to fall for that?'

'Gold is lovely but not quite my style, don't you think?'

'Have you done it to show me up?'

'Why would I do that?'

'You look like a widow.'

In not wearing her brash new necklace, earrings or bracelets, she did indeed feel half naked, thought Freya. If only she'd had the courage to abandon all her rouge as well, to reveal what lay beneath… the rawness. The plain anger. But she wouldn't do that. It would only make things worse. She had no way to account for the terrible error she had just made – it was a feeling of unsayable risk. It was like peering over the edge of a very high cliff.

She'd felt the same when she'd met Jo Wheeler high up in Gloucester Cathedral.

A similar vertigo.

'What would you have me do, James?'

'Sort yourself out. *Now*. There's a dear, while I make everyone welcome.' James quickly refolded the blue and white polka-dotted handkerchief in the breast pocket of his jacket. Nor was he entirely happy with his gold bar tie clip that held the four-in-hand to his shirt front – he really should have worn his plain blue cummerbund instead of the red. That's what came of trying to look like an American. 'And Freya, darling?'

'What?'

'Don't be long.'

But all this agitation about her appearance only exacerbated her more general worry about their house-warming tonight. Would there be enough to eat? Would there be sufficient wine and champagne, given the chronic shortage of alcohol available at off-licences nowadays? Drink might not have been rationed, as such, but it was so expensive due to the shortage of sugar that she wondered how they managed to afford it at all. Whisky was up 4s 6d per bottle to 22s 6d. Even beer was now a shilling a pint. She had to put her faith in James's dubious black market contacts of which she so disapproved.

She took a short cut through the kitchen and stopped to inspect the newly cooked venison. The whole idea of feeding their guests with fallow deer poached from the Forest absolutely horrified her. Her mother had taught her next-to-nothing about cooking, being too jealous and suspicious to impart the knowledge. As a result, she had no idea how to cope with a whole deer or even which parts of it to roast on or off the bone. Fortunately, James had hired a chef for the evening.

Still she could not help fretting. Did not any sort of game tend to taste too dry? Her instincts were to marinate the meat with wine to tenderise it in case the new oven's temperatures proved erratic, but the moustachioed chef favoured larding it with bacon instead.

'Be careful,' said Tia, appearing at her elbow. 'You might actually eat something.'

Freya stiffened.

'Maybe later.'

'Oh go on, nobody will know. Or is that black eye still bothering you?'

'Why should you care?'

Tia blinked lashings of dark mascara. Rolled her sly pupils.

'Maybe I want to help.'

'Then don't tell me what to do.'

'You scared of my big brother, or what?'

'James wants to make a good impression tonight. These people mean a lot to him. I don't want to let him down.'

'Just as I thought.'

'I don't like to see him unhappy.'

'Me, I couldn't give a damn.'

'Nevertheless I feel responsible.'

'But Freya, you didn't hire the caterers. It's not your worry. Whatever we eat tonight has to be better than Victory Sponge or 'All Clear' Sandwiches. I'm sick of all this rationing, aren't you? We're being told to make Christmas Cake without eggs now.'

Freya took a deep breath. There had been a brief time in her childhood when she *had* liked to cook, when her grandmother had let her stir soft white breadcrumbs into treacle dumplings. But the first time she'd ever tried to make one for James she had burnt it badly round the edges. At first he had given no answer, or none that mattered. Instead, she'd encountered a silent disapproval that bordered on contempt. She would never forget it: he despised her inability to be perfect. Since then their maid Betty, dressed in her striped white organdie apron, Peter Pan collar and French mob cap trimmed with fancy hemstitching had done it all – just the way he liked it.

Her hand hovered over the fruit mousse and apple pandowdy. To discover later on in the evening that the spiced apple was too sour would be devastating and dangerous. For her. Still her fingertips trembled, quivered, vacillated. She thought to sample a fruit turnover, at least. To persevere was utterly impracticable because she'd throw up for sure, she was so tense. Recklessly, she plumped for a honey biscuit and nibbled its edge like a mouse.

She liked what she tasted. It was a good sign, even if that single, little bite felt like a violent and lawless act, staking the success of the entire evening on such a small sample.

*

Freya rejoined the celebrations suitably adorned with gold chains round her throat. She tilted her head at various guests and was far too effusive. Her sole objective at this minute was to cross the room in the spotlight of everyone's curious attention; she had to do it without tripping or falling.

How to smile? She'd give it her best shot.

That's not to say she didn't feel her flesh creep in her black lace cocktail dress which James insisted she wear for the occasion; she was afraid that her peach pink slip might show under its knee-length hem. As for her hair, she had not known whether to put it up or let it down.

She could feel herself going all sticky beneath the copious amounts of verbena eau de toilette that James preferred her to wear day and night. He wasn't happy unless she reeked of its crisp lemon fragrance with mere hints of orange, rose and geranium. How was it that he didn't seem to like the smell of her any other way, so much so that she'd begun to doubt her own taste for anything different?

But it would keep trying to resurface – this other scent.

This sweat.

Dab, spray and wipe as she might, she could not entirely eradicate the warm, heady aroma that came with bare flesh which was her natural self.

'This way,' hissed James and caught her hard by one elbow. Together, they swept from person to person as her skirt clung like glue to her hips. Black lace on her bodice and sleeves, overlaid by woven bands of dense crepe in a lattice pattern, threatened to constrict her lungs.

Men and women she hardly knew said things to her, but they made no sense. What hostess went deaf at her own party?

'Well?' asked James, smoothing his freshly oiled hair. 'Is this going to be a great evening, or what?'

'I had no idea so many people owed you favours.'

At least everyone was here, thought Freya. James's sister and shady business associates all helped themselves to champagne. Over there stood public figures from local government and their wives. Their dazzling wives.

Her new home was the stage for a gaudy beauty queen pageant. And that beauty was supposed to be her. Tonight she was on display.

She was to be paraded.

Inspected.

Approved.

Most of all, she was there to legitimise everything James said and did.

Meanwhile, his latest sporting trophy stared down at her from high on the wall – a recently mounted stag's head caught the gleam from chandeliers and showed off its magnificent antlers. A cold, dead gaze formed on its glassy eyes. It honoured the fifty-year-old man who'd shot it with a curious smile, even if it was forever condemned to observe such alien surroundings. Tonight they would eat its loin and haunches.

Guests gathered by the log fire where James held court magnanimously as he passed round his cigarette case to the chosen few. Suddenly Freya's thumping heart drummed harder. The knot in her chest tightened. Lights dazzled. A waitress offered her a tray of canapés but she declined.

She couldn't do this any more.

Rather, she sought refuge under the stars on the terrace where cold winter air struck her face cruelly. Behind her, the noise of two hundred people became an excessively loud, incoherent roar. The fizzy champagne wasn't helping – it threatened to give her hiccups. She gazed back at the dark Forest that rose up to meet her while she walked alone under the moon.

Light from the house, so blindingly bright for the party, faded out half way across the turf of the newly laid lawn. A dark edge of oaks and beeches formed a ring round the clearing beyond which she had not yet strayed, not even with Ruby. She blinked hard. Surely something pale stood clothed in the silence of the sombre shadows? Her heart missed a beat as she strained to see further until she felt sure that some sort of wild animal was investigating her and the party; it was holding its snout high and smelling the rank smell of them all.

Such behaviour suggested an intelligent interest and not a chance encounter. The sheer persistence of the creature unnerved her. Those cunning red orbs conveyed some sort of menace; under their steadfast gaze she physically wilted as her courage deserted her. Her astonishment was such that she hesitated to move, should she invite the eyes to come any nearer.

Suddenly there arose the sound of voices – someone was standing at the foot of the steps to the terrace just below her. Their conversation drifted up to her in the smoke from their cigarettes.

'What the hell, Tia?'

Freya recognised James's ugly drawl.

'Relax, brother, I've got everything under control.'

'I never asked for this.'

'Me, neither.'

'If anyone finds out we're finished.'

'God, is that all you can think about now?'

'I blame you, Tia.'

'How is it my fault when Devaney's in charge of the factory floor? Who am I to say who comes and goes? I only do the accounts, remember.'

'Someone should keep a closer eye on things. No one like that should have been allowed through the door...'

'Be fair. We couldn't have predicted she would be so brazen.'

'She caught us all off guard, all right. Walked straight past everyone...'

'Is that what happened?'

'I'm not prepared to discuss it.'

'I don't even know *how* it could have happened.'

'As I've just told you, I don't want to talk about it.'

'I'm sorry, all right?'

'Damn you.'

'Oh please. Don't give me a hard time.'

'So what's it to be?'

'Not the river this time.'

'*Not* the river?'

'I'm serious, James. Rivers always give up their secrets.'

'What then?'

'I'm thinking mineshaft. The Forest is full of old coal workings. No one will ever find anything down there.'

'Doesn't mean we won't get seen.'

'I didn't say it would be easy.'

There followed a silence before James spoke again.

'You got somewhere specific in mind?'

'Yeah. Remember Dene Abbey? You recall how grandma Agatha used to keep a blunderbuss over the fireplace in case anyone tried to rob her? We all went for picnics together in the Forest during the summer holidays. We spent hours looking for slow-worms near Upper Soudley and found several old mine entrances covered with corrugated metal sheets. No coal had come out of them for years. Never will.'

'That was years ago. Any entrance will have been totally lost by now.'

'I think we'd know one if we saw it.'

'Doesn't mean we shouldn't take extra precautions. Have you?'

'Yes, I have as a matter of fact.'

'Is that a promise?'

'Absolutely.'

'What are we talking about here?'

'Sulphuric acid. That stuff's lethal. You wouldn't recognise your own mother…'

'I don't know what to say any more.'

'You could say thank you.'

'What would I do without you, Tia?'

'Don't worry, nobody will raise an eyebrow. People are coming and going all the time with this war on. Everyone will assume she has joined the Women's Land Army, or something. They'll say good riddance. No one will look for that silly bitch ever again.'

'When shall we do it?'

'Soon.'

'Accidents will happen, I suppose.'

'Talk later.'

Freya did not move. But James and Tia did – they finished their cigarettes and went back to the party. Her pulse raced. Her eyes ached to see into the Forest. She hugged herself and felt very alone. Still the beast regarded Beech Tree Grange for some malevolent purpose of its own, while its back emitted a faint phosphorescence.

Her innermost feelings of pain and abandonment rose to her throat until she found herself shedding tears. Not what she expected. But even while she attempted to deny the shape among the trees it began to grow dimmer and paler – it lost colour and disappeared gradually. Soon it had diminished to a speck in the darkness as it went back to another world. It drew all the trees together like a black cloak behind it.

'You hiding, or what?' said James, taking her by surprise. He must have seen her when he mounted the steps from the terrace. 'How long have you been out here, Freya?'

'Sorry, I don't understand.'

'You know exactly what I mean.'

'Do I?'

'You're neglecting your guests.'

'Really, I only wanted some fresh air…'

'But it's freezing. You'll catch cold.'

In her mind she could still see the beast. Eyes burned like fire and some of their boldness rubbed off on her.

'I thought I saw something. A white boar.'

'Where?' said James sceptically.

'At the edge of the Forest.'

'Is it there now?'

'No.'

He scanned the line of dark trees very briefly.

'A white boar would be really something. Imagine that on my wall. Unfortunately, no such thing exists in this country any more, not in the true sense of the word, as you well know. But it is the pannage season, after all. Farmers are turning pigs loose in the woods to forage for food – you must have seen a really big, male porker.'

Freya hugged herself so tightly she could scarcely breathe for a moment. Unbidden words rolled round her tongue. Rebellious words. Dangerous words. Imaginative words. Either she was meant to speak for the beast she had just seen, or it meant to speak for her.

Again, not what she expected.

'You've built our dream house at the heart of the Forest and you bribed all sorts of people to get round planning controls to do it. Most of all you chopped down trees hundreds of years old and now you want to excavate a swimming pool in the grounds. Is that really such a good idea, James?'

'Bullshit. I chose this place the same way I chose you. Because I can.'

She braved the smug look in his eye and refused to accompany him back indoors. Again he was trying to shame her into obedience by making her out to be a disloyal wife. But it didn't work. She'd already faced up to that particular humiliation once this evening.

'I have a bad feeling about it,' she called after him. 'I don't think we should be here. It doesn't seem right, somehow.'

There. She had voiced it. That misgiving. That unease – which came of not being loved, only wanted.

TWENTY-FOUR

Thibaut squinted at the black wall of trees that crowded the roadside this far into the Forest – he pressed his face to the narrow gap in the lorry's wooden slats for the best possible view as it chugged along. Each night he tried to memorise the route they took, but all signposts had been painted out or removed to thwart German spies.

He was bumping about in a box sixteen feet wide and six high whose rear ramp had been bolted shut and its canvas roof securely tied down. Only today had he noticed some faded letters on the driver's door that read G.H. MONK & Co. Ltd. Cattle & Meat Salesmen, CITY MEAT MARKET, BIRMINGHAM. That had to be animal dung that he could smell on the floor – he was being driven along like a beast for slaughter.

His fellow workers did what he did and tried not to slide about whenever the driver cornered too sharply on the narrow road.

Silence ruled.

Like a heaviness in the air.

It was imperative not to give into the mind-numbing atmosphere – despondent, doleful, drowsy. Muscles ached. Joints protested. So abraded by copper wire were his fingers after his long day spent working in the factory that the tips of his thumbs had split apart. The deep clefts of hardened skin did not bleed, but neither did they heal. Just to touch anything was agony.

Kevin Devaney's response had been predicable.

'Should I worry? Not really. I don't give a shit about your hands, Monsieur Thibaut.'

'But I can't work properly.'

'Don't tell me you want gloves?'

'Yes, please. We all do. Nora has a rash on her palm.'

'Fuck you, Frenchman. Who do you think you are?'

It was a question he asked himself every day. Fact was, they were all phantasms of themselves in this cattle truck.

Gradually, though, his mind filled with more pleasant tales from his childhood. Was it not in the similarly great Brecilien Forest in north-west Brittany that a fearsome Dame Blanche lived? This white lady loitered in narrow ravines or on flimsy bridges. There, any traveller who refused to dance with her was tormented by hobgoblins who took the shape of a dog or spotted pig. She guarded the great oaks ferociously and would do you many a courtesy before vanishing, but only if you came in peace.

His parched lips broke into a smile. Even now he fancied that the Dame Blanche's spirit dwelt here among these mighty trees wreathed in white mist. Such a comely creature went in fear of hunters – she destroyed their traps, filled up their pits and ripped their nets to pieces. As much human as evil spirit in appearance, she was keeper and defender of this deeply wild place, who ate leaves with deer and slaked her thirst at ponds. It was her task to withstand men's reckless destruction, misunderstandings and abuse of Nature. Perhaps every great forest needed a White Lady and her wild hog.

'Thibaut, reveille-toi, putain!'

He raised his head and opened his eyes. It was Raoul, his fellow Frenchman.

'We there already?'

'Hurry up. You know how Devaney likes to bully the last one off the truck. Don't let it be you.'

'Sorry, I was dreaming.'

'What of?'

'I was back home telling a bedtime story to my sister.'

'Oh yeah, which one?'

'I was remembering the legendary Forest of Broceliande.'

'That's typical Thibaut.'

'In French legend it's considered to be the home of King Arthur.'

'That won't do you much good in this shithole.'

'We can't just forget everything we love.'

'I'm trying to be practical here. Face reality.'

'And me?'

'You, not so much.'

*

The winter chill hit hard the minute they walked down the ramp at the back of the lorry. Thank goodness Raoul had woken him in time, thought Thibaut. Any worker who failed to fall into line was liable to feel the full force of a stock prod wielded by Kevin Devaney or his enforcer Danny Boles.

A gap-toothed cashier, who went by the name of Gordon Bates, stood ready to pay everyone their wages by the weak glow of a lantern.

Thibaut turned up his jacket collar and blew on his cold fingers as he moved up the queue.

'Hey, Mr Devaney, when do we get some decent clothes?'

'Shut up, Frenchman.'

'But it's freezing.'

'It really isn't.'

Cold mud chilled Thibaut's feet. Were these not the same leather army boots in which he had come to England three years ago? Both had large holes in their soles now. What's the betting his toes were turning blue? He saw Bates thrust a crinkly red banknote into his hand. The note was recognisable money all right, but it made little sense for all that.

'Merde! Is this what I get for a week's work?'

Bates's face turned ugly. His eyes blazed with self-justified outrage; his cheeks reddened. He stole a look at Devaney who shot a look back. In that brief exchange there was a rapid understanding.

'Can't believe you just said that, Frenchman.'

Thibaut waved the single banknote in the air.

'But it's nothing.'

Bates scowled.

'My condolences.'

'I deserve more. We all do.'

'I wish that were the case.'

'You treat us like slaves.'

'Good, that's settled then.'

'Fuck you, Bates, I quit.'

'You sure about that?'

'I didn't risk my life to come to England to live in squalor.'

'I'm really unhappy for you.'

'I want to work hard for a better future and I can't do that on ten shillings a week.'

'You get free bed and board, don't you?'

'Is this note even legal? Everyone else has the new mauve and grey money to deter counterfeiters.'

'Always something!'

'....'

Next minute a heavy blow caught Thibaut squarely between the shoulder blades. He didn't know what it was precisely, only that Devaney had walked towards a shovel a moment ago. The ring of metal on bone was like a peal of bells and pile-driver all rolled into one. His eyeballs nearly shot out of his skull. Arms and legs shook. His tongue trembled. Teeth ached. Trees, people and caravans took off round him in a strange tornado in which he whirled. Into his ears came an awful bleat. It was the sound of his own wavering cry.

He was on his knees before a second blow struck the back of his head.

After that, total blackness and stillness.

*

Where he was he hardly knew. Something rancid tasted on his swollen tongue – it had to be the stifling atmosphere. Air he breathed was musty, old, foul. The smell of sweaty, stale bodies hit his nostrils. It was the rank stench of too many men cooped up in the confines of a former Gypsy van, Thibaut realised, as he opened his eyes very slowly.

More worryingly still, it was broad daylight. How was that even possible? His spine had grown horribly stiff, too stiff to stand with ease or even at all, during the night. Something had knocked the stuffing out of him. He felt as weak as a kitten.

And his head hurt like hell.

Somebody must have dragged him to this stinking mattress on the floor?

His eyes were all double vision.

No sign of the other men with whom he shared this squalid home.

It took all his strength to work his way along the length of the cluttered caravan to a bowl where he dipped his face in cold water. His face came level with the trailer's grubby window as he rocked back on his heels. A white blur showed up among nearby oaks and beeches – it was creeping along amidst brown bracken. He opened the window's curtains wider and it faded – drew them back again and it reappeared.

'The hell!' he thought and gazed harder at the surrounding Forest.

But the spectral presence did not re-emerge.

Instead Nora skipped frozen puddles on her way to his door.

'You awake yet, Thibaut?'

'Where is everyone?'

'They've gone to work.'

'What about me?'

'No one could wake you. You just rolled your eyes and mumbled. Someone said you have concussion.'

'My head feels fit to explode and I'm seeing things. It was the same when a shell exploded near me at Dunkirk. I can't hear very well in one ear.'

'That's where he hit you.'

'Who did?'

'That bastard foreman. When you answered him back he felled you with his shovel.'

'I don't remember.'

'Sit down, I've torn a strip off a shirt for a bandage.'

'....'

To his surprise Nora pushed him about quite roughly.

'Sit down, I said. I need to wash your wound.'

'Why you?'

'I've been told to keep an eye on you, stupid.'

It was another few steps before they made it as far as the caravan's sofa, which in reality doubled as a bed.

'Ouch. Be careful.'

'Really Thibaut? Don't be such a child.'

'I can do it myself.'

'But you're still bloody.'

'Are you serious?'

'This will only take a moment.'

'So you say.'

Each dab of her hand struck his scalp carefully but firmly. She was right: his matted hair was an awful mess of mud and gore, but that was not all that bothered him. It was clear as soon as he yielded to her touch that his heart missed a beat. His arms and legs trembled. A fluttering bird took wing in his chest – he was confused, agitated and excited all in one. Most of all he felt humiliated at the hands of his enemy Devaney.

Nora bustled about but was otherwise completely calm.

'Poor Thibaut. How can this happen?'

'I blame myself. I stepped out of line.'

'Next time be more careful what you say.'

'I wish I'd never left France.'

'You mustn't talk like that. You would have been killed had you stayed.'

'I could have been killed last night.'

'There's no going back now.'

'No?'

'Not for me, either.'

Nora's long dark hair and brilliant blue eyes continued to unnerve Thibaut. Their proximity was no less alarming than the pain she inflicted on him.

'How bad is it?'

'You'll live.'

She gave him a grin, but his smile was not so bold as hers and he quickly averted his gaze again.

'Thank you.'

'I haven't finished yet. Mr Devaney wants me to empty a bucket of shit from every caravan. I'll start with yours.'

'Unbelievable.'

'That's not all. I have to clean his trailer until it's spotless.'

'Let me help you.'

'What'll *you* do? You can barely stand.'

'I can't let you do everything by yourself.'

'Just like that?'

'I can walk.'

'I don't think so.'

'Let me try.'

Once outside the caravan, Thibaut emptied his stinking slop bucket among dead leaves at the foot of the nearest trees.

'So tell me, Nora, how is it you ended up here?'

'You really want to know?'

'I do.'

'It's not a pretty story.'

'All the same?'

'Well, it goes like this. I arrived in Liverpool a year ago and did what many people do, I tried to find someone to take me in. I had no money apart from the paltry sum I'd stolen from Mother Odile's kitty in "St Mary's Mother and Baby Home". But the temporary work I found didn't pay nearly enough to keep me in board and lodging. I wasn't alone. I met a one-armed ex-soldier who worked as a caretaker in a local school, but he had to squat in churches every night because he had no home to go to.'

'What made you move to Gloucester?'

'One day, Mother Odile put the word out in Liverpool's Irish community that she was pursuing a thief and child of the Devil. Suddenly I found her sitting next to me in church one Sunday. If I didn't go back to Ireland with her she'd have me committed to a mental asylum, she said, or I'd be sent to the dreaded Magdalen Laundries for a life of never-ending drudgery washing clothes. Most of all she didn't want me telling people what I'd suffered at her hands.'

'But…'

'Let me finish. There was no way I was going back to Mass at eight every morning and eating porridge for breakfast and tea. I wasn't afraid to work hard, but I wasn't going to polish any more floors for that bitch, so I hitched a lift on a train and came south.'

'You've given her the slip ever since? Good for you.'

'It was one thing to lock up and terrify unwed mothers like me with tales of hell and damnation, but it was quite another not to give my baby son a proper burial after he passed away in my arms. He was only six months old.'

'You had a son?'

'His name was Sean. He died from gastroenteritis on Christmas Day last year.'

'I'm so sorry.'

'The nuns bound him in a cloth and threw him into the old Victorian septic tank in the grounds of our home. He wasn't the only one. Dozens of other severely malnourished and sick babies lie in those drains. Since when are nuns supposed to be experts on children, anyway? They don't have any of their own.'

'Honestly, I don't know what to say.'

'It's okay, I understand. I don't expect you to have anything to do with me now I've had a child 'on the wrong side of the blanket'.'

'….?'

'I still wake up at night hearing screams, whimpering and the murmur of prayer. The mother and baby home was a former workhouse. Its motto was "God Help To Those In Need". Can you believe it?'

'What about your parents?'

'Family, neighbours, teachers, all turned against me. I had nowhere to go except the nuns. I was banished forever.'

Thibaut used a hose to wash out his bucket. The reek of human waste rose in a steamy vapour in the cold air, like a visible exhalation. The frost-covered Forest floor vomited it back up to the surface as he added more to the dung pile.

'Everyone deserves a fresh start.'

Nora laughed.

'Yet here I am, someone's slave again. Okay, I couldn't sleep much on the streets. Some nights I was crying, it was so cold, but I could survive. I lived for better times. I just needed a chance, not this hellhole. I took Mr Boreman at his word that he'd give me a decent job.'

They walked over to the biggest trailer on site and Thibaut waited while she unlocked its door. His heart sank. Had not Devaney said Nora was his? She clearly had favoured status to be trusted with a key. It was all coming back to him now, in detail. That quarrel last night had been about her, not a ten bob note.

'Recently, in the factory, you asked me something.'

'Did I?'

'You know you did.'

Nora frowned. The neat slope of her nose, the roundness of her cheeks, the wild eyes – not to mention the lovely jet black hair – did nothing to deny her sudden look of feigned surprise.

'It's too soon.'

'To help each other escape from this place? I don't think so.'

'In case you haven't noticed, Thibaut, we have next to no money. It's not as if we can walk to the nearest train station and buy a ticket. Where would we go? It's too dangerous for someone like me to sleep rough any more. At least here I'm not about to get raped.'

'You sure about that? I don't trust Devaney. He has designs on you.'

'I'll be okay. You'll see.'

'No you won't, he's a monster.'

'So why doesn't everyone else leave?'

'Mary and Bridget are on the booze. Raoul and Nigel have been made nervous wrecks by the war. Why else do you think Devaney gives them endless black market cigarettes to keep them quiet? God knows what happened to Angela. We haven't seen her for weeks.'

Thibaut's voice died away as his eyes focused on the caravan's extensive interior. Disbelief barely described it. His eyes nearly popped out of his head. Gradually he became aware of the good quality armchairs, curtains and carpets that furnished the foreman's home. He was surely looking at the spoils of war?

'Astonishing!' he said, opening and closing the coal-fired stove on which their tormentor did his cooking. 'Mr Devaney lives like a king compared to us.'

'Just don't ask where it all comes from.'

Thibaut peeped into a bedroom and admired its down-filled bed where its owner liked to entertain his women.

'I've made up my mind. You and I are definitely leaving.'

Nora studied him hard.

'Not until you come up with a plan.'

'What am I supposed to do?'

'A *plan*. Do I make myself clear?'

Thibaut collected greasy newspapers and devoured a few dry chips left on a plate. At least Devaney and his floozies ate the same uninspiring food that he dished out to his workforce. His palate didn't extend to anything else; he didn't have the imagination.

'It's a relief, in a way, to know what I'm up against. First know your enemy.'

Not to be outdone, Nora sampled half a bar of milk chocolate from a shelf in the pantry.

'Make the most of it. Devaney has gone to buy more beer and condoms from the American base not far from here. He's taken his dog with him, but he won't be long.'

'What are you doing now?'

'He keeps all documents that he confiscates from us in a lime green, Peek Frean biscuit tin. I once saw him carrying it about by its handle. This might be our only chance – we have to do it before he returns.'

'Do what, for heaven's sake?'

'You want to get out of here, don't you? Hurry up and help me find our Ration and ID Cards. That's goes for Raoul's, too.'

TWENTY-FIVE

Since the burglary she had been a total bag of nerves. Her brain was bursting and her limbs were all at sea, as her heart raced at the abrupt apparition of the half-seen. What was that? The brume remoulded everything in blurry shapes and shadows. Now this maddening fog made a mockery of every step Jo took in the cathedral garth – she could not see to put one foot in front of the other past its murky veil.

But it was just another rose bush in the former monastery garden.

'Bella? Do NOT go near the well.'

The presentiment of danger strained her every nerve. She listened to the beat of her boots on a path that cut diagonally across the courtyard. There, she fumbled damp, cold walls in a corner to find a door, but not before she felt a total fraud.

'How can I possibly scare myself half to death in my own place of work?' she said aloud and staggered back into the cloister walk with its familiar fan-tracery ceiling. 'Just because someone stole my notebook I'm paranoid, or what?'

Next moment a hand gripped her shoulder. It was John, his shiny black shoes scraping the stone floor quite loudly.

'There you are! I've been searching for you everywhere.'

'I had to let Bella have a wee before Dean Drew goes to Morning Prayer.'

'You all right, Jo? You've gone very pale.'

'Did you see anyone come and go through here just now?'

'This weather is enough to put off even the Dean.'

'I could have sworn I saw...'

'You worried about something?'

'Not really, no.'

'In that case follow me. I have news for your ears only.'

'What? That bad, eh?'

She had not been in this part of the former monastery before, Jo realised, when John suddenly opened a door to a large, white-roofed chamber off the cloisters' east alley. The room's ancient ashlar walls were largely screened by long beige curtains as she and Bella crossed its threshold of slippery black and brown tiles. Monks might no longer gather here to listen to someone read a Chapter of the Rule of St Benedict or conduct the internal business of the abbey, but it was hard not to feel that their spirits lived on.

She admired the towering, stained glass window whose coloured panes commemorated the Gloucestershire men who had fallen in the South African War – their names were lovingly recorded on panels below – and sat down on the edge of a dais. Above her, an elaborate lierne vault with carved bosses formed the roof above the bay. She was squatting in what had once been a twelfth century apse, apparently. Meanwhile Bella sneezed at the carpet.

'So, John, tell me your bad news.'

'You want to know if James Boreman really is as crooked as you think he is?'

'I certainly do.'

'Just to warn you, the Dean has made it absolutely clear that he doesn't want us asking awkward questions about 'our man', not when he donates so much money to cathedral funds.'

'What of it?'

'Officially, he's a dead end. I'm the verger, so I should know.'

'I don't believe a word of it. Noah said that Boreman's men steal timber from the Forest of Dean, which suggests a link to Sarah's death.'

'You can't say that for sure.'

'So what can we say?'

'Again, why?'

'Because I don't like to think that a bloody spiv like him can get the better of me.'

'For a start, it turns out that a lot of the business Boreman does *is* legitimate. Right now he's building concrete roads for the army at their new base not nine miles from here in Ashchurch. This includes access to eleven very large rectilinear vehicle storage and repair buildings, plus roads to a sizeable rail terminus. His company has also concreted large areas around the sewage works.'

'For which he needs a docile workforce to do the arduous and monotonous work.'

'What's the betting it's the same sort of labour you saw in that factory in Lydney?'

'That's to say, waifs and strays. What else?'

'Just to warn you that he and his sister Tia are as thick as thieves. For a start, they own two restaurants in Gloucester. Again, everything appears to be above board, if you discount how they treat their staff. She has very good taste in clothes, by the way. You wouldn't mind her Cuban heels. Sorry, I forgot you two have already met. Her speciality, though, is sixty or so residential properties mostly in Bristol.'

'Bristol, eh? So brother and sister hide in plain sight? I suggest you hop on a train. ASAP. Check it out. Someone, somewhere, must be willing to spill a few beans.'

'….?'

Jo lit herself a cigarette, the one good reason for seeking such a quiet retreat in her opinion.

'What?'

'You know you can't smoke in here.'

'Like, that's what matters.'

'What about the baby?'

'I'm feeling so sick every morning I need to knock him or her out with something strong. Besides, I'm saving the cigarette cards for Sam. They're all pretty, green railway engines. I think he'll like them, don't you?'

'With fags the price they are I'm surprised you can afford any. Everyone else I know is trying to give up smoking to save money. Me, included.'

Jo interrupted.

'Bella? What do you think you're doing? Don't bite the carpet.'

Bella desisted, but not before she shot everyone a quizzical look. That smell on the floor had a hint of ash all right. She had already detected in the cloisters a whiff of Fine Shag tobacco. Whoever had been smoking his pipe in the cloisters had first smoked it here, too. They'd been waiting and watching.

*

John finally succumbed to temptation and pulled out a packet of Capstan Navy Cut. Such medium strength cigarettes had been all he could find in the local shop, so they'd have to do.

'What's up with Bella?'

'Never mind her, what's Boreman's background?' said Jo, looking daggers at John and dog. 'Did you even think to dig up his private life?'

'Did I say I didn't? It turns out that James and Freya move in well-heeled business circles. Before the war, they and some friends drove cars all the way to Cannes in France and the year before that they all went skiing in the Tyrol in the Austrian Alps. That new house of theirs in the Forest is pretty swanky, too. They just held a big house-warming party. I took a sneaky look. James is particularly proud of his new kitchen and newly turfed lawns.'

'Anyone can create a false show of happiness by spending money. Anybody can be just as lonely in a big house as a small one.'

'Do I detect sour grapes? Then get this. Boreman attended a well-known private school near Cirencester paid for by his parents who farmed two thousand acres at a place called Notgrove.'

'Never heard of it.'

'People say it's the coldest place on the Cotswolds. James learnt to drive tractors when he was ten. He taught himself to shoot pheasants and foxes and also rode out with the local hunt every Christmas with his mother, whose branch of the family once owned Dene Abbey in the Forest of Dean. James was hated and respected in equal measure at school, not least because he couldn't help boasting that his home had seven staircases. He excelled at sports, but he once cracked open a boy's eye socket with a cricket ball.'

'Wow, that's unpleasant.'

'The stairs or the ball?'

'What can I say? Maybe he hoped to score a six?'

John pursed his lips and blew a ring of blue smoke high in the air.

'However you look at it, he and his sister wanted for nothing when they were very young. Both rode their own ponies. It must have been idyllic.'

Jo again ordered Bella to stop digging holes in the carpet; she called her to heel.

Bella gave a growl.

'What *is* up with her?' asked John again.

Jo shot Bella a look.

'You know what dogs are like. They get ideas. So James and Tia still have an interest in the family farm, I presume?'

John drew heavily on his cigarette again.

'No, they don't.'

'They walked away from their well-heeled upbringing? Why would they?'

'It's a family tragedy. According to an old lady who cleans the station master's house at Notgrove railway station, Mr Boreman senior worked all hours of the day to look after his sheep. Thomas spoke more to his dogs than his family. Nearly died twice in snowdrifts. As I said, it can be pretty damned cold that high on the hills. That left his wife Annabelle to do everything else. For instance, it was she who rode out with the children when they went fox cubbing. She was also an exceptionally good cook. Annabelle was the cornerstone of the whole operation, no doubt about it. When she died suddenly of blood poisoning at forty everything fell apart. The publican of the Plough Inn in Cold Aston, a few miles from the farm, told me that Thomas began drinking heavily. He became violent. Couldn't cope. As a result, the farm soon went totally to pot.'

'Don't tell me he turned on his own children?'

'Thomas did a very bad thing to them. James was seventeen and Tia was only twelve when they found him hanging from a beam in the hay barn. That was the day before the farm was to be auctioned to settle mortgages and loans. Socially, it was a disaster. All their so-called friends cut them dead. It left brother and sister very close.'

'Oh bloody hell.'

'I didn't want to believe it, either.'

'Do we have any idea how they think about it all now? Perhaps they feel they have something to prove?'

John wriggled uncomfortably inside his coat.

'Christ, you don't give up, do you? Honestly, Jo, I don't know what you hope to achieve with all these questions. Is this about our friend Sarah or is it something else, because you're becoming really obsessed with the wrong people? You haven't been right since you found Sam lighting those candles in the cathedral.'

'I'm more than curious, I must admit. Fact is, Sarah was for a long time part of the Boreman's social circle, was she not? Basically, she knew everyone he did? Reveal a few secrets about him and she could finish him off. It would be the total disgrace of his father's suicide all over again.'

He gave her a hard look.

'Reveal what secrets exactly? We can rule out a bit of black marketeering. No one's going to shop someone like James when he can source them a crate of booze or a nice pair of silk stockings. The rumours of looting are more to the point, I must admit, but we know he takes care to distance himself from all that. It would have to be something more damning still. Closer to home.'

'Like murder, for instance.'

'Be serious, Jo. I know their type. The sad loss of the farm has imbued brother and sister with a sense of entitlement. They're spoilt brats who feel cheated out of their inheritance. They're nasty, but that doesn't make them killers. Basically, they've got it in for the rest of us because their parents let them down.'

She winced. John was absolutely right. You never imagined your family could be gone from your life until they were. From that day on you felt certain that, had you shown them just a little more loyalty, they might have been here for you now when you needed them most, because without family what were you?

She should have fought harder, been more courageous despite the flames.

But that's not what she had done, was it?

She had failed them.

Did that make her a coward?

That's what she still needed to know.

One day.

Did it even matter now?

Three years ago the Bristol Evening Post had called her a hero.

Keep telling herself that.

She saw the fog crowd the chamber's large, coloured window again; it pressed against the glass as though it were some living thing. It suggested itself like a face. Peered in. That mist was a physical embodiment of a creeping silence.

'As a matter of interest, who raised James and Tia after their father died?'

'Grandma Agatha. When she passed away a few years later, Dene Abbey went to another part of the family, but she bequeathed brother and sister a large amount of cash that kick-started their various commercial ventures.'

'I'd like to believe it.'

'You should. They've clawed their way back from the abyss.'

'You can say.'

'We're talking about someone who has it all,' said John, dusting ash off his new grey trousers. Since it was nigh on impossible to buy anything with turn-ups due to the shortage of cloth, he had bought his latest suit in a size too big and sewn the overlong legs into turn-ups himself. He couldn't do a thing about the awfully skimpy lapels, though. 'James keeps a fleet of cars, from a Bentley to a Riley, in his newly built garages. Tia drives a SS Jaguar 100.'

'Give me my Brough Superior, any time.'

'So now this is personal?'

'Okay, so that brings me to James's wife. How would you describe *her* role in the great Boreman business empire? Any clues yet? Is she a criminal, too?'

'Freya Boreman is a bit of a mystery, I must admit. I tracked down a picture of her looking stunning in Country Life Magazine, which recently featured her former, historic home at Drake's House on the River Severn, but she's somehow 'not there'. Perhaps it's because she's never smiling.'

'I wonder what bubbles beneath all that immaculateness and self-control?'

'You don't know me very well,' replied John, looking smug. 'Did I mention that Freya employs a cook-cum-housemaid called Betty? She can be quite the mine of information for five bob. Which reminds me. You owe me.'

'And?'

'Freya's brother Simon was killed in the 1942 Easter raid on Gloster Aircraft Factory. By then he'd worked there for a year building Hurricanes. She was very fond of him, as was Sam. The boy has been grieving for him ever since, which might explain those candles in the cathedral?'

Jo scratched her withered ear somewhat sceptically.

She'd lit candles for the dead, too.

It hadn't done any harm.

Not at all.

She didn't see how it could.

'But Freya must help run her husband's businesses, shady or otherwise?'

'I've consulted Companies House in London, but she's not listed as a director of Boreman Properties, or anything else for that matter.'

'In a way, I'm relieved.'

'Unlike Bruno Smith.'

'*What?* No, that can't be?'

'A recent entry confirms that James and Tia recently voted Bruno off the board. Which is strange because both men went to the same private school I just mentioned. Also, he and James both married much younger women who were old friends.'

'Bruno might have told us!'

'Finally, Sarah left Boreman Properties to train as a nurse some time in 1940. But you're right, everyone kept in touch socially until a couple of months ago.'

'You think it was James's child she was carrying?'

John looked alarmed.

'No reason to have her bumped off, surely?'

179

'The way I see it, James Boreman won't tolerate anything that's bad for business,' said Jo, beginning to think they might be going round in circles. It was like that fog outside the window. 'Think about it. We know James's second-in command Kevin Devaney and Sarah both worked for James before war broke out, so there's a good chance she always suspected that he did his boss's bidding, no questions asked? Maybe that's the reason she left Boreman's employment – she refused to take part in the black marketeering, unlike, say, her husband Bruno? So why go to the bother of photographing the timber thieves in action now, when she could presumably have shopped them to the police long ago? Why wait two or three years? She was a person of principle. So what triggered her sudden change of mind? If we're going to get to the truth about James Boreman we need to dig deeper. How does he manage to curry favour with all the right people?'

John stood up to go.

'This war is ruining most people but it's making a few huge fortunes. You have to hand it to him, Boreman is a bit of a star.'

'Is that how he looks to you?'

'Admit it, he looks wonderfully successful.'

'Wouldn't you be if you owned a small army of slaves?'

'So what do we do next?'

'I need to follow up on my visit to that factory in the Forest of Dean.'

'Then can I please, please, *please* go back to being cathedral verger?'

'Not promising anything.'

'And I did think this investigation would be a doddle.'

'I suppose you have a better idea?'

'Wait, I'll go with you.'

TWENTY-SIX

Sam dared not utter a single sound – he was too wide awake for that, ever since he first heard all the snorting and squealing. He should call his mother right away. Instead, here he was frozen in bed, trying to put substance to darkness.

All that gobbling and grunting he could only describe as uncannily human. The noises struck him as grotesque but not necessarily revolting.

Yes, they did.

He was alarmed and confused, not simply by what he heard, but by the great physical strength and energy it suggested – something or someone was digging at the very foundations of his new home in the Forest?

They might destroy it.

Not yet, but soon.

Still he could not bring himself to scream, but how was it that everyone else remained deaf to this terrible assault just below his window?

Sorry, but he couldn't wait.

The downstairs living room was a mass of bright moonbeams and hideous shadows.

Whatever stood there was composed of incongruous elements. Centaur, sphinx or griffin were nothing compared to the savage silhouette that loomed at the glass doors to the terrace. His lungs felt fit to burst as he cringed. He made fists of his pyjama sleeves with his fingers.

Some sort of pig was peering in at the sliding glass door to the terrace that was all whiskers and whispers. But no ordinary hog had such a hunched head and shoulders, surely? It was a malicious misrepresentation of kindness? A gentle gruesomeness? A mistake of God?

He fully expected to be set upon by this denizen of the woods the moment it clawed the door open a few inches.

Yet the more-than-mortal being did not come charging in. Rather, its shadowy profile alone probed floor, walls and ceiling.

If the roving tentacles of shade had all the attributes of arms, hands and fingers, then they were also a force for phantasmagorical trickery. He'd say he was simply imagining it but for the frightful reek of something rotten from the Forest floor.

He'd never forget it.

So why did the brute not eat him up there and then? The experience terrified him but also drew him closer. The strangest thing about this state of new wakefulness was it no longer filled him with despair. The white boar's bizarre introduction of itself proved less soul-destroying than thrilling. Instead of feeling helpless, he felt vindicated. At least now, no one would be able to call Sam Boreman, a liar.

The beast bowed its great head and let him stroke his bristles. It was strong, fierce and proud and yet lay down like a dog at his feet on the patio. A cloven hoof scratched the glass door with a squeal.

Suddenly it set teeth and eyes at him. Twin tusks curling up its face gleamed in the moonlight. It had no immediate desire to destroy – it was only the simple display of a determined opposition.

As if awaiting instructions.

Because it had been summoned.

TWENTY-SEVEN

His arm is on fire! He must have dipped his elbow too deep when he scooped that last batch of rifle bolts from the blacking tank's boiling liquid? He has somehow filled his rubber glove with hot caustic soda, Raoul realises – great blobs of red molten lava are searing him to the bone. He can see his flesh melting and peeling in the dim daylight that slants through the roof's painted out windows.

He utters a shout and the factory floor dissolves beneath him as if he's falling. His feeling is one of uncomprehending terror. For a second or two he sways over the open vat and its furnace-like heat scorches his face even more. That spell of paralysis sees him burst back into action. Those screams are his, but not as he knows them. He sheds the offending glove with a single shake. Sends it flying.

Run Raoul, *run* and you might outrun the agony.

Now he's scratching blindly at the brass tap fixed to the wall. He's discharging water on to his crimson skin as fast as he can.

He should go for help?

He can't take that chance.

At least this water is cold.

He can hold out for a bit longer, tame the pain.

No he can't.

There follows more frantic action. Bowing his head to the splashing water, he feels a stinging heat in his eye. Something intends to gouge it from its socket. He must have splashed his face, too?

To stop washing now is to give into fear. Violent muscular contractions send him this way and that. Every gut-wrenching stab of hurt leaves him dizzier, maddened, crazed. He whimpers like a dog even as other hands grip his shoulders.

'Rip his shirt off,' cries Thibaut, 'or he'll burn alive.'

Raoul falls sideways and his eyes roll white in his head. A big bubble of spit soaps his lips.

'I'm really disappointed in you, Frenchman,' says Devaney, directing water from a hose on to his arms, face and chest. 'How can you be so bloody stupid? You could have fallen right in.'

But he doesn't reply. He's thinking he must take up Thibaut's offer and find a way to flee this place. Only, he has already fainted.

TWENTY-EIGHT

'Wow, you look a bit cream crackered,' said John and squeezed his broad backside into the Brough Superior's sidecar with some difficulty. He fussed about tying a blue and white, polka-dotted scarf round his neck. 'You not sleeping again, or what?'

Jo gave a snort and pulled on her gauntlets and goggles. He was right, she'd had a bad night worrying about her father's urgent summons. Did she have a choice? She had to admit she hadn't seen that one coming. Her mother really was ill. Damn it. What she needed right now was a fast bike ride in the country to clear her head.

'I've started going to Ashtanga yoga after work every Wednesday and Friday.'

'You didn't tell me you had a job.'

'It's shift work sewing military uniforms in the Gloucester Shirt factory in Magdala Road. My arms are killing me.'

'So why bother?'

'What with? The yoga or the shirts?'

'The yoga, of course.'

'It's my latest exercise regime.'

'Must you drive yourself so hard? It can't be healthy.'

'Bella! Come!'

At the sound of Jo's call Bella raced across the cathedral car park where she had been digging for more coffin nails under the cover of blackout. She leapt on to John's lap and prepared to peer through the sidecar's dusty windscreen.

'You'll have to forgive her,' said Jo. 'She likes to see where she's going.'

'Don't we all.'

They were off to the Forest of Dean, to check up on how James Boreman really made his living.

Bella did her best to perch on John's knees as the motorcycle's V-twin engines misfired, stuttered and roared into life. They sounded like firecrackers beneath her tail. It was quite a surprise, in a way, to make it out of the car park so easily. She permitted John to stroke her head but not her nose. What could possibly go wrong? No dog wished to be seen as an obstacle to her owner's latest best friend – effective opposition required subtler, guerrilla-style actions – so she was choosing to play along.

John gripped his grey Homburg in the slipstream.

'So how *is* the yoga? You stomach churning yet?'

'It turns out that you shouldn't do that sort of thing if your blood pressure is as high as mine,' said Jo with a cautious twist of the throttle. Not everyone appreciated the full-throated roar of a motorcycle engine down a suburban street.

'No more abdominal perfection?'

'No.'

'Goodbye Nauli, hallo gym.'

'You may mock, but Ashtanga Vinyasa is based on an ancient palm leaf manuscript called the Yoga Korunta. It was discovered by the healer and scholar Tirumalai Krishnamacharya in the National Archives of India.'

'So it's all written down somewhere just like the Bible?'

'It was.'

'What happened?'

'Ants ate the palms.'

'Never mind, I'm sure it will improve your clarity of thought and harmonise your body's energy.'

'That's not me. You should see my standing asanas. All I get is a headache.'

John snuggled inside the collars of his coat. He didn't know what to do about it, but there was a cruel draught up his sleeves sitting this low to the road.

'Seriously, I'm the one who should get more exercise. Who knows, it might work miracles.'

'So why don't you?'

'The way I see it, what with this war and all, I might as well die the way I am.'

'Relax, I'll buy you a set of dumb-bells for Christmas.'

John looked solemn.

'I didn't know how cliquey and competitive men could be in a gym. All I want to do is lose weight for Christ's sake.'

'Welcome to my world.'

'I am too heavy, though. Everyone thinks I'm fiddling my coupons.'

'You should try getting pregnant. I get first choice of fruit, a daily pint of milk and a double supply of eggs.'

'I said *lose* weight, not gain it.'

'You know what?' said Jan, eager to give the Brough its head on the open road at last. 'I should jog round the cloisters with you. We should do it with Bella before Holy Communion, shouldn't we, Bella?'

Bella blinked. Whatever they decided it had better not interfere with her daily trip to the Cadena café to collect her free sausage every morning.

*

In the beginning she'd thought she would ask a few questions for Bruno Smith's sake in order to put paid to his doubts and that would be that, thought Jo. She should have known better. The moon-lit river looked positively mercurial as they rode up the steep hill out of Westbury-on-Severn. She followed its silvery, snake-like bends and kept the dark, brooding Forest on their right before they entered Harbour Road in Lydney.

John could see she was worried.

'What time did Noah say the workers get to leave?'

Jo parked their motorcycle and sidecar within sight of the unlit dock. From there they could observe the entrance to James Boreman's factory.

'Devaney drives everyone home at eight p.m.'

'Long day.'

'About twelve hours usually.'

'How far do we go with this?'

'Truth is we won't know until it happens.'

'So what do we do now?'

'We wait for them to come out, of course. Please pass my coffee.'

John felt about in the cramped sidecar and handed up a metal Thermos.

'You think this GI boyfriend of yours will marry you as soon as the war ends, then? You think you'll go to the U.S.A. with him and live happily ever after?'

Jo unscrewed the top off her flask and sniffed its lashings of whisky.

'In America, black and white don't mix very well.'

'Will your family take you back?'

'Unlikely.'

'If you ask me, you should…'

'Did I ask your advice?'

'No, but don't stop now.'

'I guess I've failed to live up to my mother's perfect ways.'

'Seems harsh.'

'No really, I have a compulsion *not* to do as I'm bidden. It drives her wild. Primrose can't abide the idea of me having a one-night stand with any man who isn't as lily-white as she is. As for my father, he mostly does as he's told.'

'War changes a lot of things.'

'As I keep saying, it's what lies beneath the outward layer of immaculacy and self control that really matters.'

It really did.

If she had embarked on a reckless bid to dance and drink her days away, it was only to forget the screams of husband and child. Hundreds of people had died and many more had been maimed in those first raids on Bristol. She still dreamt of Jack and their burning baby —he called to her from the smoke and ruins every night, but she could never quite reach them because she wasn't that brave.

John scratched Bella's ears. He gave up on any hope of any coffee. Jo never shared food with him, only the very occasional cigarette. It had to be a health thing?

'It's easy to shoot and bomb someone. It's those who find love in the midst of carnage who are the real heroes.'

Jo smiled. That shot of whisky just kicked in and she felt calmer.

'Please don't go all profound on me.'

'These are exceptional times. All I'm saying is that we can't always be what other people want us to be.'

'Amen to that. I really shouldn't keep nagging you about your weight, should I? I'm sorry. We should just strive to be happy, no matter what.'

'Are you?'

'I guess I'd be lost without Bella.'

'Have you always been plain Jo or something else?'

'Oh that? That's short for Jolantha. Thanks to my mother I'm supposedly named after Iolanthe. In Greek it means 'violet flower'. I shed the legend when I left home. I suppose I didn't want to be anyone's pretty bloom any longer.'

'So will your family ever get to see the baby?'

'I haven't the foggiest idea.'

'You seem to be blaming yourself for no reason.'

'I blame myself because my first child is dead and I'm not.'

'That's not what I meant and you know it.'

'Wait. Something's happening.'

Several men and women were helping a half-naked young man into the back of a cattle truck, Jo observed through her binoculars. All over one side of his face and down his arm she could make out ugly red burns. Someone else shut and bolted the lorry's ramp after them, then marched round to the driver's cab. The injured passenger screwed up his face with pain as he was driven away.

'Okay, I have questions.'

'I guess it's up to us now.'

'You said it. That driver is Kevin Devaney.'

'We go after him. Pronto.'

*

They followed the river for two or three miles, at times behind a US military convoy, before they turned north at Blakeney.

Once in the heart of the Forest the narrow roads were all sharp bends and hills.

Jo kept her distance.

'So what's his name?' shouted John, looking up from the sidecar.

'Who?'

'The father of your child, of course.'

'Which one?'

'The GI, silly?'

'He's called Joshua Jackson.'

'I hope it all works out.'

'Don't concern yourself, it's probably all over and done with already.'

'*It* may be over, but are you?'

'Hang on, Devaney's braking.'

While the road out of Upper Soudley continued towards Ruspidge and Cinderford, the cattle truck suddenly steered left on to a Forestry track that was all mud, stones and fallen pinecones.

Jo hadn't expected to subject her motorcycle to such a barrage of bumps.

They came thick and fast like John's questions.

Better to avoid them at all costs.

Honestly, some people!

'This won't do. I sincerely hope we don't break any springs on these ruts.'

John could almost guarantee it.

'Anyone who rides a motorcycle this recklessly has serious problems.'

'You have to go on about that now?'

Trees closed over them like a tunnel. From here on in, only the lorry's single red taillight provided any clue as to where they were going through the thousands of larches, oaks, beeches and pines.

But she kept up.

She had the situation under control.

In a very broad sense.

The track climbed and fell relentlessly in the gloom. John had to cling to the sidecar simply to stay in his seat as they lurched violently along. With his other hand he gripped Bella who was not amused.

'Be careful, he's slowing again.'

Even as he spoke, Devaney chose to stop in some sort of clearing.

'Any idea where the hell we are?' asked Jo, bringing the Brough combination to a halt immediately.

John lit his cigarette lighter in the depths of the sidecar and hoped its flame would go unnoticed.

'According to my map we're in a part of the Forest called Staple-edge Wood. There's nothing here except disused mines and quarries.'

'And a lot of bloody trees.'

'So how do we proceed?'

'I suggest we leave Bella behind.'

Don't do this, thought Bella, it's beneath you. On the other hand, the motorcycle she did regard as her owner's territory. It fell to her to guard it during everyone's absence. Or she might have a snooze.

'What if someone spots us?' said John, stamping his frozen toes.

'We use the trees for cover. Go round.'

'Devaney may have noticed us following him. He could tell others. They might be waiting for us with knives or something.'

'Well, yes, but don't worry about it.'

She couldn't stop thinking about what John had said to her earlier with his stupid questions.

Did he have any idea what it meant not to have someone's love?

Let him hope he never did.

*

'Well, I'll be damned,' said Jo. 'This has to be some sort of camp, or what?'

She didn't like the look of it. Not one bit. Lights shone in a corral of static caravans, while all about them stood a number of sheds, piles of rubbish and the skeletal remains of partly dismantled vehicles. The newly arrived cattle truck's bonnet clicked like a clock as it cooled in the cold. Someone had already placed a piece of cardboard on its windscreen to prevent it freezing over.

John stubbed out his cigarette on a tree in a hurry.

'You haven't said what we're going to do.'

'Trust me, I'll think of something.'

'You haven't a clue, have you?'

'No more than you do.'

'We need to see inside these homes.'

'That's a totally insane idea.'

'Can't be helped.'

'I could be wrong, but I thought I heard a dog.'

'I don't see any. You?'

'Not so far.'

At which point a caravan's door flew open and the reek of pipe smoke hit the freezing air. Kevin Devaney leaned out. There came the crackle of a two-way radio in his hand.

'Might be too late, boss. It's worse than I thought… No, literally I didn't…. I thought you should know he's gone into extreme shock. No, it was an accident this time… Yes, boss, I understand…. Of course we don't want any repercussions.'

From the trailer behind him there issued a series of loud moans. Devaney went back inside and shut the door on the cold. John left the shelter of the trees and positioned himself close to the caravan's curtainless window even as Jo crept along to a neighbouring vehicle. Suddenly he signalled to her frantically that he could hear voices coming from inside.

'For fuck's sake Thibaut, it's just a few burns.'

'Please, Mr Devaney, he needs an ambulance. He should go to hospital.'

'You can't be serious.'

'What else is there?'

'Plaster him with more lanolin.'

'What if his wounds get infected? We don't have any bandages.'

'Then use newspaper.'

'I beg you, Mr Devaney, you're a sensible man. Summon someone on your radio or drive me to the nearest phone box.'

'You know you're not allowed to make any calls. Boss's orders. That goes for you, too, Nora.'

'That can't be right – Raoul needs proper help.'

'Remember what happened to Angela. You all saw her dip her tea mug in that tank before anyone could lift a finger to stop her. God knows why she did it. As if a bit of hard work ever hurt anyone! Now it's as though she never existed. Like her, you are no one and nothing. You work for Mr Boreman and he owns you. Right? So keep your mouths well and truly zipped.'

'Yes, Mr Devaney.'

'Good, because I have to go now. Give Raoul plenty of Anadin and water to drink.'

John signalled madly to Jo to rejoin him. Next minute, Devaney emerged from the caravan in a hurry, looking pale. He came down the steps and strode across the ice-covered yard, all the while sucking hard on his Bakelite pipe.

'We should go,' said Jo. 'You were right. There is an Alsatian. It's in the big trailer.'

'What else did you see?'

'Devaney may be living deep in the Forest but his home is all Persian rugs, cushions and even antique clocks. What are the odds that they're stolen from bombed-out houses? He's been robbing the dead, I reckon.'

'That burnt worker we saw is seriously hurt. We should call for an ambulance.'

'Now might not be the right time.'

'From what I heard, he's in agony.'

'Tough call John, I admit, but Bruno is still saying his wife was murdered.'

'I'm not forgetting. Actually I do believe it could be connected to James Boreman.'

'You do?'

'I heard Devaney refer to someone called Angela. It seems she committed suicide. If so, James may be prepared to risk everything to cover his tracks, after all?'

They beat a white, frosty path back to motorcycle and sidecar.

'Well, we have something,' said Jo, 'even if it is something we didn't expect.'

'So what do we do next?'

She lowered her goggles over her eyes.

'We stick to Sarah. Who was the mystery last person she spoke to before her 'accident'?'

'You do know we have a cathedral to run, don't you? We have to get ready for the Christmas Coffee Concert in aid of the choir on the 2nd of December.'

'I'm sure it'll be fine.'

TWENTY-NINE

Each gut-wrenching bump along the Forest trail shook Jo to the core, as she banged about behind her motorcycle's pitching handlebars. The sooner they got away from here the better. There was no knowing if it was the scene they had just witnessed at the squalid caravan site that unnerved her so, or something else – she could only say that she was conscious of perceiving, or seeming to perceive, some other danger in the night.

Next moment a stag broke cover to cross the track right in front of her. Its nostrils blew frosty whispers in the freezing air.

The Brough Superior skidded downhill when she slammed on its brakes.

'Christ, that was close.'

John peered after the animal's white rump as it bounded left and right among the pines.

'Did you see its eyes?'

'They were electric.'

'I think we startled it.'

'No, something else did.'

What could she say? It didn't make any sense. Her ribs were aching. Her stomach was heaving. Most of all her heart raced like a steam train.

The Forest didn't look any different.

Not in that way.

But she'd begun to feel differently about it. This time of year the stags battled for access to the does to mate. You often heard them bellowing and making fearsome grunts.

But that other fear just now re-entered her soul.

They were not only being observed but tracked?

Don't be ridiculous.

She didn't know any more.

Did she hear that?

She wasn't sure. Whatever it was – this odd sensation – it wasn't going away. It was so easy to feel stalked in a dark forest by some brooding, portentous presence. Something other than a stag was crashing through the Forest and pounding a parallel trail. Broken bracken shed showers of ice to indicate its otherwise invisible progress.

'I really need to take the blackout tape off our headlamp to see better.'

'What we *need*, Jo, is a jeep.'

'Was this track really this bad when we drove it before?'

Everything was thumps and bangs from the combination's suspension. She feared grounding the sidecar on an icy rut at any minute.

'Can't be that far now to the main road,' said John, holding onto his hat.

'Don't you get what I'm saying? I'm sure we've taken a wrong turn.'

'I'm damned if I can see the wood for the trees.'

'Oh drat.'

'Maybe that stag was trying to tell us something.'

Jo hit the brakes and performed an abrupt about-turn in a muddy clearing. Back at a snowy crossroads, they drove a different trail.

'You're right, John, it is all about seeing the wood for the trees. That goes for Sarah especially.'

John clung madly to dog and sidecar.

'Sorry, you've lost me.'

'We can't presume her death *wasn't* an accident.'

'Now you tell me.'

'No, honestly, it might have been…'

Jo broke off abruptly. Her driving mirror had lit up with light. She could disregard the chance proximity of some sort of truck behind her, but not such a persistent dazzle. This was phosphorescent. She was completely distracted. Her breathing quickened as her eyes burned in their sockets.

'What the hell!'

John gripped the sidecar's mudguard and turning his body half way round, he tried desperately to see who was tailgating them.

'They can't be serious.'

Jo came to the end of the tree-lined track in a slew of mud and pinecones. Sure enough, headlamps blazed again the moment both vehicles hit the paved road. One thought especially rushed through her head: those hostile lights should have been masked like hers. Too late now. Whoever was chasing them was just getting going.

Ear-splitting blasts of the lorry's hooter rent the air.

'What are they hoping for?'

John hugged Bella tighter on his lap.

'They want to cut us off before the next bend.'

'I believe you.'

'Go faster!'

'I can't. That last lot of fuel I bought is rubbish. Full of grit. It's a waste of my petrol coupons. Not enough fuel is getting through the carburettor.'

'They could be just another very bad driver?'

'Not to me they're not.'

Sweat broke out all over her body. There was no way she was going to let this idiot of a driver push them into the ditch. She leaned lower as she positively willed the Brough Superior through the next twist in the road, but she couldn't reach full power. She could hear pinking and knocking as they ascended the hill. Really, the engine needed decarbonising. John threw his weight left and right to help them corner. A railway line appeared alongside them and then ran into a tunnel – otherwise trees crowded the verge with nowhere to go. Still their pursuers kept close to the motorcycle's back wheel. They sped after them despite the B road's increasingly severe, serpentine curves.

Bella reacted to this human fun and games by doing what she always did – that's to say, she flattened her ears and bared her teeth. It was not a pet's prerogative to criticise her betters, but it did seem to her that some people could be guaranteed to get themselves into awkward scrapes. And they said a dog should always be kept on the lead in public.

'Now what?' cried Jo.

John looked back again, aghast.

'They're still flashing their headlights like crazy.'

'Someone must have seen us leave the caravan site, all right. They must have followed us through the Forest. Now they're trying to scare the shit out of us, or worse.'

'Look out,' cried John. 'They're pulling round us.'

'Right on the bend?'

Jo gave a shriek as the truck driver drew level with her motorcycle's front wheel. A blank, fixed smile creased his lips when he glanced her way.

John squirmed in his seat.

'He'll push us into these trees if he doesn't watch out.'

The ugly throbbing grew to a drumbeat in Jo's head and everything turned into a perilous blur.

How much longer could this go on? John was her only friend; she couldn't let anything happen to him, or Bella.

Side by side with them, the lorry kept coming within inches of the Brough's handlebars. John hung out the sidecar again to help steer through the next corner.

'Damn it, he'll wreck us all.' Jo glanced through her goggles at the juggernaut's cab in which a thin-faced, grey-haired driver clung like crazy to his steering wheel. The long sideburns, the thin moustache, the slightly built arms and shoulders suggested, if not some maniac then a very impatient man. She didn't know the half of it. Or did she? That had to be someone she knew?

Next minute the Vulcan 5 ton, dropside truck had gained a slight lead. Its driver worked its Gardner 4LK diesel engine very hard. He kept up his attack yard by yard in small advances while resuming ear-splitting blasts on his horn. The very road swayed to and fro at each squeal of a wheel.

And so they entered the next hairpin bend neck and neck, but not before he squeezed past.

'Thank God, he's leaving us behind,' said John, rolling his sore neck in his hand.

Seconds later they saw why. A US army jeep tore past them in the opposite direction with an urgent wail of its horn.

Jo eased her grip on the Brough's throttle, aware of the steep bank down which they had been about to plunge.

'Wow, that was scary.'

'Was the truck driver at the caravan site, do you think?'

'Like to think not. Our road hog has the luck of the Devil, though. Had that jeep not come along just at the right moment he would have pushed us off the road for sure.'

'But what if he did recognise us? What if he tells Boreman?'

'What matters is that I've seen both lorry and driver before.'

'You have?'

'I should say so. Its rear number plate is broken but has 442 on it. That's the same truck Sarah took so much trouble to photograph in the Forest.'

'You saying we were about to suffer the same fate as her?'

'Tell me I'm wrong.'

THIRTY

Nothing Sam saw quite explained that curious whispering that hung in the trees. Each murmur spat, hissed and rattled at him from dark branches. It wasn't just the falling snowflakes. His ears imbued the gloomy silence with language, but what could be better than a walk through the Forest with his grandfather while the old man explained its secret ways? Any other child his age might have been frightened, but Jim Wilde knew a lot of good things. He was so easy to listen to, unlike other people. That's how he saw it anyway.

Right now they were following the course of an old tramway that led to a hole in the side of the hill. They trod the square stone blocks that once supported the rails – they hopped from one to the other like stepping stones as they imagined wagons of freshly dug coal being hauled along by tough little ponies a hundred years ago.

'Tell me again about the magic boar, granddad.'

Jim Wilde sat down on a log to rest his weary legs at the mine's barricaded entrance. He scratched his long white hair somewhat thoughtfully. Many a day he sat here eating his lunch and watching snakes sunbathe on the rails as he remembered his time in the underground workings. This part of the Forest in particular was honeycombed with abandoned adits. Where anyone else might hear nothing, he detected the slightest cracks of post and sling, or the faintest creaks from the wooden chocks supporting a tunnel's roof. Occasionally he envisaged legions of dead men toiling forever in their very own kingdom of inky darkness not far beneath his feet; sometimes he made out the sound of tapping and shovelling.

By comparison with Hades, a tale or two about wild boars was nothing.

'Well Sam, in Irish folklore you could ride a wild pig from this world to the next and return unharmed.'

Sam dipped his toe in a stream that gushed from the coal mine like a small river.

'Is that where uncle Simon went when he got blown up by a bomb?'

'I like to think so. Anyway, as I was saying, even swine herders were considered magicians. Once upon a time the lord of the otherworld was depicted with a pig on his shoulder. Druids and Wiccan still worship wild boar as the protector and giver of plenty. Sometimes when the Celts buried a loved one they placed boar bones in their grave.'

'If only I had a boar of my own,' said Sam, with a sigh. 'Then things might be different.'

Jim Wilde dipped his face to his grandson with a smile because he did not want to frighten him with any overt look of concern. Once alarmed, the boy became totally unmanageable – he would retreat into himself. He'd buzz like a bee if disturbed. Always.

'Then you would be like the reborn son of the Welsh goddess Cerridwen.'

'Who's that?'

'People called her The White Lady of Inspiration and Death. Her son Taliesin rode a wild boar. Like the Roman Diana. Like the Norse goddess Freya.'

That rushing water that flowed past his feet suddenly grew louder, Sam realised. The stream was coming from deep, deep in the Earth, from its most hidden places; its feverish bubbling filled his ears with cries, moans and mysterious laughter. It was not unlike those whispers he'd heard high in the trees a moment ago.

'Freya, as in my mother?'

'Your grandmother and I chose that name because Freya belongs to the Vanir. They were gods and goddesses who represented forests and other untamed places, animals and secret realms. What do you think of that?'

'I think it's very cool.'

'I'm glad to hear you say it.'

It was also true that Freya was a goddess of wild love-making. No man could resist her advances when she was wearing her magic necklace called the Brisingamen. This piece of enchanted jewellery had been made for her by four dwarves. As repayment she was honour-bound to spend a night with each of them. None of this was very suitable for a ten-year-old boy's tender ears, however, so he kept that part of the story to himself.

But his daughter had cast a spell on James Boreman all right, thought Jim

Wilde. There were other dangerous parallels, too. Although the Norse goddess loved many people, she refused to desert her husband. Even when she discovered that he had become an ugly sea monster, she stayed at his side and became enraged with the gods when he was murdered.

Again, he said none of that to Sam.

Instead he winked.

'Freya had a magic cloak made of feathers which meant she could fly. She could shape-shift into a bird and go anywhere she wished. Isn't that cool, too?'

Sam turned to the mine and shook its flimsy metal gate. Beyond the bars, night drank up the day inside the rocky tunnel. It was a special kind of blackness, profound, absolute. He imagined it might lead to hell.

'You don't know anything, granddad. You're making it all up.'

Jim Wilde flexed his arthritic knee.

'How's that?'

'No one can ride a wild boar. They're too savage.'

'Not to say bristly. But Freya did. Her boar's name was Hildisvini. It means battle swine. She also rode a chariot hauled by two blue cats given to her by Thor, but that's another story.'

'I wish my mother was a real goddess. Then we could fly away together.'

Jim Wilde wished the same, but Freya would never leave James Boreman, not unless she could rescue her son as well. In that respect she was as stubbornly loyal as her namesake, though he very much doubted if she would shed tears of gold should her husband ever be hacked to pieces.

He had never liked James Boreman. That man's obsessive passion for his daughter had cast a long shadow over them all. And he was far too old for her. It was hard to say who had bewitched whom.

'Better get going now, Sam.'

'But you said you'd take me down the mine today.'

'We'll do that another time. Besides, I don't have the key on me to unlock the gate right now.'

'But it's already open.'

202

'No way! That's not possible.'

Jim Wilde hobbled over to the mine's entrance and tugged at its padlock. Sure enough it fell apart in his hand. A rusty spade lay at his feet – someone had used its metal blade to strike hook from hasp.

'Maybe that's a good sign,' said Sam. 'Maybe one of those supernatural boars has come up from the underworld?'

But Jim Wilde was staring speechlessly into the adit. He literally had the impression that someone was down there *at this very moment*. That voice of icy cold water that exited from deep underground just grew more urgent; he tried to hear it all the way to the centre of the Earth.

'There must be some mistake,' he said firmly and clamped one hand on Sam's shoulder. 'Come away at once. It's not safe.'

'I say we investigate.'

'Why?'

'Because it might be magic.'

'You don't know anything, Sam.'

'We should at least say a prayer. We should call on Freya to send us her war boar to ride.'

'Why?'

Sam put his face to the gates' cold metal bars and peered intently into the gloom beyond. Then he picked up the mysterious spade, ready to take it home.

'So we can defend ourselves, of course.'

*

'Hurry up,' cried Freya as soon as she saw Sam arrive back at Tunnel Cottage. 'Run inside immediately and fetch your things.'

Jim Wilde frowned; he could see how flustered she was; he could rightly read the signs.

'How long can this go on, Freya?'

'Where were you, dad? James thinks I've gone shopping in Gloucester. You know how he doesn't like me coming to see you for too long.'

'Your own father!'

'You two will never get along.'

'I can't abide someone who doesn't respect his own wife.'

'Shush. Not in front of Sam.'

'As if he doesn't know.'

Freya stood with one foot on the running board of her green Riley 9 Lynx Tourer.

'James is under a lot of strain right now. He doesn't mean to lash out the way he does and he's always so sorry afterwards.'

To Jim Wilde the words issued from Freya's bruised mouth as if they were dreamy and unreal. They seemed not to belong to anyone he knew, but to someone else – to a ghost of her real self.

'How did this happen? If only your brother were still alive…'

'Well, he's not,' said Freya frostily.

'More's the pity.'

The loud ringing of a phone startled them from inside the house, suddenly.

'That'll be James wondering where I am.'

At that moment Sam saw his chance to throw his newly acquired spade aboard the black-hooded sports car. There was only one way to describe the awful panic that came into his mother's face. It was an expression of utter dismay – he could have been looking at a hunted animal.

But he knew this deadly game well enough.

'Let's go, mum. I won't breathe a word to dad about where we've been. I'll be as silent as the Forest.'

'You mean as secret as the grave.'

'That, too.'

For once Jim Wilde wasn't sorry to see his family depart. He had to get back to his coal mine as quickly as possible – he wouldn't be able to rest until he knew who or what was in there, but first he had to lie through his teeth down the phone.

His cheery wave was almost desperate.

What on earth had Sam meant when he said he wanted to defend himself? And what could he possibly want with a spade?

THIRTY-ONE

Really? At this hour! She couldn't have looked worse if she'd tried. Jo opened the door in her pink fluffy slippers, ready to retrieve a pint of milk from her doorstep, in Edwy Parade. It was only 8 a.m. With her hair tied in a towel and dressed in her shabby dressing gown, she cringed as she saw Tia Boreman cruise to a halt in her gleaming, two-seater red sports car. A rhinestone butterfly clip sparkled in the driver's immaculate red beret.

'I do hope this is absolutely necessary, Mrs Wheeler.'

Jo couldn't help thinking how terribly incongruous such an expensive vehicle looked outside the front garden of her modest, redbrick home. It was too sleek, black and aggressive. Too like its driver. Jaguar sprang to mind, of course. So did panther and puma. Cougar was no less a possibility. The large silver headlights observed her like eyes. The streamlined bonnet that housed the straight-6, overhead valve engine built for speed filled her with the vague expectation of menace.

'It really is, Miss Boreman.'

Tia must know by now that she was investigating her brother?

Hadn't John told her they were as thick as thieves?

That was no reason why she need lose the initiative. Not if she did this right. This was her chance to get the measure of her rival. All she had to do was to feign outraged innocence. Play the fool. Not show her hand too soon.

Yeah, like Tia was any better.

'As I explained on the phone, Miss Boreman, whoever gained entry to my home the other night broke the window to the scullery. I'll need a new pane of glass as soon as you can arrange it.'

Tia stepped gracefully from the Jaguar SS 100's running board and advanced up the short garden path. As she did so, she scooped the pint of milk from the step and in one fluid motion marched inside the house. A bird had been pecking at the bottle's cardboard top to reach the cream.

'One thing at a time, Mrs Wheeler. Guess what? In Birmingham, dairies are printing *SAVE for Victory* and *SAVE FOR MUNITIONS* on all milk bottles. We should do that here.'

Jo watched nervously as her landlord deposited her find in the hall and pulled off her soft leather driving gloves. Her elegant knee-length, fox fur coat with square, padded shoulders and silk-lined sleeves was a perfect example of the furrier's art, she noted. Tia's faintly smiling face, aloof and disdainful, had in it an impatience that went beyond mere time wasted as she clicked her black, daywear shoes with ankle straps and chunky heels; dyed pale blue inside, they were made from robust black calf with reptile trim. Her dark eyebrows and strawberry-coloured lips were all frown and pout, her walk a proud strut.

Meanwhile Bella sniffed a fresh hole in the skirting board.

Tia's attention was similarly focused on dark, squishy things on the floor.

'Really you should sweep up more, Mrs Wheeler.'

She was worried about her heels?

You bet.

'Yesterday I found rats' droppings all along the windowsill in the kitchen,' said Jo. 'This place is infested.'

Tia clutched her coat below her chin as if she might choke.

'How awful. Are you sure it's not squirrels?'

'I hear them every night, scratching and clawing. Bella has killed several already.'

'Show me.'

'I can't. She eats the evidence.'

'Did you know that none of us is ever more than a hundred feet from a rat? I heard it on the radio. Rats outnumber us two to one. Particularly in Paris.'

'Is that supposed to make it okay?'

Tia sidled past grubby walls and peeling paper. She gave a flick of her blue linen scarf printed with gold, green, purple and blue Armed Forces badges. In so doing, the words 'Into Battle' showed up all round its hand-rolled hem.

'Believe me, Mrs Wheeler, as senior representative of Boreman Properties,

I'm on your side.'

'So what are you going to do about it?'

'The rats or the burglary?'

'Both, of course.'

'Here's the thing, Boreman Properties can't be held responsible for an act of God.'

'Which is?'

'Those rats are migrating up from the sewers. It's an instance of uncontrollable, natural forces in action.'

'That it? That's all you have to say?'

'Technically, the problem is not on our land.'

'I beg to differ.'

'If I were you, Mrs Wheeler, I'd pay to have a one-way valve fitted to the soil pipe. Then, whenever you flush the toilet things will go out but won't come in.'

Jo was all raised eyebrows for a moment.

'But the house is so dirty and germ-ridden as to be insanitary.'

Tia took from her shoulder bag a thick wad of papers.

'I have here a copy of your rental agreement. The lease clearly states that you will undertake to pay for all necessary internal and external repairs. That goes for break-ins, by rats or otherwise.'

Jo felt her heartbeat quicken. Most of all she mustn't lose her temper.

'How about the loose tiles on the roof?'

'Believe me, this is one of our finer properties. Is it not 'on the phone'?'

'No chance you'll fix the copper, then? It sprang a leak yesterday.'

'You know I can't do that.'

'But the parlour walls are so cold and damp that the plaster is all blisters and bubbles. You can smell it.'

'Again, what's a little damp here and there? Don't get me wrong, Mrs Wheeler, I like you a lot. But do please remember that the houses in this street were built a hundred years ago without any proper foundations. Those Victorians were real cheapskates.'

'At least let me show you where the burglar broke in.'

But Tia refused to proceed another step.

'To solve your particular damp problem a trench several metres deep will have to be dug at the front of the house and filled with granite chippings. That should soak up the rain. Dry out your walls. Then you can redecorate.'

'So you'll do it?'

'The window pane or the trench?'

'Both.'

'No.'

'I had no idea that a house this small could be so unsound.'

'No one ever does.'

'That's it then, I'm leaving. I'll go and stay in the Station Hotel. I'll not pay a penny of rent until the problems are fixed.'

Tia turned on her heel.

'You wouldn't dare be so inconsiderate. You signed up for three years.'

'Who else will you find to live in a dump like this?'

'Believe me, Mrs Wheeler, some homeless evacuees will pay almost anything to get temporary accommodation, now that bombing has reduced their own houses to piles of rubble.'

'That your only answer? To profit from other people's misfortunes?'

'Yeah, long story.'

'Hey, slow down.'

But Tia had already walked out of the house in order to resume her place behind the wheel of her car. While her lips half curled in a smile, her eyes did not look kind.

'Please do pay the rent on time, Mrs Wheeler. Or else.'

Jo scowled.

'Or else what?'

'The bailiffs will take away that beloved Brough Superior Combination of yours.'

'I'll go to the press. I'll ruin your good name.'

'You're forgetting one thing, Mrs Wheeler.'

'I am?'

'This little meeting of ours never happened.'

'Surely you're a person of some principle?'

'We both know I'm not.'

*

Jo had just slammed the front door when the phone rang on the table in the hall. To her astonishment it was Freya Boreman.

'Hello Jo, I called the cathedral and the verger gave me your number. Is this a bad time?'

'No, not at all.'

Clearly Freya still had that card she'd given her on the day of Sarah's funeral.

That was good to know.

Never thought she'd keep it.

Bella pricked up her ears. Alerted to her owner's uncharacteristically delicate tone, she eyed Jo's face intensely – she noted her wide-eyed expression and reacted accordingly. That's to say, she was suspicious.

It wasn't as if she had rushed to contact Freya.

But she'd wanted to.

Bella barked a loud bark.

This was her helping.

Jo held the heavy black telephone receiver closer to her ear and its voice came across as hushed and cautious.

'It's like this, Mrs Wheeler. I've been thinking about your offer to show

Sam and me round the Cathedral crypt.'

'I thought you were against it.'

'Not exactly against.'

'….'

'Of course, it must seem like a waste of your valuable time.'

'Not to me it doesn't. One of the radiating chapels is full of switches for the cathedral's electric lighting, but the other four are perfectly accessible and very impressive. You can see where the pillars have settled due to the heavy weight of the choir above.'

'Can I ask you something?'

'Go ahead.'

'Meet me by the prayer candles. The sooner the better.'

Suddenly another voice – a male one – butted in.

'Who are you ringing?'

'No one.'

'Don't lie to me.'

'It's just a friend. Not even that.'

'Give me the phone.'

'I'm not finished yet.'

Jo called down the line.

'Is something wrong, Mrs Boreman?'

'Sorry Jo, but I have to go.'

'You wanted to arrange a meeting?'

'Not now.'

'Is that another woman on the line?'

'Think what you want, James.'

Jo spoke again into the phone.

'Are you in trouble, Mrs Boreman?'

'I can't explain right now.'

'Who's this?'

The voice was both rushed and aggressive. Almost breathless. Someone had snatched the phone from Freya's hand.

'Mr Boreman?'

'I said who's this?'

'....'

'Are you Fire Guard Jo Wheeler?'

'I am.'

'I don't know what you want, Mrs Wheeler, but stop interfering in my affairs. That includes my wife. Understood?'

'I hardly know her.'

'She's none of your business. None of it is.'

'What have you got against me?'

'You know very well.'

'Excuse me, what?'

That was it, the line went dead, but not in a way that made Jo feel any better – she felt outraged. She hung up the receiver while Bella tucked her tail between her legs and looked at her with her head on one side. In so doing she best captured her own low, feeble sound indicative of shock, pain and disappointment.

THIRTY-TWO

'How's he doing now?' asked Thibaut and banged the caravan's door shut on the snowstorm. Something told him that this wasn't going to end well.

Nora grimaced and went on mopping Raoul's hot forehead. The injured man looked horribly pale as he tossed and turned relentlessly on the dirty mattress. Didn't exactly help. Not at present.

'Do I really have to say it?'

'He seemed to be doing so much better yesterday.'

'Luckily that cold water he poured over himself limited some skin damage.'

'I'm glad to hear it.'

'So why is he running such a nasty temperature?'

'We should never have wrapped him in newspaper. I think ink from the print may have infected his wounds.'

Nora unfolded Raoul's bare arm and rested it flat on her knee. The hideously red flesh was spotted with big hollow blisters from shoulder to wrist; the bubbles of skin were thin, bloated and transparent. Each one had a hideously unnatural, whitish appearance as if large areas of the limb were already dead or diseased. He began to roll his eyes at her the moment she wielded her needle.

'Mon Dieu,' said Thibaut. 'Are you literally pricking each blister?'

'I'm just not sure there's much more I can do. Hold him still for me, will you?'

'We should have taken him to hospital long ago.'

'An obvious point.'

'A point lost on our employers.'

Thibaut wrung his hands. Did they even know where to start? Raoul had wrenched off one glove in his haste to stem the terrible burning sensation but in so doing had sent a dollop of red-hot lava flying on to his other, upper arm. In his panic and pain he had thought only to hose down the flesh that he could see was melting – he hadn't realised that it was this other limb that was really suffering, under his shirt. That hot, sticky caustic mixture had seared through muscle and tendon which were now doing their best to turn gangrenous.

'Some blisters might not leave too much of a mark, but he'll have a nasty scar on his right biceps. He'll have an ugly lump of hard skin above his elbow for life.'

'Since when are you the expert?' asked Nora, popping another bubble like bubblegum.

'I saw people get cooked alive in burning tanks on the battlefield.'

Raoul uttered a moan. More beads of perspiration stood out on his brow.

'Am I hurting you?' asked Nora.

'No, but I feel funny.'

'The sooner you stop fighting me, the sooner we'll be finished here.'

'If I don't get back to work I won't get paid.'

'We need to go on cleaning your wounds as well as we can.'

'Devaney's going crazy,' said Thibaut. 'Raoul's the only one of us who knows how to work that caustic soda vat properly – only he can turn rifle bolts black. Everyone else makes them go red or green.'

'You have to get the temperature and mixture just right,' said Raoul, responding with a hoarse whisper. 'Not too much water. Not too hot. It's just like cooking.'

'So I have to ask myself,' said Nora, laughing. 'How do you do it?'

'As a boy I helped my uncle bake bread in his village.'

'There, I'm done. Now lie back and rest. You'll feel much better in a moment. You went faint on me, that's all. Needles have that effect on some people. Here, try one of these.'

'What are they?'

'Fruit gums. I found them in the foreman's trailer. Normally they cost 7d and 4 points on your Ration Card for four ounces.'

'You thought anymore about what we said?' asked Thibaut, the instant he joined Nora in the bitterly cold air outside the caravan. He passed her a cigarette. 'If we don't do it soon we could both end up like Raoul.'

'We can't leave him, not now he has taken a turn for the worse.'

'He got careless. He said so himself.'

'Are you making excuses? You blaming Raoul?'

'Don't be an idiot, of course I don't blame Raoul…'

'You know how hard Devaney drives us all. We hardly ever get a break.'

'But accidents will happen.'

'Who else will look after him if we don't?'

'We should do it while everyone's distracted.'

'And how exactly do you plan getting away?'

'We'll go through the Forest.'

'But it's so dark we won't see anything.'

'It's simple. You can come with me or stay here and suffer.'

'Says who?'

'You've seen what happens to workers who can't or won't work any more. They vanish. We should go tonight.'

'What makes you think that?'

'We can't risk not to.'

'It's not that simple.'

'This has to end.'

Nora's eyes met his. To the everyday hazards of their surroundings, the 'disappearances' were an added, unspoken terror that she understood only too well.

'You honestly telling me that you can find your way through the Forest, Thibaut?'

'Yes, I think I can.'

THIRTY-THREE

'Everything tickety-boo?' asked John, doing his best to duck and squeeze up the narrow, stone staircase. Were medieval monks really this small, he wondered, banging his head on the curved wall? Not slopping water from his bucket was virtually impossible, as he led the way over the vault of the south transept to reach a platform just outside the cathedral tower. 'How's the high intensity training coming along?'

Every time Jo made this climb she still found it a maze. The tiny steps seemed to go on for ever and ever – they could have been on their way to the roof of the world.

'Very funny, I'm sure.'

To clamber about in these elevated nooks and crannies was to be like a rat or mouse. A door gave them access to the Ringing Chamber from which the peal should have been rung. She shone a torch into the cobwebby vaulting above the choir. At the very least, they were disturbing sleepy jackdaws and pigeons.

They were in the shadow of the massive 'Great Peter of Gloucester'. Where better? But tonight it hung silent over the city, waiting for the day of final victory when, as the largest medieval bell in England, it would once more ring out for joy at last?

The clock, too, had stopped working inside its glass case, as if time stood still.

She huffed and puffed with her stirrup pump, hose and a bucket of sand.

John took a breather before going on.

'You still doing all those backstrokes to stretch your pectoral muscles with "The Women's League Of Health And Beauty?"'

'*You* going to that gym yet?'

'It's a scientific fact that men have more fat cells at the sides of their bellies – it's where we store excess weight in our love handles.'

'By the sound of it, you're not long for this world.'

'And it's your business, how?'

'I worry about you, that's all.'

'You're the one who's pregnant.'

'Me and 100,000 others.'

'Nice to see you're in your customary bad mood tonight – like a grumpy bear.'

'I'm losing the battle of rats and roaches at home.'

Ascending as far as the next chamber, they arrived at the peal of ten bells and the accompanying machinery by which the chimes were set in motion at one, five and eight o'clock.

'No one forced you to move into that lousy old house in Edwy Parade, Jo. Besides, you bought a humane rat trap, remember.'

'Those devilish rodents have learned how to avoid it.'

'Can't you creep up on them and squish them?'

'They post sentries.'

'Isn't Bella a ratter?'

'She's doing her best, I suppose.'

Precisely, thought Bella, carrying her bone. John might try to accuse her of slouching, sleeping or scrounging sausages, but he should never question her willingness to go for the kill. It was not her fault if those damned rodents kept popping out the drains by the dozen.

'So move back in with your parents,' said John.

'And you can go to hell.'

The view from the roof of the tower was all moon and stars. There was not a Heinkel He III or Junkers 88 bomber in sight, as Jo placed her bucket of water at the base of one of the tower's four knobbly stone pinnacles. John did the same. Directly below them stretched the cathedral's gardens and residential houses, while to the north-west the Malvern Hills arched their dragon humps along the horizon. Elsewhere, the River Severn glinted silver in the moonlight as it snaked towards Wales, the Forest of Dean and Herefordshire Hills. It was all very beautiful, not like a world at war at all –

except not a single light shone anywhere in the blacked out city that lay before them.

Meanwhile Bella chewed the old fibula that she had recently disinterred. Any other dog might question why pets had to endure human small talk at all. Jo and John should have been kindred spirits, but they had an insatiable need to be rude to each other, apparently. Should she worry? It was just a silly habit. Not dog-like at all. That's not to say she didn't need to keep an eye on him and his indelicate ways.

Jo gave John a precious cigarette.

'You don't mind spending nights up here alone with a fallen woman, then?'

You see my point, thought Bella.

Surprised, John scanned the horizon through his binoculars.

'It would take a polar bear to feel amorous in these temperatures.'

'The whole world has grown cold. I don't think I'll be able to truly love anyone else ever again.'

'So it's GI Joe or nobody for you, then?'

'Shut up and make yourself useful.'

'There's a new film on at the flicks called "Outlaw". We should go and see it some time. It stars Jane Russell.'

'More to the point, did you get to Bristol all right?'

'I took a Midland Railway train, which reminds me…'

'Put it on the bill.'

John cupped his cold hands together and blew hard on his knuckles.

'I did a tour of the St Paul's area.'

'And?'

'It's as we thought. James and Tia Boreman own many a decrepit house there – those that haven't been obliterated by German bombs, that is. They're landlords to one of the five most dangerous streets in the city. It has it all. Lots of black market dealing. Violent crime. Whores. There's a hostel at one end of it that caters for men fresh out of jail. But here's the thing: some ex-cons go on to work as labourers for Boreman Properties.'

'How convenient. Many prisoners won't know which way to turn when they finish their sentences. So James rides to the rescue. Hurrah.'

John paused to give Bella a friendly nudge with his toe. She growled. People should know better than to disturb a dog when they have a bone. Even a human one.

'Nothing suggests the hostel is in any way involved in anything illegal. The workers sign up to work for James voluntarily. Only then does it get dodgy. Nobody will even think of going to the police, though. I only learnt what I did by buying one or two people a lot of beers in the local pub. Which reminds me…'

'I know, I *owe* you. So it's exactly as Noah says? The authorities turn a blind eye to Boreman or even encourage him, because they want ex-criminals, ex-soldiers and anyone else seriously down on their luck to find jobs? Any jobs. Also, he gets them to do vital war work such as building that new army base at Ashchurch. In some very important people's eyes James is doing us all a big favour by hiring 'slave' labour?'

'You said it. He's untouchable. No questions asked. It's a matter of national pride.'

'By taking human eyesores off the streets?'

John held out a few potato chips in a fold of greasy newspaper.

'Want some?'

'Please,' said Jo. After all, from now on it was her duty to eat for two.

'Noah was right about a few other things as well. I can confirm that James plies his recruits with just enough drink, cigarettes and false promises to keep them pliant. Most of all he exerts the constant threat of violence. He also confiscates their ID and Ration Cards. The result is a degree of secrecy that amounts to total and profound silence.'

Jo grew thoughtful as she poured coffee and whiskey from her flask. She was listening out for the sound of heavy guns. Midnight was peak time for bombers as they flew up the River Severn as far as Chepstow and then turned for the short run from north to south towards Bristol's dockland and city centre. All that pretty moonlight was not quite as idyllic as it seemed – German pilots used the glint on the water to navigate their way to their target just thirty miles away.

'Looks like we're in for another quiet night.'

John listened out, too.

'I don't like it. I feel something is brewing.'

'Don't worry, the Luftwaffe hasn't hit Gloucester for months now.'

'Perhaps all *our* bombing of *their* cities is paying off?'

Confident or not, Jo did not risk lighting any more cigarettes.

'Okay, so we're getting somewhere with James Boreman, but we have yet to find any obvious chink in his armour? Here's what we're going to do. First thing tomorrow morning, we go back to Bruno. I don't think our widower has been entirely honest with us about Sarah.'

'The Dean wants to talk to me about the Free Children's Christmas Trail. It starts December 16. He wants the kids to collect stars hidden in the cathedral. Each star will tell part of the Christmas Story all the way to the altar. He thinks we should discuss whether or not any part of the building should be closed off on grounds of safety…'

'Not to disappoint Dean Drew but perhaps right now is not the best time.'

'By the way, where did Bella find this bone?'

'Don't even ask.'

*

It was early afternoon before Jo set eyes on John again outside the cathedral, but that wasn't the worst of it.

'What time do you call this?'

'Your point is?'

'I said twelve. Where the hell have you been?'

'Sorry. I couldn't escape Dean Drew, after all. Did you know that he's writing a book called "The Dean's Handbook To Gloucester Cathedral"? He says it's going to be a definitive new guide to everything of real beauty and historic interest within its walls.'

'Who for? The Germans?'

'He wanted my opinion on some floor tiles in the quoir, no less.'

Jo paced up and down beside her Brough combination in front of the South Porch. She was furious. She hated delays of any kind. They'd wasted a whole morning, damn it.

'Jump in.'

John peeled back the snowy covers on the sidecar.

'I said sorry, didn't I?'

'At this rate it will be dark before we even get there.'

To ride out of Gloucester this way was to skirt its prison, docks and the remains of an old priory. Everything was overshadowed by the fickle presence of the River Severn which still defended the west side of the city with its three muddy channels. Soon they were high on the road above the low-lying meadowland of Alney Island where their medieval forebears had attended fairs and bet on racehorses.

'What are the chances that this turns out to be a waste of precious petrol?' asked John, holding on tightly to his hat. 'We don't even know if Bruno's at home.'

Bella barked in agreement. She sat on his lap and held her head out round the sidecar's small windscreen. To have the wind whistle in her teeth was to feel both free and alive. Exuberant. It brought tears to her eyes.

Jo peered through her goggles as she changed gear and steered fast past Highnam.

'Then we'll just have to wait for him.'

'Don't act the innocent with me. Have you thought this through?'

'....'

'Have you thought about this at all?'

'On the day of his wife's funeral Bruno was the perfect, grief-stricken mourner, but actually we now know Sarah wasn't the angel she seemed. She was plotting something.'

Bella barked again. Gave a snarl. That's because John was nodding but not really listening. He was screwing up his eyes at something. Suddenly he raised his arm to the vehicle ahead and pointed.

'Well, I'll be damned. Does that say what I think it does?'

Jo squinted, too. The rear number plate on a green Vulcan lorry right in front of them said 442.

'No wonder Bella's so agitated.'

Don't mention it, thought Bella.

'So what do we do now?'

'We keep a safe distance.'

'What about Bruno?'

'Forget about Bruno.'

'Why do you say that?'

'You don't need to know.'

'You're about to do something really stupid, aren't you?'

Jo kept the dropside truck firmly in view. Otherwise she said nothing.

*

Fifteen miles later they were cruising past rows of identically built, red-brick terraced houses in the little coal mining town of Cinderford. She knew how this looked, thought Jo, but sometimes you just had to go with the flow. The short winter day was drawing in fast and streets were busier than expected. That was because although the biggest mine at nearby Lightmoor had closed in 1940, the deep mine at Northern United and a host of smaller collieries were working doubly hard to hack out coal for the war effort.

'This it?' said John, seeing the lorry turn off the road.

Jo slowed the combination to a crawl.

'Let me see.'

'There, between those parked cars.'

'Looks like the entrance to some sort of yard. It says Forest Scrap Metals.'

'We'll stop at the crossroads and walk back.'

'Try not to look too self-conscious. In these quiet streets the locals will soon pick us out as strangers.'

'Don't worry, we're just a loving couple going for a stroll.'

'Easy to say.'

'That trip to the flicks still on?'

'….?'

'Just asking.'

'Stay where you are, Bella. Don't let anyone near.'

Not this again, thought Bella. No dog liked to see their owner walk away and leave them behind. There had been a time when she would have torn the sidecar's seat to pieces to register her anxiety. But not now. *Now* she'd make do with shredding today's newspaper with her teeth and claws.

After that she'd stare unforgivingly down the street for the first glimpse of Jo's return.

She'd do her lost toddler impersonation.

'If anyone asks, we're here to find a replacement headlight rim for my motorcycle,' said Jo.

'…!'

'No, actually, I really could do with one.'

He was still smarting at her apparent rebuff.

A high steel gate on wheels stood half open to a cobbled yard.

'Doesn't seem to be anyone about.'

'Good. Let's hope it stays that way.'

'Ready to go?'

'Do we have a choice?'

'After you.'

They walked in past the hulks of old cars, two steamrollers and a grey, double-decker electric car from Gloucester Corporation's redundant tramways that awaited scrapping. Each wreck propped its neighbour somewhat alarmingly. Beyond it stood some sort of brick-built office and the five-tonner.

'We need to go closer.'

John took a good look round.

'I don't see any guard dogs.'

But there was no time to take stock, Jo was already on the move. She ducked her head, ran across the yard and crouched in the lee of the truck. John swore to himself and followed suit.

She was already passing her hand over the vehicle's green bodywork.

Nothing on that.

Not a blooming thing.

She just didn't get it.

Unless.

That had to be it?

'See here. This lorry has had a new radiator grill fitted.'

John screwed up his face.

'You reckon?'

'And I'd say the wheel arch on this side of the cab has been hammered flat, too, wouldn't you?'

'That's still not a lot to go on,' said John, sidestepping iridescent puddles of oil. 'So what if it has had a recent repair and repaint? Nothing ties it to Sarah's car crash as such.'

'They must link somehow. I feel sure of it.'

Next moment someone emerged from the office. The cold eye of a torch lit the remains of windowless and doorless vehicles; each yellowish flash dispelled the winter gloom to bathe sorry remnants of glass, metal and rubber in the full glare of untimely illumination. With it came the sound of gruff voices.

Jo beat a hasty retreat. John waited a few seconds and then darted after her – they met up again among the teetering pyramids of metal.

'Damn and blast. Now what do we do?'

'I reckon more timber will be collected tonight from the Forest. What better place to hide their lorry than in a scrapyard? Time to go. Somebody's climbing into that mobile crane.'

Sure enough, the crane rolled into action on its noisy caterpillar tracks. Its ugly metal hooks made a grab for something like greedy fingers – they clawed the cab off a steam roller and dropped it onto a pile of loose scrap with a loud bang. It was picking at wreckage to feed its hunger.

John pulled Jo back by her oilskins.

'Wait.'

Although they could see their way clear to the street, that crane driver might notice them at any moment from his high cabin. He could knock them down with his hydraulic claws if he chose to.

'We have no choice, said Jo. 'We have to make a run for it.'

'What happened to your headlamp ruse?'

'I still want to look round.'

'Not now we can't. See. That man is shutting the gate.'

Well, they had to do something.

There had to be another way.

So they hoped.

Okay, which?

'Through here,' said John. 'Hurry.'

The scrapyard was as much muddle as maze. They kept going, only to find themselves at a brick wall blocked by a pile of cars at the end of a narrow, metal canyon. At the top of the heap balanced a Ford Model T with no mudguards.

Jo ducked and dived.

'So where to next, clever Dick?'

'We climb,' cried John, reaching for the spiral steps that led up the back of the Gloucester Corporation tram car.

'I hardly think so.'

'You got a better plan?'

But Jo stopped dead. Something resembling disbelief filled her face in the shadows. She didn't know what to say. What else could it be? There could be no other answer. Not that she knew of.

'Something wrong?' said John, baffled.

'Like to think so.'

'Say that again.'

Jo peered into the squashed remains of a small red car that was sandwiched between the electric tram and the huge metal flywheel of a traction engine.

'Sarah Smith was driving her red ACA Pearl Austin Seven Cabriolet on the night she died, was she not? This is it. I recognise the number plate COM 278. I'll stake my life on it.'

'You might have to. Now please can we go? That crane's coming our way.'

'I think we should take a look while we can.'

'No time, Jo.'

But her head was already all twists and turns as she stretched her hand carefully past crumpled bodywork. The car's bonnet had disappeared to expose a hopelessly mangled engine, the headlights had been torn loose from their black-painted wings and one wire-spoke wheel was minus its tyre on a broken axle. The steering wheel was bent double. Both doors were also missing. Its folding, black fabric soft-top had been torn aside and its seating had been cut in half. The back of the car, however, was more or less intact.

'A proper saloon might have given poor Sarah more protection – I'm guessing the folding roof sheered off and took her head with it.'

John leaned into the wreck after her.

'A friend of mine owns one of these. The visibility isn't great when you have the hood right up.'

'You mean she might have been slow to see someone overtake her fast from behind?'

John fingered glass from the shattered windscreen that littered seats streaked black with dried blood. Suddenly the door to the boot fell open as he withdrew his arm.

He was completely speechless.

'What is it?' said Jo.

Immediately they both began to haul a grey suitcase from the wreckage.

'We should open it at once.'

Instead, Jo snatched the bag from his hand and made for the stair rail of the double-decker tram car as he'd first suggested. She ran all the way up to its top deck and leapt on to one of its wooden, slatted seats open to the sky. She stood there for a moment at the summit of the scrap mountain.

The crane, all the while, rumbled closer and closer. Rattling metal chattered and churred. It shook the ground like a tank. It could have been heading straight for the Pearl Austin Seven.

John joined Jo and looked over the wall that surrounded the yard. He could hear her lungs blowing like bellows. Or were they his own? He could see it was a bit of a drop on to someone's allotment. They had to aim for a compost heap or nothing.

'You'll regret this,' he said, but she was already gone.

*

Back at their Brough Superior Combination, Jo opened their find – she only broke off to borrow John's handkerchief to bind a cut in her hand.

'What does it look like to you?' she asked, her hair shedding dead leaves into the suitcase.

'It's full of clothes.'

'So was Sarah going on holiday, or what?'

'It's hard to say.'

Bella sniffed the contents and whined. To have her owner back with her saw her anxiety fade to almost nothing. If she was at all worried it was because someone had yet to find out where she had stuffed the torn-up copy of 'The Forester' in the sidecar.

'How do you mean?' asked Jo, glancing nervously up and down the street.

'There's really not much here. Just a few clothes and what has to be a bundle of photographs.'

'So why did Bruno not retrieve all this from the wreckage when he had the chance?'

'He might have been too upset.'

'Or he didn't want to face what it meant?'

'Hurry. Let's get out of here.'

With that, they strapped the suitcase to the sidecar's metal luggage rack, ready to set off back to Gloucester.

'No woman goes to all the effort of packing so little for a holiday,' said Jo, kick-starting the Brough into action.

'Looks like she grabbed what she could in an awful hurry.'

'But somebody didn't want her to reach her destination that evening.'

'Violent husband? Jealous lover? Or Sarah was closing in on James Boreman. We have motive and opportunity. Simple as that.'

Jo peered through the sidecar's windscreen and kept an anxious eye on her mirror; she monitored the dark road behind them for signs of pursuit.

'Yes, could be, but I do wonder.'

'Why's that?'

'I really did expect to see scrapes of green paint on the Austin Seven, didn't you? As it happens, there's no hard evidence that the lorry ever actually hit it.'

'Isn't that the truth.'

'I know Susie Grossman says differently, but what if Sarah was in the act of *leaving her husband* for good when the accident happened?'

'Whatever are you implying?'

'What are the odds? Somebody knew she would make a run for it that night. We need to find them and do it fast. That's why we're stopping in Westbury-on Severn.'

'We are?'

'It seems we have something to ask Bruno, after all.'

With that, she opened the throttle wide.

THIRTY-FOUR

Something was wrong, that much Freya knew. James was sitting stock-still at the oak table in their brand new red and black kitchen. He had not eaten his bacon and eggs that Betty had prepared for him as usual for breakfast. As a result, the maid had made herself scarce.

A cold light blazed in his eyes; the pallor of his cheeks was no less icy. The fact of not mentioning a thing was itself an expression of greatest unpredictability. Of greatest outrage. To know a man by his silence was to know him by fear.

That wasn't all. A 12-gauge shotgun and half a dozen black cartridges full of lead lay before him. He had lined up all six in a row ever so neatly. His knuckles turned white on his spread-eagled hands, upon which he leaned with considerable pressure. He thrust out his chin as he breathed very quickly.

Freya stood there for a minute.

A minute could be a long time.

For that's what it felt like now, this frenzy of staring.

This furious civility.

This ordering of live ammunition at the edge of the table.

When she did move across the room, she did so like a ghost. Nothing about the way her husband behaved could be said to be calm or impartial when suddenly he rose to his feet. Whereas before he dug his fingers into his palms, now he tore at his bristly white hair.

'Can you fucking believe it?'

Her decision to join him at the window was risky, but not without hope.

'What is it, James? What's going on?'

He would have her sympathy about something? He clasped her hand with violent apprehension; he was agitated, shocked, disturbed. There were tears in his eyes.

'See for yourself.'

Freya heard him grind his teeth and froth at the mouth. It was as if all his emotions had to be hers for a moment. Then she looked outside and saw why. The newly laid lawn below the terrace of Beech Tree Grange was green no longer. Rather, an area half the size of a football pitch had been thoroughly turned over and uprooted, each flap of newly laid turf had been flipped on its back to expose brown earth underneath. Something or someone had dug up the ground quite methodically.

'Whoever did this came in the night,' said James. The full force of his criticism bore down on her as he began to squeeze her fingers.

'What do you mean? *Who*ever?'

Soon the smallest twist would hurt horribly.

'Somebody wants to take us on.'

'It doesn't look like that to me.'

'Whatever do you mean?'

'A great many animals live in the Forest.'

'You think?'

She winced at the pain from her crushed thumb.

'I'm sure there's a perfectly logical explanation.'

'Logical, be damned.'

'But James, you said it yourself. Farmers turn their pigs out to roam in the Forest at this time of the year. They eat the acorns and beechmast and use their snouts to root for worms. Many a garden and graveyard get raided, as you know.'

'I can't believe you just said that.'

'Call it a gut feeling.'

'You can't shoot feelings, but you can jolly well shoot a stray pig. I'm going after the bastard if it ever it shows up here again. Meanwhile I'll erect a great big fence to keep us secure.'

Freya said nothing. There could be no talking him out of the notion of some hostile neighbour. That an intruder had come on to their property could not be denied. It made her think of Sam's strange nightmares, except in his dreams his visitor was as much human as animal?

James finally thought to release her sore hand. What possible point was there asking her anything, anyway? In his eyes, she could no more put a face to their mischievous vandal than he could.

THIRTY-FIVE

'That's not Sarah's, I tell you,' said Bruno flatly and averted his bloodshot, brown eyes. His face looked drained, dismal and demoralized.

Undaunted, John continued to hold up a red, cap-sleeved sweater in the dining room; he exposed its heavy, hand-knitted and silky yarn with three pearl buttons to the light at the window for everyone to see. In the distance the sparkling river snaked past Westbury-on Severn on its way to Bristol.

'You sure about that? Red has to have been your wife's favourite colour?'

'You think this is easy for me?'

'How about this, then?' asked Jo and selected a matching, red-suede Dorothy Bag from the grey suitcase on the table. She opened its purse and inside were a lot of blue and pink one pound notes. She was already secretly angry. Either the widower was genuinely confused or there was something else he was not saying.

She really didn't like Bruno's attitude, at all.

He couldn't just tell them?

Really, this was not him helping.

Bella rolled her eyes, too. While it did not become a dog to brag, there were certain things that she could do far better than humans. She wasn't thinking of how she could jump higher, run faster and catch rats, she was thinking how superior was her sense of smell. Her nose twitched at an eau de toilette she recognized all too well. The top notes were crisp lemon and orange. At the other end of the scale her nostrils quivered at a trace of rose and geranium. Between the two extremes floated the distinct aroma of verbena. But Bruno ran his hand through his uncombed mop of reddish hair and remained thoroughly lost for words. His cheeks were all stubble and he had nicked his chin in two places with his blunt razor – no one could buy new razor blades in the shops for love or money these days. One set of shoelaces had come undone and he displayed the drawn look of a hunted man. That's to say, she also smelt fear on him.

'I should know, shouldn't I?' he said petulantly.

'Is that all you have to say?'

'What do you care, Mrs Wheeler?'

'We found this suitcase in the boot of Sarah's mangled car. The wreck is about to be cut up in a scrapyard a few miles from here, as we speak.'

'And I tell you Sarah didn't own a grey suitcase.'

'So what's it doing in her Austin Seven?'

'How many times must I say it, none of this stuff is hers.'

'So whose is it?'

Bella pawed Jo's leather motorcycle boot. Alas, a dog had no voice. Or, to put it another way, humans had no bark.

'How should I know?' said Bruno. 'Honestly, this whole business is insane.'

With no great hope Jo replaced the bottle of eau de toilette in the handbag. Then she shot John a hard look. He also pulled a face.

It couldn't be a coincidence.

Somebody else put that suitcase in Sarah's car, but who?

'Maybe, then, you can explain these photographs which we found with the clothes?'

Bruno went off to pour himself a glass of neat whisky. His third.

'What photos?'

'Take a close look, because they're all of your wife,' said John. 'They show Sarah with a friend called Susie Grossman. Here they are aboard Susie's canal boat. Another print shows the two of them laughing and smiling in a restaurant. Here they are again buying hats in Gloucester. Think about it. Did you take these photographs by any chance? Were you using them to frighten somebody? Did you stalk your own wife with her lover? You knew about their affair all along, didn't you?'

'Not in a hundred years.'

'That's not what I heard. Susie told us that you stopped Sarah going to a monthly book club with her because you suspected that they were more than devotees of literature. That's how patriarchal and jealous you really are. Or did you want your wife dead, Mr Smith, because I think maybe you did?'

'Okay, so I did know of their affair, but I didn't photograph them together. Not ever.'

'You do realise Sarah was never going to leave you, don't you? Or was she?'

Bruno shut his lips and swallowed hard. His face grew stonier. But no matter how obdurate his stance he could not deny his pounding heart.

'So what if I knew of Susie's existence? Sarah and I still loved each other. I was willing to do anything for her. She told me lots about her. I even suggested that Susie move in with us for a trial period. Whoever took those photos meant us *all* no good.'

Jo snapped shut the suitcase's catches. She didn't know what John had just done exactly, but it sounded bang out of order.

'So the presence of this luggage in Sarah's car on the night she died doesn't indicate she was leaving home? Well, all right then, but if these aren't her things, whose are they?'

'….'

'Damn it, Bruno, who else was Sarah seeing? It wasn't Susie – she told us they already broke up.'

'Really? I didn't know.'

Jo muscled in again.

'It seems there's a lot you don't know.'

Bella clawed Jo's foot.

'Stop it Bella, don't be a nuisance.'

Unable to confute the evidence, Bruno's confusion grew.

'I doubt it's connected to that boar's head that Sarah found on the bonnet of her car. You should be looking into that, not a few useless photographs.'

'Not to alarm you, but I think it might be.'

'But you don't know.'

'I know this,' said Jo. 'As I just said, we've found Sarah's car in a scrapyard in Cinderford. Well, we have reason to believe that the yard is owned by James Boreman.'

'So? That car has to be scrapped somewhere. It's an absolute write-off. Covered in blood…'

'But you and Boreman have a long history together, don't you? You were old school friends as well as business partners. That's how you knew where to go to get rid of the wrecked car in a hurry?'

'Everyone knows everyone in the Forest.'

'You were happy to work for him for years, but recently you and he fell out big-time, did you not?'

'Who's been talking behind my back?'

'Doesn't mean I'm wrong.'

Bruno clenched his fist to his mouth. Looked uncomfortable.

'James is absolutely ruthless. You have no idea. He'll sell his soul to the Devil to get what he wants. I couldn't stand idly by and watch his criminal wheeling and dealing on the black market any longer, I had to have it out with him, man to man, on account of his greed. After all, there's a war on.'

'You mean he refused to cut you in on the excessive profits to be made?' said Jo.

'I left while I still had the chance. That's a fact. Everything else is opinion.'

'You do bear him some sort of grudge, though?'

'It won't be me who ends up in the fourth circle of hell.'

John interrupted – he feared they were going up a blind alley again.

'Admit it Bruno. Is it not highly likely that Sarah was with someone on the night of the accident – someone who suffered only minor injuries and then walked away from the crash scene?'

'Please don't say that, it only confuses.'

'Suppose it doesn't? Sarah met up with Susie Grossman again a few weeks ago. Over coffee Sarah told her she was in serious trouble.'

'That would explain one thing. Did I not tell you, Mrs Wheeler, how my wife and I were walking through Gloucester one afternoon when she became quite panicky? She positively ran off into the cathedral to hide from somebody.'

'Yes, I remember. She acted as if she were being followed?'

'Susie offered to let Sarah lie low on her boat for a while,' added John, 'but Sarah said she was more concerned for *someone else's* safety than her own.'

'Yes,' added Jo, 'and I bet you *that very same person's* things are staring us in the face right now. These are her clothes.'

Bella pricked up her ears at everything she said, whereupon she displayed a rare show of solidarity – that is, she barked and wagged her tail.

*

'That could have gone better,' said John as he lowered himself into the Brough Superior's sidecar and sat Bella squarely on his lap. To say it was a tight squeeze was an understatement.

'You wait,' said Jo, wincing as she pulled on her cap and goggles. She'd forgotten her cut hand. 'Bruno will be on the blower to me again in a minute bending my ear about not performing bloody miracles. You heard him. He thinks I'm not doing nearly enough to find Sarah's alleged murderer, as if I should be his own private detective or something. It's all bullshit.'

'Yeah, he wants our help but won't come clean.'

'Not surprising since you were so nasty to him.'

'Is that what you think?'

'You as good as accused him of murdering his own wife, for Christ's sake.'

'Is that so bad?'

'….'

'Okay, so I went too far.'

'Susie was right about one thing, though.'

'She was?'

'Bruno was hoping for a threesome.'

'In his dreams.'

'He's not necessarily all wrong. Sarah's car could have been run off the road by a rival lover.'

'You keep changing your tune, don't you?'

Jo looked hurt.

'What? How do you mean?'

'It's not long ago you said her death was most likely an accident.'

'I did say that, didn't I.'

'Both theories can't be correct.'

'What if they can? What if she was in such a hurry to get away from someone that she misjudged the bend in the road and crashed? What if she and her passenger argued about something?'

John reached in desperation for a cigarette.

'Now you're really scaring me.'

'The car was new to her and she might not have been wholly familiar with its steering. Nor was she, according to Bruno, a fast driver. So why speed in the blackout with masked headlights? There are no street lights in the Forest, but there is constant military traffic taking American troops to and from camps and rifle ranges. Not to mention the bulldozers and timber lorries that are working all hours of day and night felling trees. It's a dangerous place for the best of drivers.'

'My point exactly. So what do we do now?'

'We go straight back to James Boreman's factory in Lydney.'

'I should say so. It's about time we gathered more damning evidence of the flagrant abuse of workers' rights?'

'No, I need to pick up the newly chromed badge off my motorcycle.'

THIRTY-SIX

The closer Jim Wilde went to the abandoned pithead, the more his legs turned to lead. The best years of his life had been spent here, earning a reasonable living, until the day it nearly killed him. Since then he had convinced himself that it was not safe to descend into the adit alone ever again. He'd walked away for Freya's sake twenty-six years ago, not long after she had entered this world. He was now seventy-two.

Raising his daughter single-handedly had not been easy – nobody much had wanted to employ someone who was half-blind. No matter that tunnellers like him had once been afforded the greatest honours by medieval kings. Had not Edward I confirmed that the 'customes and franchises' of the miners had existed since 'tyme out of mynde'? He'd given the Foresters special status to dig for minerals because their skills had enabled him to recapture Berwick-upon-Tweed in 1296 by undermining the city's walls.

His was quite a story. Most of the people he knew were employed in freemining, he reminded himself proudly as he picked his way over his pithead's grass-covered remnants. He peered into the winching house, no more than a tin shack, to see where cobwebs and birds' droppings coated its idle machinery. A cord strung on poles led to the coalface, somewhere out of sight down the slope behind him. The string worked a bell to control the movement of coal trucks in and out of the mine. One ring for STOP. Two for START. Three for ….

He gave an involuntary shudder. He'd once tugged on that string for dear life. Cable drums, hawsers, lever brake, rails and coal trucks were all just as he had left them when he lost his eye. Even the tipper and its extendable chute looked ready to discharge the next lot of coal into sacks in the yard. He wasn't bitter. His only regret was that he couldn't help power the steam engines needed to keep Britain moving at this critical time.

A rusty metal hawser stretched from roller to roller down the centre of the tramway he was treading. It had once hauled heavily loaded trucks from a hole in the hillside. Foxgloves grew here by the hundred in summer in a place largely invisible and secret. If you knew where to look you could find wild daffodils, too. Come winter, the flowers were long gone and even the grass and bracken were dying, which made it much easier to let the rotten wooden sleepers guide his feet through the dead weeds and leaves.

Next, he struggled to unlock the heavy padlock on a metal gate which guarded another way underground.

Was this honestly a good idea?

What if it turned out to be true? What if someone really was down here? What would he say to that?

But he had to do something.

Immediately an overwhelming sense of cold, dank blackness closed over him. Total blindness ruled for a moment. He was all set to turn up the dial on his helmet and switch on its reserve lamp when he felt a wind hit his face.

He knew that wind. The mine had been dug in a circle by Victorian workers to facilitate natural ventilation. Once upon a time a furnace had burned all day in the wall to draw fresh air through the labyrinthine workings; in very hot summers it had been a pleasant relief to feel the cool subterranean breeze on his cheeks this far from the sun.

Yet today he could not but help feel that the icy blast was somehow unnatural. Not only was it cooled by cold rock deep underground, but it blew with a force that could have been driven by something living. The very lungs of the Earth heaved at him. His sightless eye began to throb. His feet slipped and slithered. It was as if he had never been into this adit before in his life. He wondered how it could be so, or if he was about to revisit his own terror.

That unspoken reason for not returning.

'Is this what happens when you bury your greatest dread for years,' he wondered, 'only to have it claw its way back to the surface of your mind?'

Already the light at the mine's entrance had shrunk to a small glow far behind him. It was like looking the wrong way through a telescope. This was the oldest part of the workings, predating his own modest efforts to hack out coal and for some reason the roof sagged low at this point. He had struck his helmet more than once on the stone ceiling with a loud clang. This ancient way into the hill was a minor work of art, however. Each stone pressed snugly against the other without mortar or cement whose unseen counter pressures kept it together like a vast Roman mosaic. Like a catacomb.

With the continued rush of cold air came the gushing of water along the shallow channel beside his feet. He was treading the narrow ledge where pit ponies had once hauled coal, ready to load it into boats and barges at nearby Lydney Pill and Newnham. No animal would set off unless it was towing exactly the right number of wagons hooked together in the train behind it, so in tune were they with the demands of their daily toil. He'd nailed three rusty horseshoes, fished from the stream, to the tunnel wall as a reminder. He reckoned they had to be as old as 1840 or 1850.

What with the bubbling water and the whistle in the wind, it was hard to say what else he was hearing; his overwrought imagination almost led him to believe it could be human voices.

He couldn't allow that.

Every now and then his lamp lit up a bright, crimson rock face. That was because the Forest above him lay in a basin formed by carboniferous strata whose fields of black coal met red iron ore. But it was hard for a moment not to believe that these passageways were haemorrhaging real blood.

'Okay, that's enough crazy thoughts for now, Jim Wilde,' he said sternly and lit himself a candle.

He watched the wick's flickering flame illuminate green slime on corrugated iron sheets that lined walls round each corner, as he stood under the steel arches that kept up the roof. There was no 'Blue Boy', no methane, in this mine and so no risk of any explosion. Even after all these years the safety routine felt second nature to him.

If the candle failed to burn, then he was in big trouble.

He was testing for blackdamp.

Should he fail to get up again within a few minutes after a fall he would almost certainly die, since carbon dioxide was so much heavier than air.

But it was okay, the candle burned brightly in his hand – there was plenty of oxygen to breathe right now as he kept going forwards.

Water dripped and air moved, otherwise the beam from the light on his helmet penetrated a dark stillness quite unknown on the surface.

He frequently ducked this way and that as he put his ear to the passage ahead. The more pressing the absence of light, the greater the strangest of all possibilities – that he was not alone down here.

His thoughts raced.

His heart did the same.

A mine as old as this was a living, breathing thing. Timbers were keyed in a certain way to enable them to 'yield' slightly under pressure without pushing out the opposite wall. But the longer he stood at this fork in the tramway, the longer he sensed other just as subtle murmurs.

For it was also true to say that a mine like this had seen more than its fair share of the dead. He could run his fingers over rock once blown by black powder. But the only light available back then had been candles, not lamps. Sometimes a flame had sparked an explosion in miners' faces with terrible results. Did those eyeless and lipless ghosts wait for him now, in the depths below?

Was it they who silently screamed in this netherworld?

Their sweat filled his nostrils?

Their boots sounded in his ears as they shuffled towards him?

Soon he began to fancy that the drip, drip, drip that seeped from the sandstone was the blood of these mutilated men from a hundred years ago. He could still touch the gouges left by their hammers and chisels in the walls.

'It's been a while,' he thought nervously. 'How shall I put it? Am I afraid of my own ghost?'

In reality the adit was simply wetter and its drips noisier than he remembered, now that big mine towards Cinderford had finally closed. That was because a deep pit like that required so much pumping that it lowered the water level everywhere else quite drastically.

Which way should he go? One tunnel curved steeply to his left, the other carried straight on. He breathed a sigh of relief – here, at least, there was room to stand straight under the ceiling.

That's when he truly heard them.

Those awful whispers.

Not close at hand. In fact, they had to be beyond reach down the track that dipped to his right.

He immediately began to make his way past a stationary coal truck. More recollections flooded back. A fellow miner had once pushed a tub by its top instead of its coupling. He'd crushed his hands on the low ceiling. He'd had to let the truck run back to release his fingers. Lost his toes.

It was the same with your elbows. If you weren't careful you soon crushed them on the props that shored up the roof.

But this danger was something else. The hairs rose on the back of his neck as he prepared to round the next bend on his way to the place where he had last cut coal.

Someone or something hissed at him from the gloom.

In an instant he was on his back in the side of the tunnel, years ago; he was lying in an undercut in thirty inches of coal as he chipped black slabs from a seam with his pick. The tap, tap, tap of his axe drummed in his head when he heard the jagged roof crack and crash against his skull. He had only managed to crawl out at all because he had already dug himself an escape hole that looped back to the main bore. That was the trouble with slicing into an adit's side, all the pressures immediately wanted to seal the gap.

Such forces rose from below not from above; it was contrary to logic, given the weight of rock over his head, but it was so.

'I'll just go a bit further,' he told himself cautiously.

For coal mines were not the only tunnels down here, he remembered. Many centuries ago, men digging for iron ore had exhausted all deposits near the surface. Then subsequent miners had dug deeper still to gouge out huge caverns hundreds of feet below. Now one labyrinthine set of workings sat on top of the other and acted as a soundboard to whatever else it was he could hear right now.

The Earth itself could resorb its own sounds. Next minute whispers metamorphosed into snorts and growls. One snarl echoed another.

He lifted his head and peered steadfastly into the baleful darkness.

'Who's there?'

The snorts stopped, or rather they became by repetition and imitation the echo of his own fierce breathing.

'My name is Jim Wilde. This is my mine. Show yourself, at once!'

He squinted and peered past the light from his lamp when it lit eyes, nose, jaw…

'What the devil!'

Next minute he knocked his helmet askew as he tripped on something that lay on the rails. He should never have forgotten to duck his head to miss the post and sling in the roof. He was on the floor, confused. He gave a loud groan. Hard, cold tramway bent his back – he was too shaken to stand. That stupid stumble of his left him totally breathless; his chest tightened; he was badly winded.

Then, from out of the black, impenetrable night a pair of red-rimmed eyes gleamed at him with a certain malevolence. Their owner towered over him, curious and calm, commanding his undivided attention, only to lose momentum – the ghastly threat changed to caution. That said, he made out a large head, white bristly hair and a powerful back that was humped or hunched in the confines of the tunnel.

Whoever confronted him this far below the Forest jumped to his blindside. Not that he could stop him. Nor could he bend his left leg. A sharp pain hit his thigh, like the slash from a weapon. He cried out from the depths of his soul – he thought he might have snapped his hip in half when he fell.

An odd noise confounded him as he felt dizzy.

It had to be the grinding of teeth?

Possibly.

'Wait! Don't you see? It's me, Jim Wilde.'

The shadow did not answer him, only stepped back behind its veil of darkness.

But he felt stricken by his own predicament.

He lay there unable to move.

Damn it.

His unwelcome companion was abandoning him to his own devices? It was neither a good act nor a dire one. Rather, there hung in the air a strange mixture of cruelty and indifference in the midst of mutual astonishment.

Icy drops of water that dripped from the roof hit his face like the jabs of a knife. Each skin-bursting splash sent a shiver through his cramped body while, at the same time, he was breathing fast and already sweating. It was the pain. The awful pain.

He did his best to straighten the lamp on his brow, after which he braced one hand against a metal rail.

That blood-curdling scream was his own. He heard it carry for miles along the abandoned passageways to infinity, deep underground; he heard it die somewhere in the back of beyond. Like a pebble down a well. Cupped in his hand lay the head of a young woman. There was a gaping hole in her face where skin had peeled to reveal white skull beneath. Fingertips were absent from each hand as if they, too, had been devoured by sharp teeth.

Or someone had done their best to erase her identity?

Why?

To hide it from people like him.

Congealed flesh had the consistency of mud or clay. Then he realised. It was melted and burnt, but not by fire. That's when an almighty blow hit him full in the face.

After that, black nothing.

THIRTY-SEVEN

No one had better disturb him while he sketches like crazy, thought Sam – he sits cross-legged on the floor with his back pressed hard against the bedroom door so that no one can open it. His pencil hits paper and his pupils dilate, his breathing quickens and he feels butterflies in his stomach.

His compulsion to draw stems from some unlit place deep within himself; it's like trying to depict darkness itself.

Each stroke of black lead is an investigation by experiment.

He first traces snout and ears.

Next he adds the outline of a massive head. Every pattern is a projection of the thing in the Forest and the thing in his thoughts – every heartfelt squiggle corresponds with something that must be recorded before it disappears into a barely discernible fancy or feeling.

The instant he goes wrong he rips the page to pieces and begins again from the beginning. In no way must he neglect the beast's muscular shoulders and haunches. Also, the arched back has to rise into a hump to throw the whole weight and force of the body forward. The neck, he knows, is short and inflexible while the broad nostrils are strong enough to bulldoze grassy or frozen ground.

Well, that wasn't so difficult, was it – he soon traces the legs quite well? He gives each foot two main toes enclosed in layers of horn. A third, much smaller toe projects from each hoof – he knows this from having studied the tracks left behind in the woodland's muddy ground.

Except it's not that simple.

His drawing looks hopelessly rough and unfinished; it's at best a very crude portrayal of the Forest's most mysterious inhabitant.

In no way does the sketch capture its emotions.

He should show, not tell.

For what he wants is to summon forth a living creature from the grave.

But how to convey its acute sense of smell? Its poor eyesight? It's amazing hearing?

Those pricked, forward-pointing ears have to quiver.

The small, angry, reddish eyes must glow like deep, transparent garnets.

He has better luck with the teeth.

The lower canines make formidable weapons.

His fingers work in a frenzy to capture the froth that foams from the creature's jaws as it hones its bottom tusks against its upper ones to deadly points.

Slowly the beast begins to breathe.

It stamps its hooves.

Snorts and squeals.

This is a creature that can use its internal sense of direction to orient itself using the Earth's magnetic compass.

But how to make its white bristles shine in the dark? He has not yet mastered any of that because that is magic. But he's hopeful – he wants to conjure up from the surrounding trees his very own battle-swine.

Once he has his enchanted boar he'll do what the goddess Freya did and fly across the sky or swim the ocean. He'll use his magic mount to shine a light wherever he goes. He'll cling to its razorback mane and run at tremendous speed. He'll overtake his enemies, or he'll lure them forever deeper into the Forest and then round on them to take them by surprise.

He sits back and regards all versions of his creation that litter the floor so far. Seen together, the pages are quite something.

This is as much about his own feelings as the boar's.

He has to be that brutish and stubborn.

He must be furious but also courageous.

He must spit fire from his jaws.

The object of his ire is someone who has forfeited the right to call himself either a father or a husband. No excuses. No mitigating circumstances. Patriarchy means nothing. Filial loyalty must be overcome.

The longer he regards his artist's savage impression, the more he feels compelled to act to make it real.

It falls to the son to avenge the mother against the father.

He knows now what must be done.

Come boar, be me.

THIRTY-EIGHT

Freya peered harder through the kitchen window at the white wall of woodland that surrounded Beech Tree Grange. Was it only the morning mist among the ancient oaks and beeches playing tricks on her? The fact that she couldn't see over the foggy treetops, no matter how high she teetered on her toes, brought to the surface hitherto suppressed reservations. She and James had finally moved into their new home – hence the smell of fresh paint in her nostrils – but already the very air she breathed felt leaden and stuck in her throat.

The Forest's silence was an exact mirror of her own. Storms might break branches, rains might lash leaves, birds might scream, but the inscrutable trees stayed mute. A shiver licked her limbs. To stand here stock-still was to stand in almost total seclusion, not just physically but mentally. She wanted to curl like a foetus in this dark, cold, cheerless place. Yet she was intrigued by the uncanny suggestion of a constant presence. In the Forest's wilful taciturnity, in the fact of not mentioning a thing and non-betrayal of its own secrets, there lurked a mysterious invitation.

How could it possibly know so much about her, so soon? The gently swaying trees would have her ask herself previously unimaginable questions.

What do you most want from your life?

Time to myself.

Why is that?

Time equals freedom.

Freedom for what?

To do what I want.

Next minute James entered the kitchen directly behind her – she could tell at once that he was in the mood to make demands.

Always he had to psych himself up to get what he wanted. It was the same in bed. Everything had to be done his way. In brutal silence.

'I've decided that Sam should definitely undergo electroconvulsive therapy.'

Freya froze. She thought they'd already settled this once and for all.

'You talk as if he has some great affliction.'

'I'm only thinking of what's best for our son.'

'Or it's your way of avoiding responsibility for who he really is.'

James's face fell. Working late had left his eyelids redder than usual. He never liked it when she pushed back, not even slightly, but he was a reasonable man and he'd give her a second chance today.

'What exactly are you trying to say, Freya?'

'Just because Sam occasionally skips school to watch trains doesn't make him ill.'

'What else can it be?'

'Consider this then. I've met parents at his school who are almost glad that their child has been diagnosed as mildly autistic. They boast about it.'

'I'll never crow about my son's self-destructive, anti-social behaviour.'

'Don't you get it, James? Some mums and dads are happy to say that their children may be a bit on the odd side but are really quite brainy. They see some kudos in it.'

'I don't care what you say, Sam is going to America.'

'No, he isn't.'

'He's my son, I'll decide what's best for him.'

'You can't send him. It's too dangerous. German U-boats prowl the Atlantic. He could end up at the bottom of the ocean.'

James began to perspire. He stretched his fingers. Tapped his toe. His attention wandered as he found it hard to keep still.

Why couldn't she just accept what he said?

What had got into her?

Why did she have to disagree?

She knew he hated it when they argued.

'Isn't it obvious Sam needs help?' said James. 'It's very difficult to have a proper conversation with him. He simply goes off at a tangent. For instance, he talks endlessly about his own train set but won't play trains with any other children. At school he can't even follow simple instructions.'

'That's because he finds it hard to interact with the teachers.'

'So he falls behind with his work.'

'That doesn't make him stupid.'

'Only socially inept.'

'Teachers have to learn how to handle him, that's all.'

'Meanwhile he's a total loner. He shows absolutely no interest in games with his fellow pupils.'

'So what if he can't see the point, I never could either.'

There she went again, resisting him. On a scale of one to ten the danger level was fast approaching eight or nine. James stared out the window and the silent Forest stared straight back at him. He hunched his shoulders and scratched his bristly white hair.

'Here's what we'll do, Freya. We'll try one course of treatment and see if he benefits.'

'What do you mean by 'benefits'?'

'Electric shocks might make him more normal.'

'Normal? What's that?'

'Conforming to a standard. Regular. Usual.'

'Is that even a good thing?'

James rolled his great, square head at her.

'What else could it be?'

'No,' said Freya, 'I won't allow it.'

'*You* won't allow it?'

'How can we be sure that such a treatment is even suitable for children with very mild behavioural difficulties? Might they not be mistaken for something else?'

'Why do you say that?'

'I'm his mother.'

'Never mind that you're acting irrationally?'

'I'm trying to give Sam a say in his own life, that's all. I'm trying to be rational about it.'

'That's strange, because we both know that you haven't exactly been yourself lately, have you?'

'I don't know what you mean.'

'You tried to go behind my back. You believed a lot of lies from that so-called friend of yours. I warned you to stay clear of her, but no, you wouldn't listen. She's better off dead. Thank your lucky stars that you're not too.'

Freya stepped away from the window. He wouldn't take her seriously now because this was no longer about Sam but about her. That's what happened when he couldn't get his own way, he tried to discredit her. Question her sanity. Instinct kicked in and she shut down. She was that foetus again protected by tall trees. The only real safety lay in quiescence.

'If it wasn't for me you'd have gone totally off the rails,' said James, jabbing his finger in her face. 'You didn't think of Sam then, did you?'

That much was true. The world for a while had opened up. She had seen great possibilities. It was like finding a way clear through the Forest.

But that wasn't why James mentioned it. He said it to hurt her. Probe a festering wound.

Of pain and grief.

Of loss.

A few weeks ago she'd had a dear friend to help her, but not any more.

'Don't give me that sullen look,' cried James. 'Don't be so damned cold.'

Still Freya said nothing because she knew what was coming.

'Repeat after me,' yelled James, '*so cold.*'

Beyond the window that bothersome wall of hitherto mute oaks and beeches suddenly began to swish and sway more violently – grew agitated. She could only say that it was like a rip tide in an otherwise calm sea of bare branches.

'Thanks, but I'd rather make up my own mind about Sam.'

James sucked air through his teeth. This surge of fury that he felt not only buoyed his whole body, but impelled it forwards – drove it so hard that he did not look where he was going. Meanwhile Ruby leapt from her basket and began yapping at him very loudly. For a Chihuahua to take him on like that had to be either comical or suicidal. It had the odd effect of prolonging the moment. He seemed to fly through the air in slow motion. There was a mad spinning in his head. His chest felt ready to rupture. His heart pounded. He had to wonder if this was him or if he was in another place and time altogether.

His knuckles slammed into Freya with a sickening crump.

The thud hit home between breasts and pelvis.

She doubled up and clutched the windowsill before she went down.

A second blow caught her on the cheek.

It broke her hold and sent her flying.

'Stop coming between me and Sam,' James screamed in her face. All he could think about was how to vent his frustration and impatience via his rage. He had to burn it like fuel until it was expended. Still Ruby kept yapping at his ankles. His ears burst. His lungs could not breathe quickly enough. He was gasping. The blows were nothing to him, but he was exhausted. Drained. He stood over Freya and panted. What he most wanted in those first few seconds was for her to fight back so that he could finish her off, but it was a perilous moment when he might overstep the mark.

He had to pull back from the edge and withdraw his fists because she was too smart for him. She wouldn't give him the excuse he needed; she wouldn't provide him with a ghost of a reason to give in to his bad temper.

'Why do you do it?' cried James. 'Why do you deliberately provoke me so?'

'....'

'I just want to do what's best for our son,' he continued, his chest heaving.

Hitting someone was like running a marathon.

'Damn it, Freya, this isn't what I intended.'

'....'

Freya hugged herself to halve the pain. That gut-pummelling punch to the stomach made her want to vomit – that blow on the mouth saw her taste blood.

Meanwhile Ruby was still trying to come between man and woman. James landed her his best kick; he sent her rolling like a football into a corner where she lay very still.

Freya gave a scream.

'Not my dog!'

'You're fucking insane, you bitch. If it wasn't for me, you'd be dead on the street.'

So that's what he was referring to, thought Freya, crawling towards the limp Chihuahua. There had been a time when she had needed his help, just after she'd learnt that her brother had burned to death on that bus in Gloucester. But she wasn't clinically depressed now. It only suited him to discredit the past to own the future.

He came at her again with fists flailing, then stopped dead in his tracks. After all, she was down already. Instead he felt the wilful need to stand right over her. Intentionally, deliberately, he had to teach her a lesson due to her sheer perversity. He forgot about his own mad compulsion for which there could be no excuse. Next minute the muscles in his face grew slacker. That twisted, ugly look – that animality – resumed a guise more human.

Freya waited.

For the reaction.

Sure enough, James let his arms slump by his side, then squinted at her as if he were somehow ignorant of her 'accident'. It was his turn to be shocked, outraged and speechless; his face filled with horror; he despaired to see how hurt she was.

It was always the same. Already he had forgotten why he hit her. Had there ever been a reason?

'Oh Freya, what have you done?'

Flowers would surely arrive in the next few days. Perhaps new shoes, too. She already had a cupboard lined with the best Oxfords, pumps and sandals, most of which she rarely ever wore nowadays. She'd rather go barefoot than be seen in one of his 'presents'.

His fists were free, but the gifts weren't.

'Oh God, I'm so terribly sorry, Freya. I don't know how it happened.'

Yes, you do.

'Oh God, let me help you. You know how I hate to see you hurt.'

No you don't.

Her head still swam from that sideswipe to her solar plexus. But she didn't cry tears any more – they literally filled her eyes with pain, but she didn't consciously shed them. She would no longer give him that satisfaction. He was weaker than she was, which was why he had to resort to violence. She realised that now.

He paced to and fro as he tried to work out what best to do next, though she was not about to discuss it. Her steely reticence came to his rescue. To thwart him was forever to be his enemy. Instead she nursed Ruby back to life with numerous kisses.

It gave James his cue to make a hurried exit.

He'd make it up to her because today had only been a lapse on his part.

Like all the other times.

She would come round again soon enough, since she knew how much he loved her.

*

Sam slid down the oak tree from which he kept regular vigil in the garden. He tracked his father via the kitchen past the patio door and followed him to the edge of the terrace. If he had not heard much, then he had seen it all. On his way by the window he watched Freya stagger to the sink and reach for a glass of water.

Clearly she needed to drink something in a great hurry. James's apologies had not been as profuse as usual. Even his father could grow ashamed of his own excuses?

She raised the tumbler shakily to her blood-soaked lip, whereupon its contents clouded pink with her first sip.

Which was when she caught sight of him under the window.

She shook her head twice, quite violently.

Sam frowned.

Freya was turning her head from side to side, there could be no doubt about it.

She'd seen the hatchet clenched in his fist.

Which was when his eyes narrowed.

He snorted.

He stamped his feet.

He ground his teeth up and down.

His mouth frothed a few white bubbles and scum.

But it was no use.

She was telling him very firmly that now was not the right time.

THIRTY-NINE

Just to look at so much whiteness was totally exhausting. His eyeballs ached. He felt sick. Thibaut literally thought he might go blind any minute. Each step across the snowy Forest floor almost failed him as he dared to walk on the crusty, milky-coloured tundra. His worn out army boots cracked the icy carpet underfoot like glass.

It was not as if heavy snow did not fall where he came from in France, but he had never before been so lost in it. His lungs felt on fire. The very air he breathed filled with needle-like crystals.

Nora picked up the pace. To her, this bewildering wilderness seemed less of a hindrance?

'There's not a minute to lose.'

'Where are we going, exactly?'

'Can't answer that right now.'

'What if someone saw us leave the caravan site?'

'We didn't have a choice.'

'You're the one who said we need a plan.'

'Keep your voice down, will you? Sound travels a long way in these woods.'

Thibaut stopped short suddenly and listened to the night. They should never have left Raoul behind and he was feeling guilty.

'What's that?'

'The hell if I know.'

'I thought I heard a vehicle or something.'

'Might be nothing.'

Didn't he realise they could both freeze to death out here, thought Nora, hurrying on. The raw air deadened her face and fingers while her shoes no longer even pretended to protect her wet toes. Suddenly the trees trembled.

Something stirred. Icicles rained down from snow-laden boughs. The whole Forest had just whispered to them.

Thibaut shuddered. Someone was coming after them, all right. The White Lady, supernatural guardian of the trees, was breathing her frost-wind? They would have to dance with her and do her bidding in order to pass.

Or she had sent her hobgoblin in the guise of a spotted pig, to torment them for thinking only of themselves?

But it was one owl greeting another high in the branches.

'You all right?' asked Nora, laughing.

'This moon is bad news.'

'At least we're able to see where we're going.'

'If we can see, so can others. They'll follow our tracks in the snow for sure.'

'Whatever happens I'm with you, Thibaut.'

'Better keep moving, as you say.'

On they went over the glade's silvery surface; the Forest floor was littered with treasure for them to tread. Each sparkling jewel promised objects of great beauty and worth. They scooped up handfuls of precious stones as they passed; they saw them dance and dim at their toes, even if it was only hoar frost.

The confusion of rimy trunks did more than mislead them, it mixed things up in their minds. Shadows assumed the shapes of assassins and goggled at them like ghouls. Thibaut was deeply afraid of this primeval place where the worst of men's instincts could be given free rein. If the cold didn't kill them tonight, their pursuers would.

'Look,' said Nora excitedly. 'Is that a path over there, or what?'

Sure enough, a broad band of untrammelled snow cut through the Forest.

'More like a railway line,' said Thibaut. 'Perhaps now we can make proper progress on the level.'

'No more walking in circles. This track must lead somewhere.'

'Wait.'

'What is it?'

'You hear that?'

The rumble of an approaching vehicle filled their ears. A headlamp dazzled. It was heading straight for them.

That was no train.

'Duck!' cried Nora, diving back into the bushes.

The roar of an engine burst upon them. Its noise broke the vast cave of silence that had until now been strangely protective.

Thibaut crouched lower among dead bracken.

'We should run.'

'Too late.'

Next moment two men slowed to a crawl on their Norton motorcycle. While the noise of the 490cc side valve engine faded, crunching tyres filled the night as they freewheeled over snow.

The driver stopped, planted both feet firmly on the ground and let his machine tick over for a moment. While he directed a powerful flashlight into the oaks and larches, his pillion rider scanned the woods through the scope on his hunting rifle.

Those were neither US soldiers nor a local Timber Supply Department patrol.

'See anything, Phil?'

'The hell if I know.'

'Keep working at it.'

'Might have been a deer.'

A beam of light scythed the undergrowth just above Thibaut's head as he recognised the voices of Kevin Devaney and the moustached Phil Cotter – they'd left the trees and used the narrow footpath beside the railway track to get along faster, gain the advantage.

Devaney pulled out the aerial on his two-way walkie-talkie and put it to his ear.

'No, nothing yet, boss, but they can't have gone far… Yeah, I get your drift. Do what we have to? You betcha.'

Next minute he revved the Norton again. As if on cue, Phil sat back down in his seat and slung his gun back over his shoulder.

'What happens when we don't find them?'

'You heard the boss. That's not an option.'

Devaney pulled his cap lower down his eyes. What he really wanted right now was a nice warm puff on his pipe. Hungry for revenge, blinded by rage, the hunters moved on to another part of the Forest.

Snow slid down Thibaut's neck. He couldn't feel his bloodless fingers where he had lain face down on the ground and hugged its ice like a wild animal.

But Nora was quick, almost reckless. She trod tyre marks left by their pursuers. The idea was to fool the enemy by retracing the way they'd just come.

Soon they broke into a run.

They ran for their lives.

FORTY

This ghastly pong of other people's cigarettes and damp woollen clothes wasn't helping, as Jo took another sip of Guinness under the medieval arches of THE MONKS' RETREAT bar. Her hammering heart would jump right out of her chest. Her cheeks felt unbelievably hot and her hair was plastered to her scalp. Her head hurt. Her feet ached, but she liked to think that her compulsion to drink was not out of proportion to the guilt she felt.

It took the black patent malt to settle her morning sickness.

However, she would be lying to herself if she didn't admit that her interest in Sarah Smith's death was preoccupying her to an alarming and chilling extent – no matter how much she imbibed, she couldn't forget.

So what was she missing?

What connection, exactly?

Could Sarah's bloody decapitation not simply be a massive distraction from something else equally serious?

Sadly no.

Not that she wanted to go out of her way to establish anything was murder, as such, she didn't want it to be that gruesome.

You bet.

Why else did she and Bella squeeze into this corner with three empty stout bottles already secreted at her feet? The harder she concentrated, the thirstier she felt. Give her a few more minutes to down all she could and she was bound to come up with a theory. She uttered a loud belch. At times like this pride could be overrated.

As could pregnancy.

She threw Bella a Jaffa Cake. It was either that or suffer her look of insufferable indignation.

Boldly, almost defiantly, she stood up to go to the bar. In actual fact she should be sending a telegram to her mother to tell her to go to hell or otherwise not trouble her again. That was her best option. Something like that.

'If you have anything to say, now's the time.'

Jo blinked her blurry eyes and sat straight back down again. John Curtis was scrutinising the line of empties on the floor, to her shame.

'What?'

'Ready to buy another round, are we?'

'Pregnant women are advised to drink Guinness. It's very healthy. That's official. Doctors tell the same thing to post-operative patients, blood donors and nursing mothers, so there.'

'No regrets then.'

'I'll get drunk tonight if it kills me.'

'How is this any different?'

'I thought you said you were going to the gym?'

'That's it,' said John, 'rub it in.'

'What's up? Getting fit too good for you now?'

'It turns out I'm a 'non-responder'.'

'And that's because?'

'No, really, one day it will be a scientifically proven fact that some people do not respond well to all physical exercises. For instance, no matter how much weight-lifting I do, I don't get any slimmer or fitter...'

'No body beautiful for you, then.'

'It's more a case of finding the right workout just for me.'

'I think we've been over this ground already.'

'I've ruled out squat jumps, sit-ups, pull-ups and 300 yard runs.'

'Again, *because*?'

'All those short, sharp workouts only do more harm than good.'

'You, in your opinion.'

'So what are you doing here, Mrs Wheeler, all alone?'

'I just told you. I'm imbibing.'

'I'll overlook your intemperance if you'll let me take you to the flicks.'

'Lose five stone and I might let you.'

'That's not fair, that's blackmail.'

'Let's face it, we're both basket cases.'

'Nonsense.'

'So prove me wrong.'

'You'll see. In six months' time I'll be a new person.'

'Maybe not even then.'

John admitted defeat, visited the bar and returned with two beers.

Suddenly he pulled a note from his pocket.

'I have something to show you.'

'What is it?'

'It's from Susie Grossman. I thought she and I were done. Now she wants to meet me again on that awful canal boat of hers.'

'When?'

'As soon as possible. Says it's urgent.'

'Does she say why?'

'No idea.'

'Drink up. We'll go together.'

'Now? In the blackout?'

'Why not?'

'Fine, but I'll do most of the talking. Knowing you, you'll scare her off with that sozzled, bear-like growl of yours.'

'I appreciate that.'

Jo downed her Guinness and her favourite drinking den's lopsided, stone arches seriously wobbled. She didn't indicate what else was troubling her, except to say that drowning her sorrows had to be of small comfort.

FORTY-ONE

'What did I tell you?' said James, shining his torch on flattened fencing that littered the snowy garden. 'This is where it broke in, all right.'

Sam trod ground that still seemed to shake beneath him. He surprised himself – the sheer brute force that had gone into breaching Beech Tree Grange's newly created outer defences demonstrated strength beyond his wildest imagination. At his feet lay splintered pales.

Someone with an axe couldn't have done a better job, he thought proudly.

'Wow, it must be big.'

'About twenty stone, I reckon.'

'That is big.'

'Bigger the better.'

'What are we going to do, dad?'

'We're going to set a trap.'

'Are we going to kill it?'

'You got a problem with that?'

Sam sucked his lip and said nothing. Instead he hummed like a bee. James walked on ahead of him with alarming rapidity. He followed in his father's footsteps, his feet wading bracken. One. Two. Three... They were soon some distance from their brash new house and its smoky chimneys. He made a mental note of the number of paces. Creaking trees ousted every other noise with the swish of a bough or a shower of dead leaves in their ears. Every twig began to swirl, groan or sing at their approach in the gathering darkness. The more the Forest protested, the more he felt himself carried along by the vast, eddying motion of their branches.

James hardly stopped to study the ground.

'How far now?' asked Sam.

'To wherever we can.'

'To wherever we can.'

'Must you repeat everything I say?'

'Must I?'

'Don't try to be clever. Don't make me regret this.'

Never had Sam trodden such deep snow. Starry flakes stuck to his face like icy moths, while his knees sank out of sight in a mass of white crystals.

'We're going to find its den, are we?'

'You think?' said James, shouldering a hammer and wood saw in his bag. 'Whatever attacked us might not have a permanent dwelling place at all, it might wander for miles in the Forest every night. That said, it might yet circle back to where it began, if we're lucky.'

Sam smiled sweetly, even if he was quite sure that his father did not really believe what he said, since no wild boar had roamed the Forest for hundreds of years. Yet there was a glint in James's eye that said he was genuinely intrigued, that he did want to capture whatever it was that had invaded his property. He, too, had not totally dismissed the notion of some local farmer's domestic boar gone rogue. When pigs were turned loose in the Forest, it was not unknown for one or two to 'disappear'. All the more reason to go with the plan. The roll of thin galvanized wire was beginning to drag on his arm, though. He could feel it biting through his tweed shooting jacket, but he said nothing. He did not want to be seen to let his dad down.

Flashes of red, setting sun winked at them like gunfire through gaps in the trees. The bright eyes of light gleamed and glowed at their feet like stepping stones. They could have been treading on shafts of sky.

'Well, I'll be damned,' said James.

Sam paused, glad to unload his metal burden.

'Are we on its trail yet?'

'Yes, practically.'

'I don't see how.'

'I suggest you look here.'

To be included in such a mission was a real piece of luck, thought Sam. His father's bloodlust was contagious. He was beginning to feel as if they were in the presence of some invisible power – he was so sure that something would steal up on them at any moment, from which direction he could only guess, only fear.

James pointed excitedly at the non-descript, dish-shaped circle at their feet.

'This is where a very large animal has built a lying-up place in dry grass. No doubt about it. See how it has scraped away the snow.'

'What now?' asked Sam slyly.

'Better keep going. We need to see where these prints lead us.'

He was not wrong. The search for more tracks in this awe-inspiring place suggested something both mysterious and mystic in the polar cold. It was like living one of those scary fairy tales that his grandfather had told him in Tunnel Cottage.

'Here,' he cried in a stage whisper and halted before a muddy puddle. 'That's a boar's print?'

'No, actually it isn't,' said James, 'that's a deer. The two cleaves look the same, but the dew claws at the back of a boar's hoof are set lower and further to each side of the foot. They stick out at quite an angle.'

Quite so, thought Sam to himself. Naturally he feigned disappointment but not surprise. Why should a beast as magical as the white boar leave tracks at all? Surely it moved about by illusion. Of this conviction, however, he spoke not at all but trudged obediently along.

Tiredness soon set in. It was all right for his father, he could take longer strides. 1005, 1006, 1007.... Also the soft layers of soggy leaves sucked at his heels beneath the snow – he felt them try to pull him down to caves deep below; he expected, very soon, to be devoured by the displeased Forest.

Nor did James wait long for him to catch up.

At least his father had thought to bring his .303 B.S.A. sporting rifle.

'Go easy, Sam. You might want to see this.'

James crouched on a patch of snow beside a pond.

'Is it another print?'

'I guess so.'

'Are those the dew claws you mentioned?'

'Never seen a print so big. Look here, son. See how rounded the cleaves are. Note the length of its stride.'

'Is that good?'

'In younger pigs the cleaves are more pointed. If I didn't know better, I'd say this is a very large, very old hog of some kind.'

'A champion.'

'We don't know that.'

But Sam did. He already had in mind something or someone who fought for a cause. An athlete. A hero. A warrior.

'Remind me what to do again, dad.'

'Here might be the best place.'

'How can you tell?'

'I think we'll soon know.'

'Know what?'

'That our enemy is still in the area planning his next attack.'

'What kind of attack?'

'To drive us out of the Forest.'

'You can't be serious.'

'Who knows what it wants?' They had somehow circled back to the breach in their homestead's defences. 'This is where we'll place the trap, Sam. Still want to help?'

'Yes, please.'

So saying, they set about sawing down and trimming twigs off a sapling.

'How will we kill it?' asked Sam.

'Been through this.'

'I remember now. We bayonet it to death.'

'That's all there is to it.'

James cut and sharpened a short wooden spear that he tied at right angles to the sapling's thinner, more flexible end – the other, thicker end he anchored to three spikes that he hammered into the Forest floor.

'But dad, why don't we wait for the boar and then shoot it?'

'You can't shoot at night.'

'Why not?' said Sam, watching James bend the branch to test its springiness at groin height above the ground.

'We might shoot each other.'

James ran a wire to the bait. Once tripped, it released a peg which freed the branch under formidable tension – the spear sped straight at the breach in the fence in a successful rehearsal.

'Any wild animal is bound to be very wily. It'll smell us a mile off. Chances are, though, it will try to pass through this gap to dig up our grass again. With a cunning adversary you have to think both tactically and strategically. This spear will hit him right between the eyes.'

Sam could not follow everything his father did, but he was bolstered by one thought especially. James did not hear the innumerable sounds of the wooded dean, so intent was he on pursuing things of his own making. As always. The source of the noises was no more than a brief gleam of light here or a slight lifting of leaves there. Something passed close by as if to show him its presence.

Show him how?

Could he see anything?

The answer was no.

Whatever it was, it ran grunting and slobbering to the remotest, least accessible place where it lay down unseen on the Forest floor.

There it fed on bones.

FORTY-TWO

'Dislike dogs, do we?' said John and doffed his Homburg, politely.

Susie Grossman was all bluster and fluster. She stood holding an oil lamp astride the narrowboat's counter and blocked the way past the cabin doors' crudely painted castles and roses. She gazed narrow-eyed at her callers as if they were the enemy.

Bella was all frown, too. She let her tongue hang out and worked her tail very hard. Any feelings of dislike were definitely mutual. She didn't much care for this boatie in her late twenties wearing a baggy blue boiler suit – she had her hair tied up in a blush-coloured Jacqmar scarf and had coal dust on her cheeks and hands. Noting everything about the boat owner's tense little features and awkward posture, she responded the same way any good, canine sleuth would – that's to say, she sniffed animal phobia.

But no one could like a dog that was all ferocity and no fun. Consequently, she adopted the vain, empty-headed gaze of a six-week-old puppy.

Had there been room on deck she might have rolled.

'Bella can stay on the quayside,' added John hurriedly. Clearly he should have told Susie to expect someone else. Perhaps they should have come bearing gifts or something. That really didn't matter now.

Susie's hazel eyes still offered unhappy and pointed resistance.

'Who's your friend?'

'Meet Fire Guard Jo Wheeler.'

'I've heard of you. You fixed the carburettor on Sarah's Austin Seven for her?'

'Cars can be as much trouble as motorcycles, what with petrol the way it is these days.'

'Sarah liked you a lot.'

'It was so sad losing her like that.'

Susie nodded.

'You'd better come aboard, then.'

'About what happened to Sarah in the Forest…'

Jo saw John stop her with a pout. Susie had to trust them both or their task was hopeless. *So don't rush her.* They'd already got off to bad start. The narrowboat's low roof left very little room to duck and squirm. For someone as tall as she was, it was a tight squeeze as she tried not to knock anything off the shelves with the padded shoulders of her bolero jacket. She had to let him ask the questions as he looked round for somewhere wide enough to sit down.

'You okay, Jo?'

'It's so hot in here.'

'Maybe it's your condition.'

'I'm expecting a baby, not a seizure.'

'It is a bit confined, you have to admit.'

'Or you're taking up too much bloody room.'

'So what's all this about, Susie?' John piped up. 'I thought you'd done talking to me?'

It was Jo's turn to make a rude face.

This was him treading carefully?

She pursed her lips in her own pucker of protest.

John mimed back, fanning himself rapidly with a napkin. He was all for sparing Susie's feelings. Like hell he was.

That scowl on her face screwed up her freckles again as she hung up her lamp and moved to the stove. Her breathing quickened. A defiant toss of her head saw a loop of ash-blonde hair fall from her scarf and curl on her cheek.

'I lied to you about Sarah.'

John promptly hit his head on a shelf draped with lacy doilies.

'Why would you do that?'

'Because I didn't think it was any of your damned business.'

'So what changed?' asked Jo, moving to a dog box bench and bolster.

'I guess I got scared.'

'We're listening.'

Susie banged a kettle about on the hot plate.

'I told you that I bumped into Sarah in a café shortly before she died.'

'A chance encounter, you said, shortly after you two broke up.'

'That's not how it was at all.'

'You arranged to meet?'

'More than that. We were going to get back together.'

John and Jo traded glances. They were definitely not leaving now. Sorry, but nothing was making sense any more.

'Good to know,' said John, 'but how does this have anything to do with Sarah's death?'

Susie busied herself pouring tea into cups with her coal-blackened fingers.

'Because she said she was terrified, that's why. She realised that the person she'd left me for was not the loving woman she expected.'

'She?'

'Freya Boreman.'

John stopped fanning himself immediately.

'Freya Boreman? We sort of assumed that Sarah left you for...'

'Well, you assumed wrong.'

'Say what you have to, we're listening.'

Susie sat on a stool of her own and passed the sugar.

That didn't prevent Jo finding the tea absolutely revolting.

'Yeah, perhaps it's best if you tell us everything you can.'

'Sarah didn't realise it at first, but then she saw the pictures.'

'Pictures? What pictures?'

'For instance, they were photos of us when we were shopping in Gloucester.'

'Are these what you're talking about, by any chance?' said Jo, pulling prints from her jacket pocket.

Susie paled. She began to fiddle with a big silver hoop in one ear; she knocked her knees together.

'There must be some mistake. Where did you get these?'

'You're not going to believe it.'

'These are the snaps that Freya took of me and Sarah before we broke up, all right. She said she'd show them to all and sundry if I didn't back off. She'd create a real scandal.'

'Back off?'

'That bitch was always stalking us. She followed us everywhere, for Christ's sake.'

'Just like that?'

'Freya was madly jealous of me, or she wanted to weigh up the opposition.'

Jo set down her cup before she dropped it.

Some things you never saw coming.

Everyone knew that.

Except her, apparently.

'That can't be right. Are you saying that Freya took a shine to Sarah?'

'Sarah worked for a while for Freya's hubby James, as did her own husband, Bruno.'

'That much we know already.'

'Bruno was sacked from his job by James and his sister Tia who own everything. Suddenly Sarah couldn't stand the sight of James any more.'

'And?'

John shot Jo a warning look. Had they not just agreed to leave the questioning to him? Now here she was again, rolling her eyes and pressing too hard with her husky tones in her best grizzly bear fashion.

'At first Sarah was totally bowled over. She was so excited. I could see it in her eyes, whereas when she was with me she suddenly became restless and bored. It was going to be a grand passion for her as well as Freya if things worked out well.'

'You think James and Bruno quarrelled over Freya's infatuation with Sarah? You think that's the real reason why he lost his job? And Sarah couldn't forgive them?'

Susie's mouth set hard for a moment.

'Bruno blamed James for not keeping Freya 'under control'. James blamed Bruno for the same thing, but with Sarah.'

'As if it was any of their business?'

'Sarah was never the most decisive of people. She was afraid of how Freya would react when she told her she wanted to dump her and come back to me.'

'What do you mean?' asked John. 'React how?'

'How do you think? I don't doubt Freya's love for Sarah, but she has a wild shadow side. She will take what she desires. Her passion shows no reserve. It's obsessive. Sarah had little choice because Freya wouldn't take no for an answer. But Sarah didn't want to run off with her – not in that sense. She might have cared deeply for Freya, or me for that matter, but she loved her husband, too. Her home overlooks the river in Westbury-on-Severn where she was born. Her friends are there. She attended the local church. She simply didn't want to disappear to the equivalent of some desert island, or wherever. But Freya had it all worked out. She and Sarah were going to fly away like a couple of lovebirds in that silly little car of hers, only it all turned sour, *that* I do know.'

'What about Freya's son, Sam? Was he going, too?'

'Who can tell? She probably couldn't give a damn about him.'

'Oh, really?'

'In case you don't know, Freya only wants people all to herself. When Sarah said she was coming back to me, Freya was absolutely furious. She put her through hell. I tell you that bitch killed her. She ran her off the road, because if she couldn't have her then neither could anyone else.'

'*That's* what you wanted to tell us? You literally think Freya killed Sarah?'

'I don't know what to believe any more.'

*

'It doesn't look good,' said John and stepped ashore in Gloucester Docks.

Jo inhaled deeply and gave Bella a pat. Her ears stopped popping; her lungs ceased to heave – she was back on dry land at last.

'Should we even trust a word Susie says?'

'I suggest we take her seriously.'

'Then you ought to know better.'

'Since when?'

'Jealous women lie through their teeth just as well as jealous men, John.'

'We have the suitcase from Sarah's wrecked car. Now we know those photos we took from it belong to Freya, what's the betting the clothes do, too?'

'According to Susie, any feelings Sarah had for James Boreman turned to hate after he axed her husband from the business.'

'I don't doubt it.'

'But is that reason enough for her to try to bring him down? Whoever placed that boar's head on the bonnet of her car and wrote *Say Nothing* in pig's blood on its windscreen was clearly scared of her.'

'Or furious.'

'It has to be something big.'

'Like marital betrayal?'

'Bigger.'

'How much bigger?'

'Like murder.'

'You said that once already.'

'Now I'm almost certain.'

'Hey, slow down.'

'I'm better since I got off that bloody ship.'

'It's not a ship, it's a boat.'

'So let's go back to my place and grab ourselves a bite to eat. How do lemon curd sandwiches sound?'

'Are you kidding?'

'It's my latest craving.'

'And I thought you were my friend.'

FORTY-THREE

'Well, what do you reckon?' asked Thibaut, sliding one hand along the portal's slimy bricks. 'Do we lie low here for the night, or what? Boreman's men might never find us.'

Nora stepped into the tunnel and its sickly, sooty air stuck in her throat.

'Don't take them for complete fools.'

The darkness before them differed from the darkness behind. Grey smoke lingered within the enfolding walls which was acrid, bitter, gritty. They found the bare stones of the railway ballast beneath their feet quite a shock after the Forest snow.

'Where does this even go?' said Thibaut.

Nora smiled.

'I know what you're thinking.'

'What?'

'You're about to say that you're sorry you got me into this.'

'I should have known I'd get us lost.'

'No need to apologise.'

'Did I say that Devaney is bound to beat the shit out of us if he catches us?'

'You did. Several times.'

'Yet here you are.'

Nora laughed and disembodied echoes returned from the void.

'So what's stopping you? Let's go.'

She knew this fear. It was like escaping Mother Odile and Mother Martha, strictest of all Catholic nuns. Yet here she was, free and far from Ireland. That's what happened when someone failed to relock the gate after the delivery man offloaded the weekly groceries at "St Mary's Mother and Baby

Home", one rainy Wednesday afternoon.

Soon she was aware of very little beyond the sounds they made by walking, calling, breathing. Every now and then, icy droplets from the tunnel's roof hit their heads and they uttered childish squeals. She was encased in this subterranean chamber of stone and darkness in which she 'swam' at a snail's pace – she swung each arm in front of her with careful but invisible strokes of doubt and terror. She could have been drunk. Or floating. That ground beneath her had to be a guess. The wall she touched described a slight bend to the right which cut off any hope of seeing to its end.

Strange how like a game all this felt.

To live by one's wits alone.

'Is this really our best chance?' said Thibaut.

'It's too late now.'

'Hope a train doesn't come.'

At least the railway would put them on the other side of the hill in their deadly contest of hide and seek with Kevin Devaney and Phil Cotter, who had so far failed to find them.

More than once, actually.

Now the gunmen had gone haring off in the other direction.

Luckily.

But they might not be done with them yet.

Still there came that awful scrabbling sound in their ears. It was their own footsteps. Eyes wanted to pop. They breathed chilly echoes. A perpetual sense of disorientation added to the idea that they might never escape the bowels of the Earth again.

'What was that?'

Her whisper was taken up by the tunnel, magnified and then reproduced countless times through the hill.

Thibaut shivered.

'I heard it, too.'

'I bet it was a bat.'

'Oh shit.'

'Sorry, I shouldn't have said.'

Suddenly a slit of night sky opened up some way in front of them. Like a gleam. Like an eye. Observing.

Nora stopped, recovered her sense of direction and started marching.

Thibaut did the same. Rather than slide his hand all the way along the tunnel wall, he followed recklessly in his fellow escapee's quickening steps. He simply didn't want her to realise that he was afraid of dark places.

Did she know?

Of course she did.

Did she care?

He couldn't tell.

Then he, too, saw where the railway bore burned bright moon ahead.

'Now what?' said Thibaut. 'Where do we go from here?'

No sooner had he spoken than the tunnel behind them flooded with noise. A deafening, mechanical beat of a 490cc engine sounded like thunder – a cacophony of concordant pistons and side valves tore at the cochleae in their ears. The searching white glow of the motorcycle's headlamp lit the walls as it entered the bore. Clearly, its riders were making bone-breaking but steady progress right down the middle of the permanent way, this time.

'With me,' said Nora and ran along a shiny silver rail like a tightrope walker to minimise any footprints she might leave behind.

Thibaut hurried after her – she was heading for a nearby platelayers' hut constructed from old railway sleepers that stood just beyond the tunnel's exit.

'Are you serious? Don't tell me you think you can outfox them?'

'Be quiet and give me a leg up.'

He took hold of her waist even as she gripped a drainpipe at the back of the shack. She felt so slim, supple and graceful. Like a gazelle. The second Nora had climbed up onto the sloping roof, she lay down and lowered her hand his way – she practically pulled him straight after her.

She didn't mean either of them to get caught tonight.

Need she say more?

Together they lay prone on the flat roof's dirty black felt that smelt of tar, even as the piercing cold air left them panting.

'We should have kept going,' said Thibaut, his voice full of panic.

Nora stayed his arm.

'Go now and we'll leave a trail in the snow.'

That mechanical maelstrom inside the tunnel mouth became a deafening din – a cyclopean spotlight swept the portal's meeting of night and netherworld. The driver of the Norton was revving its throttle as he and his passenger rode roughshod over ballast and sleepers between more rails.

They could have come from hell.

Thibaut held Nora tight to his side. They had to keep their heads down or else they were definitely done for, should their hot breaths give them away in the freezing air.

The bounty hunters let the motorcycle tick over in the mouth of the tunnel.

'Tell me what you can see, Phil?'

'Sweet fuck all.'

'Shine the torch over here, for Christ's sake.'

'What do you think I'm doing?'

'Give me a hand to get this shed door open.'

'Try looking in the window.'

There followed much manoeuvring of the Norton to the base of the wall.

'They can't have gone far.'

'That's what you said last time.'

'Last time we didn't have any footprints to follow.'

'We don't now.'

Thibaut pulled Nora closer and her cheek warmed his. The strong smell of her raven hair filled his nostrils. Her chest heaved silently against his. Next minute a beam of torchlight scythed the edge of the shack's roof only inches from their noses. He wriggled right down and made herself smaller in her arms. He was aware how tightly she hugged him. He did the same. Arm in arm they waited.

They didn't have the slightest hope.

They couldn't make the simplest move.

Cheek to cheek they held their breaths for what seemed an eternity.

Suddenly more talking broke the shadows' stillness.

'See anything?' said Devaney, breaking out his pipe.

'Not a bloody thing.'

'No tracks?'

'How can this happen?'

'Judging by the smoke in the tunnel, a train steamed through here very recently –there's hardly any snow on the tracks to show how far they went. They must have run along the rails, then dived into the Forest. But where?'

'Mr Boreman will go ape when we tell him.'

'Look in the shed again.'

'That's what I'm doing.'

'No, you're not, you're having a fag.'

'You're the one to talk.'

'Unbelievable.'

'Get back on the bike. There's a level crossing up ahead. I bet you they made a run for it down the road.'

Nora put her finger to Thibaut's lips. They had yet to look out for a proper place to hide.

All right, where? Or they could lie low here for a while.

Until the coast was clear?

Before they could decide, the moon disappeared and bathed them both in darkness.

FORTY-FOUR

'Damn it, Jim Wilde, it's high time you got yourself out of here.'

How are you going to do that?

The teasing, taunting question floats back to him from the coal mine's deepest workings. It is the scornful echo of his own lament, which offers him no more comfort than if he were already dead in these maze-like tunnels.

The best he can do is reply out loud.

'I'll crawl.'

How can you be so sure?

'Because I nearly died in this adit once before and I'll not do it again.'

Nobody saw a thing. You could be down here until doomsday.

'Someone has to tell the police there's a dead body.'

Who cares about her?

'Check this out. She smells of overripe fruit.'

So what?

'It could be cyanide poisoning. I know about such things because I'm a miner.'

Anything else?

'She may look unidentifiable, but a small tattoo on her ankle says Angela.'

Forget her. Think about your leg. How are you going to drag yourself back to the surface?

'The pain, I have to admit, is bloody awful.'

Then stay where you are. Soon your lamp will fail anyway. Then you can sleep the sleep of the dead – abide with us all.

'All?'

Come Jim, give it a go. You'll feel so much better if you get some shut-eye first.

Those siren sneers are only part of the problem. To his horror the corpse beside him looks reasonably fresh. Whoever or whatever has gnawed eyes, lips and nose from her face might soon return.

Then he'll be helpless.

He'll be eaten, too.

In its den.

Except Angela hasn't been devoured by dogs, rats or foxes, she's been dissolved with acid.

FORTY-FIVE

She knew how it must look. Call her old-fashioned, but she had a bad feeling about this meeting – a foreboding Jo did not hesitate to call shameful. She stood in the cathedral doorway in the presence of its sombre stone statues. She had lured Freya here on false pretences, to be sure, in the presence of St Peter and St Paul and the four evangelists, but what good would it do if she still didn't trust her? She guessed it was up to her. She had frightened her off once before by being too direct and she mustn't make the same mistake now.

Freya wore her black, red-lined reefer coat wide open as she hurried towards the South Porch in the falling snow. On her way, she gripped her wine-red turban hat in both her hands, stretched its pleats and fiddled with its bow, but nothing stopped her long blonde hair, wild and wispy, blowing about her shoulders. Her face, with its narrow chin, was slightly anaemic, her lips equally washed out. For someone so pale and tired she paid scant attention to the biting air.

Jo held out her hand. Freya's grip struck her as less dismissive than efficient. Her smile was similar.

Was she pleased to see her?

It was no bad thing.

She was pretty happy to see *her*.

'So sorry I'm late,' said Freya, as Ruby ran round her heels. 'It's so good of you to wait – to go to so much trouble for so little. Hello Bella.'

Bella snarled.

'She's not really that anti-social,' said Jo apologetically.

Bella humphed. She'd thought they'd seen the last of the yappy Chihuahua. Finish. Finito. Fin. But since no dog with such bat-like ears could be taken seriously she lay down in the porch under the studious statue of St Jerome and his book of writings and covered her nose with her paw. She ignored the silly thing's deafening bark which was so out of proportion to its size.

Jo drew a small brown book from her pocket, even as the melodious chanting of Sunday's 10.30 Matins began with a prayer inside the cathedral.

'Truth is, I put it in a drawer and lost sight of it.'

'Sam can't manage without his 1943 "ABC of GWR LOCOMOTIVES". He's been asking about it every day since he mislaid it. Trains mean the world to him.'

'I guessed as much.'

Freya slipped the Ian Allan book of numbers carefully into her pocket. Her whole posture was that of earnest and breathless desire to depart as she tapped her chunky heels on the pavement.

But she didn't.

'Doesn't the minster look beautiful today in the snow? I imagine you can see all the way downriver to the ocean from the top of its tower?'

'Almost.'

'Fire watchers get all the best views.'

'And the coldest.'

'That, too, I suppose.'

As Freya dithered, she leaned her head back in the direction of some noisy pigeons that settled in rows on the cathedral's roof, whereupon her throat revealed a black and yellow discolouration inside the collar of her coat. The skin was not broken, exactly, but clearly visible were the burns and bruises from some hostile hand. Shadowy fingermarks traced the spot, not long after the bout of actual violence.

Jo braved the falling snow, too. Those wheals on Freya's neck panicked her. They literally did. What was going on? Why had someone done that to her? Would they escape undeterred?

Would she, was all that mattered now.

'How about I buy you a cup of coffee in the Cadena? It'll be so much warmer.'

'No need, Jo.'

'No? Well then, how is Sam?'

'Why do you ask?'

'Is he happy?'

'Why wouldn't he be?'

'He was lighting rather a lot of candles in the cathedral, you must admit.'

'You'll have to excuse him.'

'Please don't think we don't want him to return.'

'Sam's behaviour can be – how shall I put it – a bit obsessive at times.'

'The thing is, Mrs Boreman, he was snuffing out other people's candles to light his own.'

'As I say, he can be very focused.'

'He was coming every day and Dean Drew began to worry.'

As Freya opened her eyes wide to floating snowflakes, her pale green irises flashed specks of blue and yellow. These were in no way blemishes, but managed to convey in their brilliance a strange lack of something essential to their completeness, which was not helped by her dark, sunken sockets. Their strained look hinted at a darkness about her that could not be solved or dissolved very easily, thought Jo.

Nor did she take offence from it, since Freya's glare was aggressive only in so far as it was protective of herself and her dog.

Still she seemed to be about to say something to her.

Did she even know where to start?

'This snow's getting worse. At least step back inside the porch.'

Freya tightened her eyebrows with regret. It could also have been an expression of physical pain or constant struggle.

'Goodbye Jo.'

'Forgive me, you must be very busy. But do please tell me one thing before you go. How well do you know Susie Grossman?'

Freya executed an abrupt about-turn. She did it in an act of rash petulance. For someone in their mid-twenties she was strangely lizard-like. Observing how loosely the reefer coat sat upon her shoulders, Jo had to conclude that she was not so much slim as wiry. Her wrists and ankles were lean, tough and sinewy. She was no less striking for all that. But in her smile there was a sudden fury that she couldn't hide.

'Go to hell.'

From inside the cathedral there rose the joyous sound of a psalm.

Jo couldn't resist one last try.

'The thing is, Susie says Sarah Smith was in some kind of trouble. So does her husband Bruno – in fact, he doesn't think she died accidently, at all. I've been looking into the circumstances of the car crash. I thought you might be able to shed some light on your friend's last movements? As I say, why don't we have a chat over coffee?'

But it made no difference.

Freya glared at her with all the fury of some captive animal.

This was her decision.

'I can never have coffee with you or anyone else, Jo.'

'That sounds very final.'

Her smile was oh, so sweet and oh, so bitter. Her eyes flashed angrily.

'I'm sorry, that's just how it is.'

FORTY-SIX

'Careful,' said Nora and stopped dead in the moon-lit shadows. Her teeth bit crystals. Her breathing came in sharp, shallow bursts. Ice encrusted her eyelashes. 'Is that a house I can see up ahead?'

Thibaut took her hand beside the railway track and waited – should they go straight on or go round? He honestly had no idea. Something told him that they were about to make a terrible mistake. Suddenly there came that blood-curdling shriek from the Forest again. His knees went weak. The hairs rose on the back of his neck. He worried that those men on the Norton motorcycle would return any minute.

'We should keep our distance.'

No need to. That's not what Nora was saying. That shout just now had nothing to do with them. It was not even an owl this time – it was just a fox's scream magnified by the black mouth of the railway tunnel close behind them. Good for her. She had better nerves than him. As they advanced again, very slowly, they saw how the little home stood all alone. That's because its tenant operated the nearby railway level crossing whose heavy white gates blocked the road? The name over the brown, wooden porch said Tunnel Cottage.

Nora ducked and dived by a hedge alongside a small garden.

'I don't see any lights in the windows, do you?'

'What of it?'

'We should look for food. This snow isn't slackening. We'll die if we spend any longer in the cold.'

After the noisy fox, everywhere had an unruffled, hushed tranquillity in the bitter landscape. Frosted wires sagged between telegraph poles like heavy spiders' webs.

'What do you think it all means?' asked Thibaut.

'Whoever lives here won't be gone for long.'

'So what do we do?'

'Maybe get in via the back, somewhere?'

'Makes sense.'

The view through the window of a brick outhouse revealed an oil stove, a sack of potatoes, a shovel and a wringer. A man's newly washed clothes hung from two strings while a few cups and plates sat in a wooden rack and drained into an adjacent sink, in some sort of scullery. Its door was not much more than a crudely assembled, ill-fitting series of planks, they discovered. It could have been the entrance to a garden shed.

Nora gripped the crude metal latch.

Thibaut stayed her hand.

'Is this such a good idea?'

'I don't know where else we can go.'

'What if there's a dog? We could get bitten to death.'

'Don't I know it.'

'Okay, give it a try.'

To their astonishment the latch lifted.

'Wow,' said Nora, 'that's lucky.'

Thibaut followed her inside and the sandstone cottage seemed as peaceful as the grave. Only the soothing tick-tock of a large pendulum clock in the narrow passageway broke the stillness.

Next moment he put a warning finger to his lips. A black oil lamp had consumed all its paraffin in its reservoir and burnt out on the table. It was still warm. A few red coals glowed very low in a cast iron fireplace in the parlour, but there was no sign of any occupant in any of the chairs. He pointed silently upstairs, then took a deep breath as he began to mount their bare, wooden steps. He was certain to give himself away at the next creak in the treads?

Near total darkness wrapped him from head to toe with its monkish cloak – he was soon groping his way higher and higher in a grotesque shadow of himself.

At the head of the staircase he stopped and listened intently.

No sound of anyone dreaming or snoring issued from the one tiny bedroom.

But that didn't prove a thing.

Only by approaching the black, iron bedstead itself could he see if anyone lay asleep under its covers.

Once more he trod knotted wooden planks that squeaked and protested.

Nearly there.

He was not sure removing his shoes would be much help.

A railway timetable lay open on a table, with some trains ringed with black ink to remind the reader to open the level crossing gates at the correct hour to let them pass.

Anything else?

Oh, scarcely. He stood by the empty bedstead's brass knobs, but not before his foot struck something made of china. He froze at the loud clang. Held his breath. Too late, a hand took his arm.

He should turn, fight and wrestle his opponent to the ground.

So why didn't he?

'I found this in the kitchen.'

It was Nora. She was clutching a National Loaf of the sort that everyone had been eating for over a year now, ever since shortages had made it virtually impossible to bake bread with anything except wholemeal flour. The result was more grey than brown.

Thibaut felt himself deflate like a balloon.

Her presence was still quite alarming.

'Say that again.'

'There's more food in the kitchen larder. And I found some money in a wooden tea caddy. We can eat and move on.'

'Yeah, I suppose we can.'

'What's wrong?'

'Never said a word.'

'Then why are you standing with one foot in a potty.'

Thibaut came to his senses. He and Nora were alone together in this house of shadows.

So why worry?

In point of fact they had temporary shelter.

They had food.

They had money.

Most of all they had each other. Anything else had to be sheer conjecture.

FORTY-SEVEN

'Three, four, five, six....'

Jo inhaled as much air as possible without pausing in the icy morning. "The Women's League Of Health And Beauty's" idea of a perfect body was definitely a more curvaceous shape, which meant improving her bust. It certainly bust her gut. She was a balloon about to burst as she rotated her torso back and forth from her hips.

'Seven, eight, nine…'

Such early exercises should do her some good in the cloister garth. Where better? A healthy body was a healthy mind. She just didn't know it yet. She had gone as far as sending her mother a get well card without promising to visit her any time soon. She hadn't ruled it out, either, only found refuge in silence. Now she felt a terrible coward. If she could just put the whole matter out of her head with her keep fit routine?

'Ten, eleven, twelve…'

Bella ignored her owner's ghastly facial expressions, her tortured limbs and her childlike moans as she did her best to bite falling snowflakes. She chased icy dust-devils that whipped up powdery white drifts in corners of the courtyard and punched holes with her paws. Losing half your hair in an air raid could wear the best of dogs down, but it would take more than a German bomb to destroy her desire to jump for the heavens. Much the same could be said of her one-eared owner.

Suddenly Jo exhaled forcefully past her chapped lips; she let go an audible breath expressive of tension.

Should she go to the next level? She just did. First she swung one arm like a propeller before rotating both while bent at the elbow. Honestly, she was better suited to her mother's waif, breast-less look of the 1930s.

'Unbelievable.'

John Curtis stepped from the long shadows cast by the minster's tower; he stood with arms akimbo and arched a dark, ironical eyebrow her way. He brought all his grim authority as verger to bear as he looked down his long red nose at her.

'I know what you're thinking,' said Jo, still churning her arms.

'I hope not.'

'You think I'm a lost cause.'

'Yeah, I suppose I am.'

'They told me in hospital that I get too stressed by little things – I drive myself too hard.'

'And this helps how, exactly?' asked John, hugging himself in his black gown.

'I'm vacuuming my stomach.'

'Don't flatter yourself. At this rate the only thing you'll do is give yourself a hernia.'

'Everyone should do it for at least a minute a day.'

'You don't say?'

'It works the transverse abdominis muscle that pulls in the abdominal wall. You should try it.'

'Not in a hundred years.'

'This way I get to pull in my waist and push out my boobs. Of course I'm not saying you have b…'

'Let's keep it that way. You ready to go to the flicks with me yet?'

'Hurry up and pass me my towel.'

John tossed a snowball to Bella who caught it in mid-air and bit it to pieces. Then he threw her another one. She 'killed' that one, too, stone-dead. The third snowball she ignored. For a dog to demonstrate that she was not an automaton should have been sufficient.

'I gave Sam's book of train numbers to Freya,' said Jo, mopping her brow.

'And?'

'She walked off the minute I mentioned Susie Grossman.'

'You mean you failed to win her over.'

291

'Don't give me that look, that's not very nice.'

'Don't mention it.'

Jo sought relief from the icy wind inside the cloister alley.

'She obviously knows a lot more than she's telling.'

John banged snow off his boots – his toes were already going numb.

'Suppose Freya really was in that car with Sarah on the night she died, what went so horribly wrong? My bet is still on James who tried to stop her leaving.'

'I agree. I've seen the bruises.'

'What bruises?'

'On Freya's neck. She's been half throttled by him, I'm sure. What's more, I think she meant me to see them.'

'A man like that?'

'You're right, I should have called his bluff by now.'

'How so?'

Jo whistled Bella.

'I'm sorry I've stayed silent this long.'

'You should be.'

'Okay, to be fair, it's no one's business but theirs.'

'Isn't that what everyone says? We keep too damned quiet…'

'Freya wouldn't even go for a drink with me.'

'…to spare our own feelings.'

'I asked her before and she said she walked into a door.'

John raised his eyebrows.

'So we assume she stays with her husband for the sake of her son.'

'Wouldn't you?'

'It wasn't a question.'

'All this business about returning Sam's book suggests that Freya loves him very much.'

'Yet Susie Grossman says she couldn't care less about him.'

'To run away with Sarah was to escape serious abuse at home.'

'We can't blame her if she put herself first for once.'

Jo scratched her mutilated ear.

'To recap: Bruno's quite sure that Sarah discovered something big on James Boreman – big enough to get her killed. She told Freya about it and they joined forces to make a run for it, which is when James struck? So far so good. However, Bruno definitely bears James a grudge. He wants us to see him as the grieving husband, but what if he's using us to 'fit up' his former business partner and greatest enemy? He'd like us to accuse James of foul play to prove a private theory? He's assuming this ghastly war has somehow brought out the worst in him? He wouldn't be the first.'

'Let's face it,' said John, leading the way along the cloister, 'James looks to be a thoroughly nasty piece of work. He deserves his comeuppance. But to say he had Sarah bumped off is a big step to take.'

'Bigger than saying Freya did it?'

'In Susie's opinion! We only have her word for it that Sarah wanted to ditch Freya and go back to her.'

'What else do we have?'

Jo opened her wallet and drew from it a piece of paper.

'We have this 'killer diller'.'

'What can I say? It looks like how I feel after a night on the tiles.'

Together they stopped in the echoing cloister walk and studied the bristly head, small eyes and square snout of a wild animal.

It had to be some sort of pig.

They could agree on that at least.

You had to see it to believe it.

They shared a bad feeling about it.

But what was it *exactly*?

The hell if they knew.

'Where did you get it?' asked John.

'Sam drew it for me when we first met in the cathedral.'

'And you show it to me now?'

'I can't pretend ever to have seen anything quite like it.'

'Because it's obviously not a real creature.'

'I think he'd know.'

'Yeah, right.'

'Which means he really has met something?'

John studied the ferocious eyes and sharp tusks and could only marvel at the little boy's remarkable ability to set such a lifelike vision down on paper. It looked so *angry*. That wasn't all. The beast was uncannily like one of those wild boars carved on the ledges-cum-seats against which weary monks once leaned while singing for hours in the choir stalls – it was equally scary.

'What's this drawing got to do with Sarah Smith?'

'We have a possible pig connection, remember. Someone left a boar's head on her car and wrote '*Say Nothing*' in its blood on the windscreen.'

'Oh come on, what have we got here, really?'

'Suppose Sam lights candles to keep this what-d'you-call-it, this monstrous *hog*, at bay? He's trying to banish something that comes to him in the Forest? In his dreams? It's his own worst enemy?'

'A fiendish one, certainly.'

They might have been out of the snow but the cloister contained a sudden chill. With the shiver came a sense of something else. It might have been fear.

Jo folded the picture back into her wallet.

'What if it's not?'

John shuddered.

'Just put me out of my misery.'

'Forget what you know. If I were a psychiatrist...'

'Which, just to be clear, you're not.'

'...I'd say that Sam is showing us his state of mind. He's praying for superhuman strength.'

'You believe in that Freudian bullshit?'

Jo scooped Bella from the cold stone floor and began to warm each paw with her fingers. She dug ice from between her pads and claws. Dusted her ears.

'I may be wrong, but when Freya throws in her lot with Sarah it changes everything. Releases her stronger 'shadow self'. It sets free something that can't be put back in its cage. Something untameable. For the first time she has a friend who can help her escape her violent husband. Now that friend is gone *but she still wants out.* It goes beyond whatever feelings she might, or might not have had, for Sarah – from hereon it's all about survival that requires someone to come up with a new plan. Quickly. All this Sam sees every day. He's traumatised by it. What's the betting he's old enough to want to hold his father to account for his mother's never ending misery?'

Bella held up a leg – she'd failed to de-ice one paw.

'So what are we going to do?' asked John.

'We're going to show Freya this picture and see if she cracks.'

'That before she bites your head off?'

'This is what I think: Sam isn't just drawing some monster he honestly believes lives in the Forest, he's drawing his own father.'

'Boorish Boreman. Boar Man.'

'Exactly.'

'So it's a father-son thing.'

'It shouldn't be, but it is.'

John raised his bushy eyebrows.

'Or we could just leave well alone and see a film at the Picturedrome.'

Jo wrinkled her lip.

'I'm not wrong. He's revealing his rage in a drawing.'

'In your opinion.'

'This is not a picture but a prediction.'

'Whatever does it mean *in reality*, though?'

'It means we have to get to Sam before his prayers get answered.'

FORTY-EIGHT

Since when could snow be such hard going? Frosty air pricked Sam's cheeks like needles. His boots sank into frozen beech leaves and dragged him down. He blinked and struggled to focus. That's all he could do right now. If the wintry morning was a fiery red glow through the black, skeletal trees, then the ground he trod was a frozen, salt-white sea.

Most of all he was in awe of the surrounding silence.

But in a good way.

Silence was reassuring.

Oddly enough.

It was the click of a rifle's flat bolt handle and ten-shot magazine that really set his nerves on edge. Low voices were no less menacing. When the poachers pulled on their balaclavas they looked somewhat sinister. Breath from mean mouths blew ghostly clouds over his head.

Should he even have come?

He knew them all: Phil Cotter, Kevin Devaney and Gordon Bates. His fellow hunters cracked jokes among themselves as they prepared to enter a rarely explored corner of the Forest.

Their nervous banter came in hushed bursts.

'That the Mannlicher-Schonauer repeating rifle you got there?'

'Sure is.'

'I thought you were going to go for another Lee-Enfield?'

'With its full-length barrel this can take .375 rimless cartridges which pack quite a punch. It also has the extremely good Baillie-Grohmann peep-sight.'

'Makes sense, I suppose.'

Everyone had to work as a team. Sam felt it, too. The change. The thrill. The subtle alteration in his perception of himself. No longer was he the odd one out at home or in school; he felt charged, primed, prepared like one of those loaded guns – like a bullet ready to go. He was a thing of darkness. A stalker. A killer. No mere boy at all. No oddball.

That stiffening in his spine was pride. It was what his father wanted him to feel and he didn't want to let him down.

He felt big inside, like a giant, even though he was unarmed.

James's pale breath came hot in his ear.

'Stay close, Sam. Stay silent.'

'I promise.'

'We won't kill anything if you scare it away.'

'I won't make a noise, I really won't.'

'Watch, listen and learn. No humming. No buzzing like a bee.'

'I'll do what you do. I'll follow you.'

'Good boy. Who knows, today might be the day you get to have a go with my gun.'

Sam nodded vigorously, as if this was the best news ever. Then he joined the other shadows to merge with the Forest. He did wonder why his father should be so insistently happy for him, given what had just transpired.

Back home he had broken his favourite stoneware mug. He always drank from that mug and no other.

There had been a big row about it.

As a result, almost nothing liquid has passed his lips for nearly two days.

No wonder his head reeled now.

*

They walked a long time. It felt like miles, as Sam measured the distance in strides: 1037. 1038. 1039.... The world made better sense in numbers. If it hadn't been such a maze he would have counted the trees. At least his beloved book of trains was safely back in his pocket. That fire watcher from Gloucester Cathedral had been a woman of her word, after all.

His feet shovelled snow and fallen leaves on the Forest floor. Frozen puddles cracked. Snowdrifts crumbled. Each snap of a twig exploded in his ears like fire.

But none of these could account for the noises he *didn't* quite hear.

There was that rapid succession of short, sharp rattles which occurred whenever the trees shook themselves.

And there were those tuneful stalactites of ice that dangled from the underside of weeping branches or fell to the ground in sudden, brittle waterfalls.

He found each mini-avalanche thrilling. They clinked and jingled. Far from being frozen solid, the Forest was in constant, fretful motion. That's because something disturbed dead bracken close by. He looked everywhere but to no avail. Whatever it was stayed invisible. Some living creature kept pace with them in time to the ice-music. Could it be what he thought it was? His grandfather would know. He'd ask him, the next time he visited him at Tunnel Cottage.

His heart raced like a runaway rain, his lungs pumped as hard as bellows.

Suddenly he felt a heavy hand twist his shoulder as James ordered everyone to halt. Another hot whisper scorched his chilled ear.

'Look and learn, son. Tell me what you see?'

Sam recognised the voice's hard urgency. James was expecting him to rise to the challenge. To prove he wasn't stupid. Not weird. And he desperately wanted to measure up to the dare. The snowy Forest deprived him of perfect sight, confused him. Rationally, he knew this lack of vision was a trick of the light. Irrationally, he thought it an affliction. Because he could not see very well past the massive trees he felt robbed of his own judgement. His heart throbbed. His lips hummed. He didn't like to be put on the spot like this.

'I see a gap in the oaks and beeches.'

'Nothing else?'

'One silhouette is much clearer than the other.'

James screwed the heel of his boot deeper into the soft ground.

'What does that tell us, do you think?'

'I don't know. Could be a head and ears.'

'What did I say before we set out? What did I tell you to look for?'

Taking the question for the test it was, Sam racked his brains for an answer. There had been so many things that his father had said to him earlier that it was hard to know which was the priority. Instead he felt his head spin. That's because he remembered them all.

But what he feared most was to make a mistake, or worse, give himself away.

'I'm not sure. The sun is making the snow glint like glass.'

James caught him by the shoulder and shoved him roughly at the nearest tree.

'See that pale, white mark on the bark, Sam? That's where an animal has rubbed its neck quite recently.'

'Understood.'

'Nearby will be its wallowing place. Stags scrape them out with their hooves or antlers.'

'I see.'

And Sam did see. He imagined the great animal rising up from wet, steaming mud and rubbing itself against the tree trunk after its bath. They were trespassing on someone's most intimate habits.

'The thing is, son, an animal doesn't just scratch itself when it rubs against bark like this, it leaves its scent to mark its territory.'

'Which means?'

'We're on its trail.'

He breathed a big sigh of relief. He might not have said exactly the right thing, but neither had he earned his father's joyless smile. He lived in fear of that smile. It was used to hide irritation, impatience, even contempt.

Next minute, Gordon Bates returned from scouting ahead.

'Well?' asked James, impatiently.

The burly hunter cradled his rifle on his arm and pointed.

'Fresh tracks. Going north.'

No sooner had he spoken than a roar filled the air. The deep, belching groan echoed through the trees. The sound alone was ready to swallow them whole.

'What is it?' said Sam and clung to a corner of James's camouflaged jacket.

'It's a fallow buck calling.'

While falling snow had to be a bad time to hunt deer because they moved about less, all that went out of the window during the rut. They were on the move everywhere at any time of day or night. Sam could remember quite a lot about deer if he wasn't being put to the test, if he wasn't feeling 'flummoxed.' Sure enough, two magnificent stags were squaring up to each other like medieval knights in a Forest clearing.

It was enough to make the hairs stand up on the back of his neck. One majestic animal thrashed its antlers about in the ice-covered undergrowth, the other was still covered in snow from its recent wallow. Such was their preoccupation with fighting that they failed to smell the hunters. The two adversaries strutted parallel with one another to suss out their rival – he was privileged to be watching one of the Forest's most ancient rituals.

Next instant James gestured to him to stay low while he raised his rifle and prepared to fire off a bullet at 2,025 feet per second.

But Sam hardly noticed, so mesmerised was he by the clash of beasts as they went head to head in almost sacred battle. Both stags had lost their summer spots and their thicker, greyer hair had the look of winter. If only he could be that clever and change his appearance to suit time, place and mood, then he could hide like an animal, too – no more would he creep under his bed or shut himself in his wardrobe for hours on end to recover his equilibrium, when things proved too much and he couldn't cope. As it was, his ears cracked apart at the stags' head butts; his nostrils snorted at each snort. The winning stag would have the pick of the does.

He opened his mouth and would have roared his own roars if he hadn't been sworn to keep quiet.

Above all else, he could smell it. That sweaty, earthy smell. Of testosterone, or something like it. It was savage, angry, wild. An icy chill ran down his spine. Here was everything he'd ever wanted to feel but had never found a way to express, according to the unspoken laws of the dean.

At the same time perspiration broke out on his brow. Something terrible was going to happen and he would have a share in it.

One part of him wanted to jump up and wave his arms about.

'Stay still, damn you,' hissed James. 'If you want to kill something you first have to learn how to stalk it. You want to learn, don't you?'

Oh yes, thought Sam, part of him did want to learn.

It wanted to learn very much.

How to stalk.

How to kill.

FORTY-NINE

'No one can know why I'm meeting you,' said Freya, clutching her shoulder bag and gasmask in THE MONKS' RETREAT. With her went Ruby on a lead. 'Promise me.'

'My lips are sealed,' said Jo and offered to buy lunchtime drinks all round, but Freya, looking very smart in her black sweater and slacks, seemed less than keen to pull up a chair, or give her a smile. Not to her, she didn't. She appeared to be extremely on edge about something and kept casting worried glances at her wristwatch. Should she protest? She hadn't expected her to pick up her phone, let alone agree to see her again so soon after their disagreement yesterday.

If she hadn't known better, she would have said that Freya positively wanted to be seen in public right now, as if they were her alibi for something.

John stopped by the bar on his way past. 'Bag a seat for me, will you.'

Bella glared at Ruby with contempt. While a dog was often admired for being just like its owner in looks and habits, this yappy thing in its little red coat was a panicky ball of noisy trouble. Hypersensitive. That was the word. The harder it shivered the more it shook its fringed ears. She wrinkled her own ears and twitched her nose. In her eyes the Chihuahua was no better than a rat.

Sometimes one dog could not bring itself to speak to another.

She petitioned to play in the hotel yard, but was forbidden to trot up the crowded undercroft's steps and sink her teeth into fresh snow.

'I'm afraid you'll think it's all about nothing,' Jo stated matter-of-factly, the moment she found them all chairs in a corner.

Freya gave an impatient wriggle.

'Get to the point. I don't have much time.'

'Sam drew this strange drawing for me in the cathedral.'

Freya immediately took off her dark glasses to expose the remains of an ugly black bruise round one eye. Removing her scarf was no less revealing. Although she had spent considerable time backcombing her hair and kept it in place with bobby pins, combs and grips, she still could not entirely conceal the place where a tuft had been ripped from her scalp not so long ago. She looked perplexed and pale. But if her sudden rigid posture and stubborn gaze were manifestly uncooperative, her swollen face was at once a mixture of curiosity and annoyance. Even embarrassment. Some of those bruises had to be new.

'*That's* the boar Trwyth. Sam draws it every day. Once he gets an idea into his head nothing will stop him – he becomes obsessed with it.'

John suddenly set three bottles on the table.

'Sorry, no glasses.'

Jo traded frowns with him. Hadn't he heard, Freya just refused the offer of a drink? He mouthed something back, as if to say: *you think she didn't want to?* But even he had his doubts now.

Freya's hand went to her bruised mouth and she blushed.

'I may have a bit of a loose tooth.'

'Please go on,' said Jo. 'This so-called boar Trwyth, what's that all about?'

Freya set aside the beer after a couple of sips. She winced. Honestly, she reacted like someone put on the spot. This was all very difficult and complicated.

'You really want to know?'

'In your own time.'

'According to Welsh legend the cursed prince Culhwch can only marry the beautiful Olwen and no other. He falls head over heels in love with her but she is the daughter of the cruel giant Ysbaddaden Bencawr. The giant is under a curse himself should Olwen ever get wed. He therefore sets Culhwch an impossible challenge – he must comb the giant's hair and beard in preparation for the wedding ceremony, but only one combination of shears, comb and razor exists in the whole world that will cut such coarse locks. These magical instruments reside in the bristles of the enchanted Twrch Trwyth. The Welsh word 'Twrch' signifies wild boar or hog, so Twrch Trwyth means 'the boar Trwyth'. To cut a long story short, Culhwch enlists the help of the famous King Arthur and his knights of The Round Table who retrieve the magical articles in battle, one after the other. But Twrch

Trwyth escapes via the River Severn to Cornwall where he runs into the sea.'

'You trying to tell me Sam believes this mythical monster lives in the Forest of Dean?'

'On account of all the lurid stories that his grandfather keeps telling him.'

Jo held her glass of stout to her lips, thought of her baby and promptly drank its health.

'Why now? Why here?'

'Why not? The Forest is an ancient place absolutely riddled with caves and tunnels. Twrch Trwyth could have returned to take refuge there. Who's to say such a cunning, treacherous beast doesn't know the way right down into the underworld? Who's to say it won't lead some unsuspecting person to their doom there? In a ten-year-old's childish mind, that is.'

John raised his eyebrows.

'Imagine that.'

'As I said, once Sam gets hold of an idea he runs with it and won't let it go. His father blames it on his 'illness'. He can't bear his pedantry, as he calls it, whereas I think Sam's pre-occupation with narrow interests is simply part of who he is.'

John shook his head.

'Shouldn't we be concerned? When did he start drawing his monsters, exactly?'

Freya ran her tongue round her sore gum.

'I found the first one shortly after I told him that I was going to leave James.'

'Because he treats you and Sam so badly?'

'Yes.'

Jo and John traded more dark looks. Well, that wasn't so difficult, was it? Before, Freya had been downright obstructive, but now there was no stopping her?

'Go on,' said Jo, gently.

Freya looked at them both and then her wristwatch, again.

'I'm sure you'll agree that appearances can be deceptive, Jo. My husband can be friendly and jovial – the life and soul of the party. We once made a good couple, he and I. Also, he lost a parent in tragic circumstances just like me – I felt he was the only person who understood what I was going through at the time. It meant I no longer felt like a lost cause.'

'A lost cause? Surely not?'

'When my father was injured down his coal mine, things became very hard for him and my mother. My birth came along just at the wrong time. Mum managed to work in a grocer's shop to help pay for clothes for me and for my brother, Simon – we struggled on for a few years when the bank foreclosed on the loan against the house with only one month's notice. That's when things went from bad to worse. We were all set to be made homeless and my father couldn't secure a new loan based on his health and employment history. He became very hostile and moody, even violent. My parents had endless rows. Then one day my mother called him 'bloody useless'. She just lashed out. Of course I was still only a child – not yet ten. I had no idea how depressed she'd been ever since having me and I never thought she'd let me down. She didn't even leave a note to explain. That's why I don't think she planned anything, I think she suddenly saw a way out and took it.'

John cracked a knuckle.

'Her life might have been in crisis but so was yours. She had no right to put the blame on you.'

'I saw the whole thing. She stepped off the platform as the freight train steamed through Gloucester railway station. She was sliced to pieces under its wheels. But I didn't shed any tears. Not that I remember. Instead I hated her for making me see her like that. For ruining my life. I couldn't think straight any more – I couldn't bear to be in my own home.'

'How was it your fault?' asked Jo.

'I ran away twice as soon as I reached my teens.'

'Naturally you were frightened.'

'Not frightened but furious. I wanted to hit back at the world because she hadn't loved me enough to stay with me. I decided to rebel by *not* doing what I most wanted. I guess I was really hurting myself.'

'That's when you met James?'

'He was much older than me. Twenty-four years older in fact. But he was like a king. Charming. Generous. Considerate. He made me feel secure. He was already making big money from his various businesses. He was the man my father should have been. In the beginning it was wonderful because so many people admired and respected us. He wore good clothes and talked very well and he wasn't at all bad looking. Other people hung on his every word. He's an absolute wiz at the foxtrot, one-step and waltz.'

'What happened to you?'

'I fell pregnant in 1933. I was fifteen.'

'You were underage. He committed a crime. Are you sure he didn't coerce or threaten you to get what he wanted?'

'Oh no, we were madly in love. I left school to be with him.'

'You might think that he didn't force you to do what he wanted…'

'He never laid a finger on me. Not then.'

'…but he may have been controlling you psychologically because you were so young. He might have used his money to manipulate you emotionally?'

'Of course I'd say that now. Whatever it was, I did believe I was doing the right thing. Haven't you ever been madly in love, Jo?'

'….'

'James was my protection from the world.'

'Didn't your father intervene, at all?'

'He totally took to drink for a while.'

'Sorry to ask. What about you? Were you into anything as well?'

'James gave me some of his cocaine now and again.'

'Wasn't that crazy?'

'Not to me it wasn't. It made me forget.'

'Stop me if I'm wrong, but no one else stepped in to help you?'

Freya licked her split lip.

'When dad slipped behind with the rent yet again, James was very good to him. He found him a room in one of his rented properties in Gloucester for a while.'

'So if you stopped being nice to James he would stop helping your father,' said John, butting in.

'I never thought of it like that, not at the time.'

'Why would you?'

'As I say, I was madly in love.'

'And you? Where did you live?'

'I moved into Drake's House with James. In some ways it was idyllic down by the river.'

'You don't sound too certain.'

'The railway line runs between house and river. It's how Sam came to love trains, even if it did remind me too much of other things. I'd lie awake at night and feel the bed shake as heavy coal trains passed by from South Wales. In the end I'd had enough of being stuck at home all the time and badgered James to let me start training to become a nurse.'

'*Let* you?'

'He agreed to pay someone to look after Sam, but then, a year later, I fell pregnant again.'

'Wasn't that a bit careless?' said John.

'Shit happens. Anyway, isn't contraception a man's responsibility?'

'In all honesty, yes.'

'When the nursing college found out they didn't want me. A mother's place is in the home, they said. I wasn't feeling too well – I was suffering badly from morning sickness.'

'Tell me about it,' said Jo.

'By then James was holding parties for businessmen and their wives on a yacht in Bristol's Floating Harbour. Expensive holidays abroad were already the norm. Fast cars, too. He'd also joined the Freemasons. And, as I say, we had the historic home by the river. What more did I need? Then out of the blue he bought me this gorgeous diamond ring you see on my finger. He said we must be married straightaway because people were talking.'

'How did that go?'

'I had a lot to lose because the new baby was due any day. I had no job. No qualifications. I got scared, I suppose. I thought I was doing it because

James loved me and it would also be best for Sam. That's when it all started to go wrong. I wrote myself – my needs – out of the equation. Then, to cap it all, my baby was born dead. It was a boy. More horror followed. Come Easter last year Simon was killed when a bomb hit the bus park at Gloster Aircraft Factory. He was twenty-eight. It came as a terrible shock to lose my only brother like that, even though we hadn't seen much of each other for a while because he couldn't stand the sight of James. I've wanted to curl up and die ever since. I don't want to sleep in the same bed as my husband and he hates me for it. Fuels his violence. It's my cowardice that has kept me caged for so long.'

Jo sat back, overwhelmed. She remembered how she'd felt when she'd lost everything. The horror of it.

Then the silence.

That awful silence – when the screams stopped coming from the rubble.

God, what she'd do to go back now.

If only she'd been stronger and braver.

If only she'd had the strength of a giant.

To move collapsed walls and lift burning timbers.

'But you refuse to be trapped by the past any longer, right?'

Freya gave Ruby a kiss on the ear.

'One day, out of curiosity, I had a rifle through James's desk. He caught me and beat me black and blue. I was stunned. This was the man who said he adored me. At the time I kind of blamed myself – I shouldn't have been looking through his business correspondence, should I? Of course he was sorry and deeply ashamed afterwards. He bought me a rare 1933 Riley Lynx Tourer to make up.'

'But since then the blows have kept on coming?' said John.

'As I say, James in the beginning was bloody marvellous. But that's just on the surface. Underneath he can be… well… a bit of a pig.'

Jo leaned in.

'But now things have become utterly intolerable?'

John kicked her ankle.

'One thing at a time.'

Freya ignored the kerfuffle.

'James's plan to send Sam for experimental medical treatment in America has been the last straw. I'd reached a complete low over it when my old school friend Sarah Smith offered to help me. She might no longer work for James, she said, but she knew bad things about him. Very bad. If we stood together we could bring him down, but first I had to get out his house. Be safe. Sam, too. She said she could help us both escape.'

'She had proof of James dealing in black market timber, for instance?'

'Worse. Much worse.'

'Which means what, exactly?'

'When the time was right she would reveal all, Sarah said, but it would mean that James would have no choice but to pay up as well as give me a divorce.'

'But Sarah died.'

'Yes, she did.'

Jo tried to see past Freya's injuries for a moment. For too long she had thought they might be the result of a car accident, but not now. While graceful and stylish, her clothes clung to her spare frame like an extra skin. There was an elegance to her that bordered on the severe. The result was something pleasingly simple, even austere. Black would always do that to a person, yet her body exhibited a strange impatience – it strained to throw off its enforced, elegiac understatement. Something wild swelled inside all the constriction. She wondered if the wearing of mourning clothes was not only because she missed her dead friend, but would stubbornly protest her right to do so. The question was indisputable. Black was so uncompromising; it came across as an act of resistance. She knew first-hand how a person could become irreconcilable to the fact of losing someone in whom they'd invested so much love and hope.

Perhaps that's why she had never worn black herself, thought Jo. She hadn't wanted to admit it was all over.

It fell to John to break the awkward hiatus.

'Is that the reason your suitcase was in Sarah's car on the night she died?'

Freya nodded eagerly – almost too eagerly.

'Sarah was going to take me and Sam to a place of safety in Hereford.'

'She was helping you that much?'

'I couldn't do it alone.'

'But things didn't go according to plan.'

'I managed to smuggle a few of Sam's belongings out of Drake's House the day before our departure, but I couldn't take much of my own in case James noticed. He's always poking about in my wardrobe because he likes to tell me what to wear whenever we go anywhere in public. I couldn't have him see half empty cupboards, could I? I had to settle for a few mementoes and essentials. Honestly, I didn't want all those fancy shoes and smart clothes any more anyway. Too many of them had been bought with his fists and I didn't want to feel beholden to him for another minute.'

'Bold move.'

Freya's grim expression grew grimmer.

'I thought I could walk to Sarah at the end of the road just up from the river...'

'But you thought wrong?'

'Yes I did. I had my hand on the front door when James appeared and said he wanted to take Sam deer poaching in the Forest. I had to come up with a lie in a moment, so I said that my father was ill again – he has bad lungs ever since his days spent digging coal. I said I had to take Sam to see him that evening, that I might stay over, hence the suitcase. I'd done it before.'

Jo watched his beer grow warm in the cellar's smoky and muggy atmosphere and wondered if Freya ever shed a tear.

'You took a risk he'd believe you?'

'Illness or no illness, he wouldn't let Sam travel with me. They were going hunting and that was that.'

'So you had to leave him behind to maintain your lie.'

'What would you have done?'

'What did you do?'

'James watched me depart in my Riley. I drove alone up the hill from Drake's House to the end of the road, as arranged. Of course Sarah wanted me to follow her red Austin Seven there and then, all the way to Hereford, but I was sure James had arranged for someone to follow me, just as he liked to listen in to all my phone calls. I had no alternative but to go to my father's place at Tunnel Cottage. Otherwise my cover would be blown. Sarah and I had a big row about it. There was no one following me, she said, I was being paranoid. Perhaps she was right, but when you haven't led your own life for such a long time, your sense of what's real and what isn't begins to blur. As far as I'm concerned James always knows where I am to the minute – he has eyes everywhere. I couldn't take any chances. *He's in my head.* I threw my suitcase at Sarah and drove off. I said I'd call her again soon, that I couldn't leave without Sam. I didn't want James to come after us, I couldn't risk a dangerous chase through the Forest.'

Jo leaned in further. Breathed softly.

'But James did go in pursuit? He chased Sarah?'

Freya paled.

'All I know is that he acted far too normally that night. He didn't even ask to look in my suitcase, he simply took my word for it that all I had with me were a few nightclothes. He knew my plan, I'm sure. Perhaps he'd known all along?'

John flexed his hand. Cracked more knuckles. He looked Jo then Freya in the eye –her dry, unblinking eyes.

'What are we going to do about Sam?'

'John's right,' said Jo, 'Sam needs our help. So do you. We have to get you both to safety right now.'

'It might be too late.'

'But if we can help?'

'And then? How will James react, do you suppose?'

'Give yourself a chance.'

'This isn't a game, Jo. He can do things.'

'What sort of things?'

'I've already said too much.'

'Think of Sam. There's no good to be had by staying silent any longer.'

Freya seized Ruby, as if to leave at once. That glassy, empty glint in her gaze was in direct contrast to the nervous smile on her lips as she read the time on her watch for the umpteenth time.

'If you do help me he might kill you.'

Jo gave a quick smile, too.

'John and I have risked our necks several times already.'

'Then follow me.'

'Where are we going?'

'We're going to the Forest while there's still hope.'

FIFTY

Whatever he did next, he mustn't vomit.

Not right now.

Sam clutched his belly with both hands, bent double and opened his mouth wide.

Did he have a choice?

Did it feel like he did?

He really shouldn't get so worked up, but it wasn't that simple. Otherwise he stood like a statue next to his father in the ice-forest, as he squinted sideways through the 1000-yard sight on top of his B.S.A. Lee Enfield – he'd already seen him upload a Mark VI cartridge into the breach. Another nine rested in the gun's magazine.

Then James fired.

As did the other hunters.

The first stag dropped like a stone. A chill crept into Sam's hands, feet and tongue. Any terror at the unfairness of the contest soon changed to awe. As for the other animal, one bullet sheared an antler and another clipped its flank; it staggered sideways, tripped, then began to run.

Already James had his next round ready to fire. He was trying to take proper aim to make a second kill more likely.

'This one's mine. Come on, Sam, let's go get it.'

They passed the stag that bellowed like a bull as it breathed its last. The fatal bullet had sliced clean through its ribs at 700 yards to carve a great wound. With its chin resting on the ground, it stared at them in wide-eyed astonishment. It was a cold, accusing look that Sam felt at a loss to explain. His stomach tightened again as he retched violently, though he wasn't going to throw up, after all.

Not as far as he knew.

'Get a ruddy move on,' said James, 'or the other one will give us the slip.'

'But how will we find it?'

'Don't worry. That shot I fired was a .303. A round that size creates an excellent blood trail.'

He needn't have asked. They trod red, all right. A ribbon of scarlet splashes stained the snow. At every step the blots became larger and larger, like stars. He had to clasp his head in both hands because he could feel the agony. His brain beat like a drum and his eyes were on fire.

The stricken stag had managed to travel a surprising distance. Too shocked to think straight, it lay on the ground where it twitched and shivered. Every dragon-like breath it blew in the cold air was an exhalation of intense pain. There was no need to hurry; it wasn't going anywhere soon. They stood over it. Heard it panting. They could kill it whenever they chose.

'Not good,' said Sam and went to inspect the hole in the stag's hip. He could see where the bullet had exited the other side.

James pulled him away.

'What the hell! What are you doing? You'll get blood all over your clothes.'

'We should apologize.'

'To whom?'

'To the Forest.'

'Are you serious? It's just a wild animal, Sam. We can put it in the freezer and eat venison at Christmas.'

Sam nodded but said nothing. In his eyes the raw, bloody wound weighed heavily – as heavily as the silence that fell from the trees.

'You don't know anything.'

So saying, he refused to budge between stag and man. They should give it a moment in the falling snow.

Did he know why?

Not that he could think of, no.

He couldn't give a reason.

James screwed up his face, relaxed his grip on the rifle's trigger and pulled off his balaclava.

'Don't ever do that again, Sam. You could get yourself killed.'

But Sam's eyes were firmly focused on the trees all around. Other eyes saw him. Locked on. Some creature lurked just beyond the edge of the clearing, not twenty paces from where they were standing? The reddish orbs were two bright coals. Nor was it clear to him whether they could see him very well because they appeared so small. Such a look suggested an acute attentiveness that went beyond mere surprise, however. It was inquisitorial. Hostile. Malign? In the face of such scrutiny he shrank and shivered, but to raise his arm and point must surely provoke it to charge straight at them.

'Now what?' said James.

'Behind you.'

'Damn it, Sam, move out of my way. Let me cut the stag's throat.'

'I can't.'

'Why not?'

'I just can't. Something's watching…'

Again he sought to divert attention from one animal to another. His lips worked frantically but noiselessly as he tried not to surrender to the glowing pupils that were scrutinizing them with such ferocity.

'Is this another of your funny turns, Sam? Tell me.'

But Sam stood his ground. If he was going to get his father's attention, he had to be convincing. While paralysed with fear his senses worked overtime as he *saw* a large, bristly white head and fat snout rise from the bushes. He *heard* snorting. *Smelt* pig. Except no pig he had ever seen was so large. Raised hackles remained partly hidden by the rapidly deteriorating weather. He could imagine already what it would mean to be ripped apart by its long, pointed tusks. One quick swipe and his throat would be gone.

What were they supposed to do?

What did it mean?

Rooted to the spot, but making deaf and dumb signals, he waved towards dead bracken at the edge of the clearing.

'But dad, it's the white boar.'

James forgot about the deer and went on the defensive.

'Where?'

'I'm not sure.'

'Don't tell me you saw nothing.'

'It must be something.'

'Where?'

'A little to the left.'

'I don't know what to believe now.'

Still the creature studied them both in absolute silence. No matter how devilish its eyes, it had seen the gun in the hunter's hands and it was assessing how best to attack. The great head retreated into shadow; it merged with the frosted grass but somehow the threat failed to diminish, only became less visible.

'I don't see a thing,' said James.

All was silence and stillness.

'It's watching us, I tell you,' said Sam indignantly. 'I can still feel its eyes on me.'

'A boar, you say?'

'A big white one.'

James's lips curved into a smile. It wasn't mirth exactly, it was revelation.

'Don't be ridiculous, there's no such thing.'

'I saw it, I tell you.'

'Well, you saw wrong.'

'It had huge tusks and its eyes had red rims. Its head would look great on my wall.'

'Don't flatter yourself.'

'But its bristles shone with white fire, I tell you.'

'Say what you will, that was no phantom boar.'

'It saw right through me.'

'Isn't that the truth.'

James relaxed his grip on the rifle, ready to go back to work – that wounded stag had to have its throat slit. Hot guts must spill. The hunting knife weighed lightly in his hand. That's because its shaggy handle was made from the hoof of a deer. His heart pounded steadily and beat in his ears like a drum. To kill an animal by hand was the greatest feeling in the world. He was vanquisher. He was God.

But the stag was nowhere to be seen.

'What the hell...!'

They searched everywhere but the wounded animal had somehow performed a miraculous disappearing act.

'Damn you Sam Boreman, this is all your fault. You distracted me with your silly talk of wild boar.'

Sam looked crestfallen. He could only splutter and flounder.

'What did I do?'

'Don't you see, you've made me look a complete fool in front of my friends.'

This was beyond Sam's power to understand. All he could think was that the winged stag had overcome its shock and pain to live another day. It made him more excited than he could say, whereas James was suddenly downcast and moody. Disappointment clouded his eyes as he trudged back to the lorry and the three other hunters.

If James wanted to finish off that stag so badly, thought Sam, why didn't they pursue it right now? But the momentum had gone out of his father, apparently – his hitherto murderous intentions had dissolved, as if a spell had been broken. And he, Sam Boreman, was responsible.

*

Back at the dropside truck, Phil Cotter was first to light a cigarette. His moustache wrinkled as he gave a big smile.

'What happened, boss? You let it get away?'

James managed a smile of his own, a thin one. It was pure menace.

'Sam thinks we met a giant hog.'

'You killed someone's hog?' asked Gordon Bates, dragging their steaming deer carcass across the ground. 'The owner won't be pleased. It's the pannage season.'

James turned his back.

'I didn't say that.'

'What, then?'

Sam stepped forward, brimming with pride. He couldn't be sure what was going on from the tone of the men's voices, but he knew he had their full attention.

'I saw it first. It was a big white one.'

'Did you now?' said Phil and rumpled Sam's hair rather roughly.

'He doesn't know what he saw,' said James and poured himself a cup of whisky from a flask.

'Tell us,' said Devaney.

'Its eyes were full of fire,' declared Sam, 'with red rims.'

'Were they now?'

'And its bristles gleamed with a ghostly white light. It was a phantom boar. I can't think how else to describe it. Or who sent it. It could be the legendary Twrch Trwyth, as in the Welsh stories.'

'Is that a fact?'

'Take no notice,' said James. 'There hasn't been a wild boar in the Forest of Dean for hundreds of years. Let alone a white one.'

'Doesn't mean they don't exist. You get Judas deer, don't you?'

'Enough,' said James. 'Let's call it a night. That dead stag of yours in the lorry yet?'

'All done and dusted,' replied Phil.

'But dad, you don't understand…'

'Forget it.'

'But what if it's magic or something?'

'Just get in the truck.'

'But...'

'Better hear the kid out,' said Devaney as he blew smoke from his pipe.

'Yeah, give him a break for Christ's sake,' added Phil.

James lodged his gun in the lorry's cab.

'Say what you have to before I lose my temper.'

Sam stood up straight. Lifted his chin. But James wasn't listening. His head felt leaden, his hunched shoulders weighed heavily upon him. No one was saying too much because they didn't dare to, but a man didn't have to say a lot for another to know what he was thinking. He'd shot a stag and as good as missed it. These men were inwardly laughing at him. They were, in their unsubtle way, getting one over on him, their own boss. It was a direct assault on his authority.

It was all the boy's fault, but he couldn't take it out on Sam, not when he really did believe he had seen something so very unusual.

His hands shook and his anger simmered. It was the sort of frustration that soon grew into something else. People had got hurt because of it. People lived in fear of it. Such volatility lurked deep within him, but he had it under control. Above all else, he had not struck his own son in public.

Yet Sam had spoken with such certainty. If there literally were a wild boar in the Forest, then he was very anxious to be the one to kill it. Unbeknown to anyone else he would return within the hour to set some snares; he'd trap the swine once and for all, just to be on the safe side. Then he'd put a bullet through its heart – he'd make out he'd shot it while bravely stalking it all alone.

That would wipe the smirk off his men's faces.

No one would know what to say then.

Besides, Sam was right – the white boar's head would look splendid on a wall in Beech Tree Grange where it would take pride of place among his other kills. People would talk about it – and him – for years to come. Forget the mundane matter of how palatial his new home felt, or how rich he had become thanks to his black marketeering, or even how beautiful he still considered his wife to be, this was all about what he really wanted, *in his soul.*

He would demonstrate, by hook or by crook, that he was the real King of the Forest.

At the very least, he would quash all this silliness about a phantom Twrch Trwyth before it got out of hand.

Sam watched from the sidelines as his father seethed with unsated bloodlust.

Then he smiled a little smile of his own.

FIFTY-ONE

That voice, again. Tempting, coaxing, beguiling. From the depths of the disused coal mine.

Why not sit back, Jim Wilde, and wait for rescue?

'Because I'll die if I don't make an effort.'

But it hurts so much to move a muscle.

'Can't disagree with you there.'

No one saw you enter the tunnel.

'Don't I know it.'

Each mind-numbing stab of pain robs him of his breath. His cracked hip burns like fire and there is a terrible throbbing in his lower spine. His neck aches. It is virtually impossible to think straight when his whole body keeps going into agonising spasm like this.

But he has to do something.

He can't stay where he is.

He yells for help and waits for the echoes....

No one answers.

.... to fade away before he can listen.

Not a damned thing.

How long has it been? One day? Two?

Everything is quiet apart from the plop, plop, plop of dripping water from the tunnel roof – *that* seems to grow louder by the minute as if to torment him.

He clamps both hands on the cold, rusty rails of the subterranean tramway; he starts clawing and scratching. He utters little, unconfident moans as he unfolds his good leg and prepares to drag the other one after it. That way he kicks and hauls himself uphill along the narrow tunnel.

Does he dare hope that someone will think to look for him down here?

Obviously not.

So he has nothing, except that terrible smell. Pungent, acrid, bitter. And what else? Whatever it is, it wasn't there when he descended.

God forbid something is blocking his path out of the mine now.

He shouldn't even look.

It's a very bad idea.

You could say that.

But his fingers don't lie – he's touching the lifeless body of a young man that rests face up on the adit's floor. His shirt has been ripped apart on his chest where someone has pumped his heart in an attempt to revive him?

This cadaver has been dumped like rubbish.

It's truly disgusting.

He'll have to look at it to crawl by. The victim's boots have slipped half off his ankles; both arms are horribly wounded, one more so than the other. Blisters have turned green and gangrenous, with the cause of death probably being sepsis – it's hard to tell, because other damage has been done with very strong acid. That odd smell he can smell is liquefied flesh. Much of the victim's face has been melted to reveal teeth, jaw and cheek bones. The eyes are empty black sockets and he's missing the tips of his fingers.

Whatever the reason this anonymous cadaver lies here, it has to be the same as the one called Angela.

Take it easy, Jim Wilde. He's pawing at bones in what amounts to a graveyard.

All the more reason to reach the surface before he, too, expires.

It's not as though he doesn't know the way.

He'll be right there.

Unless he's somehow dead already? It is so much less painful when he stops moving. Does he really have to get back to Sam and Freya? Not yet, anyway. In this underworld he has the chance to join the spirits of the departed in his very own Hades.

In his very own grave.

He dug it himself years ago.

Pretty much.

Next minute he's pulling himself along as rapidly as he can. He doesn't look back for fear of his two grinning witnesses with each shaky grasp of metal railway.

Because he was hit on the head and left to die.

Because someone has to be told about it immediately:

Whose boneyard this is. Whose lair.

FIFTY-TWO

'Wait for me here.'

More Freya would not say, only shut the door to her Riley 9 Lynx Tourer with a loud bang. Driving hadn't been easy in the snow. Now she marched along the driveway to Beech Tree Grange with an air of stolid determination, even obstinacy. For someone not given to trusting anyone, her dogged tread through the gathering darkness demonstrated a foolish bravura, thought Jo. She felt terrible just watching. How could she not ask her to go with her? She must know that James wouldn't let Sam leave without a struggle. It was her word against his.

Didn't mean Freya wasn't in the right. But what if she wasn't? It could turn out to be worse than she thought. She might look like any other person returning home on a bleak winter afternoon, but that in no way reflected her actual circumstances. Was she not there to abscond with her son?

Meanwhile Ruby popped her head up like a periscope from her shoulder bag and sneezed when a snowflake settled on her nose.

Jo paced up and down before motorcycle and sidecar. 'How is this part of the plan?'

John dug his fingers into his coat pocket and wondered whether to light the last, precious cigarette from his packet of Player's Navy Cut No. 9. He'd queued for an hour and a half at his local tobacconist's just to buy a few fags and couldn't be sure if or when he would find any again. Might have to admit defeat and switch brands. *Again.*

'The moment James tries anything we go storming in. Agreed?'

Jo banged the Brough Superior's handlebars with her gloved fist.

'We can't just stand here.'

Bella squirmed in the sidecar. Yes, they literally could. Call it a dog's supernormal senses. Her eyes widened. Her ears pricked up. An overwhelmingly powerful odour hit her nostrils, of freshly uprooted leaves, beechmast and acorns from the Forest floor.

That had to be the smell of hog?

John offered Jo a drag on his cigarette.

She refused.

'We should probably do as she says and stay put.'

'Never mind that James could kill her? He owns a gun.'

'Freya doesn't need us to hold her hand.'

'But it's so risky.'

'Thanks, but I'm sure she'd rather make up her own mind.'

John was right, thought Jo reluctantly. Freya knew her value – she would never be drawn to her even if she already felt drawn to her. She saw her hold out one hand to clench and unclench her fingers as she strode along; she was reaching out to crush the falling flakes in her palm; she was savouring the bite of ice on bare skin. Let's face it, she was on the warpath.

'What's she doing now?' asked John, squinting hard.

Jo dusted snow off her oilskins and peered through the blizzard.

'She's at the house and crossing the patio. She's opening a door.'

'And now?'

'I don't like it. That's Boreman's lorry parked in the driveway. I can see its plate 442.'

'Take it easy.'

'You see any sign of life in the house, at all?'

'He could be lying in wait for her in the dark.'

'Why do you say that?'

'What do we really know about him?'

'We know he adores her very much.'

'Look how that turned out.'

Suddenly a light lit up the kitchen. Others followed from room to room in quick succession. Ruby started yapping. Soon the whole of Beech Tree Grange gave off a strange, eerie glow.

As if it were on fire.

Next moment Freya emerged back on to the patio with a torch clutched firmly in her hand.

Jo lodged her goggles high on her leather motoring cap.

'What the hell, John?'

'Sorry, I can't see that far in the gloom.'

To their utter astonishment, Freya set off at a march across the white lawn. Then she abruptly changed direction through the blizzard, which did less to slow her progress than breathe new life into her – she headed straight into the Forest.

'Something's wrong,' said Jo. 'I'm going after her.'

John let Bella out the sidecar.

'Wait. We're coming, too.'

'Goes without saying.'

Suddenly Freya cupped a hand to the side of her mouth and shouted.

'Sam! Where are you? Why won't you answer?'

Jo looked down at the ground. Many a footprint had been partially buried by fresh snow, but it was still possible to make out what Freya was following. There was one line of very large prints and one small. Accompanying them was a set of cloven hooves. Every foot left holes made by horn from which curled two separate toes.

Bella sniffed the tracks and growled.

That smell of hog just grew greater.

FIFTY-THREE

First he must secure the trap to a tree, then conceal wire and rope under the snow and bracken. What's not to like? Pigs often roam all night but return in a big circle to where they began. That's where he, James Boreman, will prop up the metal noose and leave it wide open. Once his prey enters it will draw tight round the neck.

The dual purpose, double-locking snare hangs heavily in his hand. He had hoped to find just the right place for it by now.

He can say that because he has read up about wild boar elsewhere in the world, as a precaution.

This time of year male pigs can be unpredictable.

Occasionally, they've been known to be unstoppable when they charge.

You never know.

While he does still wonder if he should have brought his 12 bore shotgun that fires a rifled slug, all advice suggests a shotgun might only kill a big animal at very close quarters. It takes a bigger calibre round to really stop a charging boar in its tracks. So say hunters in Europe and they're quite the experts. Before the war they used bait stations, drive hunting, stalking and fixed-point hunting to track three million wild hogs each year. That's why he carries his trusty Lee-Enfield slung over his shoulder – to execute the coup de grace. No one can remember when they last saw a white boar, though, not even in Russia.

Hard tears crystallize on his cheeks in this sub-zero temperature. If he can see signs of a herd or 'sounder', then his quarry won't be far from his family. Hanging from his belt is some deer meat which should make good bait.

That's when he'll shoot the blighter stone dead.

But before that he'll look it straight in the eye.

See it suffer.

The more it struggles, the deeper the wire will dig through any bristles to slice the hide.

He has to shine his torch carefully and light the terrain well, which is why this blizzard is proving such a nuisance.

So far, all he can identify are some deer and a fox or two. Whatever animal crosses his path disappears in stark differences of snow and shadow.

He's beginning to wish he had brought someone with him for the extra firepower. With each fresh step he takes, the Forest closes behind him. There's no going back now, though. The icy air he bites is full of bitter flakes as he tries to take longer strides through the drifts, but he can't keep his balance on the slippery, uneven ground beneath him.

This snowy glow is terribly confusing. It's not easy to judge distance when one frozen tree blocks another. He's lost as it is. Has it really been over two hours since he left home? He consults his 9-carat gold Rolex watch, but in the Forest time is only an added confusion.

Whenever he draws breath so do the oaks, beeches and pines – their deep audible sighs express sadness, weariness and aspiration which outdo his own.

It's all that ice rattling and jingling as frozen twigs blow about in the wind.

They're positively talking about him.

You can say.

Such imaginings feed his sense of aloneness. Is nothing in this Forest his friend? He has no idea. He is blind to eyes that glint in the gloom.

He presses on, but it's far from easy. Then, again, there comes that ominous crash close beside him. Something is keeping pace with him on a parallel track through the woodland? He feels rather than sees its proximity through the trees. Whatever is there observes him intently. Each snort, bark and grunt explodes the frozen silence. It could be an expression of anger, indignation or incredulity. Then, with some obstinacy, it twitches its raised tail. Suddenly it does a quick spin on its buttocks.

That's no deer.

It's possible to see where something has melted hot holes in the snow with twin blasts from its nostrils, only a moment ago. He ventures, with rifle ready, further into the icy world where few can survive; he's in the coldest cold he's ever known. He could do with a dog to sniff out the trail.

When he does hunt the hog down, though, he'll have its tusks honed into umbrella handles.

What's he waiting for?

It's true that normally only Rangers are allowed to cull animals in the Forest, but they're not here tonight. Nobody but him knows. Literally he's doing everyone a big favour. When pigs go feral they dig up fields and graveyards. They wander into villages and raid dustbins and make a thorough nuisance of themselves.

He reassures himself with the thought of the great party he'll throw at Beech Tree Grange when he has the noble head nailed to his wall. He'll quarter the rest of the hog and place it in a large ice chest filled with water to which he'll add half a cup of vinegar and real lemon juice. He'll soak it for two or three days to kill all the bugs. Not until the meat turns white will the blood have leached out.

Or why not barbecue it, in which case they'll have boar sausages?

However much his plans solidify in his head the subject of them remains an abstraction. What was that? Which way did it go? An unkind person might conclude that it is simply leading him by the nose?

Well, he's not so stupid.

There it goes again, that blur of white past the mist-wreathed trees. He must catch up with it if he's going to dispel his own worst fears.

Whatever it is, it inhabits somewhere between emptiness and absence.

The trees shed ice with its invisible yet lumbering progress.

He stops. Takes aim. Goes to fire. But the creature, on its continuously equidistant path, fails to step clear. That range and unobstructed space within which he can see anything at all renders his prey just out of sight. It blurs into bushes before he can pull the trigger. There is a foggy veil between it and him, or it is made of mist itself.

He wonders if it truly recognises who he is. Right now, not knowing has to be sufficient. Is there anyone who knows about this? He feels as if he is in the presence of some uncanny, pale intelligence, not just a farmer's pig put out to pannage. He walks faster. Trips. Stumbles. Now he's clawing at trees and hauling himself through more snow. Branches strike his face and leave bloody scratches. He's following the rustling of frozen bracken on the Forest floor.

He's back at the snare again. How did that happen? He's panting and shouting.

The next moonlit glade is suspiciously empty and silent.

'Why do you keep running away? What kind of enemy are you?'

In answer, there comes a roar not unlike a bull's snort and not at a distance. He hears a tremendous noise coming his way; his ears fill with the crunching of undergrowth as dead grass and branches get flattened.

A clatter of hooves shatters a hard, icy path nearby. It could be a small pony galloping straight at him.

It seems to originate from afar, yet a moment ago it was his most intimate shadow.

There's something about this creature that is utterly unworldly.

It comes from the future.

It has come from the past.

This is no ordinary pig, to be sure. Frankly, he's not certain what it is. It does not have the usual thick bristly coat with underlying brown pelage, nor is it the reddish-brown, dark grey or black type whose upright hairs are usually brindled with white or tan tips.

This is a rare white phenotype.

The ridge of longer hair that grows along its spine is truly distinctive. It is not the shaggy dog he thought it a moment ago, but something with a mane down the neck more like a hyena's.

It screeches to a halt to stand guard at the edge of the glade, from where it glares at him as if awaiting fresh orders. Its large head and massive shoulders slope to its smaller hind quarters. All the body weight lies forward. It stands four feet tall and is six or more feet long. Red-rimmed eyes are relentless. It certainly resembles a wild boar. How can this be? Male ones have been known to weigh twenty stone.

So he's read.

And this is massive.

He had no idea.

His grip tightens on his rifle. Immediately the boar wrinkles its huge pink snout. Such nostrils can smell a person from miles away. Those small eyes glare at him sombrely, although he'd be wrong to call them glum. Very large, hairy ears twitch when he does. Ears like that 'see' what eyes can't; they are constantly amplifying the smallest sound, to hear silence itself.

Yes, that could be it.

He cannot turn his head without being detected, nor can he raise his gun should the boar resume its charge.

'You the legendary Twrch Trwyth? Then meet your nemesis.'

The boar's lower tusks are as long as knives as it regards him with contempt.

He can't believe it, either.

Should he let the beast come closer to focus on him properly?

No, probably not.

Whatever happens he'll only get the chance to fire one shot.

Simple as that.

Immediately the boar shakes its hairy chin. A shiver ripples its razor-cut crest in a sinuous wave between its ears and over its head. Eyes burn like fire.

His own pupils ache.

'Is that a yes or a no?'

In trying to fold his finger he somehow fails to pull his trigger. Nor can he hold his breath any longer. There comes a tingling in every limb. He asks himself why he doesn't simply fire and whether the boar holds him in its spell.

Suddenly his opponent utters a gruff growl. It could be expressing discontent or dissent. Its nostrils snort dirt. The explosive noise is all anger, indignation and incredulity. Snot drips from each hole. When male boars fight, they can fight to the death. Good to know. After all, it could have ripped him apart already.

One trotter paws the snow.

But it is the eerie rubbing sound that is so mesmerising. The boar draws one tusk along another. Each scrape reverberates against hollow teeth as the lower tusks are continually sharpened. These are not just extremely sharp scimitars but daggers.

Most boar only live ten years in the wild, though in zoos they can live to twenty-five.

That's what he's been told.

So why does this one look ageless? Old wounds cover its head where bristles are missing, while the snout bears its battle honours in swollen scars. Its scabby cheeks are cracked by wind and rain. A tear runs from a blocked eye duct that hates the cold. This beast has swum wide rivers. It has climbed trees, run at thirty miles per hour or more. It has braved freezing temperatures. Feasted on autumn beechmast and acorns. Gorged on summer seeds, fruits, leaves and berries. Eaten birds, lizards and worms.

Okay, so he didn't know.

He's impressed.

He could be face to face with a prince of the night, with some feudal lord of the Forest. King Richard III sported a boar on his badge, if memory serves him right. To bend or kneel does not seem inappropriate. At least he, James Boreman, should incline his head a little in salutation?

He feels outranked.

But not that much.

He's looking at his rival self. Which is when the hog spits froth as his tusks clash and his cloven hooves claw gaping holes in snow and ice. His tail is right up and his snout right down – he's about to bulldoze him deep into the ground.

At last he fires off a shot but the boar keeps coming.

Either that bullet went wide or he's only winged it.

Twrch Trwyth charges at him blindly and heedlessly.

And the whole Forest shakes.

To loud screams and squeals.

Snow lies spattered red with gore.

It doesn't add up.

In the confusion his rifle goes flying.

It's not his blood that streaks the ground.

So why is he running?

FIFTY-FOUR

'We should get going,' said Nora, trying on the heavy, black railway coat that she had found hanging in the hallway of Tunnel Cottage. If it was one thing she and Thibaut needed right now, it was warmer clothing with which to brave the awful weather outside. 'We've been mad to stay this long, as it is. It's a miracle the owner hasn't returned. He could beat the shit out of us at any moment.'

She didn't like it one bit.

Further delay was simply not good enough.

But Thibaut stayed where he was at the parlour window – he was using his thumbnail to scratch at the thin layer of ice that was forming on the inside of the glass.

'It might not come to that.'

'Stop dilly-dallying and let's go.'

'Better take a look at this, first.'

They had scarcely dared go to sleep in case they had to make a sudden run for it.

Now the strain was beginning to tell.

And the cold.

Nora did as he asked and joined him at the frosted window. Thick drifts lay everywhere in the tiny garden as more and more flakes swirled about in the air, she observed, to her horror.

'You saying we should wait until it stops snowing?'

'That's what I'm asking.'

'If only we knew how long we have.'

'It's a big ask, I admit, but we can't freeze any longer.'

So saying, Thibaut picked a few pieces of coal from a brass scuttle and placed them in the cast iron dog grate in the parlour's fireplace.

'Please pass me that newspaper from the dresser behind you.'

He was right, thought Nora. If they were going to stay here even a few more hours they had to warm up. She knelt on the floor to help tear up sheets of 'The Daily Mirror', ready to light a new fire.

'But what if another train comes?'

'We leave the level crossing gates as they are, shut to all road vehicles. Everywhere must be pretty much impassable because we haven't seen a single car or lorry all day. We'd have to dig the gates open now for any traffic, anyway. You and I may not be going anywhere soon, but Boreman's men won't be able to reach us, either. All the more reason to stay put, I reckon.'

'I'm returning the money I found. Who knows, perhaps the owner will help us if he shows up?'

But Thibaut was no longer listening.

'I can't believe it!'

Nora peeked over his shoulder. She saw him spread part of 'The Daily Mirror' flat on the floor in front of the sooty fireplace.

'What is it?'

'C'est fantastique.'

'Fantastic, how?'

'It says here that in November French soldiers in England received enough military equipment through lend-lease to re-equip eight divisions. Not only that but the Free French Forces and Army of Africa have been merged to form the French Expeditionary Corp.'

'Does it say why?'

'Um…'

'Just answer me.'

'It says here we're going to join the Allied invasion of Italy.'

'I don't believe it. It might be propaganda.'

But Thibaut, already wild-eyed, was choking on his own voice. The words were like pebbles in his throat; he gargled and garbled. There was a strange leap in his heart. His temples began to throb. His ears buzzed. His chest tightened so hard he could barely breathe. His head was dizzy; he was shaking in every limb as his thoughts went into total confusion.

'Don't you see? This changes everything. Suddenly I have a way to be useful.'

'You want to be a soldier again?'

Thibaut felt the need to sit down on the nearest brown hide chair for a moment. At the same time, he quibbled at his own euphoria.

'I can't believe it, either.'

Nora took his hand in hers. 'I'm sure the army will want you back.'

'It's been such a long time. How can I take that chance? How can I even find the courage?'

'What do you mean?'

'I lost the will to fight after the evacuation at Dunkirk, but I never chose to desert.'

'So I'll help you.'

Thibaut looked up. Nora's eyes fixed his. Latched on. She was being serious.

'You'll do that for me?'

'I don't want to lose you.'

'But I have nothing to give you.'

'You have yourself.'

'I just want some sort of future.'

'Then have it with me.'

Her entire attitude he had to admit was marvellously appealing.

'Honestly?'

Nora relaxed her grip on his arm, with a laugh.

'We got our Identity Cards back, didn't we? James Boreman has no hold over us any longer.'

'Look, the fire has taken,' said Thibaut and left his seat to blow on hot coals in the grate.

Their kiss had lasted barely two seconds.

'There's more coal in the scullery,' said Nora. 'I'll fetch some.'

Thibaut's limbs were quivering but for a different reason. He no longer thought only about the newspaper article. Instead one emotion collided with another.

Don't you get what just happened?

What was his problem?

Honestly, he didn't know.

Was he happy?

Yes, he was.

That kiss should have lasted forever. It was a feeling he had never identified before; it was a sensation of reverential respect mixed with fear and amazement. He wondered if it might be love. If so, it had to be worth fighting for.

Next minute a scream pierced the whole house.

'Thibaut! For God's sake, help!'

There was only one possibility: Boreman's men. He spun round and knocked over the chair – he fell against the Welsh dresser and rattled its crockery. Nora had to be in serious trouble. He was so busy rushing to help her that he forgot to answer. But the scullery was empty and its door stood open. He flung himself at the snow and darkness outside; he was immediately floundering about like a stranded fish among piles of chopped wood in the backyard. Flakes of ice hit his face and the winter air scorched his lungs.

It was hard to see much more than a crumpled shape in the shadows. Nora was on her knees! She had her back to him, half buried in a drift of white.

What he thought had to be right.

'Where'd they go? Where are Boreman's men? What have the bastards done to you?'

'Not me, him.'

Thibaut kicked away dunes of powdery snow to discover that Nora was cradling an old man's head in her lap.

'Who is it?'

'I reckon it must be the owner of the cottage. Who else can it be? Oh God, I think he might be dead already. See the trail of blood behind him.'

'What's someone of his age doing out here in this weather?'

Half the stricken man's clothes were missing. He had torn open his shirt. His frozen look, wild and horrified, had the stare of someone who had been fighting a fire in his body, when in reality he was freezing to death from hypothermia. His head, as well as being covered in rime, rust and coal, was streaked with gore from a serious wound over one eye. Only the severe cold had helped to slow the massive bleeding. One leg lay twisted at an odd angle – he still clung to a branch which he had used as a crutch to come this far in a series of agonising slips and slithers.

Nora scraped ice from his eyebrows.

'Can we move him?'

'His leg looks bad.'

'You're right. We ought not to lift him?'

'Fetch a blanket. Quick! We'll make a stretcher-cum-hammock and drag him along.'

*

'Is he breathing?' asked Thibaut, tending to the fire in the parlour in a hurry.

Nora leaned closer to the corpse-like figure on the hearth rug and pressed her ear to his chest to listen.

'Yes, but his hands are icy cold, no matter how hard I rub them.'

'Keep trying.'

'He has pine needles stuck in his socks. He must have hobbled and crawled quite a way through the Forest.'

'We should go for help.'

'No time.'

'What do you mean?'

'I can't hear his heart.'

'Move away. Let me in.'

'But we don't know what we're doing.'

'Do we have a choice?'

With that, Thibaut knelt astride the prone man and pressed the palms of his hands flat on his chest. He didn't say so but he'd seen army medics do it a dozen times in bombed out streets, he'd witnessed the frantic attempts to keep oxygen flowing to a soldier's brain because his heart was beating too faintly after being wounded.

He had to do at least one hundred compressions a minute.

Or so he'd been told.

If the patient's heart really had stopped then he knew there was not much he could do. Most people he'd seen on the battlefield simply failed to respond.

He pressed thirty times and kissed the veteran's chapped, cold lips to breathe down his throat.

Nothing.

'There's a list of phone numbers on the wall in the hallway,' said Nora. 'I'm ringing his doctor right now.'

'Forget it. Remember the state of the roads. We should leave him be.'

'Why would we?'

'You know that as well as I do.'

'We left Raoul. I won't do it again.'

Thibaut tried a few more compressions, without much hope. He saw Nora lift the phone and did not attempt to stop her. Yet to make the call was to invite awkward questions.

Suddenly the victim uttered a groan.

'Stop,' said Nora. 'He's coming round.'

But Thibaut didn't stop. He'd seen would-be rescuers fooled like this before. Some apparent signs of life were only a person's final gasps for breath before they expired. To stop now could be a big mistake.

Press. Press. Press.

Breathe.

Press. Press. Press.

Next minute the old man opened his eyes. He started batting Thibaut's hands away as he uttered a bad-tempered moan.

Thibaut sat back and his face widened into one enormous grin.

'Mon Dieu. You're alive.'

FIFTY-FIVE

The ever deepening snow makes it extremely hard to keep going.

Icicles fly off low hanging branches into his face.

Like silver daggers.

All bloody.

He wanted to lure the boar into his snare to prove that he, James Boreman, will not be made a fool of. Anything else was not part of the plan.

Whenever he looks back over his shoulder he collides with another tree – his pursuer is pounding the Forest floor not far behind him? He rests for a moment, but immediately hears it snuffle his way like one with a cold. Such behaviour is unfair; it's crafty; it knows things he doesn't.

He glimpses its spear-like, white bristles that prickle the mist.

Christ, what does it have on him?

It has his guilty conscience.

'What the hell are you? Leave me alone.'

For he's no longer convinced that whatever pursues him belongs in this world.

Where does it come from?

Why won't it answer?

He jumps patchworks of paths where the bitter night unwinds its black veil. Dead twigs crackle beneath his feet where he might have hoped that the snow would muffle all sound. If anything will betray him now it will be the Forest's all-encompassing silence. It magnifies every move he makes.

He's in forbidden territory.

There are other things, too.

A wounded stag with a broken antler stands and stares.

But he can't stay here. That beast will be right behind him. His eyes drown as his face streams tears. His lungs feel fit to burst. That last snowdrift nearly dragged him down – now his knees ache. More sharp branches claw at his face and scratch his hands to ribbons. He no longer looks round at every other step. What good will it do? He's in a nowhere land between one place and another.

Because he's no longer the hunter but the hunted.

Isn't that the truth. Those are more grunts, squeals and rumbles? That's something, very briefly, in a glint of moonlight? That's the snort of a very angry creature?

It can track him effortlessly.

By sound.

Or smell.

That wild boar is not chasing but driving him. Each wrong step is corrected with the flash of an eye or stamp of a foot which doesn't in the least reassure him – this beast of uncertain appearances commands all the trails. And if he refuses?

He stumbles, runs and trots to a place within sight of felled trees and a fence. Suddenly frost flickers silver on the glass windows of a spanking new concrete and timber mansion in a freshly carved glade. Thank God! The boar has brought him back to within sight of Beech Tree Grange.

In the sliver of light at the end of the path lies his salvation, since he can now see the gap in the fence to his very own gardens.

The warmth of home is in his heart, the hope of refuge in his cries.

All things considered.

A sea of ground mist washes at his waist; it misleads and confuses. For a moment his mind is a maze and a blur. How can he be so close and yet so far from safety?

The beast is nearer, for sure. What's that? Sprouting from its hideous jaws, its tusks froth and rasp with a purpose entirely malignant. It's as if his pursuer, having secured its place in his brain, is hell-bent on working its spell from within. That must be it. What? Just say it: he doesn't pretend to know what's real and what isn't any longer.

With a yell, he runs at great speed towards the house. He'll go as fast as he can – he'll shut himself up and lock every door.

His head is down and he's dodging the last few trees within sight of the breached fence and ruined lawn. How strange are those calls across the Forest as he crashes through the frozen bracken. Those cries drive him on. Sound urgent. He and Sam were here not so long ago? That should tell him something.

A sudden giddiness grips him when the trees spin madly. The ground runs away from him until he can't catch up. Mist stops floating before it lets go. A black void erupts in his guts.

Then, with a cruel snatch, his legs vanish from under him.

Absolute agony shears him to the bone.

Next minute he's in mid-air as someone's eyes flash fire at him. Two lower teeth grind their points on two upper ones. Not so much frothing as sharpening.

That's all he can tell.

Because Sam just took to his heels.

That scream he screams after his own son is enough to shatter the silence.

Wake the dead.

FIFTY-SIX

Every few minutes Jo uttered a fresh curse, even as another flash from Freya's torch shone a way through the Forest. It winked between black branches.

'What does it look like to you, John?'

Little cascades of snow kept slipping down the back of his neck, too.

'She's following the same footprints we are.'

'And not much else.'

'We'll freeze to death out here at the end of the day.'

'You can say that again.'

'I know what you're thinking.'

'I *think* only Bella knows where the hell we're going.'

Bella breasted white waves with her broad brisket – she was soon busily bulldozing snowflakes with her broad nose.

'Come back here, Bella. Wait for me.'

Jo tried to curb her reckless enthusiasm, but Bella did not obey any of her calls or whistles. The moment she sniffed a bend in the trail, she charged ahead with every hope of tracking her quarry.

Any more shouts only got lost in the vast tract of frozen trees, as though some unsympathetic, permeable presence existed to taunt their arrival.

It was the heart-stopping backdrop of quietude.

Still Freya forged on. Her boots tore through snow with each purposeful stride. Flakes of ice settled on her hair until she no longer resembled anyone of this world but a mysterious white lady.

Her torch glinted again, then she was gone through the next gap in the oaks and beeches.

Moments later there came the clash of hooves and a furious bull-like snort.

There was much squealing and grunting in the dead bracken and ferns up ahead.

'What the hell was that?' asked John in a hushed voice.

Jo hesitated, too. They were not alone, but smelt some raw animal smell. Her nostrils were all rank bristles, spit and pheromone.

'I can't rightly tell.'

Freya was but a wisp of white fire as she crossed the next glade. Next minute she was using her torch to penetrate infinite darkness again and it made good sense to go after her while they still could. She was on a track that stretched on and on. So why didn't she speak? She had to know by now how closely they followed her.

Bella proceeded more recklessly than ever. She was definitely thinking enormous male pig. One such boar in Germany had been known to drag a Shepherd dog thirty feet when provoked. Even a sow could slash someone's belly wide open with her jaws.

She'd know she was in trouble if it stamped its foot. She'd heard the tales. When an animal could smash through fences and lift a twelve-foot long, galvanized farm gate off its hinges, you knew not to mess with it.

She could only say that she thought she'd seen something pass by a minute ago with more snorts and snuffles.

And something else.

Immediately from the trees there stepped a small figure. It was he who uttered that feverish buzzing from the back of his throat. Like bees swarming. Like bombers droning. Once he might have cried or called out for help, but not any more. Before, he hadn't known what to do. This was different.

'Sam?' said Jo in astonishment and rushed forwards.

On the little boy's head was an old school cap frayed at its peak and round its edges.

But Freya was oblivious to all that; she only wanted to calm her son and hug him closer.

For some reason she was drawing him away from something.

And Sam let himself be drawn – he no longer had any reason not to.

Freya uttered a cry and dropped her torch, even as Jo ran forward and plucked it from the snow.

Because there was something else they needed to know?

Framed in the flashlight's glow, a mouth's frozen scream lit up in the gloom. The eyes were wide open, blank, repulsive. The nose leaked blood and pieces of yellow vomit stained the chin. Jo's own stomach heaved. Her heart raced. There came a strange weakness in her legs, until she feared for a moment that she might topple backwards in sheer horror. She struggled to admit that what she was seeing could really be called a man. Behind her, John stifled a scream. Then, with a gasp, she stepped up to a tree. Carefully, tenderly, she pressed two fingers urgently to the person's neck in search of a pulse.

'It's James Boreman. He's dead.'

Sam looked on matter-of-factly.

'Did you see it happen?' asked Jo.

But Sam said nothing.

That look in the boy's eyes was troubling.

Did she know what she was asking him?

They had to go now.

They shouldn't be here.

'Do you know how your dad came to be in the Forest at this time of night?' said Jo. 'Just tell me why.'

Sam squeezed Freya's hand very hard.

'I helped him set the spear-trap to catch the phantom boar.'

John hurried over to Freya as she tried to shield her son's eyes. Sam's maddened buzzing had become a hum. But she would accept no well-meaning words of sympathy from him, or anyone else. All this she made clear on her son's behalf, since in no way would she have him blamed for a chance occurrence. Yet it seemed that it was also defiance in the face of some great wrong which, though not explained, haunted her every nerve. To the peculiarities of her son, the constant flicker of her pupils demonstrated an extra uncertainty.

She knew what he had done.

346

'Anything you want to say?' asked Jo.

Freya came out of her trance. Looked startled.

'What do you mean?'

'You don't look too surprised.'

'You've no idea.'

'Tell me.'

'I'd rather not.'

'But your husband has triggered his own trap. How is that even possible?'

'I can't explain it any more than you can.'

Jo examined the scene more closely. The wooden spear had skewered James's stomach, swept him off his feet and nailed him to the oak tree's ancient trunk. Snowflakes misted red the instant they settled at his feet. His contorted cheeks were ashen – he was gutted, disembowelled. By the smell of it, he was dangling in his own faeces.

'Please forgive my colleague,' said John. 'She shouldn't ask so many questions. Now's not a good time, not with Sam here. We should talk again later.'

Freya inhaled sharply. She straightened her shoulders and the deadly pallor momentarily faded from her face. Her mouth looked doubly determined.

'I'd rather we leave all that to the police.'

John eagerly concurred.

'I'll run back to the house and ring them right now.'

Bella's eyes, meanwhile, did not leave the trees. Something sniffed and listened to them from the Forest.

It wasn't just the intense quietude.

She hesitated to call it savage. *Free.* In a word, that's what it was. And its presence could only be a good thing.

*

It was late evening before two Gloucestershire Police cars and a doctor arrived at Beech Tree Grange.

DI Lockett was in a foul mood.

'Bloody snow. The main roads are virtually no-go.'

'Make it brief, Inspector. Mrs Boreman and her son have had a terrible shock.'

'And you are?'

'Miss Jo Wheeler.'

'It says 'Mrs' on your ID Card.'

'My husband died in the Bristol Blitz.'

'I know you. You're the daughter of Lt-Col. James Huntly Dutton, 6th Baron Sherborne.'

'Actually, everyone knows me as chief fire watcher at Gloucester Cathedral.'

'Your father is a great man. You must be very proud of him.'

'It's too late for that.'

'Even the nicest young lady can tire of tea parties and summer balls, is that it? You want to prove privilege is no excuse not to do your bit for the war effort? You can only do that by appearing to be as ordinary as everyone else?'

'I'm trying to find out.'

'Or you're some interfering, upper crust toff who thinks she can do my job as well as me?'

'Nice to meet you, too.'

The inspector's eyes were as black as his ill-fitting suit, Jo noted grimly; he had that unappealing stare in his lean face that brooked no competition. Nothing wrong with that. He was just doing his job and he was quick to spot trouble. Don't let it be her.

'Come, come, Inspector. No hard feelings.'

'I don't like people who can't adequately explain their presence at a crime scene.'

'It's quite a story, I must admit.'

'Give your statement to the constable over there. I'll be in touch if I need to speak to you again.'

'Just so you know, this death is a fluke. More or less.'

'How can you be so sure?'

'He's local businessman James Boreman.'

'So it appears.'

'What you should also know is that he owns a string of dodgy companies that employ slave labour. He's also a black marketer and wife beater. He may even be a murderer. From the look of the tracks left behind in the snow, I'd say he was running when he set off his own trap that he set to poach game.'

'Someone was chasing him?'

'Or some thing.'

'I'm sorry, I don't follow.'

Jo sucked her lip and looked grave.

'At a guess, I'd say James Boreman thought he was being pursued all right. That's not to say he wasn't correct, but it may all have been in his imagination.'

'So it *isn't* a fluke?'

'That depends on what you call fluky. Either way, he dropped his rifle and ran away.'

'Now you're making no sense at all.'

'I can only say what I saw.'

'Good luck with that, Mrs Wheeler.'

Jo and Sam traded looks as they walked with Freya back to Beech Tree Grange where she picked up the phone. They were agreed on one thing: the surest method of terrifying someone was to have them come face to face with their deepest, innermost fear.

'I can stay with you tonight, if you wish,' said Jo.

But Freya was adamant.

'I'll never sleep under this roof again.'

'So where will you go?'

'I'll drive Sam to my father's place at Tunnel Cottage. That's strange…'

'Something wrong?'

'Someone else is answering my call.'

FIFTY-SEVEN

'You read today's 'Citizen'?' asked John, as he and Jo took their seats with several hundred other carol singers in Gloucester Cathedral.

Jo peered through her pillbox hat's gossamer veil that she wore at a jaunty angle. This evening, the nave was a mixture of shapes and shadows. While a few strategically positioned lanterns twinkled atmospherically high up on stone arches, the tiny flames of candles down below rendered everyone all lit faces and little else in the deliberate dimness. They were ghosts that reeked of coal smoke, cigarettes and badly washed clothes in this enormous, medieval auditorium.

The way she saw it, this was a night for celebration. In her bag was a present for Noah.

Never mind that John was talking far too eagerly and loudly. She didn't even know what he meant.

Any headlines had to wait.

Not to John they couldn't.

'The police have acted on our investigation.'

'Good to know.'

'Is that all you can say? You should consider yourself a hero.'

Jo shivered inside her belted, double-breasted gabardine trench coat. She had taken care to fasten all ten buttons, but still the wide lapels and storm flap did not quite keep out the biting chill. Access to the cathedral this Christmas was not by the South Porch but via the cloisters. As a result, the draught was nearly killing her. She could just make out the newspaper's front page: "Police arrest sister of well-known local businessman".'

'Spare me the hero bit, please.'

'Really, you should read this. Police have raided the caravan site and factory we visited in the Forest of Dean and released the workers. Tia Boreman is to be charged with conspiracy to pervert the course of justice as well as black marketeering.'

'They're not wrong, are they.'

'How's Freya's father doing?'

It was John again, giving her another nudge in the ribs.

'The last I heard, the hospital was treating him for frostbite on two toes.'

'If Nora and Thibaut hadn't arrived in time he might not have been so lucky. And we would never have known who attacked him down that abandoned coal mine.'

'Tia denies all knowledge, of course.'

Jo's gaze wandered higher and higher in the nave. Light and darkness hung in the balance. It was both humbling and frightening. A monument to forgiveness. Hundreds of singers were gathering in the gargantuan stone cave built for people by people, but from another time.

'Whatever Tia says, it was her idea to flood the bodies in acid to render them unrecognisable. Freya overheard her discussing a plan very like it at her party.'

John traded his newspaper for the Christmas song sheet in his coat.

'I don't get it. Why dump bodies down a mine? Why take the risk?'

'Why not? Through bad luck, bad health or desertion from the armed forces most of Boreman's employees had ceased to function socially. Few people were going to miss them if they disappeared.'

'You think he had them killed?'

'As good as. They died from accidents sustained at work in his factory. I saw the conditions in Lydney – they were lethal.'

'That's all there is to it?'

'Think about it. If James paid for a doctor to tend to his injured workers, all sorts of questions would have been raised that would have led straight back to him. Angela and Raoul weren't the only ones to be dumped somewhere obscure, I bet. Doctors are a nosy lot. They like to ask how you came by your injuries. A worker only had to mention his name and he was in trouble. Don't forget he stole their ID and Ration Cards. That way everyone was rendered helpless, at his beck and call. They were never human beings to James Boreman. Not really. He always kept them at arm's length.

Better to dispose of a body or two in the Forest's most secret places where no one would ever find them, than risk ruining his business model. All that changed when he met Jim Wilde underground. That's when he tried to kill him with his own hand.'

'He made his money from fear.'

'Yet fear killed him.'

'Not before his wife suffered horribly.'

'Second that.'

'Who'd have thought it? James was held up to be such a brilliant businessman.'

'We both know he wasn't.'

John looked for tunes he knew on his song sheet and his eyes narrowed when he came to 'Hark! The herald angels sing'.

'You look terrific by the way. Pregnancy is doing you some good at last.'

'It is?'

'You look quite bonny.'

'I do?'

'Your face is a better colour. Not so pasty.'

'That's because I've stopped being so sick every morning. I put it down to not going to "The Women's League Of Health And Beauty" any more. I'm doing beer yoga instead.'

'Say that again?'

'It's all my own invention. One day it will really catch on. I do yoga and sip Guinness. It makes it less intimidating.'

'The beer or the yoga?'

'I've only dared try it a few times so far.'

'We should definitely see that film together.'

'....'

'So what *are* you going to do over Christmas?' asked John, hurriedly.

'Do?'

'Are you moving back home? What about New Year? Where will you have the baby? Or are you going into labour one night when you and I are fire watching at the top of the cathedral tower?'

'With those steps!'

'Where, then?'

'First things first. I'll go and see my brother, naturally. Meanwhile, my father wants me to help him persuade my mother to go to a tuberculosis sanatorium at Salterley Grange to help her recuperate! But will she go? Hell, no! Nor is she about to forgive my fall from grace any time soon.'

'Who'd have thought it?'

'Apparently rats in my house are what I deserve.'

'And the baby's father? What will he say when he finds out?'

'I'm beginning to think I'll go it alone.'

John flattened his song sheet back on his knee.

'It says here the Mayor of Gloucester is treating us to a talk tonight as well as the Bishop.'

'It's not so good.'

'The mayor?'

'The rats.'

'I'm glad we've got that clear.'

Suddenly Jo saw Sam and Freya take their seats in the row just in front of her. They had only spoken once since the night of James's death, when she had given Sam a dozen cigarette cards depicting trains.

One thing struck her at once – Freya was wearing a different perfume. No more smelling of verbena. She turned and gave her a smile. It was a smile the like of which she had not seen her give before. At first it baffled her totally. Then she realised. The grin was different because a shadow had lifted from her whole face. The new look spoke volumes. The routine of saying as little as possible every day for years, lest she provoke some boorish reaction in her husband, had ended. She'd had less voice because James had claimed more say in their lives. She'd had little pick of what to do, wear or how to bring up their boy because he had exercised infinite choice for them all. He'd ruled his family like some evil beast but now he was gone.

Tonight she seemed 'more her'. She was never going to regret it. As if she could finally see herself now she felt strong.

Freya had forgotten about her already. Which was only right and proper. It was a relief to see her free to enjoy the spectacle. Had she, Jo Wheeler, done the right thing, though? It was all too easy to go charging into someone else's life, but such actions had consequences. She was no King Arthur in shining armour. There were some things no one could change. James's death was one of them. Sam was another. Together, mother and son had planned it all, she had no doubt about that. They'd carefully put the idea of the phantom boar into James's head and driven him half insane. Like any caring parent, Freya had feared that Sam might not be allowed to be himself, that his father's hostility would see him sent abroad for experimental treatment only to see his ship torpedoed in mid-Atlantic.

Being different should not mean being a guinea pig.

At no time was Sam to be considered defective.

Or odd.

Only gifted?

So she'd acted.

*

'Isn't it marvellous?'

John was nudging her frantically, Jo realised. She stood up with the rest of the audience and her ears resonated – her eyes widened and her jaw fell open. The very air seemed ready to burst. Her lungs were breathing a collective awe as everyone instinctively leaned forward for a better view.

At first the weight of darkness was almost too great, too oppressive as a procession of choristers wove its way through the nave. A presentiment of foreboding came with them, until only the singers' tremulous voices, as fragile as glass, stood between her and the cavernous night that enclosed them all. Christmas trees looked lost in the void. The candle-lit procession spun web-like threads of light through the echoing gloom.

Such great echoes were themselves distorted, repeated and swallowed as the choristers attempted to use their voices to reach the towering heights above them. No single human utterance could be sufficient to fill the space that wanted to crush it?

Suddenly there came into her head the carved image of the stone mason's apprentice falling to his death in the South Transept. People had died building these walls.

But if she was struck by the fragility of those gathered together here tonight, no one's lungs failed to cry out in full agreement as they stood shoulder to shoulder.

Her own initial faltering vanished, too. It was not every day that so many ordinary folk got to sing together in their comical mixture of hats, turbans and scarves. The choir's voices were already united. What began as a trickle became a flood – sounds combined to raise the volume with unparalleled acoustics. It was not just loudness but confidence. She felt her lungs swelling. With mellifluence came strength. Men and boys singing were no longer mere performers but a great current as they sang 'Silent Night' and the congregation joined in. Together everyone's voices became bolder through clarity and pureness.

Whereas in the beginning the stone void above her was all set to diminish and swallow, now the sheer flow of sound expanded to fill the greatest of spaces – such was the power and beauty of song that grew to fill it.

Then something happened. The miracle. The scales slipped from her eyes. Next moment the darkness – that weighty adumbration – retreated and there came in its place the warmth of human company. No angry thoughts haunted these walls any longer. It was possible for light to triumph over darkness, to forgive one's self, after all?

As the Bishop of Gloucester began to deliver his sermon on the evils of war, John hissed in her ear.

'Tell me one thing.'

'What's that?'

'What on earth will we say to Bruno Smith?'

'We'll tell him he was mistaken.'

'That's not what he'll want to hear.'

'All right, just suppose we do accept that James Boreman's two timber thieves were involved in Sarah's 'accident'?' Jo reached for a cigarette, then thought better of it. 'Devaney and his moustachioed friend caused her to crash in a fit of very bad tailgating or they were acting on more lethal instructions – to give her the fright of her life. As they did us. My guess is that, in the heat of the moment, in the very act of being chased, she swerved to avoid some animal that dashed across the road right in front of her.'

'Nothing else?'

'How shall I put it? It had to be something pretty exceptional to cause her to panic like that because she was normally such a cautious driver. According to Bruno, excessive speed was the one thing she hated above all else.'

'You don't seriously think it was our mythical white boar, do you, Jo?'

'The Forest alone knows what Sarah saw that awful night. But it will never say. It'll keep its secret.'

With that, she plucked her red and gold fountain pen from her pocket and scribbled a few words at the top of his hymn sheet: *Flicks on Friday. Picturedrome. Don't be late.*

Printed in Great Britain
by Amazon